# RUMOURS

## Freya North

# WINDSOR
# PARAGON

First published 2012
by HarperCollins*Publishers*
This Large Print edition published 2013
by AudioGO Ltd
by arrangement with
HarperCollins*Publishers*

Hardcover     ISBN: 978 1 4713 2034 7
Softcover     ISBN: 978 1 4713 2035 4

British Library Cataloguing in Publication Data available

Printed and bound in Great Britain by
MPG Books Group Limited

For Daddy

. . . to misquote Bobby—thank you for holding
steady my ladder to the stars, for teaching me how
to be righteous and true, for helping me to stand
upright, to feel strong and to be courageous.
Thanks to you, my heart's joyful—
and it's your song I'll always sing.

# RUMOURS

# Prologue

## March 1790

Lord Frederick Makepeace William Fortescue, Earl of Barbary, ran his hands over the undulations of Molly's naked body, admiring the sight and relishing in the silky feel of her much as he did his favourite horse, Jepson. It gave him enormous pleasure, not in a carnal way, but for the sense of ownership. He loved to gaze, to feel, to assess what he had before he rode—either horse or woman—the delicious anticipation of how the external beauty brought with it the promise of such sublime physical rewards. He bucked into Molly hard, much as Jepson bucked after jumping a stile. Excited, he rode her energetically to the finish.

'My dear,' he said, 'though I would spend all afternoon with you, Lady Fortescue is shortly to return from Bath—and it would not do for your mistress to find you in my bed.' He slapped Molly's bottom and resisted the temptation to call it a fine rump. 'Out,' he laughed, letting his hand linger and wander, before he gave her another hearty wallop which made her giggle lasciviously and climb aboard again. 'Off!' he said. 'Away!'

Molly gave him a reproachful look that was as beguiling as it was coy. 'As you ask, My Lord,' she said, emphasizing the 'Lord' in such a way that it warranted a further slap on her buttocks. He watched her dress. She was turned away from him—not from any shyness, but actually because after the act itself she no longer wanted to see his

1

corpulent body sprawled inelegantly wasted. She felt that fornication, especially of the illicit type, was rather like gorging oneself when starving hungry. Once sated, the very sight of leftovers was repellent. Lord Fortescue didn't know this, of course. He thought it was a charming reversion of Molly from strumpet to servant; from a writhing, panting horny filly—unbridled, dirty and insatiable—to humble and reverent and back in her place. He wasn't aware how the extra coins he gave her provided her with both the last laugh *and* her growing independence and emancipation.

'I shall call for you,' he said in a low growl.

'I shall come,' she said, all meek, just the way she knew he liked.

'Molly Molly Molly,' he marvelled. She gave a demure little curtsey. 'A little something for your—exertion, a reward for your excellent fulfilment of all tasks set.' He nodded at the occasional chair, draped with hastily strewn clothing. 'Pocket,' he said softly. She slipped her hand into the pocket of his breeches as if unsure what she might find and feigned surprise and delight at the lace handkerchief knotted on its bundle of coins.

'Why, thank you, Lord Fortescue,' she said, as if payment was an unexpected bonus.

He winked. 'Be off now. I will ring down in a while and ask Mrs Fulford to send someone up to make the room afresh.'

'– because you had one of your funny turns—'

'That's my girl,' said Lord Fortescue. 'Away with you now. Shoo!'

Molly paused by the door. He was a good master. Her working conditions and remuneration were above par compared with other maids she knew.

And, actually, the extras he sought and paid for honourably didn't offend her. He was rather good at it. And preferable to the fat fingers and clumsy cock of Lord Aldbury who'd had her before her move to the Fortescue household.

'Lord Fortescue, sir,' she said. She turned. He was sitting on the edge of his bed, his stomach like a plump pink pillow partially concealing the instrument of his adultery. 'It's just—'

He waited. 'Just what?'

'Something I heard,' she said.

He raised an eyebrow for her to continue.

'Probably just tittle-tattle. But my sister—she lives in Long Dansbury. And there's all sorts of rumours in the village—so she says—about that new house you are building.'

'Oh, yes?'

'Yes,' said Molly. 'And there's rumours, too, here in Knightsbridge—amongst the staff. About positions to be lost, or country pay being lower than London. And country ways, sir—being, well, unsavoury.'

*Whoever gossips to you, gossips about you*, Lord Fortescue mused as he looked at Molly. 'Bugger Knightsbridge,' he said, 'but I am interested in what the villagers are saying out there. From a philanthropic point of view, of course.'

Molly shrugged. 'Just about the house you're building.'

'The house?'

'The style—some say it's too modern. Too big. Ugly, even. Others say that you'll be chopping down all the forests to feed the fires just to heat the place.'

'I see.'

3

'And that the barley fields will be turned fallow. And that you'll do cattle not sheep. And that the villagers won't get the jobs—us London staff will. But us London staff won't want to go all the way out there if we're not on Knightsbridge wages.'

Lord Fortescue was enjoying all this. And he could see Molly wasn't done.

'And there's more.' She reddened yet glanced at him lasciviously. 'They say none of the men will let their wives or daughters work for you—on account of your *appetite.*' She licked her lips, as if he'd whetted hers.

'Away with you, Molly,' Lord Fortescue laughed. And when she was gone, he rubbed his hands and his cock and his belly gleefully. 'Idiots! All of them! Hertfordshire is the new Knightsbridge— and those who choose not to come with me are fools. Longbridge Hall will put the village of Long Dansbury on the map—geographically and architecturally. I fully intend to touch the lives of the villagers in ways they'll never forget!'

# Chapter One

Stella knew there was a private car park at Elmfield Estates, and that a space would have been reserved for her little Fiat, but she pulled into a side street some way off and stopped the car. Adrenalin ate away at her, like lemon juice on teeth enamel; the same fresh but sour sensation, excitement and dread churning into an audible curdle in her stomach. She needed to compose herself and turned the ignition back on so she could have the radio on low, providing a comforting soft din to an otherwise loaded silence broken only by the rumble of her stomach. She hadn't eaten a thing at breakfast—usually her favourite meal of the day. This was so much more than first-day nerves. This job could be life changing. She'd done the figures and, with potential commission, they'd all added up. She checked her reflection—an early-morning hair wash and a brand-new mascara certainly made her look fresher than she felt, she thought to herself, as if judging the face of someone else. She knew she looked younger than she was, but no one else would know that she appeared brighter than she felt. If she could fool herself, hopefully she'd fool the office of new colleagues awaiting her arrival just around the corner. She ought to waltz on in and simply say, hullo! Stella Hutton! Reporting for duty! How lovely to meet you all! Right, where do I begin! After all, if ever there was a new beginning, a golden opportunity, a lifeline, then taking on this job was it.

The first day of March, the first day of the

week; the sky startlingly naked of clouds; the sun a slightly harsh white light and rather unnerving, like bare legs revealed for the first time after hibernating behind opaque tights all winter. Stella thought it must be a good omen—sunshine to signify the change from one month to another, not least because February had been alternately drenched and then frozen. A positive nod from the universe, perhaps, to say, it's a fresh start, Stella. Here's some brightness and warmth to prove it. Winter's receding, put spring in your step. Especially today. Of all days, *especially* today.

She shifted in her seat, flipped the sun visor back up, switched the radio off and the engine on, crunching the car into gear. My back aches, she thought. And then she wondered what on earth was being said behind it by the office personnel a few streets away.

I'd certainly have something to say about it, Stella thought, if I'd been told a person like me was starting today.

*　　　*　　　*

'Apparently, she has *very* little experience.'

'How can you go from being an art teacher to an estate agent?'

'Chalk and cheese, if you ask me.'

'No no—I don't think she was an art teacher—I heard she owned a gallery and it went bust.'

'How do you go from paintings to property?'

'Well, it's all sales, isn't it.'

'She did work experience here—during the summers when she was at college.'

'Well—obviously that's how she got this job. Her

father is brother to Hutton Senior—apparently they don't speak. Black sheep. Apparently she's estranged from her father but really close with *our* Huttons.'

'Dear God, You Three—you've never met the woman!' Geoff looked up at Belinda, Gill and Steve, to whom he always referred as You Three. Every day that triumvirate of three interchangeable voices gossiped the air into an oppressive cloy around him. Mostly, he was able to filter it out, like dust in his peripheral vision. But not today. Today the talk wasn't about Z-list celebrities or people he didn't know, it concerned someone about to walk in through the office door any moment. New blood in the company. It made him more nervous than curious. There'd always been only four agents working here in the Hertford branch of Elmfield Estates, excluding the chairman Douglas Hutton Senior who came into the office infrequently, and Douglas Hutton Junior his son and managing director whose door was mostly closed though he heard everything. With this new person it meant five. And as he was the eldest and his sales were down, he wondered if it was true that she was being brought in to edge him out. New blood. New bloody person.

\*     \*     \*

Belinda, Gill and Steve's eyes were glued to the door, not so much a welcoming committee, but a panel of judges. This was the most exciting thing to happen at work since Douglas Hutton Junior sold Ribstock Place for over the asking price last spring. A year, therefore, of dullness and drudgery,

7

with little selling, little coming on, prices falling and commission being squeezed lower than ever. How could Elmfield Estates afford to take on an extra staff member? What was she on, salary-wise? Commission only, Belinda reckoned. What of her bonus structure? They'd had a meeting at the beginning of the year to change from pooled to individual bonuses.

She'd better bloody well be given only the one-bedders then, this new girl, said Gill. Steve thought to himself he should have taken that position at arch rivals John Denby & Co. when it was offered to him last Christmas. But it would have only been a sideways move. He was on the up, he could feel it in his bones, he could sense it every morning when he tied his tie, when he'd decided to upgrade from polyester to silk. This Hutton niece— nothing but a blip, little more than something new to talk about. Not worth stressing over.

When she arrived, none of them thought that Stella was Stella. She looked nothing like Messrs Hutton, Senior or Junior. She had small features, a gentle waft of chestnut hair and a willing if shy smile, compared to the expressionless hard edges, the bristles which stuck both to the heads and faces of her relations, like coir matting. She was older than they'd expected—perhaps mid-thirties—but nevertheless, still younger than Belinda, Gill or Geoff were happy about. A pleasant surprise for Steve, though. Quite attractive.

'Can I help you?'

'I'm Stella—Hutton.'

She was stared at.

'I'm the new girl.'

Belinda didn't take her eyes off her when she

lifted the phone handset, tapped in four numbers and said, pointedly, 'Your *niece* is here to see you.'

Oh God, please don't let Uncle Dougie kiss me.

Douglas Hutton had no intention of doing anything of the sort.

'Welcome, Stella,' he said with a gravity that was appropriate for any new agent starting with the company. 'This is the team—Belinda, Gill, Geoff, Steve. This is your desk. You'll be with Gill this morning—she has three viewings. Geoff will come with you this afternoon. There's a one-bedder on Bullocks Lane.'

He went to the whiteboard and added Stella's name to the horizontal and vertical bands of the chart. A glance told her all she needed to know about the team. Steve storming ahead, Geoff lagging behind. Belinda and Gill side by side, neck and neck, tête-à-tête—thick as thieves, apparently.

\*       \*       \*

'I like your bag,' Stella said to Gill as they headed out to one of two dinky Minis branded with the agency logo. Gill looked at her, unconvinced. Stella was about to hone in on the woman's shoes for added praise but she stopped herself. Crazy—it's like being at school again—agonizing trepidation concerning The Older Girls. She decided not to talk, just to nod and smile a lot at the vendor, at the client, at Gill. The effort, combined with first-day nerves, was exhausting and she was glad of the silence on the drive back to the office at lunch-time.

'I like your hairstyle,' said Gill just before she opened the car door. But the compliment was tempered by a touch of resentment. 'Wish mine had a curl to it.' And then she walked on ahead of Stella, as if to say, that's as much as I can be nice to you for the time being. And don't tell the others.

*  *  *

Stella warmed to Geoff, with whom she was coupled after lunch, even though initially he was as uncommunicative as Gill had been. His silence bore no hostility, instead an air of resignation seeped out of him like a slow puncture. He looked deflated. He didn't seem to fit his sharp suit; Stella imagined that faded cords and a soft old shirt with elbow patches were his weekend wear. The Mini stalled, seemingly disappointed to have Geoff behind the wheel. She glanced at him as he waited patiently at the lights, as if he never expected to come across anything other than a red light and that now, after years of life being like this, the predictability was acceptable rather than infuriating. She detected a shyness from him towards her that mirrored how she'd felt that morning, sitting by Gill.

'Was art your thing?' he asked, tackling the main roundabout cautiously.

'Sorry?'

'That's what I heard—that art was your thing.'

'Oh. Yes. Yes, it was—I studied fine art. And then I had a little—place.'

'A gallery?'

'That makes it sound so grand. But yes—in as much as there was art on the walls and people came in to see it.'

'And to buy?'

'Not often enough.'

'It went bust,' said Geoff.

10

'Sorry?'

'That's what we—what I was told.'

'I had to close it, yes. I chose to change career.'

'And that's why you're here?'

'Yes.'

'You couldn't sell art but you think you might be able to sell houses?' He hadn't meant it to sound rude. He just couldn't fathom how someone who wanted a career in art could metamorphose into someone wanting to work as an estate agent. 'There's an art to selling houses,' he said, helpfully, 'or so we like to lead our clients to believe.'

'In these crap times—financially speaking—I suppose people don't want to spend money on art. As much as I like to believe that people need art in their lives, there's no point splashing out on a painting if you haven't four walls around you and a roof over your head.'

He looked a little nonplussed and Stella cringed at what she'd said—it sounded like a dictum she might churn out in a job interview.

'Anyway,' she said, 'that was almost two years ago. I love art—but I also really like houses. And I know you probably all think it's family favouritism—but I did two years at the St Albans branch of Tremberton & Co. It's just I moved from Watford to Hertford last autumn.'

Geoff looked at her quizzically, as if her move from one side of Hertfordshire to the other and the revelation that the gallery hadn't gone bust yesterday and nepotism played little part in her change of career, moved her up in his estimation.

'I have a John Piper etching,' he told her with an almost-smile.

11

They had just pulled up outside the Victorian conversion, where the one-bedder was on the second floor.

'A *Piper*?'

But Geoff pressed the doorbell before Stella could coax a reply.

Forty minutes later, Geoff really couldn't fault her—they had a new vendor on their books, her valuation had been spot on. The client had liked her and Geoff had liked Stella's manner—chatty, enthusiastic, supportive. He sensed if she took a potential purchaser around, they'd be lining up a second viewing just as soon as they'd seen the place. He had to concede that she'd probably sell a place like this faster than he could.

'Nicely done,' he said when they headed back to the car.

'Thank you.'

'We'd heard all sorts of things about you,' he said, as if disbelieving that reality could be so very different. She looked aghast. 'I doubt whether there was much truth in any of them,' he told her. 'Ignore them—Those Three, back in the office—they're harmless.' He paused. 'Relatively.'

The trouble with rumours, thought Stella, is that once the seed is planted, roots spread and the whole thing rampages like ground elder. As fast as you pull it up, renegade shoots are already off on tangents.

But then she thought, it's impossible for something to grow from nothing. However tiny, there's always a seed of truth that starts it all off.

A bit like Love really.

12

# Chapter Two

Jesus, do I *not* feel like doing this.

Xander reached over to whack down the alarm clock as if it was a bluebottle that had been bugging him for hours. Lying next to him, Siobhan mumbled in her reverie. He looked at her, naked and so very tempting. Outside, grey and raining. Inside, warm and cosy. Inside Siobhan, downright hot and snug. He lay back on his side of the bed, his hand lolling over his morning erection, trying to persuade himself that he had a true dilemma on his hands. But the truth was, Siobhan wasn't really the distraction and he wasn't really all that horny—he just craved any excuse not to go. He didn't want to do ten miles. Not today. Not in the rain. But it wasn't a choice; there really was no decision to make. He had to do it. And that was that. Half-marathon at the end of the month, all the won-derful people in his life effervescing on his justgiving.com page, pledging money for his chosen good cause. He dressed, steeled himself and headed out into the rain. More fool him for having believed in all that mad March sunshine yesterday. iPod on, he headed out of his house, past the other estate cottages in his terrace, and headed up Tramfield Lane at a sprint as if to prove wrong the Xander who'd woken thinking he didn't want to run today.

Within two miles he felt good. Really good. He headed his loop up Bridgeback Hill and through Dansworth Forest, pushing on hard until the gradient levelled out and he was looking down on the Georgian beauty of Longbridge Hall; the arable fields, noble woods, rolling parkland and manicured gardens of the Fortescue estate. The rain had stopped and sudden sunlight elicited caramel tones from the mansion's brickwork, glints of silver from the expansive slate roof; the high floating hornbeam hedge sparkled like a soft chuckle and the gravel driveway, from this angle, was like a swooping butter-coloured smile. Xander thought, it's been a while since I saw Lady Lydia. His instinct was still to refer to her thus if he hadn't seen her recently—though he'd been invited to call her Lydia once he'd graduated from university almost two decades ago.

I must drop her a line. It's been over a month.

He ran on and laughed out loud—remembering a conversation so clearly she could very well be running alongside him just then.

*'Have you heard of eel mails, Xander?'*

*'Email?'*

*'What a ghastly notion. Lady Ranchester told me she is now called dorothy at ranchester dot com. All lower case. How preposterous! Dot Common—that's what she is now.'*

*'Handwritten letters are now known as snail mail, Lydia.'*

*'Nonsense. If one can write—it's downright wrong not to.'*

\*      \*      \*

Ten miles in sixty-eight minutes. Not bad. Not bad.

'Xan?'

He wished Siobhan wouldn't call him that. Laura used to call him Xan. And that experience had shown him how familiarity bred contempt. Also,

14

with his mind now alert and his body charged by
endorphins, he just wanted to shower, have a quick,
quiet coffee with his bowl of muesli and be gone.
Siobhan didn't need to be here—not in his bed, not
on the scene. He had to do something about it, he
really did. Just not now.

'Xan?' she called out.

God!

'I need a shower!' he called back.

'I need to go.'

Thank God!

'OK.'

'Call me.'

'OK.'

\*       \*       \*

Xander always marvelled at the transformation. All
it took for his Lazy Git alter ego (the duvet-muffled
bloke who'd had too much red wine the night
before) to morph into Xander Fletcher with all
traces of sleep, sex, stubble and sweat erased, bright
and eager to greet the day, was a ten-mile run in
under an hour and ten minutes. Dressed neatly
in dark trousers and a pale shirt, driving sensibly
through his beloved village of Long Dansbury to
his office in Hertford twenty-five minutes away,
he thought of the process as a sort of protracted
Superman turnaround. Well, if not a super man,
a good bloke at any rate. Heading for forty in a
couple of years, Xander had no complaints at all.
He lived in a lovely cottage, he had an OK bank
balance and his own business keeping its head
above water, a close family, great friends and a
woman called Siobhan who didn't mind things

being casual. Doing those ten miles in sixty-three minutes would ice an already tasty cake. He thought about it as he headed out for his car. It was doable. Xander had been brought up to believe anything was doable. Apart from Love, which was beyond one's control. Accordingly, he'd decided not to entertain it in his life, not since Laura.

He drove through a landscape which rolled and tumbled like a soft green rucked-up quilt. Born and bred here, Xander had never fallen out of love with his environs and never stopped noticing its beauty or the changes, for better or worse. That's why, after interludes in Nottingham and London, he'd returned home at thirty.

His route took him through a handful of small villages, a few still with a shop clinging on for dear life to the local economy like a limpet to a storm-lashed rock. Most supported a pub and all of the villages heralded their approach with a profusion of daffodils along the verges in spring. Beyond each community, pastureland subtly cordoned off by barely visible electric fencing supported little gatherings of horses in weatherproof rugs, looking like the equine relatives of the Michelin Man. Woodland interrupted the swathes of fields like a patchy beard and the rivers Rib, Ash and Beane coursed through the landscape as if on a mission to deliver goodness straight to the Lea, the main artery of the area.

\* \* \*

'Good morning, Xander.'

Pauline Gregg, his PA of eight years, still wished he'd let her call him Mr Fletcher or Alexander

16

at the very least. To her, it seemed too casual, unseemly somehow. When she'd been at secretarial school all those decades ago, she'd been trained, along with other girls, in the correct way to address their future employers and their clients. Formality is fitting; that's what they learned. She felt it somehow downgraded her qualification to call her boss 'Xander'. Her daughter, who was Xander's age, told her it was a generational thing. But there again, her daughter had sent her children to a school where the pupils called their teachers by their Christian names. Moreover, the school didn't classify it thus, but as 'given names'. There again, *that* school appeared to be teaching Pauline's grandchildren more about something called Diwali than Christmas. So many things to button one's lip against—it was part of Pauline's day to declare to herself at least once, what's the world coming to?

'Morning, Mrs Gregg,' Xander said. He respected her right to be addressed like this—even though eight years on and being privy to the end of her marriage, the birth of her grandchildren and that Unfortunate Incident at the Roundabout With That Silly Car Which Wasn't Her Fault, Xander considered Mrs Gregg to be on the outer ring of his family.

'Seventy-two minutes?' she ventured. Xander cocked his head and smiled. 'Seventy?'

'Sixty-eight,' he said.

'Very good, that,' said Mrs Gregg. 'Tea?'

'Please.' They sipped in amicable silence, each leafing through the documents on their desks. Xander looked up. 'You've had your hair done.'

Mrs Gregg touched it self-consciously but smiled. 'Yes.'

17

'Very nice,' said Xander. He wished his own mother would wear her hair in a similar style— elegant and in place—instead of the unruly thatch half in, half out of a bun, invariably adorned with debris from the garden. 'Mrs Gregg, can you take this to the post office? And can you pick up a nice greetings card—blank inside?'

She glanced at him. When Xander had been steady with Laura for all those years, he'd never once asked her to help assist in the running of that relationship. He'd scoot off at lunch-time himself and return with flowers or something bulky in a bag which would sit quietly taunting her from the chair in the corner until he left in the evening. That was another part of her training going to waste—he had no need for her to alert him to Valentine's Day, or Special Occasions. Yet today he was asking her to buy a card, blank, just like his expression.

'Blank inside,' she said, writing it down and, without looking up, she asked, 'And what should be on the outside?'

'Oh,' he said, 'something soft—floral perhaps. Or a landscape.'

She wrote it down. Floral. Landscape. Unlikely to be a *special* card for a 'significant other'—or however his generation referred to girlfriends these days. She felt strangely relieved and yet somehow disappointed for him too. He's such a nice young man, she often described to her friends at bridge. It's a bit of a waste, she'd say. Perhaps he's not a *lady's man*, one of her chums might venture. Oh, he's not like *that*, Pauline would say, almost defensively. The contradiction had never confronted her—how she wanted to mother him, be at the helm of his life, yet keep the Decorum of

18

Division she'd been trained to maintain.

'Anything else?'

'Treat yourself to a Danish pastry,' said Xander.

'Why, thank you!'

With Mrs Gregg gone, Xander leafed through his diary and in-tray. Design, print and packaging wasn't a sexy business, but it was a solid one and even in the dire economic climate, Xander found his long-term clients remained loyal. He'd cut overheads instead of staff and it had been serendipitous that Keith, the designer, had asked to go part-time just when the office rent had been hiked, so Xander and Mrs Gregg moved to these smaller premises in the same building. Everything remained the same. Apart from the chair that had been in the corner of the old office, on which the flowers or the bag with the bulky object for Laura had once sat.

I don't need that chair, Mrs Gregg, Xander had said. And that's when Mrs Gregg realized Xander had broken it off with Laura—right at the point of engagement, she assumed. Though he said they could bring the chair with them, if she felt it might be useful, she'd declined. If he didn't need it, who was she to suggest he might, at some point, in the future?

\*          \*          \*

'I bought this card—it has flowers *and* a landscape and is what I'd call gentle. I have paper napkins with this very design.'

'Monet,' said Xander.

'No, no—it wasn't pricey.'

'*Monet,*' Xander said again, as if he hadn't heard

her. 'The Garden at Giverny.'

'One of my favourites,' Mrs Gregg said, as if there'd been no faux pas.

'It's most appropriate, thank you.'

Xander made a couple of calls and then, with the card open on his desk and his pen thoughtfully pursed between his lips, he gazed out of the window before beginning to write.

\* \* \*

'I'll take the post,' Mrs Gregg said at the end of the day.

'There's not much,' said Xander.

'It's not a problem.'

'I can post it on my way home.'

'Let me,' said Mrs Gregg. 'You know those country lanes—if you get stuck behind something, you'll be trundling along for hours and miss the post altogether. I'll pop it in the box outside Elmfield Estates—it's at the end of my street. It's never collected before six. Never.'

'OK,' said Xander. 'Thanks.'

She was barely out of the office door before she was leafing through the mail. Yes, yes, them, them, boring, boring. Ah! Aha!

*Lady Lydia Fortescue*
*Longbridge Hall*
*Long Dansbury*
*Hertfordshire*

Xander's handwriting: even, bold and steady, written with his trademark calligraphy fountain pen.

20

Mrs Gregg tutted at the envelope. Convene with women your own age, Xander, not an upper-class old battleaxe. Cut your ties with minor aristocracy! Venture forth into the real world—the one beyond Long Dansbury.

## *Chapter Three*

Stella didn't often go out, nor had she had her friends over that much recently. Her social life had dwindled over the last three years but this was her call because the invitations to socialize were no less forthcoming. Her close friends, her oldest friends— those she could count on the fingers of one hand who brought her all the dependable warmth and comfort of a well-fitting thermal glove—were always at the end of the phone, consistently energetic respondees to text messages and Facebook updates. Indirect contact and communication had become so easy that it was hard to remember when time was last spent together actually in person. She didn't mind; she was always busy and, with the new job, tired too. It wasn't as if she had much spare time to wonder how to fill it. But two weeks into her new position at Elmfield Estates, Stella had now settled into the routine. It was as if she'd been swamped by paperwork, floor plans and surveyors' reports and had suddenly looked up and thought, where is everyone? So tonight, butternut squash soup simmered on the stove and a baguette was ready on the breadboard awaiting the arrival of Jo, the closest Stella had to a sister. Tomorrow, she'd invited herself over to her older brother Robbie's and the day after that, their eldest brother Alistair would be hosting Sunday lunch for her on the condition she brought their mother *and* dessert. It did cross her mind that in one weekend she could conceivably regain the stone she'd lost over the last two years.

Jo arrived with a packet of tortilla chips, a jar of salsa, a great new haircut and, predictably, the suggestion of a date with some bloke who had a tenuous link to someone who knew someone who knew someone who knew Jo—and Stella had barely closed the front door.

'Come on in, madwoman.'

'You do realize I haven't actually seen you since Pancake Day?'

Stella laughed. 'Ah yes, when Stevie burnt herself on the pan, Scarlet spilled the sugar all over the floor and you referred to Michael as Tosser all evening?'

'He *was* Chief Tosser—in charge of flipping the flipping pancakes,' Jo justified. 'And I told my daughters to keep away from the stove and let me do the sugar sprinkling.'

'How are they all?'

'Fine. Gorgeous.' Jo kissed her friend three times: 'There—their kisses are delivered.'

'Thank you thank you thank you.' Stella paused and raised an eyebrow. 'I do have a bowl, you know. A veritable selection, in fact.' But Jo had already opened the tortilla chips en route to the kitchen and updated Stella on her various nightmares at work through a mouthful of crumbs.

The salsa was pretty hot, the soup was delicious and butter oozed fragrantly into the warmed baguette but Jo and Stella barely tasted any of it, their hunger for conversation outweighing what was to eat. Stella regaled Jo with the details of Elmfield Estates and it provided ample opportunity for the merry chinking of glasses.

'Any news from Charlie?' said Jo. 'Dare I ask?'

Stella chewed thoughtfully. 'Not a word. Funny how, before it all happened, you always used to call him Chuck—'

Jo interrupted. 'And when it was all kicking off, I called him Twatface.' She paused. 'I did wonder— even after all this time—with what's happening *now*, whether he'd be in touch.'

Stella shrugged. 'So did I. Yet the fact that he hasn't, well—'

Jo nodded. 'The lawyers—it'll be any day now, I expect.'

'I know,' said Stella.

'You'll call me—won't you?' Jo stretched over the crumbs, the globs of salsa and splashes of soup which now decorated the table like a minor work by Jackson Pollock. She squeezed Stella's arm. 'Call it the last piece of the jigsaw—the final nail in the coffin. It's a good thing.'

'I'll drink to that,' Stella said, raising a glass and sipping so that she didn't have to talk about it any more.

'By the way,' Jo said and, slowly, she let a lascivious smile spread, 'your hair is looking a bit mumsy.'

'Well, you look like a wee blonde elf,' Stella said, in her defence.

'That, my love, is intentional.'

'But I wear it like—this—for work,' Stella demonstrated, scooping it away from her face.

23

'That's highly appropriate for an estate agent,' Jo said measuredly, 'but a bit dull for a gorgeous, single, early-thirties gal.'

'I'm mid-thirties, practically. So what is it you suggest I do?'

'You phone Colin at Pop, that's what you do. And tell him I sent you. And don't tell him what you think you want—just put your head in his hands. Promise?'

'Yes, Mum.'

'How *is* your ma?'

'I'm seeing her on Sunday, actually. At Alistair's.'

'And how's the Robster?' Stella's brothers were as close as Jo came to having any.

'I'm seeing him tomorrow, funnily enough.'

Jo was pleased. Stella, it seemed, was emerging from her self-imposed hibernation. At long last.

*     *     *

'Mummy?' Will called. 'Mumma?'

Where *was* his rucksack? The medium-ish bluish one with the Clone Trooper design? Where had his mum *put* it? He looked in the usual places where she thought she tidied but really it was just moving his stuff to higher levels, to free up floor space. Well, it wasn't in any of those places. Nor at the back of the cupboard. Nope, not under his bed either. Where *was* it? 'Mummy!' He really didn't want to take the greenish, smallish rucksack because that had Ben 10 on and he *so* wasn't into Ben 10 any more. 'Mumm-y!' He opened his bedroom door and stood at the top of the stairs, placed a cupped hand either side of his mouth and bellowed for her again.

There was a tap on his shoulder and Will jumped out of his skin. How did she do that? That teleporting thing? Suddenly appearing right behind him with precisely what he'd been looking for all along, and that Am-I-or-Am-I-Not-the-Best-Mum-in-the-World look on her face? She was, of course, the Best Mum Ever—and he'd bought her the birthday card with a badge that said so—but she still liked to pull that particular face all the time.

'Why didn't you answer me?' Will said. 'I was yelling and yelling. I thought you'd been taken by aliens or fallen down the loo or something.'

'Thank you darling Mummy for my medium-ish bluish rucksack,' said Stella.

'Thanks, Mum.'

'Mummy,' said Stella.

'Do I really have to be forty-five before I can just call you *Mum*?'

'Absolutely. Now stuff in whatever it is you want to take to Uncle Robbie's and we'd better get going.'

Will went back into his bedroom and his mother went downstairs. 'Remember the Stickies could choke on any small pieces of Lego,' she called.

How did she know he was piling Lego into his bag? How did she *know* that? Will knew she had eyes in the back of her head—he'd known that from an early age. But how could she see through brick walls and closed doors? She said she'd tell him when he was ten—so just two years, six months and about a week of days and a zillion hours to go. He emptied out the Lego bricks and jumbled in some Bionicles pieces instead. His cousins— three-year-old Ruby and five-year-old Finn, commonly known as the Stickies on account of their constant general jamminess—were unlikely to eat Bionicles. Not once he'd explained their super powers and alarming weaponry. Anyway, his little cousins thought he was amazing in much the same way as he thought his older cousins, who he was seeing tomorrow, were incredible. And all his cousins called him Will-yum, sometimes just YumYum. Like he was delicious. And, as his mum told him he was precisely that, at least once a day, he sort of believed it too.

*       *       *

The Huttons were scattered over Hertfordshire; as if a handful of wild-flower seeds had been tossed from their mother's front doorstep in Harpenden. Alistair lived with his family in a lovely 1930s semi in a good suburb of Watford just a stroll from Cassiobury Park. Robbie had settled with his tribe in St Albans, Stella had spent almost a decade just around the corner from Alistair and was now in Hertford and Sandie, their mother, still lived in the family home in Harpenden. Their father, Stuart, had a flat in Hemel Hempstead but seemed to spend most of his time with an odd woman called Magda at her bungalow near Potters Bar, though he resurfaced each Christmas and steadfastly made no mention of her. In terms of quality time, it was pretty much on a par with how much his offspring had spent with him when he'd been married to their mother. Whenever they referred to him, it was accompanied by a roll of the eyes and a quick tut—as if mention of him caused a minor tic. But it was indeed minor, Stuart having never played a major part in their lives.

26

The following day, Will could hardly wait for his grandma to get in the car and do her seat belt before he told her about Ruby putting the Bionicle piece up her nose yesterday, and sucking the bogeys off it before giving it an almighty chewing and denting it with her small teeth. He had to keep making the incident sound like an extraordinary happening where he'd somehow been both victim and hero, to deflect attention from the fact that everyone had said to him, Don't Let Ruby Put Anything in Her Mouth. The grown-ups had given him responsibility. And though he'd failed, his expressive storytelling made it sound as though he'd saved Ruby *and* the Bionicle and he was fine about the fact that his toy was riddled with teeth marks.

His grandma was riveted. 'Can you imagine if Ruby had swallowed it?' She craned her neck to look aghast at Will in the back seat. 'There'd be some poor Bionicle chap missing a vital part of his anatomy. *Then* how would the battles be won?'

'Exactly,' marvelled Will.

'Exactly,' Sandie concurred.

'Mum!' Stella protested.

'Grandma, how old was Mummy before she could call you Mum?'

'Twenty-eight and three-quarters,' Sandie said, not missing a beat.

'I have to be forty-five.'

'That's not very fair,' said Sandie.

'Twenty-seven, then,' said Stella, glancing in the rear-view mirror at her son and giving him a wink.

'Cool,' said Will, looking out the car window.

Will assumed that, because of the family thing, he was genetically programmed to grow up and turn out like the Twins, teenagers Pauly and Tom, in much the same way as the Stickies would grow up to be just like him. And they'd all, one day in about a million years, turn into grown-ups like Alistair and Robbie. Apart, of course, from Sticky Ruby who'd turn out like her mum and Will's mum and the Twins' mum.

Much as Will felt his mother was the best, he secretly acknowledged that Aunty Juliet was the better cook, possibly the best cook in the world and, as he took his place between the Twins at the laden table he happily blocked out the boring chatter of the grown-ups, and the revolting mess of the Stickies sitting opposite him, to focus wholeheartedly on the spectacular offerings on his plate.

Stella sat by Juliet, whom she adored. Her brothers flanked their mother and Sara, Robbie's wife, sat between her toddlers and managed in her inimitably competent way to feed herself and her children, yet be utterly present in the conversation. Stella looked around the table. It was like sitting in the best seats at the theatre waiting for the play to begin. With a surge of joy she thought this was to be her afternoon. It would linger into early evening and she was happy. She'd leave, hours later, replete in body and soul. Thank God for family. Thank God for hers. The decibel level was high yet not discordant and topics bounded between them all like the ball in a bagatelle. The tangents they veered off to, all part of the colourful ricochet of joyful banter.

'It just goes back to what Gordon Brown said— but didn't do,' said Alistair.

'That goes without saying,' said Sandie, about

something else entirely.

Sara chewed thoughtfully, picking up on an earlier thread. 'I love the idea of supporting local businesses, shopping at the corner shop, buying books from a little independent bookshop. But when there's Amazon and Ocado, and special offers which I can order online at silly o'clock, then it's no contest.'

'It was the debilitating flaw in New Labour,' said Robbie to Alistair.

'I think you're probably right,' said Sandie to any of them.

'I have to agree,' Juliet said, a little forlornly. She looked thoughtfully at a roast potato. 'I bought these spuds from the farmers' market. Ridiculously expensive, weighed a ton. I'm not entirely sure they taste any different from Waitrose. Oh, and Stella—I think I've found you a man.'

'Whatsit's brother?' Alistair asked.

'Miliband?' said Robbie.

'No—who Juliet's talking about. For Stella.'

'Oh! I forgot about him,' said Juliet. '*Two* men, then,' she told the table.

'I have one for you too,' said Sara.

'Three,' Robbie whistled.

'Who's who?' asked Sandie.

'The chap that takes Sing-a-Song,' said Sara. 'The Stickies love him. He's so—smiley.' She paused. 'And he only wears the spotty trousers and silly hat when he's working. I saw him strolling through the Maltings last week. Almost didn't recognize him—really nice and normal. We had a little chat and I managed to deduce he's not attached, not gay and likes dogs.'

'I don't have a dog,' said Stella.

29

'I know,' said Sara, 'but it's a *type*, isn't it—if he likes dogs he must have that caring side to his nature. Plus, of course, he's great with kids.'

'No, thanks,' said Stella.

'Talking of great with kids,' Juliet said, 'option number one is the brother of my friend Mel. He's older—'

'How old?' Robbie interjected.

'Fifty-odd,' said Juliet.

'I don't like the "odd",' said Sandie.

'I don't like the fifty,' said Robbie.

'All right,' said Juliet, 'option number two is late thirties, never been married, split up with his girlfriend over a year ago. Has his own hair, his own teeth. He's handsome, chatty, caring and he lives in Hadley Wood, apparently.'

'He sounds promising,' said Sara.

'No, thanks,' said Stella.

'Hadley Wood is no longer a purely middle-aged enclave,' said Alistair. 'You should know that, Stella—from the property market.'

'No, thanks,' said Stella.

'Who is he?' asked Robbie.

'My gynae,' said Juliet.

'No, thanks,' said Stella.

'Stella,' Juliet said, 'don't be put off by his day job.'

'The last thing I want to do after a day at the computer screen is to come home and log on,' said Robbie darkly.

'Don't be awkward,' said Sandie.

'It's not his job,' said Stella.

'What's his name?' asked Sara.

'Bryanaston.'

'What sort of a name is Bryanaston?' asked

30

Sandie.

'That's his surname,' said Juliet. 'His first name is Henry.'

'No, thanks,' said Stella.

They looked at her with For Heaven's Sake, Why Not? written across their faces.

She shrugged.

'Not ready?' Juliet said softly.

'Not interested,' said Stella. 'I'm fine as I am.'

'For the time being?' Sandie asked her daughter, a gentle pleading edging her question like garnish.

'For the time being,' Stella said. 'Did any of you watch that new serial on the Beeb on Friday?'

'About Rembrandt?'

'With Kevin Branagh?' said Sandie.

'*Kenneth*,' said everyone else.

'Yes,' said Stella.

'We did.'

'Us too.'

'Wasn't it brilliant?'

'You and your Rembrandt,' Sandie said. 'She wrote her thesis on Rembrandt, you know. She got a first.'

They all knew that, and they all knew Sandie should be allowed to proclaim the fact as often as she liked.

\*     \*     \*

Stella found Alistair, later on, out in the garage with all the children—including the teenage Twins—looking on in awe as he set his Hornby model railway into action. She watched alongside them for a while, transfixed by the little trees she'd made for him when she was a kid, remembering again the smell of

31

the particular green paint she'd dipped the tiny torn pieces of sponge into. Remembering how they'd dried them on an old cake rack before painstakingly securing them onto matchstick trunks—her first use of Super Glue, her eldest brother coaching her, encouraging her, trusting her.

'Alistair?' Reluctantly, he looked up from controlling the points. 'Here.' She passed him a brown envelope.

'What's this?'

'My rent, silly,' she said.

'Oh.' He looked at the envelope as if he dreaded the contents.

'This month and last.'

'Stella—it's fine, you know. Juliet and I both say—it's fine.'

Stella shook her head decisively. 'No way. It's your house—and you have done me the most almighty favour in letting me live there for this amount. I know what the true rental value is, you know. My new job, Alistair—it's a lifesaver. I can make ends meet—with commission, I might even be able to tie them in a bow.'

He continued to look at the envelope. 'Charlie?' he asked, very quietly, glancing at Will who was engrossed in *Sir Nigel Gresley* belting along the tiny track trying to catch up with the *Flying Scotsman*.

Stella shook her head.

'No news?'

She shook her head again.

Alistair said Bastard under his breath, not so much for Stella's sake, but for his own.

'Please,' he held the envelope out to her.

'No, thanks,' she said. She pushed her hands

32

defiantly into her pockets, and she placed her head gently against her brother's shoulder. She looked forward to the day when those close to her were no longer irked by Charlie.

## *Chapter Four*

*3 Lime Grove Cottages*
*Tramfield Lane*
*Long Dansbury*
*Herts*

*Monday*

*Dear Lydia*
*I hope this finds you in good health and high spirits. I took in the view of Longbridge Hall on my early morning run—the rain had lifted, a soft mist rolled quietly just above ground level, a glint of sunshine, a hint of spring—it really was a wonderful sight. Did you know there's an extremely nice new Belgian patisserie recently opened in Ware? How about I treat you—or perhaps a bite of lunch at Hanbury Manor? Or just a stroll around Hatfield House? Audrey and Bert send their best—and I send my fondest.*

*Xander*

Lady Lydia Fortescue read the letter twice. First with a smile, then with her customary wry consternation. A *Belgian* patisserie? In *Ware*? Was the boy forgetting Longbridge's own Mrs Biggins whose scones and Victoria sponge and shortbread were legendary? Why buy foreign,

33

dear God? And lunch at Hanbury Manor—
preposterous! Rumour had it that New Money
went there, and frightful Hen Party girls lolled
around the place at weekends. Apparently, the
hotel now had one of those gym places where
men and women wore ridiculous get-ups and
sweated and grunted alongside each other like
toiling workhorses. A walk at *Hatfield*? During
public opening hours? Paying for the privilege
when she'd often been there as a guest of the
Salisburys? *And* he'd written 'Audrey and Bert'—
as if, had he just said 'my parents', she might be
prone to have forgotten who they were.

Lydia laughed—a little staccato rush of air
through her nostrils. Dear Xander. She would *love*
to see the boy. How long had it been? A month?
Six weeks? Atrocious! She walked from the drawing
room through the staircase hall and across the
entrance hallway over to the library. At the writing
bureau, she sat and rummaged through the chaotic
upper drawer for one of her heavy, watermarked,
monogrammed cards.

Longbridge Hall
Long Dansbury
Hertfordshire

Wednesday

My dear Xander,
A treat to hear from you. Delighted to have
provided an aesthetic backdrop to your athletic
endeavours. I must decline the foreign bakery,
and the public liability of Hanbury or Hatfield.

34

But do come to tea at Longbridge, dear. Shall we say Saturday next—at half past three?

Yours,

Lydia F


Rifling through another drawer, becoming a little sidetracked by a clutch of old thank-you cards sent to her after some dinner party or other an age ago, Lydia found a sheet of second-class stamps. And then she came across the estimate for the roof repairs which she'd hidden on purpose months ago. She glanced at the columns of figures—the grand total—and cast her eyes to the heavens. Only, the ceiling was in the way and, taunting her, the yellow watermark ominously circumnavigating the cracked plaster of the ceiling rose. She buried the paperwork in an ancient copy of *Country Life* and set off for the postbox outside the village shop.

As Lydia walked back, she chided herself for not taking the car because she was undeniably tired. And silly—it wasn't as if anyone would judge her, not at her age, not that she was remotely concerned with what anyone thought anyway. The driveway seemed to be so long these days and when did it develop this incline? Underfoot felt hard, uneven, despite her wearing her most comfortable slip-ons. She laughed—recalling a time when she refused to even glance at comfortable shoes, let alone buy them and wear them out in public.

Finally, she was home. And then she realized she'd forgotten her keys. No use knocking, it was Mrs Biggins' day off. She went to the side of the house knowing the back door was unlocked because it was so tricky to lock that they'd given up years

35

ago and just used the bolts, but she doubted it was bolted because Mrs Biggins wasn't tall enough to shunt the topmost one across, and both she and her housekeeper were now old enough to eschew using anything one had to climb upon in order to reach something.

There were seven stone steps leading down to the door and, through the frosted glass pane, Lydia could see the comforting welcome of the lights she'd accidentally left on in the house. Down one step, two—it was really quite chilly. Three, four, five. Finally! Six and—

She fell. She wasn't sure why. It didn't matter why. But her shoulder bore the brunt and she took a knock to the side of her face too. It hurt, of course it hurt. But more significant than the pain was the shock. She felt frightened and that appalled her.

Mrs Biggins, damn you and your day off! Lydia stayed still for a few minutes. Was anything broken? She'd fractured various bones in hunting accidents over the years—no, she didn't think so. Still, she felt most unsure about picking herself up. Her cheekbone was throbbing and her fingers were numb.

Hullo? Is anyone home? What a stupid question—why would there be? Mrs Biggins was probably in Bishop's Stortford with her daughter. Mercifully, the door was indeed unlocked and Lydia finally made her way shakily inside. She checked her reflection and noted a red mark on the apple of her cheek, growing darker. Frozen peas, she thought, going into the kitchen. And then the lights flickered. Oh dear God, no. Just wait until I have the wretched peas, would you! Flickered again. And then off.

Once again, something somewhere had fused. Even without the fall, Lydia wouldn't go feeling and fumbling her way to the panel down in the basement. More uneven stone steps. And an ancient and hostile fuseboard in what really was a dank dungeon. Silly old cheek—it was horribly sore. Lydia clasped her way along the kitchen wall to the dresser and located a box of matches after various things fell to the floor, one of which made the undeniable sound of something thick spilling. Lighting match after match, she managed to illuminate the safest passage to the cupboard under the sink where she knew there'd be a torch. Whether or not it had a battery in it would be another matter. Luckily, it did and its soft orange beam directed her to the freezer where she retrieved the peas and placed them in a tea towel against her cheek. Really, she should phone someone—Art or Clarence. But she didn't want to. She really didn't. Instead, she sat in the dark in the drawing room for a while, trying to read *Country Life* by the waning light of the torch until she told herself she wanted an early night anyway and didn't care for whatever it was that Mrs Biggins would have left her for her supper all the way back in the kitchen.

# Chapter Five

The longest thing about Long Dansbury village was the high street, with all other streets branching off it in short runs like the veins on a horse chestnut leaf. The high street itself, whilst not a cut-through to anywhere from anywhere, was still relatively busy in terms of traffic because along its length lay the church, the primary school, two good pubs, a Spar general store which also sold newspapers and stamps, and Michael Lazarus's ironmongery—which was more of a museum than a shop, if the number of people who ventured into the Dickensian interior simply to look rather than to buy, was anything to go by. The houses along the high street were defined as being either at Top End or else at Back End, though in fact from the centre, which was marked by the gates and long, snaking driveway to Longbridge Hall, the high street sloped upwards to either end. But Top End had always been known as such because here the finer, larger houses sat spruce and proud, like dapper Georgian gentlemen keeping an eye on things. In comparison, like a scatter of peasant children, were the cottages which defined the Back End; some standing on their own like shy sheep, some in a chatter of four or five in short terraces. What made the high street so pretty was that all the buildings, whatever their size, had frontage. Even in winter, flowers and well-tended shrubs proudly sang forth.

Beyond the cottages, a thatch of woodland bristled to either side of the road, after which the new houses stood in an embarrassed huddle.

These were, in fact, pre-war and far more sensible family homes than the old cramped cottages. But they would always be known as the New Houses in a gently dismissive way. Even the people who lived there gave their address with a slightly resigned tone.

Pride of place, not just in the village but in the wider locale itself, was Longbridge Hall, seat of the Fortescue family, the Earls of Barbary, for eight generations. It was as if Longbridge Hall had sat down so firmly, so emphatically, directly at the centre of the village, that the road to either side had been pushed upwards; rather like a portly old uncle settling himself right in the middle of a sagging sofa. The house itself was not actually visible from the high street; set some way back, its presence was nonetheless felt—the wrought-iron gates with handsome stone supports and the parade of lime trees lining the imposing driveway and heralding something undeniably grand beyond.

When Stella arrived on the Saturday morning, to meet Mrs Benton at number four Tidy Row Cottages, she couldn't believe that, as a Hertfordshire girl, she'd never once been to Long Dansbury. Parking her car, as she'd been instructed, in the gravel rectangle opposite the Spar, she was glad to be early and she walked slowly, taking in the surroundings. In fact, she was so enthralled by the houses, she wasn't actually looking where she was going. And Xander was so busy checking his pedometer as he ran, estimating he'd need to sprint up Back End, that he saw the woman only at the last minute.

The runner clipped Stella's shoulder hard, sending her Elmfield Estates folder flying.

39

'Oi!' she turned and glowered, rubbing her arm indignantly.

He ran on the spot for a step or two, held his hands up in mock surrender and panted, 'Sorry!'

'Honestly!' Stella muttered as she chased the scatter of sheets. 'You could at least help.'

He jogged in an exasperated arc back to her and gathered some of the papers, thrusting a scrunch of them at her, before belting off.

As she sifted and sorted, somewhat flustered, a passer-by stopped to help.

'Don't mind Xander,' the good Samaritan said. 'He's in training.'

'He's a public liability,' Stella muttered. 'Joggers —like caravans and big lorries—should only be allowed out after hours.'

The other woman picked up the Elmfield Estates terms and conditions and thought how Xander would have something to say about being called a jogger. 'Do you know where you're going?'

'Er, Tidy Row Cottages. Number four.'

'Mercy,' the woman muttered and for a moment Stella wondered if there was something she should know before she remembered the appointment was with a Mrs M. Benton.

'Mrs Benton,' Stella said.

'Fancy that,' said the woman, looking Stella up and down. 'John Denby won't be pleased.' John Denby's For Sale sign had been outside Mercy Benton's cottage for quite some time. Houses in Long Dansbury were only ever sold by John Denby. Fancy that. Wonder if they knew! She'd call Margaret as soon as she was home. See if she'd heard anything.

'Well, thank you for your help,' said Stella,

40

sensing slight resistance when she tried to take the Elmfield forms from the lady.

Mercy Benton's cottage was compact and immaculate and though the kitchen was old it could be modernized with minimal fuss. Stella walked around with the owner, genuinely charmed by the features and also by the owner's furniture and trinkets. It reminded her of her late grandmother's place. A porcelain ornament of a Shire horse and foal. A cut-glass lidded bowl full of stripy humbugs. Antimacassars on an olive-green velvet sofa and armchair. Photographs of family on top of the telly.

'I love it!' Stella told her.

'I do too,' said Mrs Benton. 'But it's time to go.'

'And you've found an apartment at Summerhill Place?'

'Oh, it's lovely. It really is.'

'So I've heard,' said Stella.

'You know it was once a country mansion? How grand that I'll be living there! They've done a lovely job. It's all self-contained apartments now—but with tea served in a smashing room downstairs for residents every afternoon. And a cleaner once a week. And bridge on Tuesdays. Bingo on Thursdays. Recitals and the like on Saturdays. And an emergency call button. All sorts going on. Such lovely grounds—ever so grand. Beryl went there a year ago. Loves it. We were at school together, you know.'

Stella nodded. 'Was Beryl from Long Dansbury too?'

Mercy Benton laughed. 'Of course!' She paused. 'Silly bugger.'

'Sorry?'

'That fast-talking chappy from John Denby.'

Mercy thought about it quietly. He'd expressed no interest in her home—only in the house. He couldn't see the intrinsic difference. He hadn't even asked a thing about Summerhill Place. That's why, twelve weeks later and with only a dribble of viewings, Mercy had decided to invite Elmfield Estates to cast an eye. She liked this young woman. Look at her now, peering at the face on the toby jug as if it was someone she recognized; running her fingers lightly back and forth across the tasselled edging of the tapestry cushion. She had gazed and gazed at the view of the garden from the back bedroom. She'd asked Mercy what flowered out there. Made notes on her pad of all Mercy told her.

'Would you be considering Elmfield as joint agents? Alongside Denby?'

'What do you suggest, dear?'

'Between you and me, Mrs Benton, if you haven't had an offer in three months, they are showing the wrong people around. Off the top of my head, I have two clients on my list—this beautiful home would suit either of them down to the ground. Also, if you give Elmfield a crack as sole agents, the commission you pay is much less.'

'Will it be you?'

'I wish I could afford it. I'd love to live here.'

'No, dear—I mean, will it be you who does all of the everything?'

'*All of the everything*,' Stella smiled. 'Yes, it'll be me. I assure you. Everything. Phone calls, visits, negotiations. The lot. Just me, Mrs Benton.'

'Call me Mercy.'

'Well, Mercy, I'll need a couple of days to organize the particulars, photographs and red tape—and hopefully, by midweek at the latest, I'll

42

be back, with my clients.'

'Would you like a humbug?'

'I'd love one. Thank you! And Mercy—when I bring people to view, offer them a humbug too, or a cuppa. It helps.'

That brash young man from Denby's had recommended she go out when he brought anyone to her home. 'Thank you, dear.'

'Thank *you*.'

*    *    *

Despite the sprint home, Xander wasn't particularly happy with his time. And he couldn't really blame the young woman who'd all but floored him. She hadn't really slowed him down more than a few seconds. He'd rest tomorrow. Possibly the next day too. His legs felt heavy. He was heading towards the *run less run faster* period in his training which, though he knew it was sensible, today still seemed like a contradiction.

He looked in his wardrobe. Tea with Lydia. He chose a white Oxford shirt with button-down collar and looked from his choice of ties to his one good jacket. It would be one or the other. He couldn't bear both at the same time, he'd feel trussed up *and* garrotted. Ultimately, he went for the tie. It was vivid blue with a pale lemon stripe. He couldn't remember when last he'd worn it.

The afternoon was bright and the morning's breeze had subsided—a brisk walk to Longbridge in shirtsleeves would be fine, but home again later, he knew the air would have chilled considerably. He grabbed his North Face jacket and set off with it slung over his shoulder, strolling down from the Back End along the high street to the gates to Longbridge. He could have gone the back way— walked uphill to the end of his lane and along the footpath, over two fields and through the side gate hidden in the yew hedge after the farmyard. But the track could be muddy this time of year. And it was lambing season. He waved to Mercy Benton, her headscarf tied neatly under her chin, pulling her old tartan shopping trolley as if it was a reluctant, aged dog. He spoke to the Pickards, out for a stroll, and he told the Pittman kid who lived at Wisteria House to pick up the crisp packet and put it in the bin. They were dreadful, that family—money, but no manners.

Up the driveway to Longbridge, a force of habit compelled Xander to try and count each of the two hundred and fifty-two panes of glass in the twenty-one sash windows by the time the avenue of limes had ended and the formal box hedging had begun. The approach to Longbridge was an exception to the rule of distances seeming shorter, places seeming smaller, than childhood memories decreed. Though he knew the house well—even down to the one missing stone support on the balustrade parapet high up where the brick walls ended and the hipped slate roof began, or which of the window panes were new glass and not the beautiful shimmering original—familiarity had not compromised the pleasure of the sight of this grand old building. He still felt awestruck by its sedate, imposing grandeur. He never climbed the broad stone entrance steps without patting one of the stone lions that stood guarding it, he never rang the clanking great doorbell to the side of the mahogany double doors without looking up and marvelling at

44

the fanlight—vast yet as delicate as lacework.

He waited, wondered whether he should ring again or give the doors a polite rap. But he didn't want to be given short shrift—he'd been on the receiving end of that, once before, when he was a teenager and he'd seen Lydia a little way ahead of him along the high street. Yoo hoo! he'd called that day. Yoo hoo! The public dressing-down she'd exacted had been mortifying.

No. He'd wait. Up until a couple of years ago, Barnaby the black Labrador would have retaliated at the doorbell with a cacophony of howls—but he was deaf now. And it had been a long while since there'd been an excitable posse of Jack Russells at Longbridge bred, it seemed, precisely for the purpose of nipping the ankles of any visitor.

'Xander!'

But the door hadn't opened.

He turned to find Lydia standing at the bottom of the steps, swamped by an ancient waxed jacket, a headscarf neatly under her chin, a walking stick used so naturally, so deftly, that it was more like an extension of her arm than a crutch of any sort. She climbed the stairs slowly, not taking her eyes off him.

'You've grown!'

'You always say that,' Xander laughed. 'It's only been a month.'

'Five weeks. And you never say I'm shrinking,' Lydia said, 'but I'll bet you think it.'

'Not when you have that walking stick with you!' said Xander. 'Your cheek, Lydia, what have you done?'

'Nothing, just a silly knock. Looks far worse than it feels. Have you rung the bell?'

45

'Yes.'

Lydia sighed, exasperated. 'Where *is* that wretched woman!' She tapped hard against the doors with her cane and Xander noted all the little dents, flecking into the wood like rain against a windscreen. 'She's in there, you know. Reading the *Mail*.' Lydia spoke the newspaper's name with such disdain it might as well have been *Mein Kampf*.

Through the doors, they could hear footsteps and the sound of someone talking to themselves. 'Is someone at the door? I didn't hear. I'll just check.' The door was opened gingerly and Mrs Biggins' face peered out. 'Oh,' she said, glancing at Lydia, 'it's you. And Xander! Xander! Come on in!'

'You're an utterly useless woman,' Lydia told her housekeeper.

'And you're forgetful—you must remember to take your keys.'

'I have my keys!' Lydia protested.

'Then why did you knock?'

'I didn't. Xander did.'

'Xander—did you knock?'

He paused, feeling like a ping-pong ball caught in a particularly vicious rally between two dab hands in this long played-out game. 'I rang the bell,' he said.

'You see—*you* knocked. *He* rang the bell.'

'Well, *you* didn't answer the bell when he rang. He was probably standing there for yonks. You're as deaf as Barnaby.'

'I am not!'

'You were reading the *Mail*, then.' Lydia brushed past Mrs Biggins and into the entrance hall.

'You're not going to hang that stinking old coat here,' Mrs Biggins warned her.

46

'No,' said Lydia, 'you're going to hang it in the boot room.' And she stood still, while Mrs Biggins eased the coat off her, in much the same way as the butler would remove her mother's mink stole decades ago. Not that any butler who wanted to keep his job would have pulled a face such as Mrs Biggins was currently wearing.

'We'll have tea,' Lydia announced. 'In the drawing room.' And Xander thought, one day Mrs Biggins might well say get it yourself.

But not today.

*     *     *

Tea in the drawing room. It was an institution that Xander enjoyed as much now as then. The anticipation of the tray being brought in, counted down by the frustratingly slow, patient tock of the grandfather clock, while legions of Fortescues observed the event from their slightly tarnished photograph frames crowding the grand piano, the mantelpiece, the ledge in front of the glazed bookcase.

The selection was always the same: sandwiches of fish paste or butter and cucumber slices, and a plate of cakes. Today, it struck Xander how the food seemed to personify the irascible dowager and her cantankerous housekeeper—the cucumber sandwiches delicate and refined like the former, the fish paste slightly common yet comforting like the latter. Similarly, the pastries so elegantly put together with the fancy toppings, just as appealing as the plain but reassuringly doughy Chelsea buns.

'Will that be all?' Mrs Biggins asked.

'Thank you, Mrs Biggins, that will be all.'

47

'Thank you, Mrs B.'

'Lovely to see you, Xander. You send your ma my love. And don't be a stranger.'

With the large French-polished coffee table between them, Xander and Lydia sat opposite each other on matching sofas—faded, capacious rather than comfortable, fleshed out by a growing collection of daily-plumped cushions to counteract the general sag and lumpiness. Xander offered the sandwiches to Lydia and then took one of each for himself. Lydia poured the tea, the same tea cosy warming the pot that Xander remembered his mother knitting when he was still a boy. There was so much about Longbridge that stayed the same. There were the sounds—the clocks, different in each room, the water in the crunking old pipes complaining its way around the house, the whistle of the kettle on the Aga as dramatic as an air-raid warning. And the smells—Assam tea, ancient tobacco, a faint mustiness from old soft furnishings, a subtle drift of floral arrangements that needed changing, of vegetables cooking in the kitchen, or lavender secreted in little muslin pouches in between cushion and cover. And there was the set-up of each room—the photograph frames and various porcelain ornaments just so, the furniture whose configuration never changed, the heavy folds of the enormous curtains as vertical and precise as the fluting on Greek columns. And the portraits of the ancestors, positioned around the house like sentries, some gazing benignly, some fixing sternly, all staring directly.

'Little changes, Xander.'

'I'm pleased.'

'You still look from portrait to portrait, as if

answering questions asked of you in a particular order.'

'I know.'

'You're wearing a tie.'

'I could have worn a jacket.'

'Mostly, these days, I see you scampering around in all that ghastly sportswear.'

'I'm training—I have a half-marathon next week.'

'Does that mean you'll be begging me for sponsorship?'

'Most definitely.'

'African babies again?'

'Cancer, this time.'

'Jolly good. Pastry?'

Xander finished a jam tart and waited for Lydia to raise her eyebrows at the platter for him to help himself to another. 'Longbridge plums,' he said, 'incomparable.'

'Jars and jars of the bastard stuff in the pantry—help yourself when you go,' Lydia said. 'Surplus from the summer fete—the first time we've come back with unsold produce. Ever.'

'Don't take it personally,' Xander said. 'People are holding on to their pennies. Anyway, I heard it was more to do with politics within the committee.'

'That wretched bouncing castle monstrosity?'

Xander laughed. 'And the rest.'

'Personally,' said Lydia, 'I blame all that shopping people do nowadays on those computers. It's an obsession and, if you ask me, absolutely unnecessary! All those supermarket vans double parking along the high street and all those delivery companies doing the postman out of a job. More tea?'

'Please.' He offered his cup because Lydia liked to pour and she wouldn't tolerate people stretching. 'How are things here?' He looked around—it looked the same, but Longbridge was so much more than the house itself. 'I hear Mr Tringle made a good recovery—pneumonia is no laughing matter, especially not at his age.'

'I've always thought, if they dropped one of those nuclear bombs, he'd be the one creaking his way out of the debris. Extraordinary chap, really.'

'How about the barns?' asked Xander. 'Did you get anywhere with the planners?'

Lydia looked a little uncomfortable. 'I'm just going to have to let them crumble—it's too much work and too much money. And Xander, how are *you*? Are you any closer to marrying?'

Xander stirred his tea thoughtfully, despite not taking sugar. 'No.'

'Are you one of the gays?'

'No, Lydia. I'm not.'

She raised her eyebrow, archly. 'I've heard people talking.'

'Talking?'

'Village tittle-tattle.'

'And you listen to it?'

'Sometimes I like to remember dear Alice Roosevelt who used to say, *if you haven't got anything nice to say about anybody, come sit next to me.*'

'And people are saying I'm not nice?'

'Well, if you won't provide the real story of Laura—then the only option you give them is to rumour.'

'Whatever the gossip is,' said Xander, 'it's probably far more salacious and entertaining than

50

the reality. I don't care what people say about me.'

'If you're sure you haven't joined the gays—perhaps you've become a playboy?' Lydia chuckled. 'A cad?' She laughed. 'A gigolo?' And she pronounced it with hard 'g's.

Xander shrugged—coming from Lydia, none of this irritated him. 'I haven't met the right girl, Lady Lydia.'

'But you're having lots of fun with all the wrong ones, for the time being?'

He loved it when Lydia turned saucy.

'Your mother must be *so* proud.' She paused. 'I bet your mother doesn't know the half of it.'

'I sincerely hope not,' said Xander.

'Are you a two-timer?' She said it as if it was some modern phrase she wasn't entirely sure she was using correctly.

'No, Lydia, I'm not. I just don't invest much time, or importance, in—*relationships*,' Xander said, as if it was a word whose meaning he was unsure of. He loosened his tie, feeling hot under the collar.

'I hope you're a gentleman,' Lydia said sternly.

'I've never made a girl cry,' Xander said, with a theatricality that had Lydia chuckling.

'I'm sure your Laura shed a tear or two over you. I know your mother did, at the time.'

'That was well over two years ago.'

Lydia could see Xander's discomfort. 'I always said you should have tracked her down sooner. Said sorry with something sparkly from Garrard's.'

'Lydia—she moved to the States and she's married. You *know* this.'

'More fool you.'

'I have no regrets.' The Chelsea bun was sticking in this throat.

51

'You're a *catch*, young man. An eligible bachelor. You oughtn't to go to waste—that would be a travesty.'

'I'm not so young these days—I'm heading for forty. Look at all the grey.'

Lydia rubbished this with a dismissive wave of her hand. 'Very distinguished. Silver fox, we'd call it. Like my fabulously expensive coat. Which reminds me—it's still in cold storage. Don't you go putting yourself in storage, Xander, you'll grow cold. You're a whippersnapper—I'm seventy-eight.'

A phone began to ring. There were no modern cordless phones at Longbridge. In fact, there were only three telephones in the whole house; one in the kitchen, one in the staircase hallway and one in the Victorian wing. They listened to it ringing.

Lydia blasphemed under her breath.

'Why the wretched woman won't answer the telephone or the door I do not know. I should dock her pay, I really should.' And she heaved herself away from the sofa, rubbing her shoulder and wincing as she made her way. 'She's an atrocious housekeeper, that Mrs Biggins. I really ought to sack her.'

But she keeps you on your toes, Xander thought tenderly, as Lydia left the room to answer the phone. And she's company. Mrs Biggins and Lady Lydia Fortescue, practically the same age, diametrically opposed backgrounds, together longer than either of their marriages—together, realistically, for ever. He listened to Lydia curtly admonishing the caller for phoning in the first place and then barking something in the general direction of the kitchen where Mrs Biggins was no doubt still ensconced in the *Mail*.

He'd phone his mum and dad when he was home. They lived, now, in Little Dunwick five miles away and Xander wondered why he always felt compelled to phone them when he'd been to Longbridge. He'd tell them how nothing had changed apart from Lydia growing thinner and Mrs Biggins plumper, that everything at Longbridge was just ever so slightly more dusty than in the days when his mother was nanny to the Fortescue offspring and the house bustled with staff.

## *Chapter Six*

Stella was prepared for it to come and yet, when it arrived, though she knew exactly what it was, she felt thrown. She stared at the envelope and re-read her name and address carefully, underlining the words with her finger, as if to be absolutely sure that the contents were indeed intended for her. It was something she'd applied for, paid quite a lot for; waited over two years for but didn't want. Not today. Today was about other things, positive things. The Marshalls were due to exchange on Mercy Benton's little cottage in Long Dansbury—less than a month after viewing it, record time for Elmfield Estates this year. Today, Stella was viewing a large property in Cold Christmas and another in Bengeo. Today the Haddams' mortgage offer for the house in Bramfield should be through. Today should be filled with all the excitement of here and now, not sullied by then and there. And tonight, parents' evening (or parent's evening—Stella was fastidious about the correct position of the apostrophe in her case) at Will's school and there was nothing more uplifting than being nourished by the warmth of compliments and praise bestowed upon one's child. So damn you, bloody brown bloody A4 envelope with the franked mail mark and correct address.

But she knew what she had to do. She'd been prepped. She texted Jo.

it's here. Sx

A moment later, the response Jo had been waiting a long time to give.

do not open—will try to be there by 8. Jxx

She wasn't expecting Stella's response.

not poss—parent's eve. Sx

who's bbsittng? J?

Mum Sx

Jo thought, much as Stella loves her mum, she won't be opening it with her.

cant do 2moz—Mike out. Soz ☹  Can you hold on til w/end?? Jxx

Stella thought, I'd rather not open it at all.

K. Sx

U ok, babes? Jxx

Yep xx

\*  \*  \*

Everyone had told Stella that, if there was an optimum age when change would have a minimal effect on a child, then she'd taken that decision for Will at exactly the right time in his life. Home. School. Just the two of them. Stella bit the bullet and went for change. Her loved ones had praised her, as if it had been a canny choice she'd

54

systematically made and not the only angst-ridden option she'd felt she had. Actually, the only choice she'd really had was between Harpenden and Hertford and her big brother had made that an easy one, with the cut-price offer of his rental house.

That evening, listening to the teacher praising Will, the feeling of Stella's heart expanding even more for her popular, industrious and bright little boy was tempered by the presence of the little low red plastic chair empty next to the one on which she sat. It was as if the full impact of all the wonderful words was somehow reduced because it was heard by only one set of ears. Parent's evening.

Four terms in, she no longer felt conspicuous as the lone single parent in Will's year. If anything, she was pleased to have moved to a community in which stable family values were strong and she'd grown to enjoy the genuine warmth extended to her. Waiting outside the classroom, busily browsing art folders and maths books, admiring the displays of *Words Into Pictures* on the walls as if the corridor was an overflow for the Royal Academy, Stella felt happy, lucky, that she and Will were there. He had his little gang of chums—and she was now very much one of the mums.

'Mums' night out next Friday, Stella—Will can come for a sleepover if babysitting's a problem.'

'Thank you.'

'Wasn't Will fantastic in assembly last week! Quite the little actor!'

'Thank you.'

Much to be very grateful for. Just that hiccup of an envelope at home, waiting to be opened. Its contents already known yet the effect they might have, strangely unfathomable.

Whenever Douglas Hutton asked to see her in his office, Stella was never sure whether she'd find her boss or her uncle in there. When she was summoned on Friday, the morning after parent's evening, she just couldn't tell who'd be behind his desk. Belinda, Steve and Gill eyed her suspiciously; Geoff, though, didn't look. He liked Stella and had decided early on to turn a blind eye on any rumoured favouritism and focus on his files instead whenever Douglas Hutton put his head around his office door and said, Stella—a quick word.

* * *

'A strange one, this,' was Douglas's opening line. He looked at Stella quizzically, as if alternating between seeing her as his niece and as his newest member of staff who was already proving her worth. 'You've been asked for. By name.'

'Oh?'

'Really, I ought to be taking this myself—if it comes off. Being head of the company, and more experienced than any of you. And you'll have to steel yourself—if it comes off—to that lot out there baying for your blood. But whatever I want—and whatever the others won't want—has no bearing, whatsoever, on what this potential client wants.' He paused. 'Are you all right?'

Stella wasn't sure how to tell him she had absolutely no idea what he was talking about. 'I'm fine. I'm just not entirely sure I understand.'

'You can't understand,' he said gruffly. 'I haven't told you yet.' Douglas was famous for his lengthy scene-setting, whether it was an introduction to a choice anecdote recounted at Christmas dinner or a preamble to a pep talk during Monday meeting here in the office.

'Sorry.'

'I don't think you will be!' He regarded her with a rare and wry smile. He shook his head gravely, contradicting the gesture with a chuckle. 'You've been sent for—asked for *by name*. There's no achievement greater, no seal of approval more valuable, than personal recommendation. That's what you have. Your reputation precedes you already. From tiny acorns, Stella—from wee little acorns.'

She tried hard not to look confused.

'That little acorn of a cottage at Long Dansbury may have turned into the mighty oak of Longbridge Hall.' He fell silent before continuing to himself. 'Unlikely though. It's the Fortescue seat.'

She couldn't even nod. She knew of the Eames Lounger but not a Fortescue Seat. Longbridge Hall meant nothing to her. And contracts on Mercy Benton's cottage had been exchanged—so there couldn't be any problems there. She tried to think tangentially about trees—subsidence? She couldn't remember any strapping great oak that could undermine the cottage's foundation.

'You will go on Tuesday morning. Eleven o'clock—be prompt.'

'OK. I'll do that.'

'Good girl. Your mother's asked me for Sunday lunch—will you be going? I am looking forward to seeing young William.'

The sentence was said in an altogether lighter tone at a faster pace and enabled Stella to speak more freely.

'Uncle Douglas—I'm sorry to sound vague. But can you just tell me exactly where I'm going on Tuesday morning at eleven—and why?'

'Longbridge Hall, Stella. In Long Dansbury.'

'Right.'

'Right at the centre of the village, give or take a half-mile driveway.'

'OK.' She paused, hoping she didn't look bewildered. 'Oh—and why?'

'The Lady Lydia Fortescue has asked for you.'

'For *me*? Lady Fortescue?'

'It's *Lady Lydia*,' Douglas corrected. 'Actually, for a while she was The Lady Lydia Huffington-Smythe—but that was her late husband's surname and he was a commoner so when she inherited her own family seat, she was quite happy to revert to The Lady Lydia Fortescue. But her family are also the Earls of Barbary. Between you and me—they probably make it up as they go along.' Douglas could see that Stella was too confused to speak. It didn't matter, really. 'Anyway, she was rather taken with the recommendation given to her by Mrs Benton whose cottage you sold. That's all I know.'

'I see.' But Stella didn't.

'I don't know what it's about—she wouldn't say. But she owns other properties in Long Dansbury—some would say she owns the entire village. And the villagers too.'

*       *       *

Friday night. Stella reached across to the bedside

58

table to check the time. Saturday morning, really, at just gone two. The working week done, the weekend upon her. A cup of tea with Jo and her daughters after Will's football club in the morning, Sunday lunch at her mum's with any number of the extended family. Perhaps the new Pixar movie after that—she might treat herself and Will to a 3D showing. Where had she put the 3D glasses after their last outing? And why it was suddenly so important to find them, at silly o'clock, just then? She left her bed and tiptoed into Will's room, smiling at his fidget and gruffle when she leant over to kiss him. She peered into his toy box but knew the glasses were unlikely to be there. Still, though, she sat in his room, on the floor, her back to his bed, awhile longer. The most peaceful place in the world.

Downstairs she went, to look through the odds-and-sods drawer in the kitchen before having a satisfying flashback and going to the coat rack. There were the glasses, in the pocket of her Puffa. It made her realize how long it had been since their last trip to the cinema. It made her realize how much warmer the weather had become, that this billowing black padded mainstay of colder climes hadn't been worn since. She tried on each pair of glasses, then buffed the lenses as best she could before placing them, side by side, on the radiator cover near the front door. It was as if Buddy Holly and Elvis Costello had come to visit and left their specs there.

Stella went back to bed. Briefly.

She said to herself, you're seeing Jo tomorrow, remember? Remember what she said? Remember what you'd planned?

It was useless. Sleep would elude her while that envelope remained under her bed. She tried to flatter herself that it was a *Princess and the Pea* scenario. Actually, the envelope was inside the old canvas and leather suitcase, in which she'd kept all her secrets and treasures since adolescence. She pulled the case out, unbuckled the straps and jostled the slightly warped lid away. She could lose herself in teenage love letters and the doodles in her Rough Book from school. She could distract herself with old photos and hark back to the days when camera film was sent off to BonusPrint and returned fourteen days later as unique memories preserved on Kodak paper—not stored on an iPhone and randomly scrolled through, in little. She could do any of these things, while away time until she was tired enough to put it all back in the case and clamber into bed. But that envelope had put up some kind of impenetrable barrier between the Stella sitting cross-legged on the floor of her bedroom at thirty-four years old and the youthful Stella epitomized by all the keepsakes in the case. Halt! Who goes there! Access denied!

It's me.

It's Stella.

Let me in—I want my life back.

So she opened the envelope at half past two. She remarked to herself, as she did so, that the tacky adhesive could close against itself easily enough, if she lost her nerve or if she wanted Jo to think she hadn't opened it. But when it tore a little, in the last inch or so, she acknowledged she'd gone past the point of no return. She felt inside. A paper clip holding a compliment slip against just a few pages, A4 size. She knew the paper clip would be pink or red or orange. Something bright and certainly not steely. And the compliment slip would have a handwritten personal message on it. She knew the essence of what would be on the sheets behind it—just not the precise wording.

It's just going to say what it is.

It can't say anything else.

You know what it is.

You asked for it.

*       *       *

She slipped the contents out and in one movement, took off the paper clip (turquoise) and gave a cursory glance to the slip of paper (handwriting in red pen with some kind of doodle in the lower right-hand corner—how lucky she was to have such a sweet-natured solicitor). To one side, she placed a page which was a letter. In her lap, face up, lay a certificate over the other pages. She read it in an instant, absorbing all the information in the blink of an eye and then, immediately, read it again, out loud sotto voce, into the stillness of her bedroom.

'*Certificate of making Decree Nisi Absolute (Divorce).*'

The type was tiny—as if the words were shameful and should be read in a whisper.

Underneath this, the font was much larger and in upper case. Stella raised her voice a little, accordingly.

'IN THE HIGH COURT OF JUSTICE

PRINCIPAL REGISTRY OF THE FAMILY DIVISION.'

She reverted to a lower tone for the next part, as

it was in the same point size as the first.

*'Matrimonial cause proceeding in Principal Registry treated by virtue of section 42 of the Matrimonial and Family Proceedings Act 1984 as pending in a divorce county court.'*

She looked at the next part quietly before clearing her voice.

*'Between     Stella Ruth Hutton     Petitioner*
*and           Charles John Taylor     Respondent*

She read to herself again, before repeating it out loud.

*Whereby it was decreed that the marriage solemnized . . .*
*At         St Peter's Church, St Albans*
*Between the petitioner and the respondent be dissolved*

'Dissolved,' said Stella. Thinking of soluble aspirin. Of tears. Wondering if destroyed or deconstructed or even dismembered were better words.

\*       \*       \*

Out into the night she continued to read aloud. *'. . . final and absolute . . . said marriage was thereby dissolved. Dated this 13th day of April.'*

There were notes but Stella just skimmed these again. The type was small, the language dense and the content non-personal. The information she'd needed to see in black and white, that she needed to hear herself say, that she'd applied for all that time ago because it was the right thing to do, the only thing to do, had sunk in. It coursed through her blood like anaesthetic. She was surprised to simply feel numbness, not pain. She felt flat and it was bizarre. She'd assumed that in spite of it all she'd be upset, yet the tears she'd anticipated didn't come. Instead, her eyes were kept busy by the majestic, circular red crest of the court's stamp, with its emblem of lion and unicorn, just overlapping the words 'absolute' and 'dissolved'.

Divorced.

It is done. It is gone. I am a divorcee.

It was final, confirmed, official, legally binding. It was what she wanted but still, it was so blunt. Yet it didn't hurt her—there wasn't pain the way there'd been pain when she'd left Charlie. She just felt tired. Very very tired. As exhausted as if she'd scaled a mountain she'd spent so long in training for. She could sleep now. And when she woke, she'd take in the view that daylight would bring, of all that stretched ahead.


# Chapter Seven

With a dog under one arm and three-year-old Sonny wriggling under the other, Caroline Rowland manoeuvred the buggy with her foot so it didn't block the entrance to the Spar. She then plonked the dog beside it with a look that said Stay—Or Else, and into the shop she went, managing to buy only what she'd come in for and cajole Sonny into thinking the dried apricots were his idea of a snack.

Caroline made multitasking appear effortless and her willowy beauty was unruffled by the daily challenges of two very young children, a dog and a husband who commuted to London. Her self-deprecating sense of humour, delivered in her upbeat Geordie accent, helped—as did a copious supply of Nicorette gum. She was one of Xander's closest friends and that they should live in the same village, having met nearly two decades ago at Nottingham University, was no coincidence. They'd dated, briefly, or rather they fell into a bit of late-night snogging at the Students' Union disco in Freshers' Week, but neither of them could remember much about that. It wasn't long after that that Caroline met Andrew and adopted the role of older sister to Xander (though she was in fact younger by two years) and Xander, an only child, couldn't believe his luck, or what he'd been missing all those years. After university, they'd all shared a house in Highbury and then, when they finally decided that they'd be grown-ups—and Caroline married Andrew and Xander set up his own company—they all ended up in Long Dansbury.

The village's links by road and rail to London meant that Andrew had the best of both worlds— miles of track to run with Xander, as well as a tolerable commute into work. For the children, having Xander close by was brilliant because he loved watching *SpongeBob*, he was always up for kicking a ball even with a three-year-old, or rough-and-tumbling over their mum's furniture, and best of all she told him off far more than she scolded them. The Rowlands had lived in the village for six years, the children had been born there and Caroline loved the way that, despite this and despite all the activities she joined in or indeed organized, she was still frequently referred to as 'Caroline—the Northern Lass' as if Newcastle was somewhere very foreign and rather exotic.

'Hullo Caroline, dear,' Mrs Patek, shop owner,

greeted her. Deftly, Caroline chatted back whilst shaking her head before Mrs Patek could say, sweetie for Sonny? and the little boy remained none the wiser. 'It'll shake the village, wouldn't you say?'

'What—*Mother Refuses Son E-Numbers and Sugar?*'

Mrs Patek laughed. She was proficient at holding down umpteen conversations at once whilst packing the shopping, doing mental maths before the till came up with the total and managing to remain resolutely jolly all the while. 'I was just saying, dear, to Nora here, that it'll shake the village.'

'What'll shake the village, pet?' Caroline asked.

'She hasn't heard yet,' said Nora who needed drama daily and added it to most topics of conversation. She sucked her teeth thoughtfully. 'Longbridge Hall—it's for sale.'

'Never!' Caroline was surprised. Xander had said nothing about it when he'd popped over to watch the football with Andrew last night—and if anyone was to know, it would be Xander.

'Nora, dear, we really must say "apparently" until the sign goes up,' said Mrs Patek.

'*Apparently*,' Nora conceded, touching her blue-rinsed perm as if to check it was still there.

'How do you know?' asked Caroline.

'Her Ladyship was in here the other day, when Mercy was in here, and I overheard her saying "Denby's?" but Mercy said, "No, Elmfield's." And then Her Ladyship asks Mrs Patek here for a piece of paper and wrote down something about someone at Elmfield's.'

Caroline put her change in her purse, hitched

Sonny on her hip because he'd decided he couldn't possibly stand, let alone walk, and took her shopping from the counter. 'Perhaps Longbridge isn't for sale—perhaps Lady Lydia fancies a spot of gazumping.' It all sounded so far-fetched.

'Gazumping!' Nora was thrilled. 'What's that?'

'Perhaps she fancies Mercy's cottage—and is going to make a higher offer.' Caroline was jesting but Mrs Patek and Nora considered this gravely.

'The Fortescues have always thought they own the village,' said Nora.

'They mostly do,' said Mrs Patek.

'Maybe Her Ladyship is making sure of it,' said Nora. But she, too, couldn't really imagine Lady Lydia selling—she must be buying.

'She'll never sell me that plot of land opposite my shop—even though you all think it's the shop's car park.' Mrs Patek paused. 'She can't be selling. Why would you move if you owned a place like that? And anyway, she's part of things. And really, we're all part of Longbridge.'

'If Lady Lydia is doing a gazump, then I wonder if Mercy's happy about that. Mind you, if it's more money, she's likely to be. She's from Scottish stock, you know—they like their money, that lot,' said Nora.

'And I like brown ale and coal, me,' Caroline laughed. 'I'll see you ladies later. Ta-ta,' and, smiling to herself, she walked away.

'But if Longbridge is sold—what'll it mean for the village?' she heard Nora say.

As she pushed the buggy, maintained a conversation with Sonny and navigated the dog who had a tendency to wander into the path of anything, stationary or mobile, Caroline texted Xander.

66

Rumour has it Longbridge is on the market
. . . Cx
The reply came almost immediately.
Bollox! Xx
What a lot of X's he uses, thought Caroline.
Xander texted again, before she'd replied.
Where did you hear that?!
Village Shop
I rest my case . . . Xx

\*        \*        \*

'Mum?' The front door was unlocked and Xander stood in his mother's hallway thinking, if I was a burglar, I could swipe her handbag, her car keys, various pairs of shoes, library books, two terracotta plant pots and a selection of Paul Newman DVDs by barely crossing the threshold. Last week, her car keys had been in the car, actually in the ignition; the passenger seat piled high with interestingly bulky Jiffy bags ready for posting and a clutch of Steve McQueen films loaned from Mrs Patek's esoteric DVD-rental service.

'Mum?' Where *was* she?

'Hullo, darling!'

She was behind him, making her way up the garden path.

'Mother—what are you *doing*?'

'Your dad forgot his jacket—it'll be chilly later on. I don't want that bronchitis coming back.'

Monday night—card night at the pub.

'But you left your keys.'

'I didn't lock the door.'

'Exactly—you left everything in here.'

67

'Xander!' she chided and laughed. 'Stop worrying! I only popped out—I've only been gone five or ten minutes. Don't start putting the willies up me about thieves and the like. This is Little Dunwick, remember.'

'It's cloud cuckoo land.'

'Don't be cheeky.'

Xander shrugged.

'You think Long Dansbury is small and friendly—well, here in Little Dee, we're a tiny happy family in comparison.'

Xander smiled as if he acquiesced. His mother still needed to justify her move away to this neighbouring village over a decade ago.

'Come on in and give your old mum a kiss.'

Audrey Fletcher made herself sound ancient though she had only recently celebrated her sixty-fifth birthday and looked much younger albeit in a windswept way. She had thick, iron-grey hair worn at one length to her shoulders and a fringe she kept too long so that she blinked a lot, which gave the impression that she was always concentrating hard when actually she chose to listen only selectively. It drove Xander mad, but his father greatly appreciated it, not being one for involved conversation. If Audrey lost track of what people were saying, she never asked them to repeat themselves, she never interrupted and she never murmured, 'Hmm?'; she simply smiled and blinked in a calmingly beatific way, which gave everyone the impression that she liked them very much and was pleased for them to talk at length. This, combined with the way she dressed—loose trousers or long skirts overlaid with smocks in heavy fabric and a penchant for Native American patterns and colours—invested her with the semblance of someone worldly, wise and contemplative; a modern oracle, a latter-day soothsayer.

In her day, she'd been the only member of staff at Longbridge to resolutely refuse to wear uniform without having to say a word. Certainly, she didn't dress like the Norland Nanny who predated her there and if the Fortescues had requested a uniform, she probably didn't hear them. (Lydia was privately quite sure that the clothes Audrey wore now were the same as then—and secretly, she marvelled at the longevity of such fabric.)

Xander kissed his mother. She cupped his face in her hands and smiled at him.

'Let me look at you.' She'd seen him the week before. 'How's my boy?'

'He's fine.'

'Soup?'

\*       \*       \*

He followed her into the kitchen and sat down at the table. It came naturally to Xander to say a sentence at a time and wait for her to respond; that way nothing was wasted and everything was heard.

'If you must leave the door unlocked, please don't leave your valuables in the hallway.'

'It's leek and potato.'

He didn't respond.

'I'll try to do that, Xander—for you, rather than to fox any neighbourhood villain.'

Good. 'Leek and potato sounds good.'

'How's work?'

'Not bad. How's Dad?'

69

'Very good.'

'This is delicious.'

'You can come again!'

'Thanks, Mum.'

'You saw Lydia recently?'

'Yes—and Caroline overheard some village gossip about Longbridge going up for sale.'

'Longbridge?' Audrey laughed. 'How absurd.'

'I thought it would tickle you.' Xander laughed with her. 'But you know what Nora's like—if there's no real gossip, she'll invent some.'

'I'm visiting Lydia later this week—I'll ask her. Mind you, a rumour without a leg to stand on still gets around somehow.'

'I can imagine her response,' said Xander. It was not unknown for Lydia to hiss the word *'peasants'*.

'I thought I'd take a stew. I don't like the thought of Mrs Biggins lifting heavy pots—despite the size of her we have to remember she's nearly as ancient as Lydia and not nearly as strong as her mass would suggest.'

'You'll say it's leftovers.'

'Yes—and Lydia will laugh and be very rude to me but she'll eat it all up and never let me know if she liked it.' She looked at her son thoughtfully. 'Will you take some soup home with you?'

'It's delicious—but I'm out most evenings this week.'

She looked at him again. 'Oh, yes?'

'Clients.'

'Clients—oh, yes?'

'No one you know,' he said and they laughed at his pat answer.

'One day you'll surprise me,' Audrey said. 'One day you'll come over and say, Mum! Meet

70

Amanda!'

'Who the hell is Amanda?'

'Amanda is simply generic, Xander. You know what I mean.'

'Mother—will you please just leave it?' He was serious. Why was everyone so concerned with marrying him off? 'I should have married Verity Fortescue when she proposed to me when I was seven years old.'

'I had a letter from her last week. Which reminds me—did I post my reply?' Audrey tailed off to rummage through a pile of paper on the dresser and found the postcard she'd written Verity. 'Blast.'

'I'll post it—and yes, I'll put a stamp on it for you!' Xander said wearily, but in jest. He noted the postcard depicted an illustration from an old Enid Blyton book. He skimmed over his mother's blowsy handwriting, not dissimilar from Verity's.

'When did I last see Verity?' Xander said quietly.

'She didn't come at Christmas.'

'She doesn't "do" Christmas any more,' Xander said.

He and Audrey shared a wistful moment, quietly recalling those long halcyon days of his childhood when he and Verity were together from sun up to sun down. Playing and laughing and climbing and swimming and imagining a time when they'd be grown-ups and Longbridge would be theirs and they'd paint everywhere purple and green and pink and blue and there'd be lollipop trees in the garden and the hens would lay chocolate eggs and there'd be cows in the meadows who'd give them strawberry milkshakes.

\*　　　\*　　　\*

Xander dreamt of Verity that night. They were in the clock tower above the stable courtyard at Longbridge only it wasn't Longbridge, not that it mattered. In the dream, he was young again—he could see himself with his ridiculous pudding-bowl haircut and his knock knees and some dreadful knitted sleeveless pullover his gran had made for him. He could taste the musty air that squeezed through the gaps in the tower as skeins dancing with dust. The silken waft of Verity's strawberry-blonde hair as refined as his tank top was coarse. Their laughter peeling out like the long-gone bell in the tower. The day speeding away and yet time, up there, standing still. But it was grown-up Xander inside young Xander's head, watching Verity. Smiling and laughing along with her but watching her closely, careful to make her feel equal and relaxed and normal, while all the time guarding her as if, at any moment, she might fall, or she might fly away or, worse, just fade from view and simply disappear. Verity—ethereal and beautiful and so very vivid—saying, *Xander! Xander! Come this way!* She was going for a door he'd never seen before. *Come with me, Xander!* But she disappeared beyond it before he could say, Verity—no, don't! Please stay.

## Chapter Eight

If one didn't know of Longbridge Hall then one might well assume the gates off the high street heralded a country park. Certainly, Stella was surprised that in all her visits to Mercy Benton's cottage in Long Dansbury, she'd never given more than a passing glance at them. On the Tuesday morning, at 11.00, she drove through the gates, noting how one was slightly crooked and both needed painting black again. Halfway up the drive, she said, oh God, where on earth is the house—I was here at 11.00, I've been going for miles and now I'm going to be late. However, even in the April shower that had suddenly descended, when the house came into view it was a breathtaking sight. Stella followed the driveway around it, until it ended in a flourish: a vast turning circle the size of a roundabout, with a small maze of box hedging at the centre. Stella checked her reflection and smoothed her hair and wondered if she should use the main front doors or what looked like a tradesmen's entrance off to one side. She also wondered whether she should curtsey. Clearing her throat, she made her way past the two stone lions at the base of the steps leading up to the front door. She gave the bell pole a pull and then did so again, with more force, and heard it clanging inside the house.

'Open the door, woman! Open the door!'

Stella panicked that the voice was shouting at her but even though she heaved her shoulder against them, the front doors were definitely shut.

Did she dare ring that bell again?

Luckily, a plump woman, wearing what her mother would call a pinny, opened one of the doors a fraction. She said nothing.

'Hullo,' said Stella.

'Hullo.'

'I'm expected.'

'Who are you?'

'I'm Stella—Hutton.'

'One moment.' The woman left the door ajar and disappeared. Was that Lydia? Lady Fortescue? Mrs Barbary?

'Is it Elmfield?' she could hear another voice asking.

'No, it's Stella Someone.'

'Well, it's probably Stella Someone from Elmfield's. Gracious me!'

*That* must be Lady Fortescue.

The plump woman returned. 'Are you from Elmfield's?'

'Yes,' said Stella. 'Sorry—I should have said.'

'Come this way, please. Coat.'

But what Stella really wanted to do was stand still for a moment and take it all in. Beyond the entrance hall was the grand stairwell, lit from above by a beautiful glass lantern roof, a swooping double staircase leading upwards to a galleried landing. But her coat was being all but wrenched from her back.

'I'm Mrs Biggins—I'm housekeeper here. Lady Lydia takes coffee at this time—would you like coffee?'

'No, thanks. Well—just a glass of water, please.'

'Or tea?'

'Tea! Oh yes, please—I'm gasping for a cup.'

The woman looked her up and down. 'You'll

74

take it strong—like me.' Stella was unsure whether she was referring to her own strength or a well-brewed cup, whether the woman's remark was an observation, or a statement not open to dispute. If the housekeeper was this disarming, what could Lady Fortescue be like? Mrs Biggins opened the soaring double doors in front of them and gave Stella a little shove. The room was so stunning, in a thoroughly *Alice in Wonderland* way with everything oversized, that momentarily Stella forgot all about locating the owner of the house and making her introduction. It was dual aspect, occupying three bays of the east front of the house and one bay south, and the four magnificent sash windows, at least eighteen feet high, flooded the room with light despite the dreary day outside. Stella was, quite literally, dazzled.

'Good morning.'

Sitting in a wingback leather chair, Lydia slowly folded the *Telegraph* and placed it across her lap. Her knees were together, her legs neatly at an elegant angle; hair in a chignon with stray strands like spun silver. She wore a woollen skirt the colour of peat and a twinset the colour of heather. Her shoes were buffed and the decorative buckles shone. Neutral hosiery gathered just perceptibly in creases around the ankle—like a ploughed field seen from a distance.

'Mrs Fortescue, I'm Stella Hutton.' And immediately, Stella thought, oh God, I've addressed her incorrectly already. 'Lady.' No! That sounded plain rude.

Lydia did not rise. Indeed, she sat motionless and expressionless. 'I see.'

'I'm here on behalf of Elmfield Estates.'

'Yes.'

Should she backtrack and apologize for the botched greeting? Stella was unsure. She didn't know what she was meant to do next. Sit, stand, talk, wait, what? She was being looked at, assessed; she could feel it. It was as nerve-wracking as the one time she'd been hauled in front of the headmistress at the age of thirteen. She felt hot and self-conscious. Did she appear suitably estate-agenty? Or was the fact that she really didn't do the navy skirt-suit and court-shoe thing actually in her favour? She was today wearing slim-fitting black trousers and black suede ankle boots with a Cuban heel and a white shirt. Perhaps she looked too much like a waitress. Damn it! She'd been in the pale blue shirt first thing, but had changed at the last minute. Perhaps Mrs Lady Barbary-Fortescue was waiting for her to be a little more estate-agenty. Perhaps she should deliver the Elmfield Estates mission statement.

What Stella really wanted to do was to sink into one of the sofas and say, wow, what an extraordinary place, how long have you lived here, tell me about the house, who is the lady in the painting—is it School of Reynolds? The rug is Persian, isn't it?

She was enamoured by everything: the carved frieze above the fireplace of cherubs apparently hunting down a deer; the wealth of photos from sepia, to tinted, to full colour, in a crowd on the grand piano, the thick velvet drapes, the Chinese paintings on silk. The glass-fronted book cabinet. The vast silk rug—yes, most certainly Persian—threadbare in one or two places but still magnificent, yet which went only some way in

76

covering the impressive run of wide floorboards. Huge, heavy columnar curtains with flamboyant pelmets that reminded her of a theatre. More furniture than she, her brothers and her mother had between them. Finally, she noticed the archaic-looking electric bar heater standing in front of the capacious fireplace, trying valiantly to take the chill off the room and adding a warm down-to-earthness too. If there was so much to look at even in this one room, what delights could the rest of the house hold?

'Let me look at you.'

Stella felt like Tess being summoned by Mrs d'Urberville. But then she thought she remembered Mrs d'Urberville being blind and suddenly she felt very self-conscious that she really wasn't smart enough and why had she popped her slightly greasy hair into a hasty pony-tail when she'd had the time to wash and dry it? As she approached, Stella decided to polish up her vowels and use words like 'frightfully' and 'splendid'.

'You're not as I expected.' Lady Lydia sounded disappointed. 'But then, Mercy Benton's powers of description have always been limited. She described her own daughter's wedding dress as simply a "nice frock" and her son-in-law as a "nice lad". She said you were a "fine woman" and "everything one could hope for" in an agent.' She paused, as if waiting for Stella to take the bait. But Stella just nodded with a wry smile in a 'Gosh, well—you know Mercy Benton' kind of way.

Lydia rose a little shakily. 'You look like a girl—a waitress.' She was not impressed.

'That's probably why my clients like me, Lady Fortescue,' Stella said meekly. 'I don't boss them around. I take their order—be it for a house or a sale—and I deliver it to them.' Stella thought about it. 'With no spillage.'

The women regarded each other. Though Lydia was pretty much the same height as Stella, her aquiline haughtiness made her appear far taller. Or perhaps Stella just felt small in this grand room in this phenomenal old house and, for the first time in her life, in the presence of someone titled.

'And have you ever been in a house like this?'

Stella was diplomatic. 'There can't possibly be another like it.'

Lydia looked at her as if she'd seen straight through her words. 'Mrs Biggins, wretched woman—she never came with my coffee. Would you care for a sherry?'

'It's a little early for me,' Stella said as if she didn't take her sherry until after lunch. Lydia looked at her witheringly, as if she'd heard sarcasm. She walked over to the walnut drinks cabinet and inadvertently chinked the crystal stopper against the decanter and then the decanter against the glass. She took her sherry and walked to the sofa, spilling a little on her skirt as she sat herself down. She motioned to the companion sofa opposite and Stella sat. Lydia took a thoughtful sip. And then another.

'I detest Asians.'

'I'm sorry?'

'*All* agents—whatever their industry.'

'Oh—*agents*.' Stella's relief was worn as an expansive smile which Lydia appeared to baulk at.

'I am going to sell Longbridge,' she said levelly, 'or at least, *you* are.'

Stella felt herself sinking into the sofa, as if her

78

surroundings were suddenly growing and she was shrinking under the weight of the realization that this is why she was here. This couldn't be real—this had to be Lewis Carroll. A joke. A dream.

But Lydia was continuing. 'I have been thinking about selling Longbridge for some time. Sometimes I stop thinking about it—but not because I've changed my mind. The whole concept is so very tiresome.' She stared at Stella, who tried to nod purposefully and to stop gawping, wishing she'd said yes to sherry, just to have something to hold instead of her hands feeling like clodden sponges awkward in her lap.

'I'm haemorrhaging cash in upkeep.' Lady Lydia gave a little cough for emphasis. 'It's preposterous! All that money just to keep the rain out and the heat in.'

The look she threw Stella as she knocked back her sherry suggested she was waiting for a response.

'I hope I don't sound ignorant or nosy—' Or obsequious, Stella thought to herself. 'But would a house like this not be handed down to the next generation?'

'There is no next generation,' Lady Lydia barked before going heavily silent, staring into her sherry glass as if, usually, it refilled spontaneously. 'I am the eldest of four girls. Cordelia died young. Anne never bred. She was a lesbian—still is, I believe, though at her age that's quite unnecessary. Margaret moved to Connecticut and remained barren despite landing herself three American husbands in quick succession.'

'You have no children—offspring?' She shouldn't have said that—it sounded intrusive, impudent.

'I had a son,' Lydia said quietly. 'And I have a daughter. She doesn't want to live here. She lives with the Welsh.' She made it sound as though her daughter had converted to an extreme religion and was living as part of a cult in a compound.

What could Stella say to that? Though desperate to know more, she bit her tongue and looked at her hands. Lydia's were bony and long; papery skin over navy veins like very old corduroy. A signet ring loose on the little finger of her right hand, an antique diamond ring and thin gold wedding band on her left. Stella had a very strange impulse to lean right over the coffee table and take Lady Lydia's hands in hers, give them a gentle rub. Perhaps Lydia sensed it because she took to her feet and demanded that Stella follow her on a tour of the house.

Sell? Sell all *this*? Is that really why I'm here? *Me*? Can't be.

'Of course, we're the wrong way around,' Lydia said of the drawing room. 'When I was a girl, this was the dining room—one never had a south-facing drawing room because all the oil paintings would take a thrashing by the sun. That's why the good paintings are currently in the dining room—which was once the drawing room because it's north facing. That's what my father told me—though my mother told me it was because my Fortescue ancestors were atrociously ugly.' The slicing look Lydia sent Stella informed her that her giggle was inappropriate. 'Hence them being consigned to a room less used.' She was leading on, along the flagstone hallway, to the room in question. The same beautiful tall double doors and fanlight as the drawing room, the same lofty windows, but just two

80

of them in here, east facing. The room was light but undeniably cold. The fireplace was bereft of logs, nor was there an electric heater in its place. The cherubs on the plaster frieze weren't hunting stags here, but hefting urns about. Their naked little bodies made Stella feel the cold on their behalf. The eyes of generations of Fortescues appeared to glower at her from the confines of their florid gilt frames as if to say, who on earth do you think you are to sell our ancestral seat as though it's a commodity akin to a sack of apples?

'They're not so ugly,' Stella remarked diplomatically, 'they just look a little—humourless.'

She checked Lady Lydia's expression. She looked horrified. Stella shivered.

'Bastard!'

'Oh God—I'm so sorry—I didn't mean . . . I only meant—'

'Bastard bastard bloody dog! Barnaby! Mrs Biggins!'

It was then that Stella noticed a furl of turd that had been deposited (quite some time ago, it seemed) on the floor just by the head of the table.

'It's testimony to the airiness of the room that one cannot—*detect* it,' Stella said.

Lydia stared at her, unblinkingly, before nodding slowly. 'You are most certainly an estate agent,' she said, but Stella was unable to tell whether this was a compliment or an insult. 'You call it *spin*, don't you. This way.' They left the door open and the dog mess for Mrs Biggins to deal with; crossed the staircase and entrance hallway and went into the library. This room was as warm and inviting as the dining room was cold and uncongenial. Stella thought, I don't care how common I might appear—and she said

81

'Wow!' out loud as she beamed at the three walls given over almost entirely to handsome mahogany bookcases—mostly carrying leather-bound volumes. Stella estimated the longest was at least twenty feet. Three leather Chesterton sofas at right angles to each other were set around a low table in front of the fireplace stacked with logs. A desk with a dark green leather inlay was positioned by one window, a writing bureau at the other. Stella perused the titles. French and English novels, encyclopaedias, dictionaries, atlases, monographs and a whole section of art books.

'I studied art,' she said quietly, as if to remind herself. She ran her fingertips gently over the routered wooden shelves right to the end. She stopped. It couldn't be! She looked at Lydia and smiled.

'May I?' but she didn't wait for an answer. Where the bookcase ended in a long, slim vertical column, Stella gave a little press and a pull and the front of the column popped open like a secret door to reveal that it was a false front—behind it, the shelves continued, with just three books' width, for the full height of the bookcase. There were books on these hidden shelves too, but their spines were blank. 'Are they *very* rude?' Stella asked.

Lydia laughed. It was an unexpected warm, earthy cackle. 'Eye-wateringly so—that is, if you were a dainty eighteenth-century lady prone to fainting at the very thought of even a naked forearm. Hardly the *Kama Sutra*. They're frightfully tame to me, so goodness knows what you'd make of them.' Insult or compliment—again Stella wasn't sure and Lydia's voice had become cool by the end of her sentence.

82

'Have you had them valued?'

'Don't be ridiculous! Cart the lot off to Christie's for them to be pored over so publicly? *Lady Lydia, your collection of two hundred years of pornography might fetch one hundred pounds at auction.*' Stella laughed—but Lydia gave her a look to silence her. She led on, back through the hallways and up one side of the double staircase.

'Now that,' Stella murmured, 'is a backside to behold.'

'You insolent young woman.' Lydia rounded on Stella who, for a split second, feared she might be pushed down the stairs. She'd already tripped over a threadbare section of runner.

'Lady Lydia—no! I didn't mean—! I was referring to—*that.*' Stella was holding on to the banister with both hands so she moved her head fast as if banging it against an imaginary wall, to signify where she was looking. It was a huge oil painting of a horse and rider, portrayed from behind. Only an eye and an ear of the horse were visible, while the rider looked most uncomfortable turning around in an already cumbersome military get-up. It was the horse's rump which all but filled the canvas, its tail mid-swish, revealing its arsehole.

'I'm sorry, I—' Stella glanced at Lydia who was staring at her. 'I studied art. It was my world before I—' And then Stella thought, Oh, for God's sake, the woman's not going to bite you. And then she thought, I studied art before all the shit fell on me from a great height and I clawed my way out and am where I am today. And then she thought, But this woman doesn't need to know that. 'Before I went into property.' She made it sound like a sensible choice, that her current career was as dignified and hallowed as the study of art. Lydia's ice-pale blue eyes were still scoring straight through her, like a welder's flame through sheet metal.

'This painting was a gift—to Lord Frederick Makepeace William Fortescue, the first Earl of Barbary, who built this house.'

'Is it Mallory Beckinsford?'

'As I just said,' Lydia said slowly, witheringly, as if Stella was dim as well as deaf, 'Lord Frederick Makepeace William Fortescue, the first Earl of Barbary, who built this house.'

'I'm so sorry, I meant the artist—is it Mallory Beckinsford?' Stella could tell Lydia hadn't a clue who the artist was, and hitherto hadn't been remotely interested.

'Beckinsford,' Lydia said, in what she thought was a cleverly non-committal way. 'It's a portrait of the Prince Regent.'

Stella dared to take one hand from the banister. 'It's just Beckinsford was taught by Reynolds—and Reynolds painted a similar portrait of the Prince Regent.'

Lydia brushed the air. 'Longbridge is full of portraits. Fortescues, royalty, Fortescues with royalty, with swords, guns, with horses, dogs—it's who we are.'

Stella worked hard to keep her tone conversational, but she was excited. 'I think this painting would have been given to Lord Frederick Makepeace William Fortescue, the first Earl of Barbary—but as a rather barbed gift. It's a slur—an elegantly concealed two fingers—from the Prince Regent. He did it to others. A very nicely painted insult, quite literally shoving his horse's great big bum in the face of Lord Fortescue. But no doubt the Earl knew that and turned the joke on its head by graciously accepting it and hanging it right here, pride of place.'

Lydia was looking at the painting again, her eyes travelling over it in little bursts. She turned to Stella and nodded.

'So one oughtn't to look a gift horse in the mouth—but up the arse?'

'Something like that,' Stella smiled at the painting. 'You might want to have it valued. Do you know of any fracas between the Prince and the Earl?'

'There is some salacious family rumour about the Earl and one of the Prince's mistresses and the billiards table right here at Longbridge.' Lydia's tone suggested it was all beyond ridiculous. 'I'll be sure to call Christie's,' she said. 'They can come and sift through all the historic backsides at Longbridge—human and equine—whether hidden in the library or hanging, bold as brass, right here.'

She sounded sharp and Stella felt deflated. Best leave all art in the past—her own as well as the Fortescues'. Leave it behind. Move on. Here to sell the house, remember. Then a notion sent a shot of adrenalin which almost winded her.

'How many bedrooms?' Stella asked, taking a sweeping glance at a queue of closed doors and that was just in this semicircular landing of the house.

'Five.'

'Sorry?'

'Sorry?'

'Only five bedrooms? Here? At Longbridge?'

'What are you talking about? Twelve bedrooms including the three in the Victorian wing,' Lady Lydia said.

'Pardon me, I thought you said five and I thought to myself surely not—'

'You are pedantic—it's tiresome,' she barked. 'These days, *five* of the rooms have *beds* in them—so the other rooms are *not* bedrooms, are they?'

Stella was tempted not to bite her tongue, she was tempted to say, well, if I'm pedantic, you're downright rude. 'Logical,' she said instead. 'It's the estate agent in me—we're trained to call even a store cupboard a bedroom if the headroom is sufficient and it is physically possible for someone to stand and also sleep in it.'

'The more bedrooms, the higher the price?'

'Square footage is the priority,' Stella said, 'and you certainly have that at Longbridge Hall—never mind the quota of bed frames.'

'Well,' said Lydia, 'you'd better see if the servants' rooms right at the top count too.'

'How many bathrooms?'

'Three.'

'I don't mean with baths—I mean, rooms in which there is the relevant plumbing.'

'Three,' Lydia said loudly, giving the 'r' a good roll around her tongue, as if Stella had reverted to dim and deaf again. 'Mind you, there was only one until after the War.'

Oh dear, Stella thought. Three bathrooms? That's *it*?

'Chop chop,' said Lydia, leading on; opening door after door and giving Stella just enough time to walk to the windows and back. 'Do keep up.'

'In there?' Stella motioned to a door they passed that Lydia didn't open.

'Slaves.'

'What?'

86

'Don't say "What", say "I beg your pardon",' Lydia snapped. 'It's one of the slaves' quarters. We don't have them any more—not even Mrs Biggins. She's a useless slave because she won't do a thing I ask. But the house was once full of them.'

'Staff,' Stella said, relieved, when she went into the room and realized it was a sizeable store for linen and laundry.

'The Fortescues have always called them "slaves"—in jest, of course. No one has ever minded,' said Lydia. She ran her hand lightly over the butler's sink by the window. 'At least, no one said they minded.' She looked around the room. 'We didn't call them slaves to their faces—we didn't say, "Slave! Come here!" The youngsters were called by their first names, which was fairly liberal of the Fortescues. And the senior staff by their surnames. Apart from the housekeeper, who was allowed to keep her title. Hence, Mrs Biggins—though, really, she ought to be called Useless Woman.'

'I love this,' said Stella, fingering the embossed brass plate above the three taps. 'Hot. Cold. Soft.'

'For rainwater,' said Lydia. She ran the tap and placed her hand under the water. She kept it there, as if the feel of it hastened a memory just coming back into focus and one that she wanted to revisit. 'All the children had their hair washed in this sink—rinsed again and again with the water from "Soft".'

Corridors that started poker straight and then suddenly veered off at angles with stairs to trip and confuse. Room after room after room. With clever wording in the particulars and positioning of furniture for the photos, Stella reckoned she

87

could list twelve bedrooms at least. The three bathrooms were a worry though, not least because the most modern of them all, the only en-suite, was a homage to 1970s design with a corner bath, bidet, basin and toilet in a dull avocado shade.

It surprised her to find they were back on the ground floor. She'd quite lost her bearings.

'Kitchen,' Lydia said, opening a door and revealing a space so sizeable that even Mrs Biggins, ensconced in the *Daily Mail*, looked diminutive. Stella's heart sank a little. Of all the rooms she'd been fascinated to see, this was the one she'd built up in her imagination. She'd anticipated flagstones and a vast range, scullery, pantry, cold store, gleaming copperware and all manner of utensils of historical importance. Instead, she stood in a large space in which rather nondescript units varnished an unpleasant amber sat haphazardly under a melamine worktop, like bad teeth. The fridge and the oven were free-standing and akin to those she remembered her grandmother having in her small flat in Wheathampstead. At least there was an Aga, if a relatively small one. It was some consolation finally to be shown a sort of pantry with lines of shelves painted soft white and an impressive run of slate worktop. Most of the shelves were empty; the ones that weren't were stacked with jars of all sizes filled with jam.

'I'm tired now so you must go,' Lady Lydia announced, still walking ahead and not turning to look at Stella. 'You will come back again tomorrow. To see the grounds. To see Art. Eleven a.m. Prompt, please. Mrs Biggins, show Miss Hutton out please. Goodbye.'

And with that, Lydia went.

88

'Coat,' said Mrs Biggins, bundling it into Stella's arms. 'Ta-ta, duck.' And she chortled a little as if, perhaps, this was a scenario that had been re-enacted many times over the years.

The rain had stopped, everything glistened and shone but Stella shivered and put her coat on, hugging it tightly around herself as she walked across the driveway to her car. Inside, she put the heat on high and realized how that old house had quite chilled her to the bone. She thought again of Tess Durbeyfield, how Tess had wondered about Mrs d'Urberville.

*'If there is such a lady, it would be enough for us if she were friendly . . .'*

## *Chapter Nine*

Stella gave herself a stern talking-to as she raced to pick up Will from after-school club.

Lady Whatnot didn't say you *won't* be representing Longbridge.

She said you're to come back tomorrow.

Money she may have—manners she has none.

She's just an old dragon.

But Stella felt despondent—as if she'd failed a test and a carrot that had been dangled in front of her had been snatched away in a harsh peal of upper-class laughter; as if she'd been one of the balls hit around in a game of croquet. Why would she want to work for the old battleaxe anyway? She felt impotent—it seemed she didn't have a choice. It appeared if Lady Up-Her-Bum wanted Stella, then Stella she would have.

'Shall we go over and see the Twins? Aunty Ju said it's fish and chips for supper.'

Will was delighted. Actually, Stella had food prepared at home for Will but her need for adult company—sane, sweet, adult company—overrode her usual timetable of homework, supper, telly, bath, bed and a long evening alone muttering at the telly. She'd phoned Juliet who was only too pleased to hear from her and to be able to help.

'But it's a school night, Mummy.'

'I know!' Stella said, as if it was the coolest, most daring concept ever.

With Will upstairs with Pauly and Tom, happy not to touch a thing, just to look at their stuff and be in their company as if hoping their cred was catching, Juliet had Stella to herself downstairs.

'You all right, chook?' Juliet asked nonchalantly while rooting around the cupboard for the ketchup.

'Can I borrow a suit, do you think? One of yours?'

'Well, I hardly thought you meant Alistair's. Yes, of course.' She looked at Stella, who looked glum and distracted. 'But why? There's not a funeral I don't know about, is there? Uncle MacKenzie?'

'No—Uncle Mac is still hanging on. I just need to look a bit more formal and estate-agenty tomorrow.'

'Charming! Is that your sartorial judgement of me, then?' Juliet gave her a long look, up and down, as if assessing which suit Stella would be entitled to. 'You're not wearing my Paul Smith then—I'll dig out my old one from Wallis for that!'

Stella laughed. 'You know what I mean—and I just need *not* to look like a waitress in a gastro pub.'

90

'Firstly—you don't, you look lovely. Secondly—why?'

'Awkward client.'

'Oh?'

'Lady Up-Her-Bum Fortescue-Barbary OK-Yah Di-Fucking-Da.'

'Oh,' said Juliet. '*Her.*' She paused. 'Who?'

'Lives in a Georgian pile over at Long Dansbury. It's worth millions. She called for me—and then spent most of this morning being rude yet demanded I come back tomorrow.'

'Can't you send someone else from the office?'

'She asked for me by name.'

'Perhaps it's just her manner.'

'She may be a Lady—but she has no manners. She's horrible.'

'Yes, but blimey, Stella—have you calculated the commission?'

'Exactly—it could be the solution to everything. That's why I have to go. I'll have to swallow my morals and sell my soul to the old devil—but hence the need for your suit.'

'And you think she'll be more polite if you dress the part?'

'She said I was to see the grounds and art.'

'Then you ought to go in wellies and a Puffa—with your own clothes underneath. Not your worky-waitressy garb—your off-duty clothes.'

'Why?'

'Because first and foremost you're an art historian—and that's who you are. Not a suity person. Dress as the real You.'

'I'm an estate agent.'

'In the interim.' Juliet looked at her sternly. 'Remember—that's your game plan.'

Stella's head dropped a little as she nodded. She fiddled with a frozen oven chip that had missed its place on the tray.

'And my divorce came through.'

And then Juliet thought, sod the suit—that's not why she's here. 'Good,' Juliet said. She wiped her hands on her jeans and put her arms around Stella. 'At long bloody last.'

'I know.' And Stella was shocked to feel tears scorch the back of her throat. She attempted to cough them away. 'Actually, it came last week.'

'Why didn't you say?' Juliet was upset.

'I felt OK about it. Flat—but OK.' Her throat still ached. A tear dropped. 'Shit. I can't believe I'm going to cry.' She groaned at herself and stamped.

'You haven't heard from him, I suppose?'

Stella shook her head and then reached for some kitchen roll to blow her nose. 'I've been fine—and I'm absolutely fine.' She was frustrated—more at her tears and herself than at any number of the transgressions that could be pinned on Charlie. 'Why am I crying *now*? I'm not really.'

'I know you're not. It's just relief and closure and you've waited a long time for it. Welcome to the rest of your life. Come on, chook. Let's go and raid my dressing-up box.' Juliet led the way upstairs, pausing with Stella to watch, unseen, Will sitting on Pauly's bed in utter heaven as one cousin strummed a few chords on his guitar and the other chewed gum and texted on his phone.

'Try the Paul Smith,' Juliet said, proffering it for Stella's approval like a maître d' presenting a Dover sole.

'Is that because you feel sorry for me?' Stella asked wryly, hauling herself back on form—a person who, once a good cry had been had, gathered herself together, dug deep for a smile and wore it until it worked independently.

'Yes,' said Juliet. 'Of course not! Just try it on—the more it's worn, the more the cost-per-wear goes down and the quicker I can justify the purchase.'

Stella undressed and, though she stood there in black socks and mismatched underwear, Juliet thought what a cracking figure she had. 'Promise not to bite my head off?'

'Pardon?'

'Just—promise.'

'I promise.'

'Not to bite my head off.'

'I promise not to bite your head off!'

'Please let me sort out a date for you—please?'

'When? To do what?'

'No—a *date*, date.'

Stella wanted to bite Juliet's head off but as a girl who'd never break a promise, she fell silent and just sent Juliet a black look instead.

'Do you not feel ready, Stella—is that it?'

Stella didn't answer, didn't appear to have heard.

'It's been over three years, lovely.'

Stella shrugged. 'I'm busy. I have Will. I'm fine. Actually, I'm just not interested.'

'Then you ought to go to your GP and have your hormone levels assessed.' Juliet thought that might have sounded a little sharp. 'You're bloody gorgeous—it's a waste! And you're denying yourself the chance to have someone really lovely in your life—not to fill a gap, just to enhance it.'

'My life is good,' Stella said and she really believed it.

'Not all men are like Charlie,' Juliet said quietly.

'In fact, few of them are. You know that deep down. I know you know that.'

Stella turned for Juliet to zip up the skirt.

'Look at your peachy bum, missus!'

Stella looked at herself in the mirror. 'That's the genius of Paul Smith tailoring,' she said.

'Rubbish!' said Juliet. 'It doesn't look half as good on me, you cow.' She held the jacket as Stella slipped it on. 'Just look at you!'

Stella looked. And had to grin. 'Blimey.'

'That's an understatement,' Juliet said. 'It would be nice for you to have a little fun,' she said softly. 'You deserve it. It'll be good for you—for your self-esteem.'

'You sound just like Jo—different vocabulary. She witters on about my mojo.'

'Go, Jo.'

Stella didn't want to be drawn. 'I just don't think I'm that bothered any more.'

'If that's the case, you've let bloody Charlie define the rest of your life—and yet he's now *out* of your life. You're really good in a couple, even when the other half was a prize shit. Don't let what you went through change something that naturally suits you.'

Stella hadn't thought about it that way. 'But— Will,' she explained, as if Juliet (like Jo) had missed the point. 'It's too complicated.'

'No,' said Juliet strongly. 'That's an excuse. It needn't be complicated—and there's no reason for Will to be involved. You need to have *you-time*, doing grown-up stuff. You need to pep up your self-confidence. You think your divorce has diminished you—but actually, it gives you your life back. You've probably forgotten what that's like.'

94

Stella sighed. She stroked the suit as if it was living. 'If I say yes, will you stop lecturing me?'

'Yes,' said Juliet.

'But no gynaes.'

'Roger.'

'And no one called Roger.'

'Noted.'

'And no one too much older or too much younger.'

'No grandpas, no toyboys.'

'No facial hair.'

'No?'

'No!'

Juliet counted off on her fingers. 'Mid- to late thirties. Height and weight proportionate. Clean-shaven. Anything else?'

'No addictions,' Stella said quietly.

Juliet took her hand and gave it a little squeeze as if to say, you needn't even think it, let alone say it out loud.

\*     \*     \*

Siobhan was late, but there again, she'd never been on time. Xander thought about it while he waited— if she'd been a girlfriend, officially, it would be a bone of contention to grind between them; but keeping it casual meant the irritation he felt came also with a sense of relief that no tiresome confrontation was necessary. He hadn't seen her for a couple of weeks, hadn't had any contact. But she'd sent him a text which he'd received at lunch-time, alone in the office when Mrs Gregg was taking her hour. Mrs Gregg always took exactly fifty-five minutes so that she had sufficient time to sit back at her desk, pat her hair, wriggle her fingers, look around her desk and then say, 'So!' in a bright voice.

The text came through when Xander was thinking, not bloody tuna mayo again, and wondering whether to see what sandwiches Caffe Nero had instead.

Horny. SEx

Siobhan Elliot. Always signed herself SE, the strategically placed kiss turning the whole thing licentious.

I have a cure for that. X

It remained unclear to Siobhan whether that was X for Xander, or a kiss.

They always met at a pub in Standon that neither of them went to at any other time; they always had bar food and a glass of wine, Xander always paid. If they went back to Siobhan's, Xander left after sex. If Siobhan came to his, she usually stayed the night but not for breakfast. Neither had met the other's friends nor even knew much of their lives beyond their rendezvous. They'd been seeing each other a couple of times a month for the past six months and the arrangement suited them both.

Her customary lateness was premeditated as it presented her with the opportunity to sashay in, swish her way across to him, sit herself down sinuously. Everything about her was consciously feline. A performance, an act. Everything was about calculated seduction but Xander had done his sums and it all added up. He was therefore a little taken aback at a pair of cold hands covering his eyes when Siobhan came up behind him without him noticing. But there again, a gaggle of women had just come in and he hadn't thought to look amongst them for her. He encircled her wrists and pulled her hands away from his eyes.

Only it wasn't Siobhan.

It was Caroline.

At any other time, Xander would have been delighted to see Caroline. But not here, not tonight and not when Siobhan's arrival was imminent.

'Hullo, monkey,' she said.

'What the fuck are you doing here?' said Xander.

'Bloody charming!' she laughed.

'Sorry, Cazza, I meant—'

'You can buy me a pint for that, tosser,' and Caroline swept her patterned shawl over her shoulder, catching Xander across the cheek with the soft bobble fringing. 'You're lucky I don't give you a slap. Pint, please!' she said to the barman. 'He's paying.'

The landlord gave Xander an odd look as if to say, this isn't a pick-up joint, you know. And Caroline gave Xander an odd look because she'd never seen him appear so awkward.

'What are you doing here?' he asked.

'Mums' Night Out,' Caroline said. 'We're bored of Dansbury pubs and your dad's probably playing dominoes in Little Dee. Pet—are you feeling all right?' Caroline placed the back of her hand across his brow before stroking his cheek. And that's what Siobhan saw when she walked in. And that was the moment Caroline clocked the two glasses of wine in front of Xander. She grabbed her pint and look a long drink. 'Bloody hell—you're on a date!'

'Xander?' Siobhan was here.

Neither Siobhan nor Caroline had ever known Xander to redden nor heard him tongue-tied. Caroline thought it most amusing. Siobhan didn't.

'I'm Caroline,' and she offered her hand, slightly wet with beer, to Siobhan.

'Siobhan,' Siobhan said, declining to take it.

'Siobhan—Caroline, Caroline—Siobhan,' Xander said, wearily. Caroline was beaming sunnily at Siobhan, as much as Siobhan was staring unimpressed at Xander. Caroline was just about to ask Siobhan a checklist of questions when one of the other mums called her to take her seat at the table and suddenly Xander didn't know whether he'd rather she stayed rather than went. Or whether he'd rather he and Siobhan went rather than stayed. He drank his wine and couldn't think what to say to either of them.

'Right, well, I'll be leaving you two lovebirds to enjoy your evening then,' Caroline said and slipped off the bar stool, offering it theatrically to Siobhan who took the seat without acknowledgement. As Caroline backed away, she pointed from her eyes to Xander and then back again. She winked lasciviously and made a telephone gesture with her hand and, with a big grin, joined her party.

'Old friend,' said Xander, though Siobhan hadn't asked. 'Best friend, really.' She raised an eyebrow. 'Married, two kids, lives in the village.'

He'd never mentioned Caroline to Siobhan. He didn't think he'd mentioned anyone in his life to Siobhan, not by name. And, just then, he thought perhaps that was disrespectful—not to Siobhan as much as to Caroline. And then he thought, I'm not here to think.

\*  \*  \*

Siobhan had lasagne with garlic bread and Xander

98

had cottage pie. He'd quite fancied a pudding but the innuendo of spotted dick put him off and he wasn't keen on anything else. The two of them always arrived and left separately, which made the whole thing slightly detached and clinical but part of their dynamic. No banter in the car, no hand on leg, no sudden eye contact, or sensing the other person's physical presence. Just a quick look, every now and then, in the rear-view mirror to check that they were still together. And, six months on, together they still were in this ever so liberal, coolly casual way.

They parked and then walked together to Xander's house in separate silence, Siobhan behind while Xander unlocked the door. She could sense detachment in him—a physical detachment which was not what this whole game was about. The emotional detachment, yes—but hitherto that had enhanced the physical side. Tonight, though, something was different. Usually, they'd be all over each other before the door had closed behind them. Though they always made it into the bedroom, it was having romped and humped their way there from the sitting room, up against all the walls en route and usually a bit of doggy-style halfway up the stairs. But tonight, Xander walked ahead, going straight through to his kitchen, keeping his back to Siobhan, filling a pint glass with water and drinking it down in agitated gulps. He hadn't let the tap run and the water was unpleasantly tepid. Siobhan stood self-consciously on the boundary of the sitting room and the open-plan kitchen, as if unsure of what came next in this change to the script. Was there to be dialogue? A scene change? There were no stage directions and she felt a little stuck. He was still standing there, his back to her. Did she want a glass of water, she asked herself? No, she didn't think so. At that moment, it struck her how unnatural all of this was and, just then, she didn't like the way it made her feel.

Still drinking, Xander turned and faced her and they looked at each other silently. He offered her the glass and she stepped forward to take it. She took a dainty sip and then, locking eyes with Xander, she trickled the rest down her neck where it reached her silk top and spread quickly like ink on blotting paper, turning the silvery tone into gunmetal grey and causing the fabric to cling to her body, her nipples to harden and stand proud. Xander knocked the glass out of her hands and onto the floor where it landed on the rug with a muffled thud. He nudged it away, where it rolled off onto the wooden floor and knocked against the skirting board. And then all was silent again and Siobhan had moved up close to Xander, grabbing fistfuls of his shirt as she reached for his mouth with hers. His hands moved across her body, feeling her flesh through the silk, wet or dry. She was rubbing at his groin where his erection was tantalizingly restricted. Falling onto her knees, she unbuckled his belt, hoicked down the zip and pulled sharply on his jeans and his boxers in one fell swoop. He could feel her breath hot above his cock and could sense how agonizingly close her mouth was, trying to stand steady while the sensation of her caressing his balls with one hand and tracing the crack between his buttocks with the other threatened his balance. And then he was between her lips, deeper into the sucking wet cavity of her mouth; it felt as if she was swallowing

100

him whole.

She pulled away and looked up at him beseechingly. 'Do you want to come in my mouth? Or my cunt?'

He pulled her to her feet and pressed his tongue into her mouth where it met hers. He grabbed at her skirt and delved his hands up her thighs, foraging through her knickers and into the slippery promise behind. And then he thought, she absolutely reeks of garlic. And then he thought, I don't have any condoms. And then he thought, oh God, I'm losing my hard-on.

'In your mouth,' he whispered as they folded down onto the rug, clawed away the remaining clothing and settled head to toe, tonguing and sucking at each other until they were sated.

Don't stay the night. Not this time.

'I'm exhausted,' Siobhan said. And she headed off to Xander's bedroom before he could suggest otherwise.

\*　　　\*　　　\*

He looked around the sitting room. Strewn clothes. A severely rucked rug. A discarded glass on the floor with a crack now visible. A woman's shoes—one here, one there. His shirt, in a scrunch and flung onto the kitchen like a wiping-round rag. What had seemed such a good idea had left him with an odd taste in his mouth—akin to feeling nauseous but unable to pinpoint the offending food. Pulling his boxers back up from his ankles, he went to sit in his leather tub chair, taking the phone from his jeans pocket. Two texts. Both from Caroline.

So . . . you dark horse. Dish the dirt—who is she?

She'd sent another, about ten minutes ago.

Want to come to dinner Fri? With your lady friend?

How to reply? His closest friends—who'd always supported him, who wanted only the best for him and who'd been there for him when his relationship with Laura came to grief. Xander knew, quite categorically, that he didn't want them to be part of this—this *thing*—with Siobhan. And that in itself made this thing with Siobhan not quite right.

## *Chapter Ten*

Stella arrived back at Longbridge Hall at two minutes before eleven o'clock and sat in her car listening to the radio for the pips on the hour. She imagined that, for people like the Fortescues, it was considered as impudent to turn up early as it was decreed discourteous to turn up late. She rang the bell and gave a lively knock at precisely eleven o'clock.

'You're back?' Mrs Biggins said, as if Stella might not be of sound mind.

'I'm expected,' said Stella, taking off her coat and giving it to Mrs Biggins.

'One moment,' Mrs Biggins said and Stella thought she could detect a glint of approval.

When Lydia appeared, Stella felt grateful for Paul Smith and high heels because she both looked and felt taller and more imposing than she had the day before and it was obvious that Lady Lydia had noticed. The woman bristled slightly, tipped her chin upwards as if competing for height. 'What are you doing here?'

'As you asked—eleven o'clock prompt.' And then Stella saw a flicker of confusion scuttle across Lydia's face and settle as dull discomfort behind her eyes. She softened her tone. 'To see the grounds?' Stella prompted in her more usual voice, 'And art?'

Lydia gathered herself. 'I'll take you.'

However, the art wasn't Beckinsford or any other painter remotely connected with Reynolds, nor was it portraits or landscapes or equine backsides. The Art Lydia took Stella to see was short for Arthur, a wizened old man little younger than Lady Lydia. He lived in an apartment in a wing of the stable courtyard which was some way from the main house and cordoned from view by the mighty wall of the kitchen garden. Made from the same rosy-hued bricks as the main house, the buildings ran three sides of a square, with a central archway crowned by a clock tower. The clock face itself was greening, the hands fixed at ten past three as if it had been dredged up from the pond where it had lain for some time and fish had feasted upon a great many of the numbers. The wing to the right had been converted into two dwellings. To the left, above what must have been the coach bays, appeared to be another apartment—Stella noted curtains at the windows but the glass was so dusty she was sure it was derelict.

Lydia rapped on the door. 'He's as deaf as a post,' she said, with the same exasperation she extended to Mrs Biggins. 'Art,' she said when he

103

appeared, 'please be a dear and take Miss Elmfield around.'

'It's Miss Hutton,' said Stella.

'He doesn't need to know, he won't be interested and he won't remember,' Lydia said bitingly whilst smiling benevolently to Art, whose eyes shone like small beads of jet. He disappeared back into his home. 'And you do *not* mention why you are here.'

Stella was taken aback.

'You can be an historian, or a writer—something like that. But *not* an estate agent. Make it up.' And she walked away, banging down her stick every stride as if expecting to find part of her land hollow.

\*     \*     \*

'Hullo!' Stella said loudly. 'Lovely day!'

'It is,' said Art in a soft voice which suggested she really needn't raise hers. 'Where would you like to see first?'

'Everywhere,' said Stella.

'Where in Everywhere?' Art asked measuredly. 'Longbridge sits in over five hundred acres.'

'Seriously!' Stella had assumed the grounds extended to a posh garden and perhaps a paddock or two.

'Four hundred arable, the rest pasture—used to be for cattle, just for ponies now—also woodland and the grounds around the house. Formal gardens, pool, kitchen garden, orchard, tennis. Which way to Everywhere do you want to go?'

She liked him instantly. She really liked him; the pared-down way he spoke, his shapeless clothing, old boots, unflattering cap and dark little eyes set into a craggy, haphazardly shaven face. She

104

reckoned Art was either spoken at, or ignored, these days. And perhaps in those days too, if the current Lady's manner was in any way a family trait.

Silently, Stella cursed Paul Smith and her high heels, not least because Art's stride was surprisingly assertive and fast. He described the lay of the land, took her on a whistle-stop tour of the livery yard, which was modern and spruce, and an area of old barns the least dilapidated of which were now rented out as workshops. She felt herself being peered at—two young geeky-looking guys in one barn, from another a cabinetmaker whose face was the colour of mahogany. The third had an array of tree stumps outside—whether this was a tree surgeon or a sculptor Stella was unsure. All these people will have to find new premises, she thought to herself. And she thought how odd it would be to rent somewhere purpose built, modern, after being treated to barns like these. And Art would need to find somewhere to live too. And he's been here decades. But she said nothing and just enthused, instead, about all he showed her.

The formal gardens, which ran in a curvaceous swoop around the house, were shielded from the drive by magnificent rhododendrons. They were set out as manicured swathes of lawn plotted and pieced by rolling herbaceous borders and grand specimen trees. There was a pond, which was really too large to be called such but a lake would sound too ostentatious, also a swimming pool which could have been bigger and, Stella noted, cleaner. Garden seats, small stone obelisks and spheres and statuary were positioned here and there, providing either focal points or surprises. All the while, the house itself appeared pompously to survey all that lay around it. The kitchen garden, however, was its own private world, shielded from the house by a long stone building whose purpose Art explained to Stella.

'Boiler was here,' he said. 'They should never've tinkered with the heating of the house now. It worked fine when it was the old way—the boiler and the boys. Now Lady's got a cold house only with them electronical heaters what don't work and cost a king's ransom to run.' He took her inside the long barrack-like building, now empty of its original purpose, housing instead garden tools and a proliferation of terracotta pots, most of which appeared to be too chipped to be of any use. 'Boiler'd take up all that section there,' he indicated. 'Boys'd be here, around the clock, keeping it going. Bunks were over there. Hollow walls, see, taking the heat to the house. Couldn't let the boiler go out. Ever.'

'Boys?'

'Couldn't let it go out, the boiler, that'd never do. Most important job, really, of all the workers. Invisible though. And hot. So hot. Noisy like you wouldn't believe.'

'Were you a boy? A boiler boy?' She didn't know why she'd asked, what relevance it had—but Art spoke with such wistful authority she wanted to know.

'I was. My family's been Longbridge people all through. Only me now. My boy gone off to Manchester. Insurance. His choice, makes sense. Sad, though.' They stood in the building a while longer, Art remembering, Stella imagining. 'Show you the kitchen garden now.'

Pale shingle paths ran energetically amongst

106

the raised beds busy with new growth; the walls festooned with canes and lattices. Everything in tidy, neat little rows, labelled with miniature signposts. Every now and then, a floral profusion purely aesthetic. Art went through the long, seasonal list of everything ever grown at Longbridge. These days, the selection was slimmer, increasing only during the summer months and then primarily to assist the coffers of the village fete. Beyond the kitchen garden, accessed through a door set into the far wall, another garden. And, Stella was stunned to discover, another house.

'They call it Garden House,' said Art. 'It's a dower house—where the widow takes up if she's outlived the Lord. Lady Lydia's ma was here, for many years.'

'Who's in it now?'

'Rented properly now—I mean, now there's no family member wanting it. Folk come and stay a year or so while they're looking for somewhere to buy. Had Japanese in here last year—very quiet. Never saw them. Current lot are all right. Churchgoers, so that's something. Keep themselves private—that's the key. That's what Lady Lydia requires, see.'

'Is it big? Inside?'

'Three bed. I been in once or twice, when the old Countess was near her time. Went to say goodbye.'

He looked misty eyed.

'Was she lovely?' Stella ventured. 'Lady Lydia's mother?'

Art smiled and turned to Stella. 'They're sharp, the Barbary ladyfolk. But good at heart. It's a quality, really. Called feminitism these days, I believe.'

Stella gave him a sage nod. Then a structure caught her eye.

'What's that?'

'Apple store.'

It was a windowless building too large, too grand to be a shed, constructed almost entirely from very slim, dense thatch. 'I've never seen anything like this.'

'Don't reckon to there being many left, these days,' said Art, opening the door and allowing the light in so that Stella could see the slatted wooden shelving, running floor to ceiling all the way around.

'It's beautiful!' said Stella. It really was. And so peaceful. Not dusty or spooky as another windowless building might be, but a soft and serene interior instead.

'It was an ammunitions store in the War,' Art told her. 'Smelled bad—funny like—for many years after.'

'Were the army stationed here at Longbridge?'

'Yes—in the west fields. Poor buggers. Begged for eggs. For anything, really.'

'Was the house billeted?'

'Yes—hotchpotch of families lived alongside the Fortescues. From all over. Lady Lydia's mother and grandmother—they were mortified at first. But everyone rubbed along just fine. What you'd liken to a commune these days—all these women and a scamper of little 'uns. The feminitists.'

'Were you here? In the War?'

'Yes, me and my ma—same house. Always the same for us. I was old enough to join up—I'd'a liked to but I'm half blind.' And Art turned to Stella and though he stared at her intently, she found it impossible to tell which was his good eye.

108

He laughed to himself. 'Seen enough?'

'Not really!' she enthused. It was fascinating, more intriguing than the main house, all of this.

He looked alarmed. 'Nothing else to show you—you seen Everywhere now.'

'I meant, I could stay for hours. There's so much to see, so much that's special.'

'Have a walk yourself—won't get lost. Impossible. Just line up the clock tower with your right shoulder and walk forwards—you'll be back at the door in the kitchen garden wall. Have your back to the tower, walk diagonally—you'll be back at the lily pond before long. If you get stuck, find the clock tower and you'll find me.'

'Thank you so much.' Stella extended her hand to shake but Art looked as embarrassed as if she'd tried to give him a tip. He turned and walked off. 'Art,' she called after him, 'Art?' On purpose, she didn't say it loudly, just her regular speaking voice. He turned, cocked his head. 'Why does she say you're deaf when you're not?'

'She doesn't know I'm not.'

'She doesn't know?'

'I find it—helpful—for her to think me so.' And he winked, thereby alerting Stella to which eye was his good one.

'Does she know you're half blind?'

'No. Mustn't know—she'd'a never let me drive the Roller, let alone the fancy ride-on mowers.' He shrugged, tipped his cap and went on his way.

Stella returned to the apple store once Art was gone from sight and stood in the dimly lit interior, thinking about apples and gunpowder and how, for such a long time, Longbridge Hall had been a fully functioning, self-sufficient vibrant world-in-little;

109

somehow sheltered by, yet also providing for, a small village in Hertfordshire.

*　　　*　　　*

Xander was halfway through a second lap around what he termed the Killer Loop which circumnavigated Long Dansbury and skirted Little Dunwick in seven and a half arduous hilly miles. He didn't usually take much notice of specifics when he was running, especially not if he was going against the clock; instead he'd tick off a mental checklist of landmarks. Today, though, from the hill high above Longbridge Hall, a glint coming off a mirror-like slab caught his eye. It was the sunroof of a Mini, parked in the driveway. Deludedly, for a moment he thought it might be Verity—but the last car she'd had was a clapped-out, orange VW Beetle whose bodywork had no shine left and as far as he knew, she'd had no cause to change it since. As he ran on, he glanced again at the vehicle and, as he dropped downhill a little, the company's branding emblazoned along the side came into view.

Elmfield Estates.

What the—!

He remembered Caroline's text a couple of weeks ago. It couldn't be! Bang outside Longbridge Hall? Where was Lydia? Did she know? Thank goodness he'd decided to work from home today. He ran fast—too fast for the gradient, really, and for this stage in his run, with twelve miles done at a pace and three left to go. But he felt strangely compelled to get there at all odds, as if expecting the whole estate to have been sold and new owners unpacking by the time he arrived.

110

Xander knew every gap in every hedge, every low part of every wall because, over the years, it appeared he was the only one who knew they were there as they'd never been fixed or filled. Down into the estate he sprinted. He ran; across a meadow, through the kitchen garden, along the drive and up to the front door. He rang and knocked but even through the great slabs of mahogany, he sensed the house was empty. Anyway, it wasn't really Lydia he needed—because he couldn't believe that this could possibly be within her control, imagining instead an idea foisted upon her and now taking hold, like an infection, with a momentum of its own. No, Lydia wouldn't be the perpetrator.

There! In the garden! Noseying near the statue of Lord Frederick Makepeace William Fortescue, the first Earl of Barbary. Some woman, walking around in a tailored suit and heels, looking frankly ridiculous—both out of place and unwelcome. Xander tempered his pace and approached.

Stella heard panting, sensed the rhythmic beat across earth of someone approaching fast. She looked over and recognized at once the jogger who'd sent her flying on her very first visit to Mercy Benton, her very first visit to the village. And as he approached, Xander recalled the woman taking up the entire pavement that day, flapping around with her papers flying, getting in his way and messing up his timing. They stared at each other, Xander feeling as if he was running on the spot for the last few yards, Stella feeling as if she'd be sent flying at any moment. He was right there. Stopped.

'What!' she said defensively, because his displeasure was worn as an emphatic frown.

'Who the hell *are* you?' Hands on his hips, his

damp hair plastered to his skull resembling a Roman emperor, his forearms all a-glisten, his chest rising and falling fast.

'I'm Stella Hutton, actually,' she said officiously. 'Elmfield Estates.' She didn't offer her hand because she had no desire to take his.

'But what are you doing *here*?' And he fixed her with his blue-grey eyes which appeared to darken the longer they kept her caught. 'Why are you snooping around?'

'Firstly, I am *not* snooping around.' Stella was indignant. 'Secondly, I've been invited, thank you very much. And thirdly, what business is it of yours?' She glanced over to the house, as if willing Mrs Biggins to come out brandishing a rolling pin or, better still, Lady Lydia to appear with her spear-sharp tongue.

'Actually, it is very much my business,' the man said. 'Leave the Fortescues alone. They've been here for generations and the last thing they need is you filling their heads with notions of millions. And the last thing Long Dansbury needs is a bloody property developer carving up the history of the place and disrupting the dynamic.' He looked thoroughly triumphant. 'Do you *know* how many lives—entire families—this estate provides for?' He'd stopped panting. His arms were crossed but still his eyes wouldn't release her.

'Who are *you*?' Stella asked, regarding him as if he might be the village lunatic. She backed up a step, feeling bolstered to be standing side by side with Lord Fortescue, the very first Earl of Barbary, even if he was bronze and looking the other way.

'I grew up here.'

'You're a *Fortescue*?'

112

'Er—no.' And he was helpless not to laugh a little. 'No.'

Stella bristled. She didn't like being shouted at and she didn't like being laughed at. 'Then I'll thank you to leave me to my work.'

'But what *are* you doing?' He scratched his head, causing his hair to stand up in jaunty spikes.

'I am here at Lady Lydia's invitation and you're in my way. You're holding me up.'

'But why?'

'Because I have work to do!' she chided.

'I mean—why are you *here*? I've heard the rumours, you know.'

'Well, you'll have to discuss it with Lady Barbary,' said Stella before thinking, No! That's not her name.

Xander snorted and Stella reddened, feeling as if he now thought her more of a silly impostor than a threat. She cast her eyes down at her shoes. Stupid high heels. Muddied.

'Just don't bully her,' he said. 'She's not as steely as she likes people to think.' It was almost impossible for Stella to ally this to the Lydia she had met twice in the last twenty-four hours.

'Look, I need to work,' Stella muttered, 'and if you have some sentimental attachment to the place, then I'm sorry.'

Xander stared at her hard and then he backed away a few steps, still shrugging, before turning and running off whence he came. She didn't know why she watched after him nor why she sensed he'd turn again. But he did; timing it perfectly at the precise place just before the land climbed and the path curved and Lord Fortescue's part of the garden would disappear from his view. And then he raised

113

his hand; this weird, stroppy bloke. He raised his hand and Stella wasn't sure why, whether it was a wave or a halt sign. Either way, it threw her and she found herself raising hers back even though it conflicted with her better judgement. For goodness' sake, woman! She gave herself a shake and turned to the bronze statue of Lord Fortescue, or Lord Frederick as she now thought of him, then stood on tiptoes until she felt she was looking right at him.

'Good God, sir,' she said, 'this place is full of the most peculiar people.'

And she looked at his face and thought of him shagging the Prince Regent's mistress and building this fine house and securing this wonderful land and planting these beautiful gardens and squirrelling away his secret porn collection and staring at that horse's enormous backside every time he went up and down the stairs.

'Actually, sir, I hope a property developer doesn't buy it.'

'Longbridge without a Fortescue?' he seemed to exclaim. 'How preposterous!'

And then Stella giggled a little. In a bizarre and surreal way, all of this was ever so slightly wonderful. What on earth was she doing here, conversing with a bronze statue? Having a stand-up row with a strange man dripping with sweat? Wearing high heels and a borrowed suit, when she was slowly sinking into the soft lawn and she really wasn't warm enough. She hadn't done the final figures—how could she, she hadn't known until an hour ago about a whole other house in a whole other garden—but she could already estimate Longbridge Hall to be worth well over ten million pounds. Was she really being chosen to handle it all? She wasn't a property guru. She was a single mum, a divorcee, an erstwhile art historian currently masquerading as an estate agent because she desperately needed to claw back money and stability into her life and fast. But could an eye-watering commission really be coming her way? The difference it would make to her life. The difference the sale of this place would make to so many lives. But that simply had to be no concern of hers. She had to look after herself. And answer to her client.

'Where's the Barbary money gone? Why does Lady Lydia need to sell?' she asked Lord Frederick.

'Buggered if I know, m'dear,' he replied. 'You need to ask her yourself.'


## Chapter Eleven

'I'm not remotely interested in who gets it.'

Lydia was suddenly at Stella's side, as if butting in on the private tête-à-tête Stella and Sir Frederick had been having.

'Lady Lydia!'

'As I said, I don't care who buys Longbridge,' she said. 'It's not like selling a horse, you know. Gracious me, the hoops I'd have potential owners jump through before I'd let one of mine go. I turned down thousands for Percy—no one was quite right. He lived out his days right here in the garden, where the grass was sweetest. Used to drive Art absolutely potty.' The women gazed at the lawns awhile, as if the ghost of Percy was present. 'So don't come to me with any *"Mr and Mrs Buggerlugs will cherish this place and breathe life back into it*" nonsense,' Lydia continued. 'All I'm interested in is who's going to pay the most—then it's theirs. Plenty of rooms at Longbridge—but no room whatsoever for sentiment.'

Stella reflected quietly for a moment. Usually, she could assess a house within minutes of seeing it. But in her two lengthy visits, she felt she'd merely scratched at the surface of Longbridge, as if peering in through a dusty window at an angle and knowing she wasn't seeing all the details. Yesterday, the house itself—unexpected rooms, hidden shelving, veiled insults from a future king to a Fortescue and from a current Fortescue right back at Stella. This morning, with Art, she'd discovered that behind the crumbling walls of the old barns, in the secret garden of the dower house, in the reverential shadows of the apple store and the cold interior of the empty boiler house, a jewel was hidden. Despite the faded walls, balding rugs with dog mess, nasty kitchen and general chill in the main house and direct frostiness of the owner, today Stella sensed that Longbridge Hall had secrets and riches that had been peculiarly downplayed. It was as if someone had switched off the central heating—but if it could be put back on again, the warmth and colour would flood the place. Even the old brass nameplates, now tarnished and suffocated by ivy but still fixed to the southern wall of the kitchen garden, told a more detailed story than simply naming the long-gone espaliered fruit trees. How would she bring all this across in the particulars? A mammoth task but with potentially huge rewards.

'Longbridge Hall is worth millions,' Stella said, looking at the statue of Lord Frederick as if he'd approve.

116

'Of course it is,' Lydia rubbished, *'but how many millions?'* The breeze had lifted strands of her hair and it made her look overexcited.

'I didn't know about the dower house,' said Stella.

'The what?'

'Garden House—as you call it.'

'What is there to know?'

'Are there any other dwellings here? In addition to the apartments in the stable courtyard?'

'No,' said Lydia. Then she thought about it. 'Well, there's a groom's flat over in the livery yard—but that's not for permanent residence.' She thought about it some more. 'And then the cottages on Tramfield Lane—they fall within the Longbridge curtilage too. As does the patch of land opposite the shop where people park.' Lydia glanced at Stella, who was gawping, and looked away with barely concealed irritation. 'You're catching flies.'

Stella closed her mouth. 'And *everything*'s for sale?'

'The lot!' Lydia said, with a dismissive wave of her hand. 'The whole rotten lot. Crumbling barns. Ancient tenants. The whole shooting match!'

'You see, we could market it as an estate entire—or divide it into lots.'

'I don't want to be left having to auction off the dregs, I want the whole thing gone. It's an utter bore now—not to mention an absolute sinkhole when it comes to money.'

Stella paused. 'In that case, I'll need to see the other places—the cottages.'

Lydia stood expressionless. Then she nodded. 'Of course,' she said.

Stella glanced at Lord Frederick, who seemed to be goading her on. 'A man came up to me this morning—right here in the garden,' she told Lydia. 'He charged up to me—I thought he was going to send me flying. Extremely rude—started telling me off for being here and told me in no uncertain terms to leave you alone and that Longbridge wasn't for sale.'

'Art?'

'No, not Art. A younger bloke—all sweaty and panting and in jogging gear. He was really stroppy. I thought he might be a trespasser but he claimed to live here.' Stella paused. 'Of course, I could tell he wasn't a Fortescue. *So* ill-mannered,' she stressed, as if that in itself made him the polar opposite of a Fortescue. Fortunately, the irony was lost on Lydia and actually Stella had managed subtly to appease her. Lydia's expression had softened around the eyes and even a smile was threatening to crack out from the corners of her pursed lips.

'I see.' Lydia walked on ahead. 'There's lunch, if you care to take it,' she called over her shoulder. 'We'll go and see the cottages, and the rest, in thirty minutes.'

\* \* \*

'Where the hell is she?'

'Second day on the trot.'

'Phone her again, Belinda.'

'Her phone was off half an hour ago.'

'If she doesn't call in, I'm taking on the Bengeo property. Mr Winterton has phoned twice already, wondering what's happening with the survey.'

'I reckon the job's too much for her.'

118

'What did I tell you?'

'Well, I think we should let Douglas know. I mean, what did any of us actually know about her?'

'Those other properties she's sold—a kid could have shifted them.'

'If you're so intrigued, why don't You Three ask Douglas where she is?'

'He's not in either—or haven't you noticed, Geoff?'

'*You* phone her, Geoff—she has a soft spot for you.'

'We've heard you like a younger woman, Geoff.'

'I beg your pardon?'

'For God's sake—it's a joke.'

*       *       *

Stella was sitting down to the lunch which Mrs Biggins had presented to her with all the stroppy flourish of a celebrity chef before flouncing accordingly out of the kitchen. On a plate: a hard-boiled egg, two celery sticks, a hunk of cheddar, a whole tomato, a glob of pickle boot-polish brown, and a slice of thickly buttered wholewheat bread. She imagined lunch for the workers had been pretty much the same throughout the history of Longbridge. When her mobile rang, its jaunty polyphonic ring tone seemed vulgar, too harsh for a house which had only three old-fashioned Bakelite telephones.

'Hullo?' she answered quietly.

'Oh. Yes. Hi, Stella—it's Geoff—from the office?' It touched her, the way he turned anything about himself into a question, as if today he was unsure whether he was who he thought he was, let

119

alone whether he was in the office or not.

'Hullo, Geoff—everything OK?'

'Well, it's fine, Stella. Yes, everything in the office is fine—but we haven't seen you.'

'No—' she paused—'no, you haven't.' Her uncle had told her not to mention a thing until they knew whether or not Elmfield Estates would be representing Longbridge Hall. She could hear Belinda in the background, hissing to Geoff to ask Stella where the hell she was. 'I'm just—' she paused—'I'm just following a lead. I alerted Mr Hutton I'd be out of the office—apologies if you weren't informed.'

'Right,' said Geoff, because he'd thought it quite wrong to phone her in the first place.

'Right,' said Stella. 'I was hoping to be back after lunch, but it's unlikely now.' She looked at the tomato, punctured and deflated from where she'd sucked. Delicious.

'Mr Winterton wanted to know about the survey—at Bengeo.'

'Yes, of course,' said Stella who'd quite forgotten. 'I have his number, I'll call him directly.'

'Of course,' said Geoff, wishing the others would stop hovering. Belinda was wearing ghastly perfume today, the heavy musky type that clung to the clothing of anyone near, and Steve had had curry for lunch. 'We'll see you tomorrow then?'

'You will indeed. First thing,' said Stella. 'Thanks, Geoff.' And she was grateful it had been him calling, not one of the others. Though she'd managed to foster a workmanlike cordiality with the others, she knew it was paper thin. Geoff was kind and, in his weary way, an ally. She phoned Mr Winterton, put his mind at rest and, after that,

120

found to her consternation that she'd quite lost her appetite. What would she do if she did secure Longbridge Hall on their books? Belinda, Steve and Gill would want her head on a plate and Geoff, dear Geoff, would probably just give up.

*     *     *

'What did she say?'

'Did she say where she was?'

'Did she say where the hell she's been?'

'She said,' said Geoff, 'that she's following a lead.'

'A lead? I don't think so—I think she's up to something.'

'Yeah—funny how she scarpers as soon as she knows her uncle isn't about.'

'I think we should let him know she's not been in.'

'Me too. She can't hide behind the family shield for ever, you know.'

'You Three!'

Everyone looked at Geoff as if realizing for the first time that he was there, sitting at the desk they were crowding around. He didn't want to hear it and he didn't want to doubt Stella. He just wanted to do his job. Gossip was one thing—it was idle and it irritated him—but rumours were different. Rumours threatened to contain a modicum of truth and were unnerving.

*     *     *

Stella could hear her name being called. Leaving the kitchen, having attempted to bury the leftovers

121

under a pile of other stuff in the bin and then washed and dried her plate and cutlery, she went through to the hall where Lady Lydia was standing as though she'd been waiting for ages. She'd changed. She was now in a pair of navy trousers and a sugar-pink cashmere pullover over a high-necked blouse. She had sensible navy shoes with a little heel and her hair had been redone— no strands escaping. She also wore lipstick. If she'd been Stella's mum or someone Stella simply liked, she'd have told Lady Fortescue that it was a little smudged and offered her a tissue. She wasn't sure whether it was because she didn't dare or because it actually made her feel a little empowered, that she said nothing.

'Would you come on! I haven't all day, you know.'

'Perfect lunch,' Stella said, 'thank you very much. It was very thoughtful of you. I rarely have more than a snatched sandwich.' Her mother had taught her to bat away hostility with grace, thereby giving only softness for the aggressor to fruitlessly hit against. *Those who hit at foam balls as hard as they can will never hurt their opponent—they just squander their energy.* Stella often thought of her mother's cod psychology. In her family, though decibel levels were invariably high in whosever household they all gathered and discussions were frequently lively, arguments never raged because they were always deflected, like gunshot dampened by a silencer. She'd tried to employ the method in her marriage but found it to be the only exception to the rule. So she'd tried the opposite—but that hadn't worked either.

'My dear—are you OK?'

Stella brought herself back to the present with a shudder. 'Sorry—I was miles away.' She called me 'my dear', Stella thought and a gentle triumph coursed through her.

'Thank you, Lady Lydia.'

'I think we shall take your car,' Lydia said. 'I've phoned ahead.' She paused, not looking at Stella. 'You may call me Lydia.'

*     *     *

Lime Grove Cottages, on Tramfield Lane, were in a little terrace of three. Each had window frames and doors painted in French grey which Stella now knew to be the estate colour. The woodwork in the stable block had been painted the same, as had the door in the kitchen garden wall, the glassless window frames in the boiler building and all the barn doors, whether the buildings were derelict or now rented as workshops. Longbridge Hall, however, had its woodwork painted white, its doors in the natural rich mahogany. It gave the impression that all the other buildings were in uniform, beholden and in servitude to the Fortescues.

In number one lived Peg Gilbey, a small woman, perhaps Lydia's age but appearing more elderly She welcomed them in as if they were guests of honour and the highlight of her day. The cottage was a hotchpotch of minute rooms, furnished to the nines and with trinkets adorning every available surface.

'Your hem's down, Lydia,' she said and Stella's blood ran cold, anticipating the short shrift this might be met with. But Lydia surprised her.

'Is it? Gracious me—would you look at that!'

'Shall I see to it now?'

'Don't worry, I'll have Mrs Biggins bring you to the house. There are a couple of other things needing you, Peggy. Buttons and a tricksy zip.'

'Right you are.'

'Seen enough?' Lydia asked Stella.

'Thank you,' Stella said to Miss Gilbey. She looked around the sitting room again and nodded warmly. The curtains caught her eye—and she realized they were the same fabric, heavy silk with an embroidered floral design, as those in Lydia's bedroom.

'Miss Hutton—please!' Lydia tusked as if Stella had been loitering. Stella shook Miss Gilbey's hand and told her it had been a pleasure.

Outside, on the way to number two, Stella felt compelled to remark on the curtains. Lydia stopped in her tracks and cocked her head to hasten a memory.

'Peg's mother was maid to my mother. She was a lovely woman—she'd have me and Peg on each knee, storytelling. Mother,' Lydia said, 'sent Peg to London at the age of fourteen, to learn to be a seamstress. She was her benefactor, I suppose— but she got her money's worth.'

'Curtains and hems?'

Lydia actually smiled. 'And the rest—Peg is a magician with needle and thread. Even now. She made Mother's last bed jacket—worked on it day and night so she could have it for her last few days. It was the softest, lightest velvet in powder blue.'

Stella didn't know what overcame her, but she reached out and gave Lydia's forearm a little squeeze. Lydia appeared not to feel it. 'Number two,' she announced, 'rented to one of the teachers

124

at the primary school. Nice woman—husband's a twit. Mrs George.'

'Won't she be teaching?' Stella looked at her watch.

'She's part-time,' Lydia said witheringly.

The cottage was the same size as Peg's, but seemed larger on account of the downstairs rooms being knocked through and everything Farrow & Ball neutral with no knick-knacks on show, just soberly framed black-and-white landscape photographs.

'The upstairs lights keep flickering,' Mrs George told Lydia, apologetically. Lydia nodded. 'And the downstairs radiator makes the strangest noises.' Lydia nodded again but Stella noted a twitch to her jaw which suggested she was clenching her teeth.

'I'll have someone come by the end of the week.'

They'd barely left before Lydia hissed, 'Always complaining about something. It's a cottage! It's old! Of course lights and radiators are dicky! For the rent she pays, she should put up or shut up.'

Lydia stopped by the gate to number three.

'I don't think he's home,' she said but before Stella could beg to differ—on account of smoke being visible from the chimney—Lydia had turned and was walking back towards Stella's car where she waited for the passenger door to be opened.

'You'll have to go back there on your own. I'll phone Mr Fletcher and tell him to expect you. How about Saturday afternoon?'

Saturday afternoon—Will had a football match.

'I have another viewing Saturday afternoon,' Stella said. It was only a white lie—she always viewed Will playing.

'Morning, then,' Lydia said in such a tone that

there was to be no further discussion.

Just before Stella started the engine, she turned to Lydia. 'How long has Miss Gilbey lived there?'

'She was born there. We were born in the same year. It's a grace-and-favour cottage—not that numbers two and three bring in much rent in the light of all the repairs I have to fork out for.'

'And if the cottage is sold, where will she go?'

Lydia didn't answer. She had heard, Stella could see that, but she looked out of the window as if disturbed by the notion that she hadn't thought about that.

\*　　　\*　　　\*

Was that Lydia? Xander wondered, coming into his sitting room. He thought, I must go and see her. He thought, I need to find out what's going on. If those estate agents have hooked their claws into her, I need to know.

## Chapter Twelve

Xander broke with tradition and ignored etiquette. At the risk of incurring short shrift from Lydia—which could be icy at best, humiliating at worst—he simply turned up at Longbridge with no prior warning, never mind an invitation. Hitherto, he'd always sent a letter, resorting to the telephone only if it was urgent. Not today. There was no time for phone calls. The working day was coming to a close and, after confronting that estate agent woman in the garden at Longbridge and then thinking he'd

126

seen Lydia outside his cottage an hour ago, he decided he had to act now.

Mrs Biggins opened the door to him.

'Xander!' Then she looked confused. 'Are we expecting you?'

'No,' he said, 'but is Lady Lydia home? Might I pay a quick visit?'

'Hold on a mo', duck. Come on in.' She left him in the hall and went into the drawing room. Lydia was dozing in the wingback chair, head back and at an angle, mouth slackened, the *Telegraph* folded on the half-completed crossword, half fallen off her lap, her hands curled on top of the paper, not unlike like the claws of a dead bird.

That's how you'll look when you've snuffed it, Mrs Biggins thought.

It wasn't a malicious or irreverent thought, it was almost in preparation. She walked over, making a little unnecessary noise as she went, clearing her throat, speaking to herself, lifting a pile of magazines just to plonk them down on the coffee table. It all combined to enable Lydia to wake without being woken. With a little snort, which Mrs Biggins feigned not to notice, Lydia woke and was relieved to see her housekeeper busy plumping a cushion, seemingly unaware that she'd been anything other than wide awake and engrossed in her crossword.

'Would you like tea here or in the library?' Mrs Biggins asked.

'Here, thank you.'

'Xander is here.'

'Xander? Here? Was he invited?' Lydia paused, affronted more by her confusion than by the fact that he might simply have turned up uninvited.

'That's what I asked him. He said it was impromptu—if you weren't otherwise engaged.'

'Did he now!' Lydia's tone changed.

And Mrs Biggins noted a very strange expression on Lydia's face—as if a prior spell she'd woven had worked, or quarry had walked straight into a trap carefully set. It was glee, mischief, and she looked altogether self-satisfied and bright.

'Send him in, then,' she said with a little clap, 'and ask if he'd like tea too.'

Mrs Biggins went back out to the hall. 'She says you're to go on through and would you like tea?' Xander noted that Mrs Biggins looked confused so he said yes please to tea, put his hand briefly on her shoulder and went across to the drawing room where he knocked and poked his head around the door with a big cheery smile before Lydia could say, 'Enter.'

She was sitting poker straight on one of the sofas, looking very stern.

'Xander,' she said, not in welcome, not as a question, but as a statement underscored with consternation that demanded he qualify his presence immediately.

'I was working from home today—I thought I'd pop by.' He paused. 'I hope that's OK?' It didn't look as though it was OK at all. Lydia's lips were pursed as if invisible running thread had been sewn across and then pulled tight.

'Did you not think to phone ahead—if you profess not to have had time to drop me a note?'

This was his ticking-off, what his mother would call *being royally scolded*—when Lydia took much pleasure in wearing her airs and graces around her like an ermine cape borrowed from the Queen.

128

'I'm sorry,' Xander said. 'But actually, I really needed to see you, Lydia. It's just that—well, there's a crazy rumour circulating in the village that you're thinking of selling Longbridge.' There. That's what he'd come to say—and he'd made it sound suitably risible.

He waited. There was a long silence, during which he glanced at her to find her still sitting poker straight and seemingly emotionless.

'Rumours, eh!' Finally, she laughed—a little acidly—as if Xander was an idiot to have been seduced by them and a bore for bothering her with them.

'I rubbished it,' Xander qualified. 'I didn't trouble you with it—and it's been doing the rounds for a week or so. Apparently.' He was still standing and Lydia had made no gesture for him to sit. 'But today, I came across this woman with a clipboard, teetering around the gardens here in high heels, with some hideously emblazoned car parked on your drive.'

'Miss Hutton,' Lydia corrected. 'And you didn't come across her, Xander—you trespassed at a gallop and frightened the poor thing witless.'

He bowed his head because that part was true.

'I was concerned,' he told Lydia quietly.

'Oh, do sit down—standing there like a naughty schoolboy does not become you.'

Xander sat opposite Lydia, grateful for Mrs Biggins' appearance with the tea tray. Shortbread, dusted with icing sugar when still warm so that it formed a delicate, sparkling crust. When he was a child, Mrs Biggins had facilitated Verity and him by leaving the biscuits in an empty kitchen, cooling on a rack with a linen napkin folded

129

helpfully into an envelope to one side. Even now, Xander wondered if Lydia knew about that, and felt a surge of nostalgic gratitude towards the housekeeper—not so much for her baking skills, but for being a conspirator back then. Maybe that's why there was shortbread today—maybe Mrs Biggins wanted Xander to have something sweet to soften the dressing-down. Only she didn't know he was coming, did she, because he'd made no prior arrangement. It could be just coincidence, but as he bit gently into the biscuit and the buttery crumble of sweetness filled his mouth, he saw it as a good omen.

Unbeknownst to Lydia and Xander, Mrs Biggins had been listening at the door. She was never in the dark about anything. It was her, after all, who'd told Lydia about Mercy Benton's to-do with John Denby & Co. And it was she who'd told Mercy about Elmfield Estates in the first place. And then kept Lady Lydia abreast with the sale of Mercy's cottage.

Lydia watched Xander. He hadn't changed all that much over the years, really—look at the boy! Waiting on tenterhooks for her say-so to take another biscuit. Not too dissimilar from the spaniels they used to keep. She let him eat, she sipped her tea and then she waited for him to speak, enjoying his awkwardness when returning to the contentious subject.

'Is it?' he said. 'For sale? Longbridge?'

She stirred thoughtfully at the long-dissolved sugar in her cup and then placed it down carefully onto the table. 'Yes, Xander, it is.' Her spikiness had gone: her tone was still grave but softened now by a slight tilt of her head which Xander knew to look for.

'But why?' Xander's response surprised neither of them.

'Because I can't afford to run the place.'

He looked at her—it was the kind of statement that stood alone and one really couldn't question it further without sounding impolite, nosey, or, worse, uncouth. 'Is there no alternative?' he asked tactfully.

She shook her head. 'It's ridiculous, me rattling around the place simply because my forebears lived here.'

'What about a grant or something? National Trust, English Heritage, the Lottery—I don't know? Longbridge is listed—doesn't that help?'

'On the contrary,' Lydia said.

'How about fund-raising? You could open the house, charge an entrance fee, perhaps. Open the kitchen garden, sell produce.'

'I can't think of anything I'd like to do less,' Lydia said with utter disdain.

'Weddings?' Xander ventured. 'You can apply for a licence these days. Hold them out in the folly—or just erect a marquee.' This suggestion warranted only a look from Lydia, but Xander knew that look well enough. 'You could put our rent up? I'm sure we'd all rather pay more than find we had nowhere to live.'

Privately, Lydia was touched by Xander's response; his passion for the place, his yearning to find a solution, to save it. She drifted away for a moment, remembering too how she'd reacted when she was told little Edward's condition was terminal. The hopeful yet futile straw-clutching, the questions and ideas she bombarded the physicians

131

with, the energy and hope that underscored each flailing suggestion; but all the while receiving only the same calm, benevolent response which was essentially negative—much as she was now giving to Xander. But this was just a rotten old house, not a child. It didn't compare. An inanimate block of brickwork and a lead roof that would take a king's fortune to repair.

'It's the end of an era, I know,' she said and he saw that she didn't dare look around her, instead locking eyes fixedly with him. 'But it's not happy— this silly old house. It needs an obscene amount spending on it just to keep it going, never mind restoring it to its former glory.'

'Could you not sell off all the other bits—the farmland, the barns, the other houses?'

'And stay here? Good God, can you imagine how distasteful, how depressing, that would be? Longbridge would be *surrounded*—besieged. A fine old house tottering atop a shrinking island. The house needs its land, in the same way that the land and cottages need the house—it gives order, hierarchy, balance. Control is in the right place, proportions *and* harmony are maintained.'

She spoke eloquently with no concession to theatre and Xander had to nod. 'I know,' he said. 'I know.' He had half a shortbread left. He couldn't touch it. He'd had half a shortbread left the day Verity told him she was being sent away and he'd scoffed at her words and scoffed at the biscuit and it had lodged in his throat, curdling with the stuck tears until he threw it up later that night back at home. He shrugged. 'It's such a shame,' he said to Lydia. 'It's a worry,' he said. 'Say it falls into the wrong hands?'

132

'Not many pairs of the wrong hands have the wherewithal to purchase a place like Longbridge,' Lydia said. 'By virtue of its size, its location, it can only attract a certain type.'

Xander felt cynical but too deflated to debate. Was Lydia so naive as to think that money was still the domain of the landed gentry, of historical families with the abundant funds and the taste, the discernment and knowledge—the breeding— to invest in an estate like Longbridge? Didn't she often complain that she was one of a dying breed? But he knew now was not the time to warn Lydia of Russian oligarchs, footballers' wives or chavvy young pop stars. He knew, too, that there might never be a time appropriate to discuss it— because what business actually was it of his? None whatsoever. He loved the place because he'd grown up here, all his rites of passage had happened here, love and heartache, prosperity and poverty, safety and danger.

'OK,' he said at length. 'I do understand, Lydia.'

She drained her tea, placed cup and saucer neatly down and looked at him straight. 'Then you will understand that I need to have the whole estate valued—which includes Lime Grove Cottages.'

'The woman with the high heels and clipboard,' he said darkly, as if she was the Grim Reaper in disguise. 'Were you there today? Earlier? Outside my place?'

'Yes,' said Lydia.

'Why didn't you come in? You didn't even knock.'

'Because you were in,' she said. 'Because we had no prior arrangement.' She looked at him. 'It's terribly impolite to simply turn up, unannounced, uninvited, with no prior warning whatsoever.' Her words sounded sharp but they were edged with a glint to her eye and a wryly raised eyebrow. And when she told him to bugger off home—there's a good boy, her tone had softened and her smile was fond. Xander didn't want to wipe it from her face by asking whether or not Verity knew anything about any of this.

\*　　　\*　　　\*

Caroline had collected Millie from school and was trying to distract both children from the lure of the corner shop when she saw Xander walking on the other side of the high street in a world of his own. What was he doing back from work so early? And when did he ever go in to work dressed like that? She called and waved but he didn't hear. It was one of the busiest times on the high street, the thirty minutes after school; the slinking cortège of four-wheel-drives with darkened windows and personalized registration plates, the gaggles of mothers chatting amidst a fidget of children wanting wanting wanting. One of the mums was trying to chat to her about fund-raising, and Sonny was tugging at her, and Millie started wandering off, and God knows where the dog had gone—and although Caroline prided herself on her ability to multitask, watching Xander had to be forfeited.

Finally walking home, Caroline stopped in her tracks and stood still. Her children and her dog looked up, surprised. They'd never had cause to wonder if she knew what she was doing. But now, she was standing still, appearing to be unaware of the chill, of the three sets of eyes staring at her in growing puzzlement. She didn't say anything when she executed an about-turn and retraced their steps at quite a pace and it wasn't until they'd gone way past the school gates that she turned to them and said, we're going to see Uncle Xander. The children hooted a chorus of Xander! Xander! (because it was only Caroline who prefixed his name) and the dog barked because he thought he ought to.

She phoned him while she marched.

'Get that kettle on, pet—you have visitors.'

Oh God, thought Xander. You can't come—I've tidied the house.

This had nothing to do with any mess the children might generate. Quite the opposite: if Caroline saw the house in such extreme order, she'd know in an instant why. He only cleaned like a dervish when something was afoot. And Caroline, of all the people in his life, would be able to elicit anything and everything he was intending to keep private. He did, for a moment, consider pretending he wasn't home. But she'd phoned his landline, not his mobile. She was on a mission, she was coming over—and that was before she'd even set eyes on the spruce interior.

Even if he went out, if he knew Caroline she'd just go to the shed at the back for the spare key and let herself in anyway. Switch on the television and pop the children in front of it; root around for a Tupperware container and give the dog a drink. Make herself a cup of tea and wait for him. With an air of resignation, he set the kettle to boil and filled a plastic bowl with water which he put by the back door.

\*       \*       \*

135

'Surprise!'

'Xander!'

'Xander!'

The dog barked.

Xander looked at the posse on his doorstep, the children ruddy cheeked, Caroline beaming, the dog scrabbling halfway up Xander's leg.

'Well, hullo,' he said and he swept his arm low to invite them in. In an instant, the children tumbled around on his sofas, the dog was lapping at the water and Caroline was looking around, wryly flabbergasted.

'You're either preparing for guests, or else you're clearing up after them.'

'Yeah,' said Xander, ruffling his hair, which contradicted his lightweight laugh. 'Something like that.'

'Or,' she said, noting that she hadn't heard Xander say 'yeah' since student days. 'Or there's something going on that has nothing to do with Cillit Bang being on special offer at all.'

'Tea?'

'Go on then!' she said, with a little nudge in his ribs as if he was twisting her arm to stay.

'Pretty please may we watch the smellovision?' Millie asked, employing Xander's terminology and her mother's canny wink.

Little Sonny simply chanted, *smelly! smelly! smelly!*

Usually, Caroline would say no, that they had to chat to their Uncle Xander first. But today she walked boldly over to the set and turned it on to CBeebies. Xander knew this wasn't for her children's benefit as much as to afford her the peace and quiet to grill him to within an inch of his life. He tried to

136

deflect it by waffling on about Andrew and work and running and the next half-marathon but Caroline simply stood with her back to the wall, arms crossed and an expression that said, I'm humouring you, sunshine, and as soon as you shut up I'll be wading on in.

He handed her a mug of tea and, gave her a shrug. 'Go on then,' he said, with a measured sigh.

'Why didn't Mrs Mop go into work today?' she asked him. 'And Mrs Mop'll be you, before you get all Smart Alec on me.'

Xander thought about it.

He'd started off the day perplexed by his situation with Siobhan and that was the reason for playing hookey—yet he had given her little thought since seeing Lydia. It was the news of Longbridge which loomed largest, and darkest, for him.

'It's been a weird day,' he said.

'Go on, you dark horse you—who *is* she?'

'She's no one,' Xander said.

'That's not very nice,' said Caroline.

'She'd say the same about me,' Xander said. Caroline looked confused.

'So you weren't on a hot date yesterday?'

'Not in so many words,' said Xander. He looked at Caroline and shrugged. 'She's a hook-up,' he said, 'as I am to her. That's all.' He rinsed out his mug, filled it with cold water and drank it down. 'So it's a "no" to dinner at yours, but it was kind of you to ask.'

'Oh my God—you didn't meet on one of those sad-fucker Internet sites, did you? Shag Buddies Dot Com or some such? Oh, Xander—no!'

'No, of course I didn't,' he said. 'We met in a bar—it's been like a one-night stand on repeat.'

137

Caroline looked at him askance. 'Oh?'

'It's easy,' he said, now a little irritated. 'I like it that way. It suits me.'

The concept didn't seem to suit at all the Xander that Caroline knew so well. 'Isn't it all a bit—shallow?' she said. 'And a bit—seedy?'

Xander shrugged. 'It's preferable to having a relationship. It suits me just fine.'

Caroline wrinkled her nose in distaste. 'That's just some stupid motto you've decided to engrave onto your virtual shield of self-protection.'

'A *virtual shield of self-protection*, eh? Bollocks.'

'No, it's not. What's wrong with her, that she can't move on from one-night-standom?'

'Nothing's *wrong* with her,' Xander snapped. 'On the contrary, that's precisely what's right with her—it's balanced, what I give and get.'

'You're sounding like a tosser, mate.'

'You're sounding common.'

'Fuck off.' Caroline glanced through to the sitting area but her children hadn't heard her. 'So she's called Siobhan and—?'

'Jesus, Cazza—there is no *and*.' And then Xander thought, but there is an end. And that was this morning. 'Bloody wish you hadn't muscled in last night. And I wish you—Mum—Lydia—all had something better to do than fixate on who I'm seeing and when I'm going to settle down.'

'So it's my fault, is it?' Caroline said it softly—she could see he was struggling a little.

Xander thought about it. 'Of course not.' He paused. 'Look, I'm sorry. And you know what? You're probably right—perhaps I was kidding myself I could have this on-the-side thing and keep it all separate. Because, actually, it was disturbing when

138

the two sides of my life crossed last night. Neither fitted with the other. It just all felt—wrong.'

'How long have you been—seeing her?' Caroline paused. 'Or, rather, giving her a seeing-to?'

Xander laughed. He loved Caroline most when she was gutter-mouthed and irreverent because she put such heart and well-meaning into it.

'Couple of months,' he shrugged. 'Longer.' He was embarrassed. 'Six, I suppose.'

'Calling it quits?'

'If I have the self-control,' he said. 'It's not easy when a bloke receives a text saying fancy-a-fuck.'

'You need to pre-empt her sending you any kind of text,' Caroline said. 'For her sake as much as yours—because I'm telling you this, however much a woman may profess to want nothing more than a no-strings shag, you can bet before long she'll want the lot.'

Xander laughed, but he sensed she was right. He nodded. He thought back to Siobhan—it was so manufactured last night. Down to her extremely sonorous and long-lasting orgasm.

'Is that why you skived off work?'

'Yep,' he said. 'I just felt—crap.'

Caroline looked into her half-drained mug while considering how badly he must have felt to have skipped work. Unheard of, for Xander. She felt a wave of sad fondness. Why hadn't he told her of Siobhan? Why did he want that—rather than what the rest of them had? Why wasn't he shacked up happily, like her and Andrew and the others? Such a bloody waste of a good bloke. Bloody Laura. No, not bloody Laura—Laura was lovely. It wasn't her fault. No one was to blame.

'You OK now?' she ventured.

He shrugged. 'To be honest, Siobhan is the reason for my house being spotless—but Jesus, did the day get worse.'

'How so?'

'Lydia,' he said. 'You were right—the rumours are true. Longbridge is for sale.'

'You are not serious?'

'I am. And so is Lydia—I went round to see her this afternoon. I wasn't back long when you announced you were coming over.'

'How did you find out?'

'I went for a run this morning—did the top loop and saw one of those ridiculous estate-agent cars parked in the driveway of Longbridge. I ran down and some woman is mincing around the garden with a clipboard and a suit, sinking into the grass in high heels.'

'Were you very rude?'

'Probably,' Xander said, with a rueful smile.

'What'll happen?' said Caroline. She'd given it little thought when she'd heard it from Mrs Patek and Nora. But to hear it from Xander made it very real. 'What'll happen with everything—the house, everywhere?' She thought about it. 'Christ, it's going to turn the village upside down.'

Xander nodded, his face grave. God, he was tired.

'Will she be selling the lot? Or just the house? *Here*? But this is *yours*!'

'She needs the whole lot valued.'

'Hence the clipboard lady.'

Xander nodded. 'She's coming over here on Saturday morning, apparently.'

'Ship in a load of cockroaches! Shame you've

cleaned—make it mucky! The kids'll help. Make it stink!' He wasn't responding. Caroline tipped her head. 'You needn't be in,' she said. 'If you'd rather not be here, I'll stop in for you, if you like.' She paused. 'Perhaps Lydia will sell the cottage to you?' She paused again. 'Or maybe the agent might know of somewhere local up for grabs?' But then she thought, I may as well scatter all these straws I'm clutching at, all over the floor, to give Xander something else to clean up later when he needs the distraction.

'It's slightly pathetic for me to feel so burdened by it all, because it all seems so—futile,' Xander said. 'I mean, Lydia didn't seem that perturbed by any of it. Longbridge costs a fortune to keep going—she's broke—it's time to sell.'

'*Broke*?' Caroline baulked.

'Apparently so,' said Xander. 'So it has to go—all of it.'

'End of,' Caroline murmured.

'End of an era,' Xander said.

'The hoity-toity don't have feelings,' Caroline said.

Xander thought about it. 'I know why you're saying that—but perhaps you're wrong there. Perhaps they do and perhaps they've evolved this really clever and sensible method for both not letting it show and not letting it affect themselves.'

'Andrew's taking the children to Audley End on Saturday morning—I can come in, if you like. When the estate agent comes? If you decide you'd rather not be here?'

'I might well take you up on that,' Xander said.

*       *       *

Later that evening, sitting in his pristine front room, he stared at the screen on his phone. He'd composed a text message.

Hey. Hope you're well and your day was good. Am feeling we should perhaps just let it lie and call it quits. It's been fun—but it's time. X

He had yet to send it. He reread it. She wouldn't think that was a kiss, would she? X for Xander.

Was it cowardly? Should he phone instead? Would it be better to be doing this face to face? Yet would that not give the whole thing the gravitas that he and Siobhan had prided themselves on eschewing?

Sod it.

He sent the text.

He felt like a right bastard. Not because he imagined Siobhan would be particularly distraught or lovelorn, but because he'd been in a situation for which an ending like this was appropriate. It wasn't who he was at all, really.

Deep down, sitting there alone on a Wednesday night, he knew the whole thing had been unseemly. It had been so disconnected—from emotions, from day-to-day life, from the people who meant so much to him, from his past and the relationships he'd had. Good, long, solid ones with love and sex and sharing and laughter and the company of friends and family. Suddenly, he felt a little sickened by this alter ego he'd recently thought so cool and controlled. Stupid. I'm practically forty. I don't own my home and I'm about to be evicted. My history is about to be erased.

So design yourself a future, Xander. You design

and print packages for others, according to their specifications. And you do it very well. High time you made yourself one.

## Chapter Thirteen

'I can't see it taking me more than a couple of hours,' Stella said to Jo. 'I've already seen the other two cottages in the row—it'll be pretty straightforward. Will? Will?'

'Don't worry about Will,' Jo said, glancing up the stairs of her home where the children had disappeared moments ago and all was now ominously quiet.

'Please ask the girls not to put make-up on Will,' Stella groaned. 'Last time he came out in hives. And he has football this afternoon.'

'Facepaint?' Jo said.

'I'd rather they didn't,' said Stella. 'It's his first match for the B team.'

'Bless him,' said Jo. 'Now go, would you—see you in a while.'

Stella blew her a kiss. 'You're a star and I love you.' She walked briskly to her car, remembering the patronizing satisfaction with which Gill had announced that all the company cars were taken for Saturday. You need to be *in* the office to be *in* the know, she'd said. Whatever that meant.

What did it matter! Stella liked her little car. The last two days in the office had been awful; Geoff had been off sick and she found herself alternately batting away the sarcastic asides as to her performance and whereabouts, and fending off the heavy chill of being ignored. Even her uncle seemed a little irritated that, as yet, nothing was certain one way or the other with Longbridge Hall. He started muttering about whether he should phone the old dowager himself. Almost there, Stella had tried to assuage. Almost there. In truth, she still didn't feel she had a handle on it all. It was so big, so—involved. She needed not just one floor plan, but a number of them; not just a map but an atlas. A forest of family trees, a who's who and who's where on the estate. She'd gladly ask for her uncle's advice—but not before she knew whether or not Lydia wanted Elmfield Estates to handle the sale of Longbridge Hall.

Mr Fletcher's gate was creaky, his front garden as plain as the one next door was colourful and Miss Gilbey's, at number one, was overgrown. Just lawn at Mr Fletcher's Stella noticed; a little mossy in places, either side of a paved pathway. She rang the doorbell, checked her watch and mobile phone and thought, if I'm lucky I can grab a sandwich with Jo before we head off to football.

'Click click clickety click,' Xander muttered under his breath. 'Miss Clippity Clipboard and her clickety high heels is here.'

He slung the tea towel over his shoulder, picked up his mug of tea and went to answer the door.

'Oh,' said Stella, confused that the demon jogger should open the door.

Xander didn't answer, he just executed one of his expansive sweeping gestures with his free hand to welcome her in, as if genuflecting with his tongue firmly in his cheek.

'Is Mr Fletcher home?' Stella said. 'Lady Barbary-Fortescue told me I was to ask for him.'

144

'I am he,' said Xander, doing another sweep of his arm because Stella was still standing on the doorstep, determined to hold out for a Mr Fletcher.

'No,' she said, rather formally, 'I don't think so.' She looked through sheaves of paper on her clipboard. 'No.' She looked up. 'You're the Jogging Man.'

Xander was momentarily silenced. There was something unnerving about her conviction, her eyes unblinking. Brown. A strange brown—pale fawn flecked with auburn, striated with amber. 'Pardon?'

'The two times I've seen you, you've been out jogging—and both times you've practically tripped me up.' That should wipe that cocky smile off your face.

'I *run*, I don't "jog",' Xander said, as if he was a Michelin-starred chef being asked for a Big Mac. They stared at each other a moment longer, unsure who was quarry, who was prey. 'I am Xander Fletcher—and if you want to call me Mr Fletcher, that's fine, Mrs? Miss?'

'Hutton,' said Stella briskly. '*Ms* Hutton.' She wasn't going to pander to this pompous prick and argue the toss between jogging and running.

'Come in, *Ms* Hutton,' he said wearily, walking ahead of her. 'And it's "Lady Lydia Fortescue",' he said over his shoulder. 'Or she'll have your guts for garters.'

\*     \*     \*

To Xander, Stella today looked younger than he had first thought; less confident, less officious—and he felt a fool for having been remotely threatened in the first place. Look at her, hugging her clipboard as though it contains trade secrets or revision notes for an exam she's eagerly prepared for.

'Please, Ms Hutton,' he said, annoyed with himself. 'Let me show you around.'

You're not getting my first name out of me, thank you very much. 'I'm just here to have a quick look—I won't keep you long,' said Stella, thinking to herself, I can't believe *he's* Mr Fletcher. She thought, I bet his cupboards are full of stinky jogging trainers.

Running shoes.

She thought, I could murder a cup of tea.

'Tea?' he offered, taking a sip of his.

'No, thank you,' said Stella, primly. 'I'd like to get cracking.'

'It's no bother,' he said and she noticed his face was open, his head tilted, his offer simple and friendly. He was running his hand across his hair, smiling with grey-blue eyes.

'Well, OK then. Tea. Thank you.' She watched him walk off to the kitchen, open plan with the sitting room. She wondered whether he'd been out running today too. She wondered what exactly was the difference between jogging and running? Just speed? Or distance covered? Or some physiological distinction between types of footfall? Was he having to stay in because of her visit? He'd seemed pissed off initially, now no longer. He looked comfortable in his home, whistling softly as he made her tea. Black jeans and a long sleeved T-shirt. It was grey and had a darker grey print of a native American Indian. She wondered, what made him choose that? He looked, today, like someone she might know, like someone who might well be part of her milieu.

But she decided swiftly to un-notice all of that. And then she thought, it's silly to wonder about any of this—I have work to do and football to get to.

She loosened her hug on the clipboard and made notes on the room. It wasn't dissimilar in layout from next door's, identical in size and yet with a very different feel. Number One had appeared tiny on account of Peg Gilbey's dark furniture, swirly carpets and whatnots crammed with, well, whatnots. Number Two had seemed airier and yet cooler too with all those Farrow & Ball neutrals. Here at number three there was exposed brickwork and beams; flagstones partly covered by a rug in autumnal shades and an Aztec design, a coffee table hectic with books and newspapers and a scatter of mail. The sofa, indented from where the last person sat. An armchair with a sweatshirt draped over the back and an Iain Banks open halfway through, face down. Number Three was homely.

Stella glanced down at the page of notes. Facts. Jargon. They seemed to quash the spirit of this man's home. What was it that she suddenly felt? Not guilt—how could it be? He wasn't being forced to sell. He didn't even own it. Regret? It was disconcerting. She told herself to snap out of it—she would much rather be annoyed with him. Because he was an arrogant cock, wasn't he. But she did feel concern. And just a little intrigued. Why was he so irked about the potential sale? What exactly was Lydia to him? He said he'd been at Longbridge all his life—how so? Was it just a purely sentimental attachment? But did he really matter? Did the George family next door matter? Miss Gilbey did. And so did Art. And his neighbour, Mr Tringle. And someone else called Clarence, who lived in a little stone building in a field a way off from the stable yard. They were elderly. Longbridge was all they'd known and to an extent, it defined them. What would they be without it? She thought about Clarence—she had yet to visit him. She'd have to fudge it until they were at the stage of setting out the prospectus. These folk were dependent. Where would they go? This Xander Fletcher—he'd be OK.

Commission. Commission. Commission.

I had to leave my home. Sell it fast and for a fraction of what it might have realized in a year or two.

Damn the recession!

Damn bloody Charlie.

'Tea.'

Stella blinked. Xander, handsome in grey, looking at her quizzically, offering her tea in a mug that was telling her to *Keep Calm or Fuck Off*. She looked at it, then at him and smiled, lifted the mug as if it was a wineglass, raising it so that the message was relayed back to him.

'Thank you.' She took a sip. He didn't appear to notice which mug he'd given her. Or maybe he did. It figured. 'Lived here long?' How corny did that sound.

'I grew up on the estate—with my family.'

Stella nodded. 'I meant here—in this cottage?'

'Eight years.'

She blew rhythmically at the tea, watching intently the ripples on the surface. Eight years a home doth make. She felt at once awkward. She hadn't felt this when she visited the Georges next door.

148

'Yep,' he said, 'eight years. I could have bought one of the new houses but I wanted to be part of Longbridge again. And Lydia is very fair with the rent.'

'Peppercorn rent,' said Stella.

Xander nodded.

'I've always loved that expression—and the concept,' said Stella. That's enough talking.

The tea scorched the back of her throat. She put the mug down, on last week's *Sunday Times* which was uppermost on the pile on the coffee table. She took a broad tape measure from her bag and started to work. Bloody thing! Curling back on itself with a twang, flinging itself back into the casing as if struck by acute shyness. How amateur she must look.

'Do you want me to hold it?'

'Oh,' said Stella. 'I mean, I know the room's about seventeen by fifteen—not just because the others are. Because actually, I can estimate pretty well. But that's in feet, and I know that converts to about five by four but I have to account for every centimetre so yes—thanks.'

'Here.' Xander held the case while Stella pulled the metal ribbon to the other side of the room. 'Seventeen exactly.'

'Bang on!' she said with a triumphant thumbs-up that was artless and funny and made him laugh.

He thought, who on earth finds seventeen feet so thrilling? He thought, I don't think she's really a proper estate agent. 'Five metres eighteen centimetres,' he said deadpan.

'Just doesn't have the same ring to it, does it!'

Xander raised an eyebrow and turned away. 'Come on,' he said and he showed her elsewhere

149

downstairs. The kitchen, the cold little loo crammed with the washing machine currently in spin cycle while photographs of Xander finishing races rattled against uneven walls, as if he was running right out of the frames. The back door out to the garden.

'Veggie patch,' he said. 'I like my veggies.' And he thought, what a bloody stupid thing to say.

'Do you live here alone?' Stella asked. She didn't have to. She wasn't sure why she did.

'Yes,' said Xander, whose thoughts strayed momentarily to Siobhan and the text he'd had in response to his.

Ok. Good luck. And thanks! SEx

Upstairs, a box room with a rowing machine that could only fit on the diagonal and a windowsill heaving with trophies. Next door, a tiny bedroom with a futon sofa bed—she hadn't seen one of those in a long while. A sympathetically modernized bathroom and then, finally, the master bedroom. Stella thought, if he had owned this cottage and wanted to sell it, she'd say to him, you need to do something in here, Mr Fletcher, you need a woman's touch. Even a couple of scatter cushions would help. A throw at the end of the bed. Different linen, perhaps—not that cold white. And ironed too. His bedroom was the least attractive room in the whole house. No personality, a basic coldness. Just a bed, a closet, a mirror, a chest of drawers, a folding chair folded against the wall. And more framed photos of Xander running his socks off. Narcissistic prat! No curtains. The warmth and homeliness downstairs was utterly absent here—as if there was a downstairs bloke and an upstairs one.

150

'You have no curtains,' Stella remarked.

He looked at the window as if he'd only just noticed himself. He saw his bedroom through Stella's eyes. 'Well, I'm not getting curtains just so Lydia can get an extra bob or two for Longbridge,' he said and he walked out, so close to Stella that she had to step back to avoid being pushed into and, in the process, caught her back on the edge of the drawers. It hurt.

'I didn't imply that you had to!' Stella retorted, stomping after him. Her back was smarting and she was thoroughly irked. Xander was standing on the landing, arms crossed, with a glower on his face.

'I was just noticing, that's all!' Stella descended the stairs in front of him with a perceptible flounce. The cottage was small enough for her tea to be still hot. She gulped it, irritated by his shortness, cross with herself for feeling affronted. Cross with herself for feeling just a little compelled by all those bloody photos of him, pounding twenty-six miles out of pavements in various locations. 'Right,' she said brightly, a little spikily. 'That'll do.'

He was between her and the front door. 'Right,' he said.

'Thank you for your time, Mr Fletcher,' she said, not looking at him. 'I'll be in touch, as and when.' He noticed how she checked her bag and heard her say under her breath, *phone, tape measure, keys*.

With his hand on the latch, he stopped and turned to her. 'You know,' he said quietly, 'she's an old battleaxe but she's vulnerable too.'

'Who is?'

'Lydia,' he said.

'I don't feel that's any of my business.'

'But Lydia and the old house aside—please just

151

consider how there are so many people woven in with Longbridge,' Xander said. 'It's not about money—there's a morality bound up in the mortar.' He paused, searched her face to see if she was listening properly. 'People's lives,' he said, only now opening the front door. 'The integrity of the place. The vision Gregory Lynforth, the architect, had. The utopian plans of Frederick Makepeace William Fortescue.' Xander didn't know where he was going with all this and he knew he sounded melodramatic. 'The sale will affect so many. Past and present. There are fewer and fewer of these estates left. You lose them, you lose a way of life. You destroy balance. In this village in particular.'

'It's not my fault,' Stella said. He had to admit to himself, he had made it sound as though she was culpable.

'I'm not saying it is,' he nodded. 'You're just doing your job, and your job, ultimately, isn't about people—it's about percentages and commissions.'

Do. Not. Redden.

But it was true.

How mortifying that, deep down, she knew she'd become so mercenary. Even so, she felt he didn't have to make her sound so heartless and materialistic.

'I'm saying Lydia is old and perhaps there is a solution, an alternative, to her selling.'

Stella thought about this. 'It's not for me to advise,' she said. 'It's beyond my remit. She asked for a valuation, and that is what I'll give her. If she wants me to represent the sale, then I will gladly do so. But ultimately, I can't see what business it is of yours.'

Xander said nothing, knowing he'd said enough,

152

perhaps too much.

'You're right,' he said, stepping aside to let her pass. 'It's none of my business. It's just a shame that the human side of Longbridge—of Long Dansbury—appears to be none of your business either. Goodbye.'

*    *    *

His words ricocheted around Stella's head as she walked to her car, his garden path feeling to her like the plank on a pirate ship. She felt like saying, hey! estate agents have feelings too! But that sounded as though it belonged on a mug or a bumper sticker. Anyway, what was the point? She heard the door shut firmly. Why did she care what he believed? Why did he care so much about something Lydia seemed so level-headed about? After all, it was her place not his; her decision. And people would find new homes, other jobs.

'Get over yourself!' Stella said, as if Xander Fletcher was still in earshot. She drove off angrily, feeling affronted. And something else. What was it she felt? Why were her cheeks burning up? What was it?

A little bit ashamed.

It was true—the percentage. All those juicy zeros. They were what mattered most to Stella. Fine old house and grounds, sweet little old lady in the cottage, doddery old characters in the stables, some old boy called Clarence who appeared to live in a remote sty whom she had yet to meet, a talkative bronze statue in the garden, cartoon-perfect housekeeper, the mad old bat who owned it all. And this man—this jogging running stroppy man who's

153

against it, handsome and fit and morally upright but with a cold cold bedroom that appeared to have a story behind it. None of his business. Business is business. Sell it. Just sell it. *It's a dog eat dog world*, Geoff had said to her when one of her clients had been gazumped last week. She thought, he's right—it is. And then she thought, even so—I don't like sodding Mr Fletcher defining me as one of them. And she thought, why can't I get those bloody photos of him and his legs and the triumph and pain and achievement on his face out of my mind?

## *Chapter Fourteen*

Mrs Gregg took the call. Xander noticed she was doing a lot of listening and not much talking. 'Please hold—I shall put you through,' she said, eventually. As his desk phone rang, Xander looked over to her. 'It's a Mrs Hutchins?'

'Mrs Hutchins? I don't know a Mrs Hutchins,' but he answered the phone anyway. 'Xander Fletcher—good afternoon?'

'Oh, Xander—I wasn't sure really what to do so I decided to phone you. I'm in a bit of a tizz really—I'm just confused.'

Who was this?

'And where do I fit in?' he asked, diplomatically.

'Well, it was Len's idea, really. He said, Doreen—rather than take the rumours as gospel, why don't you speak to Xander instead of getting your knickers in a twist with all the not-knowing. He speaks like that—you know he does.'

It's *Doreen*—Doreen from the village.

154

'What is it, Doreen—are you OK?'

'It's what's being said—about Longbridge Hall. We're on a peppercorn rent here—Lydia's been very generous. But I worked all those years in her kitchen, when Len was with the Longbridge cows. We only have our pensions. What will we do if it's sold? We've been saving to go on a cruise—trip of a lifetime. Do you know anything? Will you speak to Lydia? I saw Mrs Biggins in the shop—but she pulled a zip over her lips. It's just these rumours, Xander, circling around and around—but all of us feel out of the loop.'

'I don't know what I can do,' said Xander gently, 'but let me have a think about it and I'll be in touch.'

'Please.'

'I will.'

'Thank you, Xander. Thank you.'

He hung up and shrugged at Mrs Gregg. 'Trouble at mill,' he said in a faux Yorkshire accent but she could see by his expression that he was worried. He checked his text messages and reread one sent last night from Jim—an old friend from the village. Xander took his mobile and went outside.

'Jim! It's Xander. Thanks for your text, shall we go for a pint tonight? I'm starting to get calls from the village—about Longbridge and is it, isn't it. To be honest, I probably don't know much more than they do. I think I'll phone a couple of the others— you know, with Longbridge connections. See what people feel, shoot some ideas, see if we can come up with something. Can you ask the guys in the small barn workshop—you know, the computer twins? Yeah—but I never know which is Dave and which is Dan. Thanks—I appreciate it. See you later. Black Ox at eight-ish. Bye.'

God, if ever there was a time to start smoking again, now was it. But he and Caroline had both given up over seven years ago and he prided himself on his supreme willpower and enjoyed lording it up over her chronic Nicorette habit. He took a moment to stand in the sunshine and breathe. Shake off the headache of that month's unpaid invoices whose payment he really needed. Tomorrow, he'd put Mrs Gregg onto chasing them up by phone. She had a wonderful way on the phone—officious yet non-threatening but very, very persuasive.

School was out and droves of bouncing children chattered excitedly while their mothers half listened. He watched them standing at the pedestrian lights, patiently, obediently though there wasn't much traffic. Bugger waiting for the green light, he thought—I want to go home now.

'But I want to go straight home—*Clone Wars* is almost on—almost! But Mummy—*please*.'

'We have to nip in to M and S. No buts. Come on. Percy Pigs?'

I know that voice.

Xander turned to locate it.

It's that estate agent woman. Jesus. Couldn't he get away from her? She hadn't seen him. There she is—waiting for the pedestrian green man. Stella. Known as Ms Hutton. Known too, it now transpired, as Mummy. It surprised Xander. He wasn't sure why. And it surprised him to see that she'd teamed her workaday estate agent garb with trainers. Shoddy ones at that.

'Mummy—*please*.'

156

'Poppet—no. You've probably seen the episode a million times anyway.'

'A zillion times wouldn't be too much,' the boy remonstrated.

'How about we *play* Clone Wars when we're home?'

'You and me? With Lego?'

'And Percy Pigs.'

And Xander thought, who are the Percy Pigs? Distantly related to the Ewoks, perhaps? Surely there couldn't be George Lucas characters he'd somehow missed? And he thought, so that's what an estate agent does behind closed doors.

\*　　　\*　　　\*

The Black Ox was always busy, every night of the week, and that Monday was no exception. In fact, Xander needn't have suggested rounding up the troops; most would probably have meandered in at some point, as if rewarding themselves for surviving the first day of the new working week. Eventually, pints in hand, they gravitated away from the bar to the large scrubbed wooden table which, on a Saturday night, could sit two parties of six without either feeling encroached upon. Word must have spread, Xander thought, because it wasn't just Jim and the interchangeable Dan and Dave, but Len Hutchins had come along. And Mr Patek. Then there was Xander's neighbour Tom George, and Bob Redline who'd moved away from the village but was a school governor. Xander looked around. No Art or Mr Tringle. No Clarence. They did know, didn't they—about Lydia's intentions? Had they known about tonight? Did they feel guilty—as if to

157

show up somehow made them disloyal to her? Or did they just want to think it was all hearsay? Who brings a tale takes two away, Xander recalled some old adage or other. Would Lydia get wind of this? Would she think it a cabal? Would she be furious with him?

Dan or Dave said Lydia hadn't mentioned anything to them directly—apart from informing them that some agent would be visiting 'for valuation purposes'.

'To be honest,' said one of them, 'if we're given notice to leave, then so be it. But when? And how long will we have?'

'We love it—we're attached to the place, we started up here,' said the other. 'But—there's other places to go. As long as we're given enough notice. She's not very approachable.'

'It's different for us.' It was Len Hutchins. 'You're young, Longbridge is just where your business is, you've homes to go to. But my wife and I—we've rented off Lydia for over forty years. It's our home—but it's her house. And it won't matter the years we did in service at Longbridge. She hasn't come to see us yet. Doreen's not in a good way about it.'

'What about that parking space opposite the shop?' Mr Patek's favourite subject. 'She'll never sell it to me, but if she sells the whole place, what'll come of it then? My customers depend on it. It's a silent agreement, if you like, between the Lady of Longbridge and the villagers. Someone new comes along? Who knows!'

People murmured and nodded and said 'Who knows?' over and again.

Xander thought, with some relief, that no one

158

had turned to him directly. They were here, all of them, for a sense of comradeship—an arena in which to voice fears that were shared, to pool what scant information had snagged on the grapevine like fluff on a thorn.

The landlord came over with pints all round. 'For what it's worth, what *will* it be worth—that huge house and all that land and properties?'

People were excited to toss figures around.

'For what it's worth,' he repeated, 'I think it could be a good thing—for the village. At the moment, there's no cash coming in from there. There's only a handful of folk living up on the estate itself—it's not as if my business is boosted by any of them. Mr Patek, how often does Her Ladyship come into your shop?'

'Twice a week,' Mr Patek said amiably, 'in person. But she has her daily order.'

'And how much does she spend, then, a week?'

'Well, that's seven *Telegraph*s—and seven bars of Fry's Chocolate Cream.'

The landlord sat down. 'So, say she shifts the place to some nice new millionaire—it'll inject cash into the village directly or indirectly. Jobs, quite possibly. Employ far more locals than *she* currently does—craftsmen, tradesmen. It could be good for all of us.'

Xander couldn't speak.

The landlord sensed it and it was to Xander he turned. 'Lad, I know it means everything to you—you of all people. You grew up there. You have—' he paused—'*history* with the place.' People glanced away from Xander because most of them knew to what he alluded. 'But change isn't always a bad thing, lad. It might save the place and inject

159

something positive into the village. Then that will be a good legacy—won't it?'

Xander wanted to say, but there have always been Fortescues at Longbridge. However, he wasn't a Fortescue. And he wanted to say, the place needs saving—but couldn't acknowledge, just then, that Lydia currently wasn't doing a very good job of that. And he wanted to say, but people in the village are dependent on the estate—that was true, some were here tonight. But he could see that, fundamentally, their interests weren't altruistic but for themselves really, not the Longbridge community as a whole.

He sipped his pint. 'There are so few places like Longbridge left.' He paused, thinking to himself how he was privileged to have the run of the place. He shuddered at the thought of keep-out fencing, of being suddenly shut out. 'And there are vulnerable people currently dependent on the estate, on Lady Lydia, who aren't here tonight. Other businesses operating out of the barns.' He glanced at Dave and Dan. 'The buildings themselves. The kitchen garden—a property developer would just bulldoze the lot.'

'They mightn't.'

'English village life is an endangered thing,' Xander went on, not caring that he sounded pompous. 'We have tradition and balance here— between the house and the village. It would be a travesty not to at least try to preserve it.'

Finally, after many opinions were thrown into the mix, Bob Redline spoke up. 'It's a difficult time because little is known and nothing is certain. Not everyone will be happy with whatever outcome transpires. But it is interesting to consider that the future of Longbridge might not necessarily be in the hands of the Fortescues.' He paused and looked from Xander to the landlord. 'And that is a very, very strange concept indeed for anyone who's connected with Long Dansbury, whatever their age or involvement.'

'It's a bit of a waiting game at the moment,' the landlord remarked.

And the concept was as unsettling for Xander as it was for the rest of them.


## Chapter Fifteen

'I have a date for you.'

Stella was standing in the kitchen, clearing away the supper things, when Sara rang.

'Oh, yes? Hang on,' Stella made her way to the calendar.

'A *date*, date,' Sara clarified.

Oh. One of those. But Stella knew she'd previously agreed to it in principle with both her sisters-in-law. No point protesting. She'd just have to say yes. Get on with it, get it over with—like a check-up at the dentist.

'He's called Riley.'

That is a ridiculous name.

'Which I know sounds faintly ridiculous—but it doesn't suit him.'

'You're not selling him particularly well,' said Stella.

'He's early forties and has been living abroad— recently moved back. No dependants. He's a friend of my friend Bella's husband.'

'Right.'

'Stella?'

'Yes?' Stella was looking at the calendar wishing more of the weekend boxes were taken so she could truthfully say, so kind of you to think of me but I don't have a window until July.

'How about the fifteenth? This coming Saturday night. Will could come for a sleepover—the Stickies would love that.'

This coming Saturday, 15 May. Not a jot on the calendar. Not even something crossed out that could be reinstated at a push. A gloatingly bare square saying, fill me if you dare.

'OK,' said Stella. 'Why not. Riley O'Blimey.'

'Don't take the piss before you've met him. Apparently, he's handsome and clever—and rich.'

Just what I need, Stella grumbled as she hung up. And then she thought, if he ticks so many boxes as well as fills the empty one on my calendar, why don't I feel remotely excited? She thought, perhaps I just don't need it—Riley, anyone—rich, poor, gorgeous, other. Perhaps it's everyone else's needs that I'm to take care of—some notion they have that I ought to be paired off, as if it will then cancel out the negative of my past, render Charlie non-existent. Make everyone feel better. They all felt so helpless at the time—maybe this is their own way of making amends, of feeling proactive, useful, kind.

'Perhaps,' she said quietly, 'perhaps it's just not for me. Maybe I like life; just me and my boy.' She scraped the plates and rinsed them before filling the sink with hot water and adding the washing-up liquid last so it didn't foam too much.

'It's not like I'm pining. I'm not losing sleep hoping for Mr Lovely. I don't even miss sex. My

162

life doesn't feel the poorer for the absence of these things—and maybe the presence of them would just complicate the cosy balance I have, me and Will together.'

*    *    *

'Hold on, please, I'll just transfer you.' Belinda pointed her desk phone at Stella as though it was a lance. 'It's for you.' She bashed at the numbers and Stella's phone rang. Belinda didn't hang up but Stella, sitting at the front of the office with her back to the stabbing eyes of her colleagues, didn't know this. Geoff did, but he diverted his gaze because work was trying enough without the added conflict of taking sides.

'Stella Hutton speaking.'

'You need to see the coach house apartment. And Clarence's.'

Stella hadn't heard of either development but thought they might be in Sawbridgeworth.

'Hullo?'

'Yes,' said Stella, 'could you tell me a little more? Where they are? Sale or rent? Could I take your details please, Mrs—Mrs?'

The exasperated sigh on the other end of the line hit Stella so sharply she felt winded. It was Lydia. Of course it was! The sigh said, Good God, girl—don't you know who I am!

'Lady Lydia!' Stella said. 'I'm so sorry—I've had a cold and the line isn't great.' Flimsy—but plausible.

'Yes yes,' said Lydia dismissively. 'But you'll come soon, please.'

'Saturday?' Stella said covertly, now aware that,

163

around her, ears might be open and tongues ready to lash.

'Very well,' Lydia said. 'Nine o'clock sharp.'

'Very good,' said Stella. 'Cheerio.'

There was a pause. 'Toodle pip,' said Lydia, tentatively, as if unsure whether a jaunty sign-off was her thing.

But in Longbridge and Hertford, as each woman replaced the handset, they gave it a quizzical smile. And behind Stella, in the offices of Elmfield Estates, Belinda gave Gill and Steve a sly nod. And although Geoff was relieved not to be included, he sensed it and wished he'd remained in the dark. Or just at home, off work with stress.

\*     \*     \*

'*How* posh is posh?' Will asked.

'Posher than posh,' Stella said.

'How *big* is big?' Will asked.

'Bigger than you could even imagine,' said Stella.

'Bigger than Buckingham Palace?'

'Not quite,' said Stella. She looked at her son. 'A different style of architecture.'

'But really big and really posh?' Will said.

'Yes,' said Stella, turning through the gates of Longbridge. 'Don't touch anything, remember. Just see how well you can impersonate my shadow.'

'OK,' said Will. 'Is this the way?'

'It's the driveway,' said Stella, 'their own *private* drive.'

'All of this?'

'Every inch.'

\*     \*     \*

Mrs Biggins opened the door, greeted Stella but looked horrified once she'd noticed Will.

'Are we expecting—*both*—of you?'

'I—' Stella stopped. 'It's just that—it's the weekend?' She put her hand protectively on Will's shoulder but he wriggled away.

'Hullo,' said Will, stepping forward with his hand outstretched. Mrs Biggins shook it. 'I am William, but you may call me Will.'

And then he bowed.

Mrs Biggins was visibly delighted. 'Leave it with me,' she said to Stella quietly. And she winked at Will.

They were shown to the hallway in which Will found it impossible to keep his head straight—there was a magnetic pull to tip it back, mouth agape. Nor could he walk straight, turning a constant 360 as he was led deeper into the house.

'Miss Hutton is here,' Mrs Biggins told Lydia, who was in the drawing room, standing in front of the electric bar heater in the fireplace though, being mid-May, it wasn't cold at all.

'Very good,' said Lydia.

Mrs Biggins didn't move. 'With young Master William.'

'Who?' Lydia's brow knotted into itself.

'William,' Mrs Biggins announced. 'Her son.' She paused.

'She has brought a child? A boy? *Here*?' Lydia looked appalled. 'She has a *child*?'

Mrs Biggins thought, God in heaven forgive me for lying. 'She did phone to check—it being the weekend and all. I did mention it.'

Lydia couldn't bear to acknowledge lapses in

memory. They were so undignified. So troubling. She straightened the furrows across her forehead with a swipe of her hand. 'Of course you did. Yes, of course. Very well. Show them in.'

Mrs Biggins returned to the hallway. 'You may go in,' she said. Then she said to Stella, 'Of course, I did pass on your message to Lady Lydia—when you phoned ahead and spoke to me the other day. That you'd *both* be coming.' She stared levelly at Stella but with complicity, not malice.

*Thank you*, Stella mouthed and she straightened Will's hair, a lock of which was jumping straight upwards as if electrified.

'Shadow,' Stella whispered to him and they entered the drawing room. 'Don't forget.' She placed her hands on the handles of the double-height doors and pushed them open.

'Good morning, Lady Lydia.' Stella liked to be formal when she first saw Lydia each visit.

'Good morning, Miss Hutton.' Lydia was staring at Will, like a person scared of dogs but trying not to show it.

Will thought, I'm not to say a word. He thought, I'm to be a shadow. But then he thought, the Lady lady is staring at me. He thought, it's rude to royalty not to say hullo. It's the sort of thing that they used to chop your head off for, in the olden days.

So he kept his head down and raised his hand. Glanced up. Still being stared at.

'Good morning,' Lydia said to him, an audible rasp to her voice.

'Good morning, Your Ladyship,' said Will, stepping away from Stella to bow. 'I am William Ewan Taylor-Hutton.'

Stella thought, oh, Jesus Christ, he's gone and

166

double-barrelled his surname. Will Taylor, son of Charlie Taylor and Stella Hutton. His father's surname was the most he'd ever had from the man. Every time Stella wrote or spoke Will's surname, she felt the contradiction acutely—it was so present, so fixed, yet served only to exaggerate the distance Charlie had created. The total lack of presence, let alone any valid connection.

Lydia glanced at Stella, as if unsure as to whether the boy was taking the mickey or, worse, fibbing.

'Commonly known as Will,' Will said, apologetically, stepping back just behind his mother, not daring to catch her eye. At least he'd saved his neck. No dungeon for him.

'I see,' said Lydia. 'And how old are you?'

'I am seven and just over a half, Your Ladyship.'

She looked at him warily. 'I see.'

'Yes,' said Will, with a sage nod.

'Come here!' Lydia barked. 'Will!'

Watching Will walk over to Lady Lydia, Stella recalled how she had felt like Tess first meeting Mrs d'Urberville. Now it was like watching her son take the role of Pip, summoned by Miss Havisham. Thank God Lydia called him Will, not 'boy'. Stella watched as Lydia stared down her aquiline nose and Will looked up at her in awe tinged with terror.

'I'm normal size for my age,' he said, nervously.

'Your hair is preposterous,' Lydia said and, taking him by the upper arm, she led him to the circular table on which a display of lilies and ferns was choking in a vase too small. Keeping a hand on him, she rooted through the stems for one in which the bloom was past its best. She removed it, snapped at a joint below the flower head and squeezed the gluey sap between her fingers. This

167

she then smoothed onto the errant lock of Will's hair, patted it down, tugged it and then lay her hand there for a long moment.

'That should do it,' she muttered, leaving the broken stem on the table and shooing Will back to his mother. She tapped her nose at Stella—as if she'd imparted an invaluable secret known only to the landed gentry.

'The carriage house apartment,' she said, 'and Clarence's place.'

'Yes,' said Stella.

'It is Art's day off. And I don't do those stairs any more. So I have asked Mr Fletcher to show you what you need to see.'

'Mr Fletcher?' Stella wasn't sure whether she baulked or reddened or how visible either might have been.

'Yes?' Lydia regarded her sternly. 'You've met him. Xander.'

'Yes, I know,' said Stella, 'I know who he is. He was the one who accosted me in your garden.'

'For which, I am sure, he has since apologized.'

Stella thought about him. Had he? Hardly.

Lydia looked at her watch. 9.14. She waited. 9.15. The doorbell clanged. Moments later, Mrs Biggins was showing Xander Fletcher into the room.

'Miss Hutton,' he nodded at her. Then he clocked Will and the expression on his face, which he cast to and from the boy to Lydia, could only be described as aghast.

'Hullo,' Xander said quietly, his eyes scouring the boy's face as if checking for wounds.

'I'm William Ewan Taylor-Hutton.'

'I'm Xander Fletcher.' He smiled at the boy, relieved that he appeared unscathed and seemed

168

relatively chirpy. He went over to Lydia to receive his instructions. But he glanced back to Stella and her boy, on whom Lydia's eyes remained fixed.

Will was pulling his ear, having just scratched the back of his head, rubbed his nose into the palm of his hand and quickly given a small cough. Currently he was doing peculiar arm movements as if performing some strange mime. Just then, Lydia and Xander noted he was aping his mother who had been rummaging in her bag, scratching her head, pulling her ear, rubbing her nose and leafing through papers on her clipboard.

'What *are* you doing, child!' Lydia barked.

Stella sensed Will freeze. And then she noticed Xander freeze too.

'I was . . .' Will stammered. 'I was . . . My mum told me I had to be her shadow. So I was being her shadow.'

Lydia looked from the boy to his mother, both of them standing there trying desperately to pull a mask of nonchalance over their obvious discomfort. Lydia stared levelly at Stella, imagining all she'd said to Will, prepping him on their way here this morning. Don't touch! Don't speak unless you're spoken to! Don't fidget! Just be my shadow.

Almost eight. With his hair now lying nice and even. Fair and straight. Almost the same. A pretty face. But not the same—how could another face be anywhere near as beautiful? But wide eyed and button nosed and a bloom to the cheek—not dissimilar. Less cherubic. A little skinnier. And older, of course. By a few months.

'I'm sorry, Your Ladyship,' Will said meekly, with a small bow.

'I told him not to—'

169

Lydia swatted the air as if the two of them were intensely annoying. 'Xander, show them what needs to be seen, would you.'

'Thank you, Lady Lydia,' said Stella. 'Shall I come back in, afterwards?'

'No!' Lydia said, the thought of it apparently appalling her.

'Thank you for having me, My Lady,' said William, backing out of the room as if unable to turn away from this terrifying aristocrat in her dreamlike surroundings.

*     *     *

Mrs Biggins was at the front door. She handed something to Will. It was an envelope made ingeniously out of a cloth napkin. She patted him on the head and then, just as Stella was passing, Mrs Biggins laid her hand fleetingly on her shoulder. By the time Stella looked round at her, she'd taken it away and was talking quietly to Xander.

'What's in here!' Will whispered excitedly to his mother as soon as they were outside.

'I don't know,' said Stella, glancing at Xander.

'It's shortbread,' Xander told them while Mrs Biggins shut them out. Then he grinned at Will. 'For sharing. No,' he smiled, 'don't open it here—I'll show you where.'

Though Stella was familiar now with the house, with the look and smell of the place, the slightly dank feeling of some of the rooms, the dusty celestial light in others, outside was still a mystery. The distances between places so much greater in reality than her memory recalled. The walk from the house, across the drive, up the box-lined pathway to the garden, the route across the lawns to the lavish rhododendrons, in front of which Lord Fortescue gazed out. The expansive undulations of impeccably mown grass. The size of the pond, strewn with lilies. Lake—she would definitely put 'lake' on the particulars. The long run of wall of the kitchen garden, plotted and pieced into obedient vegetable beds behind which was a forest of fruit canes and cages.

Xander led them a circuitous route from the domestic side of the exterior, through a wooded walk, to what had once been the busy stable block and was now occupied by the two doddery old boys, Art and Mr Tringle. Will walked on beside him, gazing in awe and pointing out everything around him, waiting for direction from Xander whether to go left or right or keep going. This wasn't a back garden, this was a whole county! Stella lagged behind, absorbed, trying to formulate descriptions that would do the place justice.

'So,' said Xander to Will as they walked. 'You're Will.'

'I am,' said Will.

'Must be boring to give up your Saturday to come and see an old crumbling house.'

'No, it isn't. And it isn't a house—it's a palace.'

Xander smiled, looked about, realized how he'd grown up taking all this for granted in some ways.

'The house my mum and I live in—it could fit into a cupboard at Longbridge Hall.'

My mum and I. It certainly made Stella more human.

'Where do you live?'

'Oh—in a town called Hertford. In my uncle's house. Not with him, though.'

'Ah,' said Xander, pointing out a buzzard.

'I can't wait to eat the shortbread,' said Will.

'Me too,' said Xander. 'Not long now.'

Stella caught up with them and Will scampered ahead.

'Good week?' Xander asked as they walked, because silence seemed to clash with such a beautiful day.

'Ish,' said Stella, thinking how relieved she'd been to leave the office yesterday, dirty looks striking her between the shoulder blades resulting in a stiff neck and a headache that still lingered. 'You?'

'Fine,' said Xander. She asked politely what he did and where he did it. Then she told him about Lydia and the plant sap and Will's hair and the dowager's asperity.

'God,' said Xander, 'how could I have forgotten about the *glump*.' He ran his hand over his head, as if he might find vestiges of it there. 'That's what she calls it—glump.'

'Is she really a dragon—or is it just her manner?' Stella stopped, her question was sincere. 'It's just so difficult to tell.'

Xander looked at her. He could say the former, or the latter. Neither were untrue. 'She doesn't like boys,' he said. Stella looked down as if guilt-stricken for exposing her son. 'You should have left him at home. Couldn't your husband have looked after him?'

'I—don't have a husband.' She paused. 'I'm divorced.' It was the first time she'd qualified her new status. A direct answer to an acceptable question.

'Oh,' said Xander. He found himself wondering

172

whether his question suddenly seemed intrusive and hostile. 'Sorry.'

'That's OK.'

'I didn't mean to—'

'It's *fine*,' Stella stressed, slightly snappish. She continued, calmer. 'I didn't realize bringing Will could be a problem. I should have asked first.'

'Sorry—that was a bit sharp of me,' said Xander. 'It's just I know what Lydia can be like.'

'Did she like you when you were a boy?' Stella asked, thinking how Lydia appeared to like no one.

Xander broadened his shoulders and snorted a little through his nose. 'Not at first,' he said.

'What is it with boys?'

He shouldn't really be going into all of this. He should be taking Stella only to the stable yard and on to Clarence's. But he glanced at Will, holding the package of shortbread so carefully, like a ring bearer and his cushion. 'Edward,' Xander said quietly, turning to face Stella. 'Her son. Who died.'

Stella suddenly remembered Lydia saying she *had* a son, past tense. 'How old?'

'Just seven.'

'Oh, dear God.' She paused. 'Did you know him?'

Xander shook his head. 'Before my time.'

'How?'

'Leukaemia.'

'Just too terrible.'

'Yes.'

'But you grew up here?'

'I did.'

'Did she terrorize you?' Stella said it gently, not wanting to offend. And actually, her son appeared to be unscathed and seemed rather in awe of Her

173

Ladyship.

Xander acknowledged her tone. 'Pretty much,' he said. 'But I was very—close—with Lydia's daughter, Verity, in our childhood. And that was important to Lydia. Useful, you could say.'

'Sounds very Charles Dickens,' Stella said.

Xander thought about it. 'You know something? It was.'

'Very Pip and Estella.'

'No, not like that at all. Verity was—different.' Xander called ahead to Will. Left! Through there! Straight on and through the archway! 'Is your name short for Estella?'

'No. Just Stella.'

They were at the top end of the stable yard, passing under the clock tower, Art and Mr Tringle's quarters on the left. On the right, the three sets of old arched double doors of the coach house in the French grey of the Longbridge estate. The paint flaking and brittle, like tired old horses in need of a groom. Xander walked ahead to the side of the building where exterior stone steps led up steeply to a small grey door at the top. The metal banister bent in some places, rusted in others and occasionally missing all together.

'Up here?' Stella said. Will and Xander looked at her as if she was a little dim.

'Can I unwrap the shortbread now?' Will asked.

'Almost,' Xander laughed.

He had a key in his pocket. He unlocked the door and it creaked open. He let Will in first. Held the door open for Stella next. She had to squeeze by, not anticipating how narrow it was. Had she, she would have turned away from him, gone in with her back to his body. But she didn't think. A

174

hair's breadth between them, close enough for her to notice the few dark hairs on his chest at the opening of his shirt, close enough for him to detect the fragrance of her shampoo.

Glanced up. Him looking down. Eyes, dark and intense—not grey blue today but slate navy. He hadn't shaved.

That's not a glance. That's a linger.

\*　　\*　　\*

The apartment above the coach house bays was long and appeared to be subdivided by little more than folding screens. The windows themselves, of which there were six in a long horizontal run, were wide but short and resembled pairs of eyes squinting. It wasn't dark inside, but it felt low, quiet, because one had to stoop a little to see out, as if those within the apartment could choose to hide from the outside world. It was empty, dusty, still. There were some old tea chests filled with rubbish, gingham curtains hanging limp and moth-eaten at the windows like a peasant girl's skirt. Will, automatically, was walking to the far end. Xander was not directing him otherwise. Just in front of him, Stella. She had stopped at the first of the partitions—which were indeed folding screens covered in calico.

'My dad called this place a moveable feast.'

'Your dad?'

'This is where I grew up.' Why am I telling her this?

'This? *Here?*' Stella turned and for a split second, Xander thought she was going to reach for his arm, at much the same time that Stella thought she might, too. She hugged her clipboard close. 'This is your childhood home?'

'It was,' Xander said, looking about himself. 'Unconventional—I'll say. But it was a merry place. Warm and bright—with my parents forever rejigging the layout with the screens. I can't exactly remember where my room was—it grew with me when I was a boy and needed the space to play, then it seemed to shrink when I was in my late teens and hardly ever here. And when I left for uni, it disappeared altogether and my parents went for the Ultimate Open Plan—like something you'd see on *Grand Designs* these days.'

He sat on a tea crate and watched Stella gazing about. He told her how his parents moved to Little Dunwick when they retired, but that his mother still visited Lydia regularly. He told her about Nottingham University and Caroline and Andrew and their communal, post-student existence in Highbury before they all moved to Long Dansbury. Him renting. Them buying. Marrying. Again, he wondered to himself why he was telling her any of this.

'No mortgage?' Stella asked. 'No offspring?'

'Er—no,' Xander laughed.

And then he wondered, what about you, Stella? What's your story? Divorced? When? Are you a single mum by choice? And while Will came back to them, in awe of his surroundings, asking for Xander's say-so to start the shortbread, Xander wondered why Stella should be of any interest to him. Why had he noticed the amber in her eyes, why was he interested to see what she'd make of it all, up here in the quiet shadows of his past? Why had he stopped to think that she suited being a mother to a boy like Will?

'Please, Mr Xander, can I have the biscuits now?'

'Very nearly almost.' Caroline's kids loved it when he said that. 'Come on.'

At the very far wall was a door, which opened to another door—much like between the carriages of a train. Through this door, and at right angles to the apartment and to Art and Mr Tringle's flats, ran the clock tower section, joining the two. It felt draughty, as though they shouldn't be there. There were gaps in the floor and holes in the roof and bird shit encrusting some of the rafters like barnacles on a lobster pot.

'Are there bats here?' Will asked.

'Yes, right up high in the clock tower itself.'

'Does it chime?'

'Not any more.'

'Can I eat the biscuits?'

'If you share them with your mum and me.'

'Can we go in further?'

'You'll have to ask your mum.'

'Can we, Mummy?'

'No, darling. No. I don't think so. I think it's time we went on.'

*     *     *

Xander noted how quiet Stella had become as they left the stable yard and walked through the yard with the workshops in the old barns, past the livery stables and out into the farmland.

'Are you all right?'

'I'm fine, thank you,' said Stella. She looked at her clipboard. 'Clarence's place?'

'That's right,' said Xander. 'Over there.' He

pointed, a long way off, to a stone shack.

'Who is Clarence?' Stella asked. 'The only Clarence I know of is the angel in *It's A Wonderful Life.*'

Xander smiled. 'He's a great big, soft gentle bear of a man.'

'Sounds like Hagrid,' chirped Will.

'Who?'

'You can tell you haven't got children,' Stella laughed.

'Clarence is special,' Xander said defensively. 'Of all the people still tied to Longbridge, he's the one I'll worry about most, if the estate goes. He's more than just a tenant—he's part of the land. I honestly don't know-how he'll manage.' She could feel Xander looking at her—no doubt with some confrontational expression as if to say, well, have you thought about that? She kept her eyes on Clarence's place.

The building seemed at odds with all the others on the estate. Stella thought it looked best suited to the moors. Stout and low with thick walls constructed from uneven slabs of stone. Small windows, like deep-set eyes. Clarence wasn't in. Though she stood on tiptoe and cupped her hands around her face as she pressed close to the window, Stella could see little.

'It's really an outhouse,' Xander said, now with affection. 'It's very simple inside—Clarence has made it homely. He's been here since the War. Many times Lydia's offered him different quarters, but he's happy there.'

'Since the War?' Will was all ears.

'He came with his parents from the East End of London,' Xander said. 'He was a boy. His dad was a corporation dustman—none of them had ever seen a cow before.' He paused. Will would love Clarence. Xander remembered how he'd sit for hours on an upturned bucket listening to Clarence's stories.

'Never seen a *cow*?'

'Never. His dad became head herdsman. He had a gift—passed it on to Clarence. Limousins—the cattle at Longbridge.'

'Where are Clarence's cows now?'

'Long gone.'

'But he's still here?'

'It's his home,' he told Will, whilst looking at Stella accusingly. 'He's very old.'

Stella thought, don't you look at me, you with your dark stare. But she couldn't say anything. And she couldn't look away.


## *Chapter Sixteen*

'Look!' Will showed Sara the napkin that had contained the shortbread which Xander had advised him to keep because, if Will returned it to His Lady, Mrs Biggins would be in trouble. Xander had winked at Stella at that part but Will hadn't seen so he couldn't recount that bit.

Sara fingered the embroidered crest. 'How fabulously posh,' she said.

'You should see the place,' said Stella. But tonight, Sara wasn't interested in details of cornicing and fanlights and horse's bums and men called Clarence.

'Go,' Sara said to her. 'The life of Riley awaits

you.'

'Who?' said Will.

'It's a saying,' said Stella, sensing Sara grinning at her lasciviously. 'You help Robbie and Sara with the Stickies, darling,' she said, 'and I'll see you first thing in the morning.'

\*            \*            \*

Driving home, Stella thought how bizarre the concept of going on a date seemed. She felt a little alarmed that she wasn't more excited. A blind date at the age of thirty-four, her first blind date ever, in fact. It was too long after breaking up with Charlie, not least now that the divorce was through, to consider the merits of The Rebound. A couple of her friends had proposed it, in the early days, but Stella had an intrinsic sense that it wouldn't suit her. These days, she doubted a relationship was her thing either. But there again, Saturday nights alone were rather pathetic, when they happened week in, week out, so she'd humour the good intentions of her loved ones and spend the evening with some charming, well-off, handsome chap with a silly name.

She'd been through various options of what to wear—standing critically in front of her wardrobe and mirror and sharing her thoughts via text and phone calls with Jo, Juliet and Sara. Ultimately, the women closest to her were unanimous in the pairings they suggested. Dark grey skirt not too short but sassy enough, black boots with a heel and her silky tunic top in dusky rose. Hair up, she'd been told. Drop earrings. Dark lipstick. Smokey eyes. And be five to ten minutes late. Stella was

180

slightly concerned that her own instincts were apparently so far off the mark—she'd have been on time, in stretch jeans, just a lash of mascara, just a slick of lipgloss and lower heels in case a getaway was necessary. She started to fret. Say she found Riley unattractive physically and in person? What would she do and what would she say—not to him, but to all those involved in making this evening happen? As she made her way to the restaurant, she felt utterly burdened by the expectations of others. Only then did she think, what on earth would Riley make of *her*? What was *he* expecting? Oh God—this all felt so contrived. Awful. It was little comfort knowing her domestic army was behind the scenes, rooting for her and, it had to be said, living vicariously through her too. It just felt like pressure. Jo had told her to buy new underwear—just in case you're tempted. Sara, conversely, had advised old, mismatched, shapeless—to ward against temptation on a first date. If those closest to her couldn't agree on how she was to behave, what chance did Stella have to decide for herself? Stop bloody thinking! The one thing she did hope was that either they would both find the other attractive—or else that neither of them would.

\*       \*       \*

She was five minutes late, but there again her watch was set five minutes fast. Riley, however, was not on time. On entering the restaurant, aware that it was full and feeling too intimidated to even glance around to assess whom he might be, Stella polarized her vision and made straight for the maître d' who appeared to take pleasure in leading her, very slowly, to an empty table, nodding to his diners left and right as he went.

She thought, I'm not remotely hungry. She glanced at the menu and couldn't see a thing that whetted her appetite. She thought, what am I meant to do now? She wasn't going to be stood up, was she? She didn't dare look around her. She ordered a vodka and tonic. Soon after, a Bloody Mary. She took out her phone, nervously playing Solitaire which she won in two minutes seventeen seconds. New best time! New fewest moves! Well— that made the evening a success, if nothing else. No texts. She checked the news headlines, the weather. Nothing surprising there. No texts. Phone on vibrate. She scrolled through photographs and gazed at Will, wishing with a pang that the two of them were snuggled up doing their usual Saturday evening thing but then realizing, sadly, that it was his bedtime and if she had been at home, she'd have been curled on the sofa, with a glass of wine, watching rubbish TV and hoping to feel tired enough for an early night. A text came through. Jo. A barrage of larky Emoji images. She couldn't find any appropriate to fire back so she left the text unanswered. Fourteen minutes late. She did have the right time, didn't she? And date? And location? Another voddie?

'Miss Stella!' Riley had missed Stella. He'd already had a good scout around the restaurant wondering which of the three lone female diners might have been his blind date. Missed Stella. 'God—am I late? Sorry. Couldn't get parked.'

'That's OK, I was a little late myself,' she said. She half stood to greet him while he sat down, leaving her stooped so it looked as though she had

182

gut ache. They shook hands a little gingerly, having to negotiate the candle, the condiments, the small vase with the single gerbera—the spiral of wire around its stem seeming to garrotte the flower as much as support it.

'How *are* you?' he asked, as if she'd been on some epic worldwide adventure and he was ready and waiting to be fascinated by her.

'I'm fine!' She remembered to smile, do the eye-contact thing. He was good-looking, and she was relieved. She didn't want to not fancy him—Sara wouldn't accept that as an excuse. And he looked nothing like Charlie, thank goodness. An open-necked shirt rolled up to just below the elbow. Nice forearms. A quality watch a little clunky for her liking. A neatly trimmed goatee, dark hair, green eyes. Slim, tanned, obviously fit.

'Come here often?' He laughed as if the cliché was beyond witty. She laughed for him.

'A first for me,' she said. She paused. Did that sound pathetic? Be yourself. Be honest. 'All of this is a first for me.'

'I'm starving,' he said and overlooking her awkwardness to peruse the menu was helpful. 'Do you drink?' he asked.

'Yes, please,' she said, draining her glass and crunching the ice.

He gave the wine list great attention, muttering names under his breath as though they were players in a football team it was his duty to rank.

When the waiter came to take their order and Riley looked expectantly to Stella to place hers, she realized that each dish she liked contained words she was unsure how to pronounce. So she changed her mind said, green salad to start, please.

And then the risotto. It was sage and broad beans. She didn't like broad beans but the dish was a better option than Agneau de Lait which sounded barbaric. Riley pronounced quinoa *key-noir*. Stella thought that was incorrect. Or else she'd made a fool of herself in the past. She hadn't fancied it tonight. It was with something called Noix de Ris de Veau and she wasn't even going to ask what that was. Riley ordered the steak for his entrée.

'So, tell me about yourself,' Riley said which, to Stella, was on a par with a job interviewer asking where she saw herself five years hence.

'I—er—'

Luckily, he interrupted. 'The only Stella I know is Artois,' he chortled. 'And I've had a very chequered time with that one!'

Again, she laughed for him. And told him, in one breath, the details she thought sold herself well.

'Property, eh?'

She nodded. 'And you?'

'Sales.'

She could have guessed.

'Global,' he stressed and then Stella relaxed because she knew she could repeat this to Jo and they'd fall about laughing. He's in sales, you know . . . *global*.

'And you have a kid?'

She hated that word.

'I have a son,' she said. 'Will. He's seven and a half.'

'How old are you? If it's not too rude to enquire?'

Oh God, had Sara shaved a few years off her and forgotten to mention it? Be honest, remember. 'I'm thirty-four.'

He stared at her. The candlelight making his eyes shine like jade. 'You look younger,' he said, impressed. Stella felt chuffed and happily munched her way through the green salad. He raised his glass at her, and his eyebrow. She busied herself sipping wine to keep a blush at bay.

'So you're a dating virgin, then?' His gaze lingered and Stella thought, what the hell, and lingered hers back at him whilst nodding with a coy smile. After that, he didn't ask her any further direct questions, choosing instead to talk about himself. She drank as he spoke and, at opportune moments raised her glass as much for a refill as to toast his many accolades. His monologue also gave her the perfect opportunity, when the main course arrived, to surreptitiously conceal the broad beans under a duvet of risotto. He was soon preoccupied filling his mouth with fillet steak and, bolstered by the wine, Stella felt happy talking at him. As she did so, every now and then he gurned a little, obviously dislodging something a little too fibrous and Stella deduced the meat was not as butter soft as the menu had claimed. When the dessert menu was presented, she was draining her third glass of Merlot or Shiraz or something—or was it her fourth—while nodding for Riley to refill it. She did think she oughtn't to have had the vodkas whilst she'd been waiting. And she vaguely recalled some pithy saying about grape-and-grain but she couldn't remember what, let alone which order was the safe one, which was the danger.

Crêpes Suzette. She loved Crêpes Suzette. Splash on the Grand Marnier! Go on, give it a good slosh! Shit—something hot down her top. Really hot. The Suzette bit of the crêpe. How awful!

How mortifying! Really not funny—certainly not something to start giggling about. OK. You can stop laughing now. Stop. Laughing. Now.

'I could eat that all over again!' she laughed, moments later. She reached for the wineglass and somehow, the water glass tipped over. Oops. Silly glass. Don't ask for the bill yet, Riley.

Riley Riley not very smiley.

She linked arms with him on their way out, because that's OK to do on a date, isn't it? With a handsome man who's in global sales. Who pays for dinner *à deux* without even checking the bill. Do we look like a couple, sauntering out of here? He's very handsome. Do we suit each other? What happens next?

It was a surprisingly chilly evening—which the day had not hinted at. Stella's weather app hadn't warned her. The cool air sobered her up only so much as to make her suddenly aware just how woozy she was. She'd done as she was told and worn her high-heeled boots but now she felt unstable and each time she teetered she felt just a little more unwell in that annoying, stupid, car-sicky way.

And then she thought, I just really want to go home.

Lie down.

Be asleep.

I really want to be home.

'Where do you live? Nearby?'

I don't want you to come home with me. I don't want you to be with me just now at all.

'Nearby.'

'I think I'd better run you home.'

She meant to say, 'It's OK.' But only the 'OK' bit

186

came out of her mouth.

'I'll go and get the car.' He sounded like a cross parent. 'Just wait here—I'll be five minutes.'

As he walked away from her, briskly crossing the road, she saw him checking his phone. Making a call. She tried to focus on him but he was moving too much. She tried to focus on anything but everything was moving. Riley didn't look back. Oh Goddo Goddo God. Don't want to be sick. Not here. Not at all. I don't feel well. I don't feel happy. I don't feel safe. I don't like tonight. I want to be home.

Images of the meal just eaten churned in and out of her mind's eye accompanied by waves of nausea. Stop the pictures. Stop the feeling. Hold on to the wall. Just stare fixedly as possible at that tree over there. Common sense says that tree trunks are categorically stable things. Leaves flitter and branches sway but tree trunks are nice and solid and steady. Keep staring at it. Don't let it out of your sight.

*     *     *

'Stella?'

That's not Riley.

Stella knew she'd turned her head but her eyes had yet to catch up.

'Stella?'

That's Xander.

And a tall blonde lady.

And another man.

And another lady.

And another—oh God, double vision, triple vision.

Just lots of people. Only one of whom she knew

and who was the last person she wanted to be here right now.

'Stella?'

Xander. Rude Xander who jogs and runs and annoys her because he hates her.

*     *     *

'Do you know her?' Caroline asked quietly.

'Yes,' said Xander, evenly.

'She looks ropey, poor monkey,' said Caroline. 'Are you OK, chicken?'

*     *     *

Monkey. Chicken. I'm a stupid cow.

Stella didn't dare nod. She needed to keep her head very still because she was wobbling on her heels like one of those children's toys which can sway precariously. Please just let everyone disappear. All these Xander people. And that Riley man.

'Are you waiting for someone?' That was Xander again. She tried to focus on his face, gave up and just stared blurrily into the middle distance.

'I had a date,' she said. 'He's gone to get his car.' She burped. 'I don't want him to drive me home.' She started to cry. 'I just want to be at home.'

'We can't let some bloke drive her back in this state,' Caroline said to Xander, shuddering at not-so-distant memories of throwing up into her handbag in Andrew's car—and he was her husband. Xander just thought that no way should some bloke Stella had just met be allowed to drive her off, let alone go anywhere near her home.

188

'Would you like us to take you home, pet?'

Stella reached her hand towards Caroline.

'I'm Caroline.'

'I don't feel well.' And Stella quietly sobbed.

'Come on,' said Caroline but she said it to Xander. Then Stella vaguely heard the Caroline person saying something to the other people whose shadowy figures were registering on her peripheral vision. Something about pappadams and bhajis. But she really couldn't afford to think about food so she stopped listening and just stared at the pavement which was mysteriously revolving.

'Hold on,' Caroline said. Stella thought she was giving her an instruction. And Xander was the nearest thing for her to hold on to. So she reached for him. Stella's eyes were half-closed and her head was lolling and all Xander could do was put an arm around her waist, an arm close across her shoulders and hold her up, hold her steady. Caroline went to speak to Andrew and their friends to say, don't worry, Xander and I will just deal with his friend then we'll meet you at the Raj.

It wasn't late. It wasn't even ten o'clock. And they glanced over to Xander who was standing still and steady, tall and strong. And thoughtful. His arms around the drunk girl as if he was embracing her, not steadying her. It was a strange sight, a good sight. A sight Caroline and Andrew hadn't seen, hadn't associated with him, for a few years now.

'Do you know where she lives?' Caroline asked Xander quietly, now the others had gone. He shook his head. 'But you know her name.' She paused. 'Stella, can you tell us where you live? Xander and I will take you home.'

As Caroline and Xander removed Stella from the

189

scene, Stella felt she was on a hovercraft because there appeared to be no pavement beneath her feet. Riley drove up some minutes later. He parked but left the engine running, opened the driver's door and stood in the gutter looking quickly up and down the street. No sign of her. Well, that was a blessing in disguise, wasn't it. He looked around again. She was local, wasn't she. She'd probably gone home. Or gone to chuck up behind a wall. He phoned her mobile—relieved when it rang through to voicemail. What a dire evening. Oh, well. Chalk it all up. Another Saturday night, another date. Pretty enough—but not his type.

Vaguely, Stella could hear questions being asked of her, her voice discombobulated when it came, giving out the components of her address in an order she hoped would be pieced together and make sense. She kept burping. And it made her feel worse at first and then better straight after so it seemed silly to say sorry or to stifle them. And certainly the Caroline woman kept telling her not to be silly and not be sorry. She was wearing a floaty wrappy sort of thing with bits on which tickled the side of Stella's face, comforting and annoying.

And Xander's arm around her waist. Xander, hearing her burping and slurring. Oh, the shame of it! Xander and Caroline. Stella so drunk that she had no option than to allow her nemesis and his friend, the Good Samaritan, to escort her right to her front door.

'We're here!' Stella's head rolled around as if it was on a pivot. 'Thank you so much!' She started to cry again, with a little hiccup ever now and then.

'We have to take her in,' said Caroline. 'Where's

190

your key, monkey? Can I look in your bag? Here—'
She passed the girl to Xander who held her steady
and held her close.

'Smell nice,' Stella murmured.

'Pardon?' Xander pretended he hadn't heard.

'Nice,' she muttered. He felt her cold nose
against his neck. She felt his skin, warm, fragrant.
The smell of him made her feel better. Just want to
stand like this for a little longer.

'Got them!' said Caroline. 'Come on, pet.'

'Stella,' Stella corrected.

Caroline unlocked her door and Stella was back
in her world.

Oh, the relief.

'Is your bedroom upstairs?'

A very difficult word to repeat when drunk,
but Stella gave it her best. She was clinging on to
Xander's shoulder trying desperately to focus on
the framed photos of Will yet the sight of her little
boy filled her suddenly with acute shame. How she
wished her evening had been the simple Saturday
night she was used to. Why veer from the tried and
tested? Something had been broken so she'd fixed
it—divorced Charlie. Why had she tinkered with
the status quo? Will and her together. Supper on
their laps. Telly. Never again. Never drink again.
Never go on dates, blind or otherwise, ever again.

Caroline was in the kitchen, fetching water,
the washing-up bowl, old newspaper to lay out
strategically; going upstairs to prepare Stella's
bedroom. Stella looked up forlornly at Xander.

'I had a date,' she said. 'I never have a date. I
never want to have another date again. Stupid.
Stupid. Stupid.' She pressed the side of her face
against Xander's chest because it made the room

191

spin less. 'What a numpty.' And then she heard him laugh. Actually, she didn't hear him—she felt him. Soft low vibrations thrumming comfortingly against her head.

'I know what you mean,' he said, knowing that Caroline couldn't hear him and that Stella wouldn't remember. 'There's some woman loitering for me with my mates at the Raj curry house.'

'But you can run away,' Stella said sleepily. 'Because you're very good at running.'

Very good at running away, Xander thought quietly.

'Ready,' Caroline called down.

Slowly, Xander brought Stella upstairs, leaving her sitting on the edge of her bed with Caroline tending to her. Before he left the women to it, he glanced around the room. It was small but homely. And he couldn't help but notice the fragrance and, for a split second, he recalled how she'd passed by so close to him when he'd opened the door for her into his childhood home that morning.

'Good night, Stella,' he said but she didn't respond, sitting there on her bed with her head hung low, possibly asleep already or simply comatose. He went downstairs and waited for Caroline.

'Ready?' She appeared a few minutes later.

'Will she be OK?'

'Yeah,' said Caroline. 'When it comes to the drunken element of the female race, I'm an expert.'

'Takes one to know one,' Xander said.

'Cheeky!' said Caroline. 'Come on—there's a hot dish with your name on at the Raj.'

'About that,' said Xander as they left Stella's place and checked the door was closed. 'She's not

192

my type.'

'I was referring to a chicken jalfrezi—madras hot, pilau rice, a plain nan, Bombay potato,' said Caroline pointedly. 'Not Penny.'

'She's not my type,' Xander persisted.

'For God's sake, Xander,' said Caroline, 'just get over yourself, pet. And live a little.'


## Chapter Seventeen

When Lydia entered Elmfield Estates, unannounced at eleven o'clock on the Monday morning, Geoff was on the phone, and Belinda appeared to be checking notes between her phone and her desk diary though actually she was browsing Facebook updates. Steve and Gill had just glanced at each other and were busily rifling through papers on their desks, lest their colleagues should guess that they went home together on Friday and spent that night and most of the weekend in torrid entwinings on Steve's black leather sofa. Mr Hutton was in his office. And Stella was in the kitchenette on mid-morning teas duty.

'Can I help you?' said Belinda, it being on the tip of her tongue to tell the old dear that this was an estate agent's and that the Citizens Advice Bureau was two doors along.

'Miss Hutton,' said Lydia in a voice a great deal lower than Belinda expected. The timbre was such as to cause the others to look up.

'You mean Mr Hutton?' Belinda corrected.

'No,' said Lydia, as if the woman was boring her, '*Miss*.'

'Stella?' Belinda said it as if the notion that anyone really wanted Stella was preposterous.

Lydia merely raised an eyebrow.

'She's out the back, making tea,' said Belinda, returning to Facebook, assuming Lydia to be an aged aunt, thus foregoing any formality or indeed politeness. 'She'll be through in a minute—sit yourself down, love.'

Lydia was so affronted that though her knees would have benefited indeed from a taking a seat, every muscle in her body locked and she stared witheringly at Belinda and coldly at the rest of the staff.

'Bugger,' Stella muttered to herself, watching as each mug splashed a little of its contents onto the tray. She couldn't still be hungover, could she? Not after all the Alka-Seltzer she'd had yesterday. If she was, the sight of Lydia standing rigid and in full glower soon snapped Stella out of it.

'Lady Lydia!'

'Miss Hutton,' said Lydia gravely.

'Lady Lydia! Was I—expecting you?'

'No.' Lydia paused. 'I thought I'd call in. I wasn't passing—I have made a special journey.'

'Of course,' said Stella, 'of course.' She put the tray down and quickly took each mug to each desk, placing them wetly on the surfaces. 'Would you like a cup of tea—or coffee?'

'No. I want to sign on the dotted line. That's why I'm here. It seemed appropriate.'

Stella stood there, gawping. Her colleagues were riveted.

'Providing you have a guide price for me. You should have, by now, after all the time you've spent at Longbridge Hall.'

'Yes,' said Stella. 'Yes,' she said, a scurry of thoughts in her mind, the first being how to remove Lydia out of sight and earshot of the rest of the office. 'Please, come with me.' She led the way to her uncle's office. Knocked, entered. He was on the phone. 'Lady Lydia Fortescue is here to put the Longbridge estate on our books and I suggested the privacy of your office,' she said loudly, in one long breath so that Mr Hutton hung up his call straight away.

'Lady Lydia, delighted! Delighted!' he said in an obsequious tone that was unbecoming and visibly irked Lydia. 'We have met—a little while back.'

'Yes,' she said, underwhelmed, 'I remember.'

'Douglas Hutton is my uncle,' Stella turned to Lydia. 'As managing director of Elmfield Estates, he will sit in on this.'

'Very well,' said Lydia. She took off her light summer jacket, handed it to Stella and sat herself down.

'Very well,' Stella echoed quietly, her adrenalin rising as she thought how ill prepared she was. Lydia waited for her to continue. Douglas just looked levelly at his niece, giving the impression he knew exactly what she was going to say because he was at the helm of everything. 'Lady Lydia,' said Stella, 'I would value the Longbridge estate— as a whole, rather than separate lots—at fourteen million pounds. All land, all buildings. But I would suggest we put it to market at fifteen million.' Her uncle fought hard to clear his throat as discreetly as possible.

'Fifteen million,' said Lydia, but her emotion was illegible.

'Yes,' said Stella. 'These days, the feeling of a

195

bargain is what secures a sale. Hence putting it on at fifteen but I would advise you to be content with between thirteen and fourteen.' She paused. 'Million.'

'And have you clients suitable?'

'Yes,' Stella lied whilst smiling gamely at her uncle. 'Oh, yes.'

Lydia looked at Stella. Behind the ice blue of her eyes, a faint mist of entreatment was legible. 'I have made it quite plain, my dear, that I care not who gets it.' She paused. 'But that's not to say I am not entrusting you to handle the sale—elegantly.'

Stella nodded earnestly, and smiled gently. 'I understand.'

'I know you do,' said Lydia, sounding tired. 'Where do I sign—and what happens next?'

*    *    *

What happened next was that Lydia went home, inviting Mrs Biggins to join her in an early lunch, with wine, over which she confirmed her plans. With Stella at his side, Mr Hutton made an announcement about the Longbridge estate to the staff before disappearing back into his office to put word about to his contacts in the industry. Steve resigned on the spot and flounced out of the office. Belinda and Gill both felt they wanted alternately to kill Stella yet suddenly befriend her. And Geoff just sat at his desk and looked bleakly through his flimsy portfolio of properties.

Stella asked her remaining colleagues whether she could pass all new clients to them and then spent the rest of the day phoning photographers, land agents, her contacts in the Planning Office and private property search connections, speaking with as much discretion as she was able while allowing herself to rejoice in the upward curve her path appeared now to be taking. It was real. It was happening.

Geoff was given Steve's clients. Gill received a text from Steve telling her to fake an appointment, to meet him at his so he could shag her senseless all afternoon. Belinda put on Facebook that she was going to get hammered that evening and who's up for joining her. At the start of the year, long before Stella's time, the agents at Elmfield Estates had voted unanimously to change the commission structure from group to individual. They could all resent Stella as much as they wanted for having secured Longbridge and for standing to make substantial commission on the sale—but each had to admit that they wouldn't have put the effort Stella invested in Mercy Benton's little cottage in the first place and that, realistically, Lady Lydia Fortescue would never have come by any of them.

*       *       *

There was home, and then there was Longbridge. There was Will, and then there was Lydia. For Stella, nothing else mattered. Nothing else warranted, or could be afforded, more than a passing thought. Every hour was so taken with one or the other, it provided a wonderful opportunity for only the briefest post-mortem with Sara about Riley. A slightly lengthier dissection with Jo which involved laughter and cringing on both sides and much mention of the word 'global'. And that business with Xander and

197

His Friend? Well, all that was best forgotten.

So, Stella met the photographer at Longbridge on the Wednesday, which dawned fortuitously clear and sunny, the lawns mown as neat as baize the previous day by Art. Stella's brief to the photographer wasn't dissimilar from any regular property she'd marketed—she was specific about wide angles and lighting and, in this case, panoramic views of the extensive parkland. Lydia had warned her she wouldn't be there. Lydia might want as much money as possible from the sale—but that wasn't to say that, privately, Stella intended to work flat out to secure a buyer who also had the necessary taste and moral fibre to take on such a property.

Mrs Biggins let them in, then disappeared. It was strange for Stella to have the house to herself; it was as if the old place had no idea what was about to befall it and she found she couldn't look at the Fortescue portraits directly and felt as if Lord Frederick had told the Prince Regent to be a sport and place his horse's rump right in her face to make his feelings plain. It was unnerving and, giving some flimsy judgement on the quality of light, Stella suggested to the photographer that they start with exterior shots. She was acting as photographer's assistant, wanting to be behind every element of Longbridge's epic journey to the market. She caught sight of Art mooching around with a wheelbarrow. Did he know? And how about Clarence, whom she had yet to meet? He was out again, his dwelling locked but, as the photographer said, while the building added great rustic charm to his shot of the farmland, you really wouldn't want to concede that it was used for human habitation.

Nor did he feel the peculiar thatched apple store was worth including in the brochure—but he took a few shots to humour Stella who was in paroxysms over it.

'I'm starving,' he said.

'Why don't I nip to the village to buy us something,' said Stella, seeing it was nearly noon and Mrs Biggins had made no mention of the classic Longbridge ploughman's lunch.

'I'll do the walled garden in the meantime,' he said.

'Make sure you get the little nameplates of all the long-gone fruit trees,' she said.

The photographer was finding her tiresome. The tiny tarnished brass plaques wouldn't show in the photograph—and what was the point of a close-up? There were no trees—it was in blatant disregard of the Trade Descriptions Act. There again, she'd wanted him to photograph a bronze statue, imploring him to "show the Lord's best side". It's a bronze statue! he'd said. We don't even know if it's included in the sale! Stella was taken aback at the thought of the first Earl of Barbary being separated from his estate. Photograph him anyway, she said. 'It,' said the photographer. 'It's an *it*.'

It was in the car alone, heading for the village, that Stella suddenly thought of Xander. She was still on the Longbridge driveway and slowed the car down to a crawl. Her recall of Saturday night existed only as a series of hazy stills, but her memories of the daytime earlier, of Xander showing Will and her around, remained vivid. Seeing Longbridge through Will's eyes. The taste of the buttery shortbread. The way she held her breath and Xander held her gaze as she squeezed past him. The feeling of being watched from the great house—Lydia shadowy in an upper window, Mrs Biggins with hands on hips at the back doorway. The way he spoke—lucid and with passion. Anyway, it's Wednesday so Xander should be at work and now that everything's official with Longbridge and she's seen everywhere that needs to be seen, their paths needn't cross again and there's no point recalling the way he laughed with Will.

She drove to the village, couldn't park in the area opposite the shop so drove on a little and crept her car up on to the kerb, as other motorists had done. She passed by Mercy Benton's cottage and waved at the new owner who was just entering. It's not Mercy Benton's cottage, Stella thought, it's Mr and Mrs Marshall's now. Would she feel that about Longbridge too, some day? Could the words Fortescue and Longbridge really be divorced? She realized how she felt a certain kinship with the village now. Look! Michael Lazarus's shop was open—it had always been closed when she'd been by. Stella went in, wanting nothing other than a nosey but came out with a padlock and four small paintbrushes and some black shoe polish. Marvellous place. However wide the catchment of the out-of-town hypermarkets, hopefully there'd always be a place for a shop like Michael Lazarus's in a village like Long Dansbury. Stella went into the Spar, amazed at how busy it was. Lots of mothers and toddlers. Must be end of session at the nursery. She placed sandwiches, cans of soft drinks, crisps and a packet of biscuits in the basket and went to join the queue.

'Sonny, you little monkey—put that back!'

The melodious Geordie tone was known at once to Stella. It belonged to the woman right in front of her; the woman who'd been so kind to her on Saturday. The woman who'd been with Xander. Who'd helped her home. And now, she was right in front of Stella.

Please please don't turn around. Come on queue—move! Goodness, could the shopkeeper talk for Britain. Stella thought about putting all the stuff back and leaving empty-handed. But found herself hemmed in by a display of canned goods and two shoppers now queuing behind her.

'What's that?'

The little Sonny boy had surreptitiously plonked into Stella's basket the tube of sweets his mother had told him to put back. Now he was pointing to the biscuits and gazing up at Stella, expectant for her answer. Just pretend you didn't hear.

'What's *that*?' He was more insistent.

'Biscuits,' Stella all but whispered.

'Biscuits?'

She nodded.

'What's that?' he asked, pointing to the can of Coke.

What do you think it is!

'What's *that*?' He wasn't taking Stella's non-committal smile for an answer.

'Sonny,' his mother turned, her eyes on her son, her focus on the items in the basket of the shopper behind her. 'It's the lady's shopping.'

He took the biscuits out of Stella's basket. 'Biscuits, Mummy!'

'I am so sorry,' said Caroline, finally looking up at Stella whilst trying to wrest the package from her son's determined grip.

201

I know you. I *know* you!

I know you too. But feel free to pretend you don't.

You're Xander's friend—Stella. Oh my God!

It was a rare occasion for Caroline to be stunned into silence.

'Hullo,' said Stella. Then she winced. Then she rambled. 'Look, I'm so sorry—and grateful. And fancy seeing you here. And you'll have to forgive me but I can't recall your name.'

'I'm Caroline,' she said warmly while Stella nodded and grimaced again. 'It's Stella—isn't it?'

'Yes,' said Stella, 'and—again—I am so sorry. And I can't thank you enough.'

Caroline laughed. 'That's quite all right. I wish I'd had the opportunity to thank my many saviours who've come to my rescue over the years, I can tell you.' Stella still looked shamefaced. 'The number of times Xander or Andrew—he's my husband, we're all old friends—had to give me a fireman's lift home from some club or other. I'd say you were very demure.'

'Hardly,' Stella groaned.

'You'd been on a date,' Caroline said, as if it were explanation enough.

'A disaster, more like,' said Stella.

'Don't you like him?' Caroline asked.

'Well, I'm sure he's a lovely bloke once you get to know him—but to be honest, he's nearly bulldozed me down twice round here whilst he's been running. And he can be moody. Quite rude, actually.' Then she thought about Xander, up in his childhood home by the clock tower. And the shortbread. And the lonely chill of his bedroom. And her cold nose against his warm skin. The

202

feeling of his laughter.

'I didn't mean Xander,' said Caroline, regarding her oddly, 'I meant the guy you were on a date with.'

'Oh,' said Stella. 'Oh.' Mortified. 'Him.' She paused. Caroline's gentle, friendly face was creasing into a grin. 'Between you and me,' said Stella, 'he was a tosser.' She glanced down at her basket. Sonny was still fingering the biscuits. Nice. They were called Nice. She was never sure whether that was 'nice' as in the adjective, or Nice as in the place. She'd chosen them because they were comfortingly nostalgic, those sugar-encrusted oblong thins with a subtle coconutty hint. 'Xander,' she said, 'I mean—sorry—yes, he's a nice chap too, I'm sure. Your friend.'

'How do you know Xander?'

And though Caroline was chatty and light, Stella wasn't sure what to say because though the sale of Longbridge was official, it wasn't yet on the open market. 'Oh. I just know him—from around.'

Caroline thought, with some consternation, oh, you're not one of his fuck-buddies, are you? And then she thought, no, you're not. And she thought, I know you're not because unlike when I walked in on Xander at that pub in Standon, he wasn't the least bit embarrassed to come across you on Saturday night, despite the state you were in. An image of Xander quietly holding Stella steady, Stella's head against his chest, confronted Caroline. And Caroline thought, oh yeah?

'Hope I didn't ruin your evening,' Stella said, bashfully.

'Hope you didn't ruin your Sunday,' Caroline laughed. 'Did you chuck?'

Stella nodded, ruefully. 'Thanks for the strategically placed washing-up bowl.'

'All part of the service,' said Caroline. 'What are you doing here, by the way?'

Stella liked this woman and wished she could be honest. 'Some business, nearby,' she said. 'I'm working with a photographer today.' That sounded good. And it was true. 'So I just nipped in to buy some snacks.'

Caroline nodded. 'Well, it's nice to see you again,' she said.

'You too,' said Stella. 'And thanks. And sorry.'

'No problem,' said Caroline. 'Any time!'

'There won't be another time,' Stella said grimly.

'Oh, I always say I'm never going to touch a drop again,' Caroline said, opening a pack of Nicorette not yet paid for and chewing as if her life depended on it.

'Not that—the dating. First one in two years—a nightmare. Never again.'

Suddenly, Caroline thought how she'd love to know more, that she'd probably enjoy chatting to Stella over a coffee; imagined them putting the world to rights, bantering; imagined it all getting gloriously salacious. But Mrs Patek was telling Caroline it was £7.42 but to call it £7.40 and Sonny was dangerously near the racks of chocolate. And she'd been queuing for ages. It really was time to go.

'Ta-ta,' said Caroline. 'It's nice to see you. Say bye-bye to Stella,' she told Sonny.

'Bye-bye, Stella.'

'Bye-bye, Sonny,' said Stella and Caroline really liked the way she waved to her son, opening and closing her hand methodically, just like he did.

The shopkeeper rang through Stella's items. 'Oh, that's not mine,' Stella said, as the tube of sweets Sonny had placed in her basket were put into the bag.

'You want me to refund it? It's 10p.'

'No,' Stella laughed, 'no, of course not. It's OK. It's fine.'

And she put them into the glove compartment in her car and drove back to Longbridge.

\*     \*     \*

'Do you know what I think?' Caroline didn't wait for Sonny to answer. 'I think, when you're having a nap, I'm going to phone Uncle Xander.'

\*     \*     \*

Lydia returned to Longbridge to find Stella and the photographer having an impromptu picnic by the statue of Lord Frederick. Stella scrambled to her feet as she approached and Lydia saw her nudge the photographer with her foot to incite him to do the same.

'Hullo!' said Stella. Lydia nodded at her. 'This is Malcolm Brown.'

'Nice place,' he said. And both Stella and Lydia cringed.

'Would you like a biscuit?' Stella said, offering the packet to Lydia who declined with a look of slight distaste. 'They're Nice.'

'I'm sure they are,' said Lydia vaguely. And Stella wondered if there was home-made shortbread waiting for Lydia in the house.

'We'll be in shortly—if that's OK.'

Lydia nodded and walked stiffly to the house.

\*     \*     \*

Malcolm and Stella were setting up the shots in the drawing room, having done the library and the dining room, when they next saw Lydia. She stood alongside Stella and they watched, quietly, Malcolm at work.

'You know, during the War, this room was out of bounds—all shut up,' Lydia said. 'Mostly empty, just dust sheets over the furniture. Tape and blackout at the windows. But I had to come in every day.' She started to laugh at the memory. 'I had to do my piano practice. The war was no excuse.' She laughed again. 'Dear God, it was cold.' She looked at Stella. 'The curtains wafted against the walls even though there was blackout and the windows were locked. It was so cold I'd come in here in full outdoor regalia—balaclava and mittens—and poke out my fingers at the very last minute.'

Stella looked at the grand piano. 'Was it the same piano?'

'Same piano, same position,' said Lydia.

'I always hated piano practice,' said Stella.

'I did too,' said Lydia. 'But during the War, I didn't mind it so much. Despite this room being the bloody North Pole.' She paused, to let the memories turn from sepia to full colour. 'I was the only one allowed in here—and I liked that, I liked having a little bit of the house all to myself, time by myself, in a room that was just mine.' She trilled a little Chopin, a little quakily. 'During the War, Longbridge was billeted—I don't know if I told

206

you. It was quite mad, really. Chaos. At one time, there were fifteen children living here. My sisters and I. My mother. My aunt and her daughter. And all these other—*people*.' She said it as if referring to a different species altogether. 'From the city. All types, my dear. We had the Smiths, from the East End—cockneys, you know! They taught me to rhyme. And the Coopers—they were East End too. They taught me to swear. And music-hall songs. And some Jews from somewhere in deepest darkest London too.' She spoke lightly, fondly.

'Fifteen children?'

'Four different families—not counting Fortescues,' Lydia said, and she said it proudly. 'Just women at the helm, of course. All the men were at war. Apart from Clarence's father. But they weren't in the house. They were with the cows.'

'With the *cows*?'

'Not *with* the cows—in the farm cottage, in those days. It's gone now. It was really rather jolly. Just blessedly cold, of course, during the winters. But actually rather gay. When any of the men came back on leave, they became everyone's father.' With that, Lydia left the room. Stella was transfixed by the piano, imagined the room covered in sheets, crosses of tape at each window pane. She conjured an image of a young Lydia, wrapped to the gills, coming in to tinkle the ivories once a day while England was at war and Longbridge was overrun with commoners.

'Here.'

Lydia was back at her side, holding a photo album open, heavy black pages, white ink annotations. It was a photograph of a line of children from tallest to smallest, outside in the

207

grounds. One by one, Lydia attempted to name each of them, substituting Youngest Cockney or Eldest Jew if she'd forgotten their names. 'That's me,' she repeated, and she touched gently where she was, the fourth tallest. 'That's me.' And there was such wistful affection in her voice Stella felt compelled to gently tap at the photograph too.

Strange to think of Lydia as a child in a white frock with hair loose and enormous ribbons like rabbit ears. Odd to think of Longbridge being noisy, of every room having a purpose—even a deserted drawing room whose function it was to provide the young Lady with a little solitude to practise piano. Stella imagined the melodies filtering through the cold, working their way out through the closed doors, bringing a little light music to all the disparate souls mucking in together in the great old house. Suddenly it struck her as unbelievable that Lydia could consider leaving it all behind. Whoever buys Longbridge needs to know these tales, thought Stella. They need to be a fixed part of the fee. They're non-negotiable.

\*     \*     \*

It was after the children's bedtime that Caroline finally had the chance to call Xander.

'Hullo, Mrs,' he said.

'Hullo, yourself,' she said.

'Good day?'

'Busy,' she said. She paused. 'About last Saturday.'

'What about last Saturday?' Xander said though he knew where this was leading.

'About Penny.'

208

'About Penny.'

'You liked?'

'I liked,' said Xander evenly, thinking back to the curry, to Penny quite surprisingly running her hand along his inner thigh under the table.

'You want to see again?'

Xander paused. 'I no want to see again.' He paused again. 'Why are we speaking in pidgin English?'

'I don't know,' said Caroline. 'Why don't you want to see Penny again? She's gorgeous and bright and you made an impression on her.'

'She's just not my type,' said Xander. 'I told you at the time.'

'You've been out of the loop long enough to no longer have the right to a choice of specific type,' Caroline said. 'Soon you'll just have to take what you can get.'

'I'm fine as I am,' said Xander, not quite so larkily. 'Stop fussing over me. I'm fine.'

'Oh?'

'Shut up, woman!'

'Charming.' Caroline paused. 'By the way—I bumped into your friend today.'

'My friend?'

'Stella.'

Caroline grinned at the long silence she'd anticipated through her sixth sense. 'Yep,' she said. 'Stella.'

'She's not my—friend.'

Is that so? Caroline thought, conjuring again the image of Stella snug against Xander's chest.

'Far from it,' Xander said.

'She was in the shop today.'

'You know why, don't you?' Xander said, curtly.

'She's from Elmfield Estates. She's the one selling Longbridge.'

Caroline had not seen that coming. Now she was silenced.

'So you see, she's really *not* my friend.'

'You might not like what she does,' said Caroline, measuredly, 'but that's not to say you can't like her.'

'She's annoying. She's an estate agent. And she's a stroppy mare. Look, what the hell—I'll call Penny. Why not. Give me her number. Must be two sides to every Penny. I'll call her.'

'OK,' said Caroline, slowly while her brain racketed around with new information and forward planning. 'I'll text it to you.'

After the call, Caroline sat looking at her phone for a long time. Penny was not exactly a friend, but on the occasions Caroline had met her, she'd liked her very much. Penny was just the kind of girl Caroline had thought it would be fun to finally have Xander partnered with; at nights out, dinner parties at theirs, pub lunches on a Sunday. But Caroline found herself thinking about Stella and staring at her phone. And then she deleted the text containing Penny's number that she was about to send Xander.

'What *are* you doing?' Andrew asked, having noticed his wife transfixed by her phone.

'Nothing,' she said. 'Just sorting out Xander's love life.'

'The words "Xander" and "love life" are a contradiction in terms,' Andrew laughed. 'Leave the poor sod alone.'

Caroline couldn't quite believe she was going to do it—but still, she felt strongly that what she was about to do was the right thing, even if she intended to keep it to herself. She tapped out a text to Xander and sent it.

Spoke to Penny—she said you're a lovely guy, but not really her type. Hey ho! Cx


## Chapter Eighteen

And so the rumour mill swung fully into action, grinding down the tiniest nibs of information into a powder so insubstantial it was carried easily on the prevailing gossip winds of Long Dansbury, where fiction mutated easily into fact and fed the tongues that wagged.

'Apparently it's Madonna.'

'Madonna? No no, she turned it down. She likes the city. No—what I heard is that it's Anton Deck.'

'Who's Anton Deck?'

'Someone off the telly—so I'm told. He was on that *Get Off My Celebrity* programme.'

'Haven't seen it.'

'You know—when they send them to an island to eat insects. Look! It's Rachel Brightey—she'll know. Mrs Brightey?'

Rachel had just said goodbye to Caroline and was walking to the postbox, by which Nora and Marjorie stood. 'Good morning, ladies.'

'I was just saying to Nora that you'd know who I mean. That Anton chap off the telly who does *Celebrity Island.*'

It didn't seem to ring a bell with Rachel.

'Anton,' Nora prompted, 'Anton Deck.'

'Ant and Dec?' Rachel looked over her shoulder,

willing Caroline to catch her eye so she could come and hear all this.

'That's the one.'

'*I'm a Celebrity, Get Me Out of Here?*'

'That's the show—not that I've seen it. Well, it's him who, apparently, is buying Longbridge. But you didn't hear it from me.'

Rachel was stumped for words and far too tickled by it all to enlighten the women so she just said, wow! and, is that so! and made a detour back to Caroline because it was too good to wait.

'They're from your neck of the woods, aren't they—Ant and Dec?' Rachel asked her. 'Good Geordie stock? You lot'll be bringing coal to Dansbury and have us all gallivanting around in T-shirts and bare legs in December, before long. I think we should have border control.'

'We're taking over the world, pet,' said Caroline. She looked at Rachel. 'You don't think one of them is really buying Longbridge, do you?'

Rachel shrugged. 'That's the rumour.'

'I wonder which?'

'Do you actually know which is which?'

Caroline thought about it. 'I can't say I do,' she said. 'Shame it's not Gary Barlow, though.'

'What about the daughter—there's a Fortescue daughter, isn't there?' Rachel had only lived in the village for a couple of years. 'Some kind of scandal, there, so I've heard.'

'Verity,' said Caroline. 'No,' she shook her head. 'It's not for her.'

'Isn't there anyone in the outer family?'

'I don't honestly know,' said Caroline.

Nora was suddenly back. 'If the boy had only lived,' she said. 'Little lad,' she spoke fondly. 'It

212

would all be different. Her Ladyship would be in the dower house—and the big house would be his. And he'd perhaps have a family—an heir, even—and—'

'—and none of this would be worrying us,' said Marjorie, joining them.

'—and you two have been watching too much *Downton Abbey*,' Caroline laughed.

'Mind you, imagine if it does go to someone *famous*. The Fortescues are posh all right—but they've never been *glam*. Wouldn't you say, Nora?'

'I wouldn't call Ant or Dec particularly glam,' said Caroline, 'they're from my stamping ground.'

Nora and Marjorie tutted sympathetically.

By the time the primary school finished for the day and Rachel and Caroline returned for pick-up, Ant and Dec were no longer in the running: the Longbridge estate was variously being bought by a premiership footballer, or a Russian oligarch or as a tax dodge for someone overseas. People had been busy, Googling and scouring Elmfield Estates' website. The guide price was now known. It was spoken of in double figures only.

Fifteen.

It's on for fifteen.

*       *       *

Lydia should have been tickled by the rumours about the buyers but actually she was irked about the gossip because, two weeks after she'd signed the forms at Elmfield Estates, Longbridge had yet to have a single viewing. Stella had given Lydia her mobile phone number and urged her to phone any time, any day. Lydia, however, who hated traditional telephones, loathed mobiles even more. She'd phoned Stella's mobile for the first time that morning—but Stella had taken the call in Tesco where, she told Lydia, she was doing her weekly shop. Lydia found that so unbearably uncouth and had hung up immediately. On a mobile phone! In Tesco! On a Sunday!

Sitting in the kitchen, picking at a scone, Lydia eyed the phone fixed to the wall whilst Mrs Biggins bustled about pretending not to notice Lydia's agitation. Stella really must phone her back soon. It might be a Sunday but it really was most important.

Finally!

'Yes?'

'Lady Lydia? It's Stella Hutton. I'm so sorry about earlier. I'm home now. What can I do for you?'

Lydia imagined her surrounded by those ghastly plastic bags, no doubt with a phone tucked under her chin as she put the shopping away and closed kitchen cupboards with her foot and mouthed things at her child. Multitasking—wasn't that what they called it? If people were better at time management, there'd be no need to do two things at once.

'I need to call a meeting and I need you to be here,' said Lydia.

'A meeting?'

'The village is chasing its tail with ridiculous tittle-tattle of who's buying Longbridge.'

'You want to host a public meeting?'

'Oh good God, girl—of course not! A meeting for those directly affected. For the people connected with Longbridge—those who work here or live in Longbridge property.'

214

'You haven't told them?'

'Don't speak to me like that!'

'I'm sorry,' said Stella, who hadn't meant her tone to sound so flabbergasted. 'I meant no offence.'

'I've been waiting for you to sell it!'

'I've been working round the clock these last ten days. I hassled the photographer and the printer as much as I could, but the packs only arrived on Friday. However, I sent out six straight away, having phoned those clients pre-emptively. They're all interested. I'm working as fast as I can. But discreetly.'

'I know!' Lydia sounded frustrated, tired, overwrought. 'I know! I just—I should have spoken to everyone by now. And I haven't. And that's just how it is. But I must—and I think I should hold a meeting for one and all.'

Stella imagined Lydia fearing some kind of peasants revolt, anticipating a flailing of pitchforks in the drawing room, the apple store being torched, the statue of Lord Freddie daubed with graffiti.

'Lady Lydia—it's a very stressful thing, selling property. Up there with death and divorce—and that's official. Let me handle as much of the hassle as possible.' Stella paused but there was no response. She wondered if she'd been hung up on again. 'Would you like me to come to the meeting? A sort of living, walking, talking voodoo doll for people to stick proverbial pins—or pitchforks—in?'

Her words were met with silence. Had she said the wrong thing? Had that sounded irreverent? Was Lydia having second thoughts? It made Stella shudder. Perhaps she ought to go over there now. Will wouldn't mind, even if Lydia did. Stella couldn't risk Longbridge being taken off the market or handed to another agent. Though she felt she'd gained Lydia's trust, she sensed how precarious it was.

'Would you?' Lydia's voice, hoarse, broke the silence just as Stella was about to end the call. Stella could sense her stiffen. 'Thank you,' Lydia continued. 'You can give them all the legal banter. Thank you, my dear.' And Lydia hung up.

Mrs Biggins continued with her generally pointless busyness in the kitchen, just casually saying, 'Shall I fetch you a nice little sherry?' as if it was simply a perky little idea and not a medicinal suggestion.

'Be a dear and do,' said Lydia, brushing away the sultanas she'd picked from the scone. 'And then you go, Mrs Biggins. Your daughter will be expecting you.'

*     *     *

Fortified by the sherry, Lydia decided she'd walk to Xander's. She'd had enough of telephones for the day. She put on her comfortable shoes and chose the cross-country route. It was a warm afternoon. It was about to be June. Passing by the statue of Lord Freddie, Lydia glanced up and said, oh, don't look at me like that, before crossing behind the kitchen garden and along the footpath that skirted the farmland, to the gate in the hedge. Down Bridgeback Hill, noticing blackberries green and tight in the hedgerow and a red kite flying low. She was heartened that they were back, the kites. Such a familiar sight in her childhood and gone from the area for so many years. Lydia steadfastly kept her eyes on Xander's cottage; she didn't want to note whether Miss Gilbey was in or out. She didn't much care where the Georges were. But Miss Gilbey—the thought of Miss Gilbey without 1 Lime Grove Cottages, or that cottage with anyone other than Miss Gilbey in it, was frankly disturbing.

'Well, hullo,' said Xander, wanting to comment on Lydia turning up unannounced and uninvited, but knowing that doing so wittily would meet with short shrift, and remarking upon it in any other way would seem petty and rude. 'Will you come in? Have a cuppa?'

'I was just passing,' said Lydia, though they both knew how unlikely that was.

Xander made tea, wondering if non-brand digestive biscuits would be an affront to Lydia. 'Biscuit?' he asked. She was standing in the middle of the sitting area, one hand gently on the oak pillar, and she appeared to be taking in the surroundings as if seen for the first time.

'You have done a lovely job in here,' she said.

'Well, you paid for it,' said Xander.

'Yes, but you *did* it,' said Lydia. 'You've made it very—homely.'

He wasn't sure what to say. She looked tired, a little disorientated. 'Biscuit?' he offered again. 'They're only digestives, I'm afraid.'

'That would be lovely,' said Lydia, remembering the uneaten scone, the scatter of sultanas strewn on the kitchen table back at the house. Lunch seemed too long ago to remember quite what she'd eaten.

Xander wasn't sure where to seat her. He didn't have a table, per se. Just a long breakfast

217

bar dividing the kitchen area from the sitting area and backless stools which were high and inelegant. The Sunday papers were on the coffee table but these he moved into a pile and gestured to the leather tub chair for Lydia to sit. He poured from a teapot and had decanted milk into a small jug, well remembering Lydia's abhorrence of milk served any other way.

'Goodness me,' said Lydia wryly, 'leafless tea— or is that a magic pot?'

'It's tea bags,' Xander admitted, sheepishly. 'Sorry. But you're very honoured to be having a cup and saucer,' he said, pouring his tea into a mug. 'It's the only one I have.'

Lydia took a sip. It was actually very good. 'They're a marvellous invention, tea bags,' she said. 'And this is a very decent brew.' She took a biscuit; looked at Xander sitting on his sofa, noticed he was in his socks and that they said Tuesday. 'It's Sunday,' she said, raising her eyebrow archly whilst looking down her nose at his feet.

'The right Sunday is holey,' he said.

She looked at him, momentarily perplexed.

'And the left Sunday is lost.'

She pursed her lips, as if to smile at such corniness was unthinkable, but the sparkle in her eyes said otherwise. They sipped in affable silence broken only by the soft munch of digestive biscuits. 'And Xander,' she said, as if they'd been conversing soundlessly, 'how are *you*?'

'I'm very well—busy at work. Running. The usual,' he shrugged.

'Why is there no woman here?' she asked, looking around her as if the heating wasn't on and it was cold and there was a window open

218

somewhere.

'How do you know there isn't a floozy whom I bundled into a cupboard when I saw it was you at the door?' he said.

'Because I know you,' she said. 'And we've been through this before.'

'Is this a pep talk or are you just being nosey?'

Both Lydia and Xander were aware how he could time his impudence so perfectly, speaking to Lydia in a way that no one else dared to but that was OK in the instant.

'Mrs Biggins said there was a rumour you had a young lady,' Lydia said blithely, 'over in Standon.'

God. Siobhan. How had such non-news travelled? He hadn't actually thought about her at all. Seemed so long ago. Slightly unsavoury, to be honest.

'Over and out,' Xander said, refilling their cups.

'You need to make yourself available,' Lydia said. 'I'm sure your mother says the same. If you're always out running, the young ladies won't be bothered to catch up, let alone wait.'

'I'm proud to be a cheetah.'

Lydia looked at him through narrowed eyes. 'Very droll,' she said, witheringly.

'Life's good,' said Xander. 'How are you? Longbridge?'

And, fleetingly, both Xander and Lydia thought of Stella.

'I'm holding a meeting,' she told him, 'to speak to those whom the sale of Longbridge will affect. It's on Wednesday evening. At seven o'clock sharp.'

Xander looked into his mug. Took a thoughtful sip. 'OK,' he said.

'It was my idea,' said Lydia brightly. She placed

219

her teacup on the saucer which she placed carefully on her lap. She looked over to Xander who was dunking a digestive. He looked a little downcast. 'Miss Hutton thinks it's a jolly good idea too,' she told him.

Xander's eyes darted up at her and she caught them like an expert fielder unfazed by a curve ball.

'Well, Miss Hutton would, wouldn't she,' he said.

They held each other's gaze a moment longer until they were released by the sound of a sodden clod of digestive biscuit dropping into his tea.

## Chapter Nineteen

Stella's mum came to babysit on Wednesday because, though Will had pleaded to come with her, Stella had said it was a school night and anyway the meeting would be boring and there wouldn't be biscuits. Will gave her strict instructions to bring home any if there were, and to tell an elaborate white lie if the pilfered napkin was mentioned. Sandie told her daughter to drive carefully, not to rush back and not to worry about anything at all. It might end with a good old shindig, her mother said. You might have fun. Stella doubted very much whether the tone would lighten beyond sombre, let alone loosen enough for cross-class socializing and merrymaking in the drawing room. She'd be leaving as soon as the meeting was over; she didn't want to be lynched by the mob and she certainly didn't want to cross paths with Xander. That he would be there was a given, but surely the gravity of the evening would deflect his memory from recalling the last time he'd seen her—

and the presence of so many others would enable her to acknowledge him politely and fleetingly. She'd just nod cordially. And if he became the spokesman for the Voices of Dissent, then she'd simply address the rabble as a whole.

Stella had arrived early, as asked. The meeting wasn't in the drawing room, it was to be in the dining room and suddenly the whole thing seemed imposingly formal. Glasses of water had been poured and plates of the lightest, crescent-shaped biscuits made with ground almonds and dusted with Mrs Biggins' ubiquitous icing sugar, were placed on plates with doilies up and down the long table. Lydia was to sit at the head of the table, in a capacious dark mahogany dining chair, with maroon leather attached by a run of small brass studs to the seat and back. The other chairs around the table were the same—but without arms. Next to Lydia's place, a simple folding chair for Stella, like a pianist's page-turner. Fundamental, but to be inconspicuous. If every seat was taken, that would be twenty-one including her.

'Are you happy with what you need to say and how you're going to say it?' Stella asked Lydia, who regarded her witheringly. 'Is there anything you'd like me to say or do?' Stella continued, unabashed.

'You will sit alongside me—as my representative. And if I look to you, then speak. If not, please don't.'

It was hard not to feel insulted, belittled. But Stella nodded and excused herself. She didn't need the loo, just a private moment to steel herself, to look herself straight in the eye and say, it's just her manner, the old battleaxe—you know by now what she's like.

She'd been in there a while, heard the bell at the front door clang a few times; Mrs Biggins saying 'Lovely' at regular intervals, a quiet thrum of voices. On the closed toilet seat, Stella sat and thought, I am really quite out of my depth. Her uncle had told her not to comment on anything beyond the remit of her being there on behalf of Elmfield Estates. She was to say, 'Lady Lydia will consult her solicitor,' or 'This is a matter for further discussion,' or 'Thank you for bringing this to our attention.' If she was unsure of how to answer, she was to say, 'We will look into it and report back.' She nodded at herself in the mirror, drew herself tall from the back of her head as her few Alexander Technique sessions had taught her. Quietly, she practised the various responses. *We will look into it and report back.* That's the one she anticipated quoting the most.

'We'll look into it and report back.'

She nodded sagely at herself. Then she frowned.

'No! *I'll* look into it and report back.' She tried that again. *'I'll look into it and report back.'*

She went over the phrases, putting them firmly into the first person, and practised them, softly, with different inflections.

'Thank you for bringing this to my attention,' she said, winking at herself in the mirror as she unlocked the door, jiggled the tricksy handle. 'I'll look into it and report back,' she said. And she opened the door to find Xander, arms crossed, standing right outside.

*       *       *

Flabbergasted and mortified; telltale redness crept

222

up from her chest to her neck.

'You're not drunk again, are you?' Xander said.

Stella didn't know how long he'd been standing outside, but obviously the old wooden door was not as thick as she thought and he'd heard a lot. 'Or is that a *matter for further discussion*?' Speechless, she could only stare at him. But in doing so, she noticed he wasn't being hostile; in fact, he was smiling.

Hostile, Stella thought, would have been a whole lot less humiliating and easier to deal with.

'I didn't need the loo—that's why you heard no flush.' Her response sounded beyond ridiculous and only compounded his comment that she might be pissed. 'Of course I'm not drunk,' she said huffily. Then she stopped. Actually, she had no right to be affronted by the accusation—and Xander, truthfully, was in line for an apology. Neither of them had moved. She was looking down, darting her eyes from her shoes to his, wondering what to say next that would shift the power back and not sound too contrite. She looked up and he cocked his head, waiting. What was she meant to say? Just say something quickly—make it a statement that warrants no response! She straightened a little and crossed her arms too.

'I'm, er, just wanted to—you know—for you to know, for me to say, I'm extremely sorry about the other week.'

'Sorry?'

'Not just sorry,' she qualified, 'grateful. Embarrassed.'

'Oh,' he said, as if the penny had only just dropped, '*that*.' He made it seem as if he'd meant 'Sorry' as in 'Pardon me'.

She gave him her best pained smile but her

223

sentiment was genuine. 'I'm mortified,' she said. 'But want to say thank you for—helping.'

'Any time,' he said.

'Oh, I don't make a habit of it,' she rushed. 'I was just nervous and I stupidly mixed my drinks.' She shuddered at the vague memories now taunting her. 'Anyway—sorry. And thanks.'

Xander shrugged. 'No problem.'

But they stood where they were.

'OK,' said Stella.

'OK,' said Xander.

And there they continued to stand.

'You have a nice home,' he said.

'Thank you—you do too,' she replied.

'Mine's rented,' he said, with a barb.

'So's mine,' she batted back.

Another pause.

'It's just I need the loo,' he said, at length.

'Oh!' said Stella, moving aside. 'Of course! Sorry.'

He closed the door, saying 'Bye' slightly awkwardly as he did so.

Stella knocked her head gently against the opposite wall.

'Everything all right?' said Lydia, suddenly appearing from goodness knows where.

'Yes,' said Stella, noting Mrs Biggins disappearing as if she'd been there all the while. 'Alexander Technique,' she added. 'Sort of.' And she gave the wall another knock with her head, as if she was giving a display, while Lydia regarded her with her eyebrows fixed high.

It seemed to Stella quite irretrievable that Lydia obviously now considered her quite the most peculiar young woman she'd ever come across. But,

224

to Stella's relief, Lydia chose not to comment. Her eyebrows had said it all anyway.

'Come along, Miss Hutton,' she sighed, walking ahead, 'people have taken their seats.'

\*　　　\*　　　\*

Watched sternly by the Fortescue ancestors presiding over the meeting from their lofty position on the walls behind gilded frames, as if in private boxes at the theatre, the current people of Longbridge asked questions one by one that really all amounted to the same thing: what would happen to either their jobs or homes—or, in the case of Art and a couple of others, their jobs *and* homes—and how much notice would they be given.

There was no raising of voices, no frayed tempers, no simmering discontent. Instead, there was a resigned air and the mood was sad but sensible and biddable. Stella found she needed to say little. Lydia handled herself superbly, calling people by their Christian names and speaking to them with direct eye contact and a softness to her voice. In fact, sometimes her voice cracked a little—and this display of her own emotion was both canny and appreciated.

Sitting by Lydia's side, listening carefully, pleased to have been able to put so many new faces to names she already knew, Stella made notes on her pad about who belonged where and what their concerns were. She was intrigued by Clarence—old yet huge, a gentle but obvious presence like the bass drum in an orchestra. Sitting beside him, Miss Gilbey looked like a harvest mouse in a dress. She wanted to know what would happen to all the soft furnishings at Longbridge and at 1 Lime Grove Cottages. Would they be included in the sale? She was wearing white gloves and a hat with a silk flower on the band. Xander sat at the opposite end of the table, next to Mrs Biggins, and Stella found many reasons not to look down there.

He spoke just the once, repeating what he'd asked Lydia privately already. 'Is there no solution other than to sell?'

'The fact of the matter is, I have to sell Longbridge because I cannot afford to live here,' said Lydia to the group. Many looked astonished. 'It's a sign of the times,' she said. And she looked down and across to Stella's lap, on which her clipboard of notes rested. 'It's sad for us all.' There was a heavy silence.

Dave and Dan informed her that they'd already started looking—and if they found somewhere, would she hold them to the three-month notice period.

'My cat is very old and confused,' said Mr Tringle. Lydia nodded and others smiled benevolently; how Mr Tringle would cope with the upheaval of moving was much more of a worry than the senility of his cat.

'Do you want us out—now?' asked the wiry cabinet maker who rented one of the workshops. 'Can we not hold on—at least see if the new owner wants us? If they don't, then we go?' Stella looked at her lap. It was horribly sad. People felt the sale defined them. That they might be seen as unwanted chattels. That their presence could somehow adversely affect the desirability of Longbridge.

'You could put our rent up?' It was Miss Gilbey herself who suddenly piped up.

226

'We're attractive as tenants, surely?' said Doreen Hutchins. 'The majority of us are—mature. We're responsible. These are homes that we have cared for. The new owner might like that—less for them to worry about.'

'But if Lydia puts our rent up, but still sells, maybe they'll hike it even higher,' said Len, worrying.

Lydia cleared her voice. 'So much is unknown, but I simply want to keep you informed even at this very early stage. And I promise you will be kept abreast of all developments.' She paused. 'I am sorry. I wish you well. I will help you as much as I can. But Longbridge is to be sold. I have made my mind up.

'Right!' she said, to break it, to gather back her steeliness as if it had been a shawl which had slipped. 'If that's all?'

'I have a question,' said Clarence, his voice a low roll, like morning mist tumbling quietly over fields.

'Yes, Clarence?'

'Never mind us,' he said, 'but *you*. What about *you*? Where will you *go*?'

Stella felt a chill zip through her.

She hadn't once asked Lydia this.

It actually hadn't occurred to her to do so.

How unprofessional. Worse—how insensitive.

There was an awkward silence and Stella glanced to Lydia who was dumbstruck.

*Thank you for bringing this to my attention*, Stella wanted to interject.

*I'll look into this first thing tomorrow.*

'Don't you worry about me, Clarence,' she heard Lydia say. 'I'll be fine.' Lydia paused. 'Downsizing, I think they call it.'

A chuckle spread like the relief of a cool breeze in enervating heat.

'I'll be absolutely fine,' Lydia repeated.

Stella looked around the table. Everyone was looking at Lydia. Everyone's eyes said, are you sure?

Actually, not everyone. Everyone but one person. Xander. He wasn't looking at Lydia. He was looking directly at Stella. And Lydia herself of course. When Stella managed to look away from Xander, she found Lydia was looking straight down the table at him.

\* \* \*

People didn't loiter. For those whose connection with the estate was longstanding, it felt like an ill wind; as if Longbridge was suddenly crumbling around them and they needed to get home, to shore up their places to weather the storm they now knew was approaching. For those who rented barn space for businesses, there was no time to waste; they needed to be Googling for commercial rentals in the area, registering on websites. Art, who already knew of Lydia's proposal, just wanted to get home. Miss Gilbey's neighbours, the Georges, were keen to be going as they had a babysitter and wanted to maximize their time with an unrushed meal at the Black Ox. Mrs Biggins wanted them all gone so she could clear up. And Lydia had a headache and didn't want it to show.

When Stella went to her car, she was taken aback by the constant crunch of gravel, by so many vehicles circling to leave, like a pod of dolphins

228

surrounding a shoal. When she'd arrived, apart from Lydia's old Vauxhall, hers had been the only car there. In fact in all her visits, she'd never seen any other cars—just Art and his crew with wheelbarrows or atop the ride-on mower. It had compounded the feeling of Longbridge being in a time warp of its own. Tonight was different— just an old house looking slightly out of place in a new age. It seemed undignified, somehow. Disrespectful. All that revving, the need to be gone. And where oh where were her bloody keys?

\*       \*       \*

'So did he call again?'

Stella turned. It was Xander, some way off, now the only person on the driveway.

Her hand was still deep inside her bag. 'Pardon?'

He walked a few steps towards her, hands in his pockets, head to one side, stopped again, keeping his distance, the setting sun brushing against one side of his face while sepia shadows settled over the other. 'Your date—the other week. Did he call again?'

Stella wondered how to answer a question she'd never anticipated being asked by this particular person. 'Would you have called?' she remarked finally, humble and slightly incredulous. 'If you'd taken out some girl who couldn't see straight let alone stand, who'd made an utter show of herself and had wasted your evening?'

'I avoid such situations like the plague,' Xander said, only now wondering why, when he'd seen her head for her car, he'd slowed his walk right down. Why converse? He could have just called 'Bye'. He

229

could have kept going. He could have said nothing at all.

'Well,' Stella answered him, 'I do too, usually.' He nodded. 'But everyone's always going on at me—and my sister-in-law set it up. I suppose I went to shut her up.' And I should shut up, myself, right now.

'And now you've brought shame upon your family,' Xander said grandly, with a wry smile.

'Indeed,' Stella laughed. 'I think they'll think twice, in future, so that's no bad thing.'

'I tripped a girl up once, on one of those types of date,' he said. 'Accidentally,' he added, scratching his head.

'Accidentally on purpose?'

'No!' He couldn't help laughing at her turn of phrase. 'Well—maybe subconsciously.' He cringed at the memory. 'She went flying.'

'Nightmare,' Stella muttered.

'There was blood,' Xander said.

'That's dreadful!' Stella gasped. 'Sorry—I shouldn't laugh. Poor woman.'

Xander nodded and they watched each other biting their lips because laughter is so tempting when it's most inappropriate. They just stood there, him a little way off, her still with her hand in her bag now with the keys firmly in her clasp. They watched as Art and Clarence sloped off homewards across the lawn; Clarence patted Art's shoulder before they went their separate ways.

'I'm not usually like that,' Stella said.

'Like what?'

'Sloshed and incapacitated.' She shrugged. 'Sorry again.'

'It wasn't a problem,' said Xander. And then he

230

said, 'I'm just glad I found you.'

Stella was struck by his words and it was physical. All this time she'd been mortified that he'd done precisely that—but now she knew how grateful she was that he had.

'Keys,' she said shyly, which sounded stupid and was all the more stupid for her jiggling them at him for proof.

'Goodnight, then,' he said and he started to walk away.

Stella opened her door and then she paused. And, on a surge of adrenalin that made her speak before thinking, she called after him. 'Would you like a lift home?'

They stood where they were, both of them feeling as fixed as the statue of Lord Frederick, peeping at them a little way off through a gap in the laurels.

'OK,' Xander shrugged. 'Thanks.' But though he'd turned, he didn't move.

His awkwardness relaxed Stella. 'Are you wanting me to drive over to you? Door-to-door service, is it?'

Though he laughed, he still made a slightly faltering passage over to her car while she busied about, chucking today's unopened post, yesterday's empty crisp packet and Will's Bionicle into the back from the front seat.

Xander seemed so big in her car. He appeared to fill it, his presence so marked. Though he was tall, he was not incredibly so, but still he had to ratchet the seat back.

You'd have squashed Will's legs, Stella thought to herself. Will would have something to say about that, she thought. And then she thought how neither she nor Will had ever been in this car with a man. Not this car. The old car—the Land Rover she'd had to sell—yes. Charlie, of course. God, how grim car journeys could be with his constant sniping at her driving and his authority over which radio station. She looked at Xander.

'Have you enough room?'

'Plenty,' he said. And actually, he didn't look squashed at all. Just big. Manly was the word that came to her mind and it made Stella both blush and cringe.

And that's all they said. Xander didn't comment when Stella unnecessarily indicated to turn from the turning circle entrance onto the main run of driveway, nor when she didn't indicate to turn right onto the high street. He could sense she was nervous but he couldn't think of what to say to make her less so because, actually, he couldn't think of anything to say because he felt nervous too. Not in a tense way, but, oddly, in a shy way.

The journey lasted all of five minutes.

'Thanks,' he said, opening the door. He stood for a moment then stooped, as if he might well get back in.

Are you rushing off anywhere?

Do you want to park up and have a half at the pub?

Would you like to come in for a drink?

A coffee?

Her hand on the gear stick, engine running, seat belt on.

'Thanks,' he said again.

'No problem,' she said again.

He closed the door, tapped the roof of the car and walked off down his garden path.

232

Are you going to turn at the door?

Are you going to wave?

Are you going to look back—even for a second?

No.

He simply went into his house.

'Bye, Xander,' Stella said, a little deflated but knowing that thinking too much about why that should be was probably not a good idea.

*       *       *

'Do you want anything for that headache?' Mrs Biggins asked Lydia.

'No—just an early night will do it.'

'Very good. Will that be all?'

'Yes, thank you. You were most helpful this evening.'

'For what it's worth, I think it went well.'

'It's going according to plan, I do believe.'

'They call it a frisson,' said Mrs Biggins, relishing the word, 'in those paperbacks from the library I like to read.'

'I was thinking more of *Pinocchio*,' Lydia mused. 'How what once were puppets come to life, take responsibility and figure out the adventure for themselves.'

'They try not to look at each other—'

'—and when they do, they don't realize how long they're at it.'

'It went well,' said Mrs Biggins.

'All will be well,' said Lydia.

'And the meeting went well.'

'And the meeting went as well as can be expected. Goodnight, Mrs Biggins.'

'Good night, Lady Lydia.'

\*       \*       \*

'Is Will asleep?'

'Yes, darling—about half an hour ago.'

Stella looked disappointed.

'How did it go?'

'It was fine, actually, Mum. Odd really—I was expecting all manner of discord and malcontent. But it was very civilized.'

'Biscuits for Will?'

'Shit, I forgot.'

'I hope you don't kiss your son with that mouth?'

'Of course not.'

'Well, I'll be off.'

'Thanks so much.'

'Any time, darling. Any time. You know that. You should get out more. But you know that too.'

'I know.'

'Are you OK?'

'Yes?'

'You suddenly look a little—I'm not sure how you look. Distracted?'

'I'm fine.'

'Something on your mind?'

'No, no—I'm just pooped. Thanks, Mum. See you Sunday.'

\*       \*       \*

'How did it go?'

'Hi, Caroline.'

'That bad?'

'No—I just spent most of the day on the phone.'

'Shall I call tomorrow, then, instead?'

234

'No, you're fine. How are you? Is Andrew back?'

'Working late.'

'Tell him—pub tomorrow night.'

'Bugger off—I'm out with the girls.'

'Friday night then.'

'We're out for dinner. You're the babysitter, remember?'

'Oh, yes. Sure. Of course. No problem.'

'So how did it go?'

*  *  *

He could tell her.

Of all the people in his life, Caroline was the person Xander really could turn to. He could tell her, I'm confused, I thought I loathed her but I like her. She stirs something in me and I don't know what. He could tell her, I've been sitting here thinking about her for half an hour straight, feeling charmed, feeling intrigued, feeling confused, feeling horny. I should be feeling outraged and frustrated that she's bulldozing Longbridge and running roughshod over any lives in the way. Guilty. Turned on. Just weird.

He could admit to Caroline, I don't know what to make of it all. He could say, why her? He could admit to Caroline, I wrote a text to bloody Siobhan to say fancy a fuck. Because Stella's left me horny and Stella's on my mind and I don't want anything complicating my life. And he could tell Caroline, but I didn't send the text. In fact, I deleted it. He could say, it's not Siobhan I want. It's not just sex, not now. And he could ask Caroline, what shall I do? He could ask her, if I said to Stella, would you like to meet up, what do

235

you think she'd say?

Caroline would tell him what to do. Caroline would be honest with him. Caroline always knew what to do. She'd been right about Laura—as painful as it had sounded at the time and as excruciating as the outcome had been. Caroline had been right. And she'd been right about Siobhan. In fact, in retrospect, it would have been no bad thing if she'd known about all of that much earlier on and given him an honest, outspoken piece of her caring mind.

'It went fine,' Xander said.

'Good turnout?'

'Packed.'

'Everyone OK?'

'Yes, actually.'

'Was, you know, Stella there?'

'Yes. Yes. She was there.'

'Was she OK?'

'Yes, she's fine.'

'I'll tell Andrew you called.'

'Cool.'

'See you Friday.'

'She gave me a lift home. Stella.'

'Oh, right?'

'I was going to ask her in for coffee but—I don't know. I didn't.'

Caroline thought, go gently here. 'Maybe next time, hey?'

'Maybe. See you Friday, Cazza.'

'Ta-ta, Xander.'

Caroline hung up the phone. Well! she thought. Well!

# Chapter Twenty

Interest in Longbridge came in much the same way as the hot water in the taps in the upper floor of the house—a trickle, a gush, apparently nothing, a trickle. Stella, who considered herself a very poor judge of character when it came to husbands, was nonetheless excellent at sorting potential clients from time-wasting nosey parkers. Those who phoned her with excessively rounded vowels and choice adverbs such as 'frightfully' and 'awfully' she knew to be phoneys whom she humoured by sending the particulars but stalled making viewings. They might feign the appropriate accent and vocabulary, but that didn't fool her. There were three clients already on her book she trusted to waste neither her time nor Lydia's. Mostly, however, potential buyers came to her via high-end property-search agents. That's how she came to take Florian and Jessamy Virenque to Longbridge, and the Hakshimi family. But Mr and Mrs Tompkins broke the mould. Longbridge had been in the Saturday *Telegraph*, the *Sunday Times* and *Country Life* that week—and that's how the Tompkins had come by Stella. When they came into the office on spec, though Gill sniggered and Geoff looked aghast, Stella felt she might well have found her buyers. They were honest, artless and obviously incredibly wealthy. They weren't social climbers, they were very steady. Most importantly, they weren't remotely like Lydia.

Mrs Tompkins was bedecked with an extraordinary array of bling—only Stella doubted whether the real thing could be called bling. It was difficult to age her, on account of her immovable facial features, but her hands suggested to Stella she was late forties. Her husband had obviously been playing a lot of golf, given his burnished complexion and expensively casual clothing. Some people look cheap and smell expensive, others smell expensive and look cheap but, to Stella, this couple spared no expense on looking and smelling the way they did. She could practically detect the scent of fine Italian leather lingering on their clothes from the seats of the Bentley in the car park.

'Come to see Miss Stella 'utton,' said Mr Tompkins, sounding like Bill Sykes.

''Bout the house,' said his wife and her Estuary inflection made it sound like she'd said 'Bat the hass'.

'The big 'un,' he said, lest Stella should be unsure which.

'This way, please,' said Stella, unruffled, while Gill snorted and Geoff thought she'd lost her mind. Her uncle was out—but he and Stella had previously agreed that, should he be in, she had only to knock and request privacy in his office and he would vacate immediately and perch awhile at her desk. She handed them each a copy of the particulars which they pored over, cooing and tutting.

'Have you somewhere to sell?' Stella asked.

'Over Northaw way,' Mr Tompkins said.

'Would you need to sell that, to fund a purchase?' Stella asked in a casually tactful tone, whilst nodding enthusiastically at the photograph of the lily pond which Mrs Tompkins was tapping

238

at, with a finger manicured to perfection in deep aubergine.

'Nah,' said Mr Tompkins. 'Property market's dead on its feet—we'll put our place on but if it don't sell, it don't sell.'

'And if you do decide to sell, I'd be thrilled to be considered,' said Stella. They both nodded at her and smiled with pristine, blue-white teeth.

'And a viewing,' Stella said, 'when would that be convenient? Weekends? Outside of office hours?'

Mr Tompkins stroked his BlackBerry as if it had a heart and feelings. 'This baby's me office,' he said.

'Lucky you!' Stella said.

He looked genuinely upset. 'It's not just luck, love—it's all down to blimmin' hard work too.'

'Oh, I meant no offence.' Stella leant forward and whispered, 'I hate working in an office—having to smell other people's bacon butties and tuna sarnies and listen to them drone on about the weekend they've just had or the night out they're going on.'

The Tompkins laughed and Mr Tompkins nodded energetically. 'Both our kids done work experience in offices, building sites—hard graft. They got to feel it—really *feel* it. When they was nippers, their mates thought they had a great house, with a great pool—and a right old sod of a dad.' He started chuckling, turned to his wife. 'Do you remember?' He wiped tears of mirth from the outer corner of his eyes. 'Right old sod of a dad.'

Stella looked a little unsettled. Mrs Tompkins came to her rescue. 'Our kids—they got a lot less pocket money than their friends, you see.'

'Made 'em work for it. Had to sweep leaves, or wash the cars. Something or other, every weekend,

239

for a quid or two.'

'And now?' Stella asked.

'Super kids.' His eyes brimmed again. 'Classy, you know? And kind. One at university, one just finished and looking for a job. Good kids—aren't they?' He turned to his wife who leant forward with her iPhone and scrolled through frame after frame depicting the smiling, open faces of a girl and a boy.

'Well,' said Stella, 'if it's work experience they want, they can come here and make the tea and do the photocopying.'

Mr Tompkins sat back in the chair and regarded her quizzically. 'I like you, I do. And I'd like to see Longbridge Hall. And it'll be you that takes us there, will it?'

'Indeed,' said Stella. 'I'll speak to Lady Lydia Fortescue and see when suits.'

Lady Lydia Fortescue! the Tompkins murmured nodding at each other as if Lady Lydia Fortescue was a value added bonus that might well swing the purchase.

'Perhaps some time later this week?' said Stella.

'Look forward to it,' he said, filling in forms while his wife smiled at the photos on her phone.

\*       \*       \*

Lydia continued to make it plain that she didn't care a jot who bought Longbridge and she was out when Stella brought the Billington-Wildes for their viewing. However, the silent conversation which passed between Stella and Mrs Biggins, mainly through rolling of eyes, pursing of lips and raising of eyebrows, said that it was a good job that she wasn't in. They'd double-barrelled their

240

surname by deed poll online, they told her. They were Lottery winners. They had the money—they had cash. They liked the thought of a house like Longbridge—buying a bit of history and class—but reality let their preconceptions down sharply. Their dismay was barely concealed.

'No dressing rooms? Only one en-suite—and it doesn't have a separate shower area, let alone a walk-in one?'

'I'm not paying good new money for old tat.'

'It's just so—*second-hand*,' Mrs Billington-Wilde complained.

'Actually,' connived Stella with a wink to Mrs Biggins unseen by the clients, 'it's ninth-hand.'

The woman shuddered, as if she'd been forced into some moth-eaten coat picked up from a jumble sale.

'I think,' said Stella, 'you might prefer buying a plot of land and building a dream house to your own specifications.'

They looked at her as if she was an oracle and then went, declining the opportunity to look around the grounds.

*    *    *

Lydia was in when the Hakshimis came to visit. Only it wasn't them, it was a representative who simply nodded at Lydia just as he nodded when anything was pointed out to him. He nodded at the statue of Lord Fortescue, he nodded at Art who kept on wheelbarrowing regardless. It was hard to reconcile what is commonly thought of as a positive gesture when it was accompanied by such an emotionless face. Even Stella's deluge of detail and delight for the thatched apple store met with no more than a single up-down motion of the man's head. Lydia phoned her later that day.

'Soul destroying,' she said, 'and an utter waste of time.'

'He's come back with an offer of eleven million,' said Stella.

*     *     *

It was Wednesday night. She'd be taking the Tompkins to Longbridge the next afternoon. Jo had come over for the evening, with tortilla chips, all manner of dips and a dense variety of topics to chat about.

'God,' she said, 'this time last week I was in Paris.'

'This time last week, I was right here, on this very seat—but without the Doritos and chat.'

'You need to get out more,' Jo said, with a laugh tempered by a joking-aside look.

'That's what my mum says,' said Stella. And then she thought, actually I wasn't sitting here this time last week—I was at Longbridge, at the meeting. And then she thought, Xander. And as soon as that thought had alighted, it was accompanied by a zip of adrenalin which surged through her body, its force giving her quite a shock.

'The salsa's not that hot!' Jo laughed, noting how flushed Stella suddenly looked; her mouth agape, a Dorito resting over her tongue like a sacramental wafer.

Stella chewed, swallowing with difficulty. Sipped at the wine.

'Stella?'

She looked at Jo. 'I wasn't here.'

'When?'

'A week ago—it was the night of the meeting at Longbridge.'

'Right,' said Jo, munching away. 'So?' She regarded Stella, now as pale on the spectrum as previously she'd been scarlet. 'What's wrong, babes? Suddenly twigged where the secret passage might be? Just remembered pocketing a silver cake fork? The Ghost of Longbridge haunting you?'

'I.'

'Aye?'

'I,' said Stella, flabbergasted. 'I've met someone.'

They sat and stared at each other for a moment, trying to make sense of what Stella had just said—words neither of them expected to hear from Stella's mouth any time soon, let alone just now. But the words were out there now, unequivocally. It was as if they'd suddenly surfaced in Stella's head, swum straight out of her mouth and were now right there in front of them, brand new, dripping wet and in need of someone to do something to protect them.

'Who?' said Jo. '*Who*!'

'Xander,' said Stella, incredulous.

'*Who the hell is Xander?*'

'The awful one—the argumentative one. The one who sent me flying the very first time I went to Long Dansbury. The one who threatened me and almost knocked me over in the garden—you know, Jo, the running jogging man. The one who hates estate agents. The one who loathes me.'

'The one who saw you drunk as a skunk after that blind date with Global Riley?'

Jo looked at Stella. Her face was pale. Her neck looked like corned beef.

'You're not selling him very well, I have to say,' said Jo, wracking her brains for someone else—anyone—she could pair Stella with.

'I know,' said Stella, laughing uncontrollably. 'What am I going to do?'

'What is there to like?'

Stella thought about it. 'Passion,' she said, 'and awkwardness.'

'I don't follow.' Jo did not like the sound of the man at all. Perhaps Stella should phone Riley. That bloody house—it was taking up too much of her time.

'He's passionate about Lydia and Longbridge—he grew up there. But there's a shyness, an awkwardness to him. When I took him home—'

'*You took him home*?'

'Gave him a lift,' Stella qualified. 'And when I squeezed past him and I looked up and he looked down—'

'When did all this squeezing and gazing go on?' Where had Jo been, she wondered, while Stella was falling for this man?

'When he took me upstairs to his old place.'

'*What*?' Jo was now as lost as Stella had been on her first visit to Longbridge. 'Can you just backtrack, please, and tell me how so many events, which hadn't even registered before you ate a spicy Dorito, are suddenly so momentous and portentous?'

Stella shrugged and grinned and her eyes danced and she had guacamole on her chin. 'I don't know!' she laughed. 'I have no idea!'

Jo remembered when Stella had first told

244

her about Charlie, how she spoke in all these carefully structured statements; essential facts and information organized into a compelling portrait, analysed her emotions cogently. Stella had delivered all of it in a rousing soliloquy. Tonight, though, it was just a tumble of disjointed anecdotes and a deluge of unstructured feelings. However, as much as it was bizarre, it was also moving and contagious. Soon enough, Jo knew about the photographs of the various marathons and races, about the lack of curtains in the bedroom. She was told about his slate-navy eyes and the scatter of chest hair. And the mud on his strong legs. Jo heard everything they'd ever said to each other as well as the loaded silence in her car. Oh, and he has this really nice friend— Caroline. She's cool. And all about his eyes (again) and the lingering gaze from the other end of Lydia's dining-room table. And his passion (again) and how Stella believed that made him a worthy man (conjecture). And he's single and he doesn't do dates (fact, apparently).

'Just like you.'

'Just like me.'

'Are you sure?' said Jo. 'That you truly feel these things.'

Stella looked at her and shrugged. 'I feel *something*,' she said, thoughtfully. 'It just feels good to feel strong, *positive* emotions, rather than suffocatingly negative ones.'

'No news from Charlie, then?'

Stella shook her head.

'I've a new word for him,' said Jo. 'Twunt.'

Stella giggled. Then she groaned. 'What shall I do?' she asked Jo. 'I know Longbridge now—and

245

the cottages. And the meeting's been and gone. There's nothing imminent at which our paths might cross again.'

'You could call him?'

'I don't have his number.'

'You could knock on his door?'

Stella considered it. And then, with a thud which pulled her down visibly in her seat, she tried to imagine walking up his path, knocking on his door, saying, hullo, Xander, just wondered whether you might like to have a drink with me. And she knew how she'd never have the courage to do any of that. The thought of it alone was terrifying. And then she thought, I'm deluded and stupid.

'It's just a crush,' she said quietly, feeling crushed. 'I *imagined* the attraction. It's probably not there. It's probably not mutual. Why would it be?'

Jo thought about that. She thought about how, if that were the case, her friend was safe. But then she thought about Xander and suddenly saw Stella through his eyes—all uppity with her clipboard, or wide-eyed over some old building, or mortified after her monologue in the loo. Stroppy back at his stroppiness. Gazing up as he gazed down. He'd've seen those amber flecks in her eyes. And he'd've seen how she is with Will. How she handles Lydia. How funny and cuddly she is when she's drunk. How she stands her ground when she's cross. And how dreamy she can become in a moment. And Jo thought, if I was Xander and I'd seen even this little of Stella and who she is—I'd want her.

'If I was Xander,' said Jo, 'I'd have a crush on you.'

Stella tipped her head to one side. 'Would you

246

call me? If you were Xander?'

'Would I have your number?'

Stella shook her head. 'But you know where I live.'

'But I think you think I'm an arrogant sod.'

'But I took you home.'

'And I was too shy to ask you in, to ask you out.'

'You're not shy, you're stroppy.'

'I was shy that night. I stumbled over my feet in the car park and stumbled over my words before I got to your car. I couldn't think what to say on the journey—it was so short.'

'What would you like me to do?' Stella stopped. 'You—Jo. What would you like to see me do?'

'Trust your instincts.' Jo was definite.

'They took a bashing.'

'Don't tar him—or anyone, for that matter—with Charlie's brush. Go with your gut feelings.'

'I don't know what the etiquette is, these days. In your mid-thirties, what are the rules?'

'They're bollocks, that's what they are,' said Jo. 'You're a grown-up. You have a history, you've loved, lost, before. You're a mother. You're single-handed. You've weathered a divorce. You're more experienced—and probably more canny—than you realize.'

'I don't have his number,' Stella said. 'Otherwise I could send a text.'

'You'll be in his neck of the woods tomorrow,' said Jo.

'Maybe I'll see him around.'

'And if he doesn't appear to be around, you know where he lives—go and see if there's a light on.'

# Chapter Twenty-One

'She's sat in her car,' Mrs Biggins told Lydia, bringing in coffee.

'I know,' said Lydia, not looking up, 'I can see.'

She was busy writing cards at the bureau in the library. The two of them looked across to the driveway where they could clearly see Stella, sitting quietly behind the wheel of her car.

'Who's this lot, then?' Mrs Biggins asked.

'I don't ask the names—Miss Hutton tells me, but I don't commit them to memory. She's told me not to be put off by the way the people coming today present themselves. Whatever that means.'

'Well, you *can* be judgemental,' murmured Mrs Biggins.

'I have every right to be,' said Lydia, affronted.

'No, you don't,' said Mrs Biggins in a sing-song voice as she left the room and went out to Stella to ask whether she'd like a cuppa brought to her car.

'Dreadful woman,' Lydia muttered, observing Mrs Biggins over her half-moon glasses. And then an enormous black brute of a car appeared, gliding its way up the drive like a bison on wheels before pulling to a standstill askew.

'Never is that a Bentley!' Lydia hissed. 'What a travesty!'

When she saw the Tompkins emerge, she clapped her hand to her forehead and thought, oh dear God, no. Mrs Tompkins looked as if she was off to audition for *Strictly Come Dancing* and Mr Tompkins looked like a tall version of that funny little chap in *Only Fools and Horses*.

A beige V-necked top with nothing underneath and a chunky necklace which, caught by the sun, appeared to be winking coarsely over to where Lydia sat unseen. Above the fireplace, her great-great-grandmother looked at her sternly as if to say, it takes all types, Lydia dear. You should know that.

Lydia watched them stand on the driveway, the woman putting on enormous sunglasses which surely only people undergoing major eye surgery would be unfortunate enough to have to wear. And the man—the man was looking at the house while he was on the phone! How very vulgar! And just look, he's patting Stella on the shoulder as though she's a paper boy or a dog! How terribly rude!

They were craning their necks and Stella was obviously speaking nineteen to the dozen, using sweeping arm gestures for emphasis. Oh, get back in the house, Mrs Biggins, lest any of them should think you somehow have greater significance to me and my house than is rightly yours. But Mrs Biggins led the party into the entrance hallway. Stella was discoursing enthusiastically about fanlights and the woman was saying, yeah? oh yeah? oh yeah? But at least it gave Lydia a moment to soundlessly shoo Mrs Biggins away and to take an imposing position in the staircase hall, under the circular roof lantern above.

'Aha!' Stella exclaimed with hushed reverence, smiling at Lydia as if stage curtains had suddenly gone back to reveal the *pièce de résistance* of Longbridge Hall. 'Lady Lydia!' She turned to the Tompkins who were gawping at Lydia. 'This is Lady Lydia Fortescue. Lady Lydia Fortescue—this is Mr and Mrs Tompkins.'

'Pleased, I'm sure!' Mrs Tompkins said,

extending a hand bejewelled on every finger. Lydia declined to take it.

Mr Tompkins stepped forward. 'Pleased to meet you,' he said, clasping her hand in both of his and giving it a good shake. 'What a bloody gorgeous house you have.'

Later, Lydia would muse over this—how someone who initially repelled her could win her over so quickly. It wasn't so much his sentiment as his choice of words which melted her icy preconceptions and broke the password she'd subconsciously set. Never mind the accent. Regardless of the fulmination. His words were simply artless and so sincere. And, thought Lydia, so very true. 'Thank you,' she said. And then, to Stella's surprise, she drew herself tall and spoke with a booming voice. 'Welcome to Longbridge Hall!'

Lydia led the way, side by side with Mr Tompkins, while Stella and Mrs Tompkins followed behind. 'The drawing room,' she announced. 'I'll have you know, this wallpaper is one hundred and twenty years old.' She looked Mr Tompkins up and down. 'Would you be so kind as to remove that painting?' She gestured to a framed, delicate Chinese painting of a heron. He lifted it away from the wall. 'That has hung there since the War. And just look—not a fade mark to be seen.' She turned to Mrs Tompkins. 'They don't make paper like *that* any more.' Lydia sat down on the sofa and her reminiscences poured out. 'Mother brought back some divine paper from a trip to America,' she said. 'It was blue, with a design in silver. Real silver leaf. Only it tarnished on the boat journey over. She still put it up though—in what was the smoking

250

room. I imagine it's still there, if you peeled back the modern layers.' She focused on Mrs Tompkins. 'Just imagine,' she said, *real silver.*'

Mrs Tompkins, who was now sitting opposite, nodded earnestly. 'We've got real suede on some of our walls. Purple, it is.'

Stella held her breath, willing Lydia not to respond too spikily.

'How very brave of you,' she said and to Stella's relief, Mrs Tompkins had graciously taken this as a compliment. They sat for a while—Mr and Mrs Tompkins and Lady Lydia, while Stella remained standing—and Lydia told them of her family's history with the house. 'Great-Grandmother loathed it,' she said. 'But from what I've been told, everyone loathed Great-Grandmother.'

'Battleaxe, was she?' Mr Tompkins said.

'*I'm* a battleaxe,' said Lydia with some pride. 'By all accounts, *she* was a merciless guillotine in comparison.'

'Her ghost don't haunt the corridors?' Mrs Tompkins said, with a nervous laugh.

'No, dear,' said Lydia. 'But Mr Wakeley's does.'

Stella couldn't help herself. 'Who's Mr Wakeley?'

'He was butler, after the War. Disappeared into thin air—' Lydia paused during which time a mischievous sparkle danced across her eyes—'or *did* he?'

'Shall we move on?' Stella suggested, noting Mrs Tompkins fiddling uneasily with her rings.

Lydia's tour of the ground floor met with Mr Tompkins' throaty approval. Stella watched his wife carefully as she gazed and gawped her way through the rooms. In the library, Lydia looked over to

251

Stella and raised an eyebrow, its meaning perfectly legible. Stella nodded and smiled.

'Mr Tompkins,' said Lydia, 'though I'm sure you are an honest man, should you ever have need of somewhere secure for something private—' she let her words hang as she popped open the bookcase column to reveal the secret shelving. To her surprise, Stella noted the pornographic volumes were gone and Lydia, it appeared, steadfastly refused to catch her eye.

Door after door, Mr Tompkins held open for Lydia and as she took them into and out of rooms, up and down stairs, through bedrooms and over landings and every once in a while lingering at a window to take in the view, her memories and anecdotes tumbled forth like an overstuffed linen cupboard bursting its doors open.

'This is Frank's boot room!' she declared in the basement, Stella never having heard of Frank.

'And this is the flower room,' she said, on the ground floor in what Stella had assumed was the pantry, where the jars of jam lined up lonely on the otherwise empty shelves. 'Or at least, it was. The vases were kept here and see this long surface? This is where Hilda would dream up her lovely sprays. And see this?' Lydia pointed to a strange piece of plaited rope attached to the wall, the free end fraying to reveal some type of narrow hosepipe within it. 'There used to be a mouthpiece attached. Black. It had a very particular smell. You could call the garage from here—have the car sent around.' Stella looked at Mr Tompkins who was simultaneously grinning yet apparently close to tears.

Stella looked at Mrs Tompkins—her shoulders

had slumped a little when she'd seen the bathrooms and even more when she'd seen the kitchen. However, venturing outside, Mrs Tompkins' spirits seemed to lift a little while her husband puffed out his chest as if he were already Lord of the Manor.

'I do love a garden,' Mrs Tompkins said, 'but I don't do gardening.'

Lydia looked at her. Mrs Tompkins waggled her slender fingers and long glossy nails and shrugged. Lydia paused. 'That will be music to Art's ears,' she said quietly, as if a thought had just taken root.

'Who's this geezer? Standing here like he owns the place!' Mr Tompkins put his hand on Lord Fortescue's shoulder and for a moment, Stella thought he might give Lord Freddie such a hearty slap on the back he'd tumble off his pedestal.

'He *did* own the place,' Lydia said, not in the least affronted. 'He was an absolute bounder—but one with vision. It's thanks to him that Longbridge stands, that I'm here today.'

'Does he come with the house?'

Lydia looked at Mrs Tompkins. 'Part and parcel, my dear.'

As they walked on, Stella lingered at the back and glanced at Lord Freddie, who appeared to be giving her a very strange look from this angle. Not hostile—but as if she'd presented him with a gift and he wasn't sure quite how it worked.

The tour had taken over two hours and Stella could see how Lydia was suddenly fatigued.

'Thank you—so very much,' Mr Tompkins said. 'It's a gem. It's a jewel. And it's been a pleasure to meet you.'

Lydia tipped her head graciously.

253

'Thank you,' said Mrs Tompkins. 'I'm all lost for words. Not me at all, is it, Barry?'

'Talk the arse off a donkey,' her husband said fondly. Stella cringed until she noted Lydia's wry smile.

'Just a bit overwhelmed,' Mrs Tompkins said. 'It's modern places, really, what I know. And that's what we've been looking at, really. Nothing like this. It's—well, a bit unbelievable.'

'*Do* come again,' Lydia said extravagantly as if they were her favourite guests in a long time. '*Do.*' With that, she went back to the house, waved from the steps and went inside.

'Gobsmacked,' was all Mr Tompkins could say to Stella while Mrs Tompkins shook her head incredulously.

'I'm sure, if you wanted a second viewing, it could easily be arranged—perhaps even for this weekend,' Stella told them. 'Lady Lydia appears to like you.'

'She's a colourful old bird, isn't she,' Mr Tompkins laughed. 'Though I wouldn't want to get on the wrong side of her.' He whistled.

With anyone else, Stella would have shuddered, thanking the stars Lydia was out of earshot. Yet with Mr Tompkins, she found herself wishing Lydia had been right there. She'd have cuffed him around the head. She'd have laughed like a drain.

\*       \*       \*

Stella followed behind the Bentley in her little car, feeling as if she was being pulled along in their slipstream. They indicated left at the high street and drove off with a merry blast of the horn. She turned right, without indicating, and headed for home, keeping her eyes fixedly on the road ahead, resolutely refusing to look left to the Spar or to Mercy Benton's cottage or, a little way along, to look right, up Tramfield Lane. Up the hill and out of the village she drove, woods to either side, on to the New Houses at the top, clustered together as if resigned not to be part of the main hub of Long Dansbury. Stella drove past. And then she slowed down, right down, until her car juddered at the point of stalling. She swung into someone's driveway and, with her head pounding and adrenalin running havoc with her heartbeat, she turned the car and headed slowly back towards the village.

What am I doing what am I doing what am I doing?

Don't be in.

Say he is in?

Don't be in. Don't be in. Be in. Be in.

She turned left into Xander's street. The postbox. The scraggly patch of rough ground. The grit bin on the left. The cottages just ahead. One two three. Everyone's recycling boxes neatly outside their gates.

Car outside the middle cottage.

Stella drove past all three, continued on to the end of the dead end.

Now what?

Now what!

She turned the car badly, backing up too quickly, brushing against the thick hedgerow. It sounded like fingernails on chalkboard.

Slowly, she drove back.

Miss Gilbey is in.

The Georges are home.

There are no lights on at Xander's.

Should she wait?

Five thirty.

What time does a person with their own business usually arrive home?

She sat in the car and switched the engine off.

But say he comes around the corner right now? What would I say?

She switched the engine half on, so that the radio and the air conditioning were active.

She phoned Jo. Straight through to answering machine. That's no use. No point sending a text. She opened the glove compartment, saw the sweets that Caroline's little boy had put in her basket and which she'd forgotten to give Will, and wolfed them down as she rooted around for paper. All she could find was the printout of her car's last service. It had cost her £214. It was blank on the other side. She used the roadmap as a surface on which to write, sucked her pen thoughtfully and then began. She phoned Jo. Straight through to answering machine. Stella would just have to read it through to herself instead.

It sounded OK.

I'd be chuffed to receive a note like that, she thought.

She was going to phone Jo one final time but she thought, no, I know what I want to do. And then she thought, it's what Jo would tell me to do anyway. And without further ado, Stella left the car, walked calmly down Xander's path and, with a slightly shaky hand, posted the folded note through his letter box. Walking back to her car she felt

256

ridiculously jubilant. Her phone was ringing. It was Jo.

I'll phone you when I'm home, Jo. I have to pick up Will. I'm running late.

*      *      *

Xander went to his parents straight from work, taking them a bag of Marks and Spencer's prepared meals which he knew they'd tut at, but enjoy. Then he dumped the car outside his cottage and strolled down to the pub for a couple of pints. Andrew was there and they discussed where they'd run and how long they'd take and what time they'd set off on Saturday morning. Xander left at last orders and strolled home. It was a beautiful night, no breeze and just slivers of high cloud inching past the moon. He'd already decided to watch *The Sopranos* all the way from the beginning—again—and was looking forward to a couple of episodes before he went to bed. He went into his house, took the boxed set of the series through to the kitchen, flicked on the kettle and read all the episode breakdowns, as if his appetite for the show wasn't whetted enough.

It was close to one in the morning when he forced himself to switch off the DVD and go to bed. It was gone two in the morning when he woke, ragingly thirsty, and went downstairs for water. Taking a glass back to bed, he suddenly noticed the folded paper on his doormat. He hadn't seen it when he came in—but there again, his mind had been focused on a good strong cuppa and all things Mafia. It was probably just some flyer about all-weather coatings for houses, for Jim and Bob's local plumbing services; but

257

something made him venture over to it anyway.

It was a handwritten note. No 'Dear Xander', just 'Xander'.

Stella. It's from Stella.

He took it to his chair and put the glass of water on the coffee table. It was chilly. He was in a pair of boxers only. He put the letter down, unread, went upstairs and pulled on a pair of socks and a sweatshirt and returned to the living room.

**Thursday 5.30**

*Xander*

*I was at Longbridge and was just passing so thought I'd just call by. Actually, that's not strictly true—I wanted to see if you were in but I bottled and drove on out of the village only finally doing a 'U-ey at the last point possible. Anyway, you're not in and I don't have your number and I wouldn't know what to say if I did. And so I thought I'd just write you a little note (I know I shouldn't start a sentence with 'and'). But—and here's the big But . . . I don't actually know what to say!! Well, I sort of do—but I just feel stupidly shy . . . Ridiculous!*

*Anyway, Lydia is well and the viewing was with a colourful couple whom she really took to. The gardens at Longbridge are looking gorgeous. Mrs Biggins made tea. And so what I actually wanted to say was I was wondering if at some point you might perhaps like to have a drink or something if you're not too busy if you wanted to and I apologize for the lack of punctuation.*

*Or if not a drink, perhaps a walk—somewhere, at some point, or something. I don't do jogging. I mean, running.*

*Anyway, that's what I wanted to say.*

*And this is my only sheet of paper—if I returned home for some fancy little notelet, the chances are I'd never deliver it. Ramble ramble—apologies . . .*

*Hope all's well.*

*Ta-ta*

*Stella*


Xander read and reread the letter. He folded it carefully and placed it on the coffee table, next to his glass of water. He sat there awhile and thought, if I looked in the mirror, I'd see I'm smiling.

Christ, he didn't want to know what time it was now. He took the letter and the water upstairs with him. His bedside light was on. He read the letter once more, switched off the light and settled himself for sleep.

Then he laughed out loud and said into the silence, 'But you didn't leave your number, you daft mare.'

But you know where she lives, came the reply.

## Chapter Twenty-Two

'She'll kill us,' Juliet said to Alistair while he patted shaving foam onto his face. 'I don't think it's right—I think we should warn her. I mean, I know if she's forewarned the risk is she won't come—but I still think it's unfair.'

Alistair looked at his wife then looked in the mirror and slicked his razor down his cheek; the swipe of smooth pink skin as satisfying as a path cleared from pristine snow. He swilled his razor under the hot tap and continued to shave, giving his wife a thoughtful 'hmm' at regular intervals while she fretted. Splashing his face with cool water, he then pressed a towel across it and, in the soothing cotton, he thought about it.

'It'll be me she wants to kill,' he said, while Juliet sluiced his bristles down the plughole. 'Rupert is my contact. You're in the clear.'

'But you're Stella's big brother—she trusts you.'

'Exactly,' said Alistair. 'And it's not like we're staging some intervention, it's not like we're going to force her into an arranged marriage there and then. It's only a dinner party. It's only a regular Saturday night. There'll be others there—she knows the Hendersons and the Griffins. Tell you what, sit her by me and sit Rupert opposite her.'

'But then it won't go girl-boy-girl-boy!' Juliet protested as if to abuse the seating plan was unthinkable. Alistair raised his eyebrows at her. 'All right,' she grumbled. 'I'll rethink it all. He's not vegetarian or anything, is he?'

'He's normal,' said Alistair. 'He's a nice guy—that's why I want my little sister to meet him.'

*       *       *

For the last few weeks, Saturday mornings had been given over to cricket and, with a play date organized for Will for afterwards, Stella had no time constraints for accompanying the Tompkins to Longbridge for their second visit. She'd thought about Xander over the last couple of days—often. But she wasn't waiting for him to call or spending time on fanciful imaginings of what might happen. As she'd said to Jo, she simply felt oddly euphoric that she'd had the courage to write that note and deliver it.

If I was Xander, said Jo, I'd be rereading it over and again, wondering how to respond. Take your time, Stella had said. Thanks babes, said Jo. And then they'd both become a little confused by their role play, as to who was who, and when had the other turned back into the real them. What Stella did know was that the laughter and fizz that all this had created was a lovely state to be in.

'Come on, Will!' She didn't want him to be late for cricket and she absolutely couldn't be late for Lydia.

'I'm just getting changed.'

'You said that an hour ago.'

'It's cricket—you have to be smart.'

You're seven years old—that's a contradiction in terms, thought Stella but she cooed when Will appeared in his whites with a big grin on his face and told her not to forget he was more than seven and a half.

261

'We need some of that flower glump,' he said, trying to pat down an errant frond of hair which refused to lie smooth. 'Like Lady Lydia Fortescue uses for royal children.'

'I don't have any flowers,' said Stella, glancing at a potted orchid that had bloomed only the once but which she couldn't bring herself to throw away. 'You can use some of Mummy's hairspray.'

'No way!'

'Just hurry up—you need your clothes for Luca's afterwards.'

'I don't know where they are,' said Will.

'Your clothes? You don't know where your *clothes* are?'

Will could never work out why his mother frequently sounded so incredulous about the things he said he didn't know about.

'I'll get them,' she huffed, taking the stairs two at a time. They really needed to be going if they were to make it to cricket and Longbridge on time and unflustered. She must go to the toilet.

The doorbell rang just as she entered Will's room.

'See this door?' she said to him. 'It's a *cupboard* door and watch! We open it and—hey presto! *Clothes*! And guess what! They fit *you*! Well I never!'

There was now knocking at the door.

'Maybe it's the postman with my Lego Hero Factory!' Will said.

'Go and answer it, pumpkin. I'll get your stuff. I must go to the loo before we go. You too, Will.'

Will slithered down the stairs on his bottom, praying that the Danish gods were looking kindly upon him.

262

But it wasn't the postman.

'Mummy?'

No answer.

'*Mummy*!'

'I'm on the loo,' Stella's voice came hollering down. She'd forgotten all about postmen.

'She's on the loo,' Will told Xander.

'Yes,' said Xander, 'I think the whole street heard.'

'My mum says that going to the loo when you really really need it is one of life's pleasures.'

Xander looked at Will. 'Does she now?' He laughed.

'Yes,' said Will. 'Hopefully it will put her in a good mood because she's always grumpy when she's in a rush.'

'Well, I'd better not hang around then—I don't want to make you late.'

'Bye! I'm going to cricket and then to Luca's. Bye!'

'Bye, Will.'

'Bye! PS—I still have that napkin!'

'Good—keep hold of it.'

'I will!' said Will. 'I am!' said Will. He thought about it. 'I! Am! Will!'

Xander laughed. 'Just tell your mum I called on the off chance—OK?'

Will saluted. Xander saluted back. And then he went.

*     *     *

'Right,' said Stella, pulling up at the cricket club. 'Have you forgotten anything?'

'Don't think so,' said Will.

'Good,' said Stella. She parked and gave Will a squeeze as they walked from the car. 'Sorry to rush you, poppet. I don't like having to work on Saturdays.'

'That's OK. Oh!'

'Oh God—what have your forgotten?'

'I forgot to tell you—it wasn't my Lego at the door.'

'The door?' She'd quite forgotten. Then she remembered. 'It'll come on Monday—I'm sure of it.' Stella was now bundling him up towards the cricket pitches which were strewn with white-clad boys in little squiggles, like scatters of spring lambs in a vast meadow. She'd never make it to Long Dansbury in quarter of an hour. She'd have to phone Lydia. And the Tompkins. She'd phone the Tompkins first. No, Lydia first.

'It was Xander.'

His mum was suddenly silent, now standing stock-still, staring at him.

'What?'

'At the door—I forgot to tell you. It was Xander at the door, not the postman. We had a chat. But then you were rushing and I'm sorry—I only just remembered.'

'Xander was at *our* door?'

'When you were on the loo—remember?' His mum was still staring at him. 'I told him you were on the loo and he said the whole street heard. Anyway, I think he just said to tell you he came over. Sorry.' Why was she standing so still? Wasn't she in a rush any more? He dragged her towards the grass. 'Bye, Mum. There's Luca's mum.'

'Bye, darling.'

My mum sounds like she's turned into a robot.

264

Will scampered off, turning to wave. Then he remembered. 'Mum!' he yelled. 'I remembered! Xander didn't say to tell you he came over. He said it was an off chance. Something like that. Bye!'

And the grown-ups turned to look at Stella. They all noted her eyes glinting and wide, the blush blooming her cheeks, and they all thought, who's Xander, Stella! And when she gave Luca's mum the bag with Will's clothes in it, Luca's mum raised her eyebrow and said, Xander eh!

\*     \*     \*

Though Stella drove sensibly to Longbridge, it felt as if she was breaking the speed limit because suddenly everything seemed super-fast. Her heartbeat, her rattle of thoughts, the replay of Xander's message. The zip of excitement, of anticipation, of wondering—what did he want, what did he want! The bare brilliant fact that he really had come to her house, on the off chance. What was the off chance? She squeaked it all out to Jo, who finally phoned her back just as she was turning up the driveway at Longbridge.

'I have to go—the Bentley's here already,' Stella laughed, overlooking the fact that she hadn't mentioned the Tompkins or their car to Jo.

There was no one outside. She skipped up the stone steps, patting one of the lions as she went, and rang the doorbell. Her prayers were answered when it was Mrs Biggins who answered it.

'I'm late!'

'I know—and I wouldn't look so happy about it,' said Mrs Biggins who thought for a terrible moment

265

the girl was going to hug her in greeting.

'I'm not! I'm appalled!' said Stella with a Cheshire cat grin.

'They're over in the Garden House,' said Mrs Biggins.

'Shall I go there?'

'Lady Lydia told me to tell you to wait here,' she said. Then she looked askance at Stella. 'Cuppa?'

'You are a star,' said Stella and Mrs Biggins liked it. She'd give her a rock cake too, she decided. She wasn't expecting Stella to follow her into the kitchen, but she didn't mind that she had. Stella watched as she made the tea.

'Mrs Biggins—how long have you worked here?'

'Since I was twenty-one. Almost fifty years. Lady Lydia tells everyone we're the same age—but there's seven years between us, in my favour. Sometimes I remind her of that.'

'Wow—do you dare?'

Stella's remark wasn't catty, it was said in awe. 'When she's frustrated,' Mrs Biggins told her. 'When she can't open a sticky door, or a jar of pickles. When she found the old iron kettle heavy.' She paused, looking over at the new electric one that she always boiled when Lydia came into the kitchen, but rarely used. 'When she feels the cold. That's when I say to her, I say, "Well, Lady Lydia—I *am* seven years younger than you." I don't say she's seven years *older* than me, you see.'

'I see,' said Stella. She sipped her tea and munched her rock cake, surprised that Mrs Biggins decided to join her in both. 'Mrs Biggins, where will you go?'

'Go?'

'When Longbridge is—' Suddenly Stella couldn't

say it out loud. It seemed so tactless, as if the plans were being kept secret from the bricks and mortar for the meantime.

Mrs Biggins ate thoughtfully. 'Depends if Lady Lydia has need of a housekeeper, I reckon.'

'She won't talk to me about where she sees herself, what type of property, which location—she keeps saying, "All in good time." I worry—partly because I don't honestly know where someone goes, when they've lived their life in a place like this.'

'Hard to imagine,' said Mrs Biggins. 'Hard to imagine not being here. Me. Her. Any of us.'

'What if the new people—whoever they might be—want you to stay on?'

Mrs Biggins looked at Stella as if the suggestion verged on barbaric. 'It's the Fortescue family I work for,' she said. She looked at once uncomfortable and Stella felt bad.

'Sorry—I didn't mean to offend you.' Mrs Biggins offered her another cake. 'Will—my son—says hullo.'

'Nice little lad—you take a cake for him.' And Mrs Biggins wrapped one in another napkin.

'A piece of kitchen paper will do,' Stella assured her.

'They're my rock cakes!' Mrs Biggins retorted. 'Kitchen paper will *not* do.' And though she put her smile against her mug of tea as if it was the shape her mouth made when she was blowing on hot liquid, she winked at Stella all the same. For a split second, Stella had the urge to tell her about Xander. Just to say his name out loud. Perhaps chat about him. But she felt shy and she thought better of it and the two of them sat there and sipped until, minutes later, they heard Lydia rattling the front door, the bell chiming out.

Mrs Biggins tutted. 'She knows the French doors are open—she does this on purpose.' And she huffed off to open the front door, with Stella following behind.

After profuse apologies brushed away by the Tompkins but sternly accepted by Lydia, Stella joined them for another tour of the house before she took the Tompkins off to see the stable courtyard. Lydia had said to her not to bother Clarence. He was under the weather, apparently. And she told Stella the Tompkins didn't have time to see the Lime Grove Cottages today, at which point Stella just stood there and grinned like an idiot.

'I've offered to take them next week,' Lydia told her.

'I can do that,' Stella said, like an annoying, over-keen school goody-goody. 'I can do that—let me!'

Lydia thought, what is wrong with the girl? She preferred Stella when she was deferential and sensible and behaving like a proper estate agent. She didn't even have a clipboard today—just the silly smile. And she was wearing the sort of pumps that used to be seen only on a tennis court.

Lydia took her leave of the Tompkins and nodded gravely at Stella. But she was quite taken aback when Stella found a moment out of earshot of the Tompkins to tell Lydia of three forthcoming viewings for the next week. It was suddenly apparent that for Lydia, the Tompkins were her favoured buyer.

'I'm sure we'll hear—shortly,' said Stella,

nodding over to the library where the Tompkins could be heard marvelling. 'Perhaps after they've seen Lime Grove Cottages.'

'The Hakshimmer people?' Lydia asked, visibly pulling herself together. 'Did you speak to them again?'

'Hakshimis,' said Stella, 'Sticking at eleven.'

\*      \*      \*

Once again, Stella followed the Bentley out as far as the high street. Once again, she turned right when they turned left. This time, however, she didn't overshoot the turning to Tramfield Lane, parking well in advance of it in a space in the lot opposite the shop. Perhaps Caroline was in there. Perhaps not. Maybe Michael Lazarus's magical shop was a hum of activity. But, passing by, she saw the sign said 'Open after lunch'. Mercy Benton's little cottage appeared quiet but Stella noted all manner of summer bedding plants lining the pathway and she was pleased the new owners were continuing to make it their home. She walked on. She'd chosen to walk because she needed to collect herself though when she saw the sign for Tramfield Lane the charge of adrenalin put paid to that.

Shall I? Can I really do this? She'd left her phone in the car so as not to be tempted to text Jo because if Jo didn't reply she might well lose her nerve. Digging her nails into the palms of her hands and taking a couple of deep breaths, she headed up the lane to the cottages, truly not knowing whether she wanted Xander to be home or not.

He heard the creak of his gate. From the back of

269

the kitchen, he could watch unseen Stella walking down his path. The real-life Stella, walking a zigzag down the straight path to his door, hair in a pony-tail, squinting in sunlight, moments away from seeing if he was at home. And he wondered, shall I be in—or not? He'd been for a short run, he was showered and changed. He had no plans. But he hadn't planned for this. He'd meticulously planned to turn up at Stella's earlier that morning and claim it was on the off chance. He'd decided on it the previous day, whilst sitting at work staring at the tuna mayo sandwich brought to him by Mrs Gregg who then asked him, intermittently during the afternoon, whether he was all right.

Xander couldn't see Stella now. She must be at the front door; perhaps hovering there as he was hovering here. Would he be able to say—to ask— what he'd primed himself to, earlier that day? Did his question have a sell-by date of that morning—a caveat that it had to be said on *her* doorstep and not his? He waited for the knock. He waited a long time for the knock. He was just wondering whether to venture over to the front door and see if perhaps she'd gone, when the knock finally came. A shy, single tap followed by two more assertive raps.

Just offer her a coffee. Or tea—she had tea last time. But look at the time. It's lunch-time. Perhaps suggest the pub. Nice weather—a walk? Or just start by saying hullo. Or hi. Or, add her name. Just open the bloody door and see what bloody happens.

Open the door.

Open the door.

Xander opened the door and they both said hullo at the same time. Then Stella made a strange and inadvertent snort sound while Xander simply stood like a lummox as he struggled with what to say or do because no thoughts came to him though he scrambled to locate any.

'Did you want the loo?'

Dear God, let her see the funny side of it.

Stella made much of biting her lip and scrunching her eyes and groaning in a genuinely mortified way, but Xander just laughed, realizing that what he assumed was such a stupid bloody thing to say was actually just fine.

'*Did* you want the loo?' he repeated, eased by Stella visibly wracking her brains for a larky response. 'Because I'm told it's the highlight of your day. Nothing comes close.'

Stella just stood there, outwardly dumbstruck while inwardly grasping for the best response. She'd told Jo that having a pee when you're bursting is better than sex. She certainly wasn't going to say *that* to Xander. Say something! 'I've just been at Longbridge,' she said. But that sounded boring so she opened her bag for him to see the napkin concealing something lumpy.

'Is that for me?'

'It's for Will, actually. Mrs Biggins' rock cake.' She wished she hadn't followed it by saying 'Yum'.

Both Xander and Stella turned when the Georges walked by and called hullo to him. Then they spent a few moments concentrating on the emptiness of the lane. Stella gave the type of sigh that said, well, I ought to get going I suppose. So Xander pulled himself together because he knew he really wanted her to stay.

'Would you like to come in?' he asked her. 'Or are you in a rush? Apparently you're stroppy when you're in a rush. So you must always be in a rush

271

because I'd assumed you were just stroppy—full stop.'

Stella huffed. 'I'm not stroppy!' she protested. '*You're* the moody one, thank you very much!' But she grinned. 'And no—I'm not in a rush.' And she all but stomped past Xander and into his house while they both laughed a little too heartily.

Xander closed his front door. The click of the latch, then simply the silence of the house. The day outside was excluded. Lydia, Will—everyone was where they should be, unaware of the two people standing quietly inside 3 Lime Grove Cottages. Xander and Stella, finding themselves together in a secret stillness away from the world. They looked at each other, heads tilted, smiles soft and instinctively they took a step closer, and closer still so that Xander could cup her face in his hands and Stella could place hers either side of his neck and slowly, very slowly, they kissed.

As their lips met, anticipation melted into relief. All the awkward clumsiness of moments ago— the talk of stroppiness and the loo and rock cakes and hullo George family—faded as they found each other's mouths and conversed wordlessly, perfectly. Noses rubbing, tongues flicking shyly at first, soon enough dancing deeply. Hands stroking and feeling. The landscape of muscled arms. Such a strong back. Maybe that word 'manly' isn't so silly. There's that fragrance—perhaps it's not her shampoo. Perhaps it's just her. This is her—this is the gentle curve of Stella's waist, the soft dip at the base of her back. It was like Braille on a human scale.

When they pulled away, a little bashful to find themselves in the here and now, they had to focus on something else for a few seconds—Xander on Stella's silver necklace, Stella on a rivet on the front pocket of Xander's jeans. And then, they looked at each other. He tucked a strand of her hair behind her ear and she placed her hand over his and pressed her cheek into it.

'*Are* you in a rush?' he asked. Tiger's Eye—that's where he'd seen the colour of Stella's eyes. She shook her head. 'Do you want to—I don't know!' He thought about it. 'Sit? Walk? Eat? Talk? God!'

'Could go for a walk? I don't know either!'

'A walk sounds good.'

'Good—I'd like a walk.'

'OK.'

'Right.'

They paused.

'Or maybe a cup of tea?' Stella said, wanting to stay right here, in this space in which some crazy magic had just been woven.

'Yes—OK. Or lunch? Are you hungry?'

'I've had a Mrs Biggins' rock cake.'

'That'll keep you going.'

'You could have the one she packed for Will, if you like.'

'What a dreadful mother you are!'

And Xander kissed her again because her indignant face made him want to.

'Please have it,' said Stella, unwrapping the napkin. 'I'll ask Mrs Biggins for the recipe.'

'She'll never give it out,' Xander said.

'Doesn't matter—I make a mean fairy cake myself,' said Stella. 'Will's favourite. Cream cheese icing. Hundreds and thousands.'

'Are you pocketing the napkin?' he asked her, going to the kitchen and putting the cake on a saucer. The atmosphere now light, both at ease; simply together at Xander's place on a Saturday lunch-time as though it was the most normal thing for both of them to do because they'd done it a hundred times before.

'You bet—I'm hoping to collect the set.'

'Look.' He showed her a delicate teaspoon engraved with an elegant F.

'You stole Lydia's silver?'

'*Acquired* when I was small. Actually, it's silver plate—see.' He traced the EPNS letters on the back. 'Apparently, a solid silver spoon *did* find its way into my trouser pocket but Lydia managed to appease me with this one.'

Stella smiled, taking the spoon from him, noticing how lovely his hands were; shapely fingers, nice nails.

'This morning,' Stella said. 'When you came to my house. On the off chance?'

'I was going to ask if you wanted to have dinner tonight. You know—if you could find a babysitter.' Xander stopped. 'Can you? A babysitter. Would you—like to have dinner?' He was properly asking a girl out on a date. When had he last done that? When had he last felt this nervous? Ridiculous how nervous he felt! Get a grip, man! 'The Black Ox in the village is really good. We could go there?'

An image of her gloriously empty kitchen calendar sprung to Stella's mind. With the one bloody Saturday—the first in June—glaringly filled in. Today. Red pen. A & J's 7.30 p.m. Her mind racketed over whether she could cancel Alistair and Juliet. If she could find a babysitter at such late notice. But what about Will? He liked to know well in advance if she was going out. He was looking

274

forward to going to his super-cool older cousins. But Stella had been asked out, on a proper date, by exactly the person she wanted; a man who'd just kissed her and awakened sensations she'd quashed for years and it was all so thrilling and she couldn't bloody go.

She looked down and rubbed the spoon as if hoping for a genie. 'I'm going to my brother's tonight—they're having a few friends over. Will and I are staying the night.' She looked forlorn. 'I can't cancel. I'm sorry.'

'So you'd've said no—if I'd asked you on your doorstep.'

'If I hadn't been on the loo,' Stella said. Then she looked at Xander. 'But that would have meant I wouldn't be here now.' She paused and smiled. 'And there'd have been no kissing. And no planning. None of this would have happened.'

He looked at Stella, sitting on his stool, in his kitchen. An odd sight indeed, but a welcome one. He went over to her and pulled her close to him, sinking his mouth into hers, wishing she didn't have to go. He wanted to talk the afternoon away, walk with her, eat with her. Take her to bed. God, he wanted to take her to bed.

'I'm going to have to go,' Stella whispered against his lips, eyes shut.

'I know,' he whispered back. 'Right now?'

'Now-ish,' she said, darting her tongue along his lips and thinking she'd rather be in a rush to collect Will if it meant she could kiss Xander for a little while longer.

'Go,' he said, kissing her fast on her cheeks, her chin, her lips. 'I don't want to make you late.'

'Will you call? Soon?'

He nodded. 'We can postpone dinner. We can rebook it.' Reluctantly, they headed away from the kitchen. Stella picked up her bag, Xander liking the way she wore it across herself, like a school satchel. And then he raised his eyebrow at her. 'Er—my spoon, madam? Are you intending to pilfer that too?'

She hadn't realized. It was so dainty and so warm and so snug in her hand. She gave it back to him and, eyes dancing, she stood on tiptoes and kissed him. 'What would Lydia think if she knew you'd been kissing me and kissing me?'

Xander looked at the spoon as he rotated the stem between his thumb and forefinger. What *would* Lydia think? What would she say—because she'd certainly have something to say about it. Sometimes, though, with Lydia, what she thought and what she said didn't necessarily correlate. And what had he just done? What was he doing, finding so attractive the woman who was wreaking havoc through the village and trampling all over his memories? He looked at her.

'I don't know,' he said thoughtfully. And he couldn't stop himself weaving her pony-tail through his fingers as he led her to the door. 'I honestly don't know.'

# Chapter Twenty-Three

Alistair felt so proud of his little sister as Stella breezed into his sitting room full of people. She looked just lovely. He wasn't sure if she'd had her hair done, or was using some new expensive magic mascara, or if she'd filled out a bit, or was wearing a new outfit, but something was different and whatever it was she looked really radiant. She greeted the Hendersons and the Griffins warmly and gave Rupert a good long handshake and easy smile when they were introduced. And she hugged Juliet tightly. She was chatty and effervescent and Alistair said to Juliet, you know what, I think she's turned a corner, I think she's back in the game, I think she's ready to put herself out there and reel them in. Juliet just slapped him on the backside and said, for God's sake, don't go on about there being plenty of fish in the sea. But Alistair just shrugged and said, Rupert is a catch, and they left it at that.

\*　　　\*　　　\*

**beans on toast. Xx**

Stella had felt her phone vibrate. Surreptitiously, she took it from her pocket, placed it in her lap and read Xander's first-ever text to her, while sitting at Alistair's table having thoroughly enjoyed Juliet's hors d'oeuvres and the lively company. She thought, how can my heart miss a beat just by someone telling me they're eating baked beans! She thought, how am I meant to reply! Rupert was talking at her about something or other and she managed to nod at him across the table while trying out sentences in her head. She tapped out a fair few, assessing how they looked on screen but deleted them all. What should she say! Come on, Inspiration!

I know!

and for pud? Sx

\* \* \*

She thought it was an accidental nudge, but when it happened again, Stella realized it was her brother kicking at her leg under the table. Juliet's incomparable roast duck had been placed in front of her and everyone else had already started, so Stella quickly slipped her phone back in her pocket hoping to feel the buzz of a reply soon.

It came in the middle of Rupert recounting something quite funny about his hiking holiday in Guatemala.

thoughts of you. Xx

The impact from the message was utterly electric. All Stella wanted to do was run; run as fast as Xander. Push back her chair and belt from this house, cover the one and a half marathons which was the distance separating Watford and Long Dansbury in the blink of an eye. Hammer on his door and fall into his arms.

Memories of the morning's kissing filled her mouth, her mind, took her far from Alistair's dining table and left no room for Juliet's duck. It was only her brother's sharp kick at her ankle that returned her to the present. That hurt! Her phone dropped to the floor. She made to move her chair back but stopped when she saw how Alistair was frowning at her and Juliet was looking from her plate to

278

her face worried, as if there might be something wrong with her cooking. The Griffins and the Hendersons were simply looking at Rupert who'd stopped mid-sentence, halfway into his Guatemalan adventure.

'Sorry,' Stella said to the table at large. 'It's just work—I have to be available to Lady Lydia at all times. Will you excuse me a mo'?' She left the room. Rupert's story ended in a damp fizzle. He'd only really recounted it for Stella's benefit and the Griffins and Hendersons, who'd been primed by Alistair and Juliet, hadn't been that enthralled by it anyway.

*       *       *

'Stella?'

Juliet had to say her name twice. Stella was standing with her back to her in the kitchen, head bowed. When Juliet went over, she saw it was because she was staring fixedly at her phone. She put her hand on Stella's shoulder.

'Everything OK? It's nine o'clock. Can't the old bat give you an evening's peace?'

But when Stella turned, Juliet was taken aback by her flushed cheeks, the pervasive sparkle which seemed to create a glow around her like the Ready-brek kid. 'Are you all right?'

Stella stared at her and then she broke into an expansive grin and stood there shaking.

'What is it?' Juliet hissed.

'Finally I've met someone!' Stella whispered and she threw her arms around Juliet and squeezed her.

'Alistair will be so pleased,' Juliet hugged her back.

'I know,' said Stella. 'I can't begin to describe how I feel!'

'Is that why you didn't eat my gorgeous, expensive, slaved-over-all-afternoon duck?'

'I'm sorry!' Stella pulled back and tried to add a sheepish edge to her broad smile. 'I'm just a bit distracted. And Al keeps kicking me. But I just feel so—' She had no words so she made a shuddery sound as if she was simultaneously boiling hot and freezing cold.

'He's lovely,' said Juliet.

'I know!'

Then Stella stopped. Who'd said what when? 'How do you know?' Had she mentioned Xander to either of her sisters-in-law?

'Because Al's known him for years.'

'You're joking!' Stella felt alternately thrilled and confused. 'Al knows Xander?' Of all the crazy coincidences.

The smile left Juliet's face like air seeping from a balloon. 'Who?'

'Who?'

'Xander?'

Stella nodded, searching Juliet's face.

'Not Rupert?' Juliet asked.

'*Rupert*?' Stella stared at Juliet. Then she clapped her hand to her mouth. 'Oh shit.' She reached for Juliet's arm. 'Oh shitting shit.'

Juliet tried to edge her own obvious disappointment with a smile, but actually she just looked bewildered. 'But he's handsome, fit, stable, single—and normal,' she pleaded.

'I thought he was gay,' Stella mouthed.

Juliet looked down but her shoulders shook and when she looked up Stella could see her biting back giggles. 'So did I,' Juliet mouthed back. Then she slammed her hands on her hips. 'So who the fuck is Alex-blinking-Xander?'

'He's just Xander,' said Stella, beaming. 'And he's at his home eating beans on toast and I asked him what he was having for pudding and this is what he replied.' She showed the text to Juliet who read it and then clapped the phone to her heart.

'Oh my *God*!' Juliet's smile was back.

'Oh my God what?' said Alistair, suddenly in the kitchen. 'What's wrong? What are you doing in here? What's going on?'

But Juliet winked quickly at Stella and said 'Just Women's Things' to Alistair, which always shut him up.

\*     \*     \*

Snuggled up to Will in Alistair and Juliet's spare bedroom, Stella scrolled back and forth through the texts. She hadn't yet replied to him. She hadn't wanted to be continually kicked by her bemused brother so she'd returned to the dinner table and had conscientiously tried her best to converse with everyone equally.

Now she was alone with her thoughts, thinking back over an extraordinary day, the morning seeming so long ago but the sensations ever present. For Xander's pudding, he'd had thoughts of her. She'd had zabaglione. He'd had the courage to tell her. It was heading for one in the morning. It all happened yesterday. Stella was exhausted, elated, wanting to reply but not knowing what to say. She just wanted there to be contact, it seemed safe to let him know she was thinking of him—after all, he'd ignored any preposterous dating etiquette or ridiculous rules and had let her know that was precisely what he was thinking.

G'nite. Sx

Xander read the text, put down his book, switched off the light and went to sleep with a smile on his face. His bedroom didn't seem quite so cold.

## Chapter Twenty-Four

Once Alistair and Robbie had swallowed their slight ignominy that their baby sister had rejected the suitors they'd worked so hard to put her way in favour of some bloke they'd never heard of, Stella's family banded together to assist the fledgling romance with offers of babysitting. Initially, Stella had felt a little reluctant to accept and was somewhat vexed that details, let alone the simple fact that at long last, she'd found someone she wanted to see, were now to be shared. But babysitting was expensive and hitherto she had rarely called upon anyone other than her family or her closest friends anyway. *I don't get out much* was one adage that Stella was famous for—said in a self-deprecating way. But the truth was, over the last two years, she really hadn't much wanted to go out, to leave Will. The last two years had been given over to building a safe fortress for herself and her son and, despite the dragging loneliness which ensued once Will was asleep, there'd also been the sense of relief that evenings need never again revolve around wondering where Charlie was and whether or not he'd be coming home.

So, when on the Monday Xander phoned and asked whether she might be free for dinner two days later, Stella knew she'd have three offers of babysitting—four, if she asked Jo too. She called upon her mother in this first instance, not merely because it was the right thing to do but also because she knew her mum would skirt around details and be happy enough if her daughter was smiling. Stella was also aware that it was giving her mother two gifts for the price of one: an evening with her grandson as well as relief and joy that at long last her daughter was Out There, taking tentative steps towards a chap she really liked.

Xander, too, had his little army in the wings. When he phoned Stella, Mrs Gregg was sitting at her desk preparing invoices, unable to believe that what she was hearing was as simple as it sounded. Surely Xander must be arranging an after-hours business meeting! But his voice sounded so soft. She considered this alongside the periods in which he didn't seem to working at all, just sitting there gazing into the middle distance. It was all a little peculiar. She couldn't quite believe what it could equate to.

'Well, Wednesday it is then,' she heard him say and glanced up to see him grinning, revolving around on his chair. 'Lovely. Yes. Ha! Stroppy mare.'

Had he suddenly become interested in horses? Perhaps that was it. Off to see some stroppy mare.

'The Black Ox.'

Or cattle.

'OK. Ha! No. I'll run first—can we make it eight?'

Eight oxen? Or eight o'clock? Sounded late to be

viewing livestock.

'Come to mine—I'll see you at mine. We'll stroll down together.'

Who! Who! Who is Xander Fletcher going to be 'together' with?

'Everything all right with those invoices, Mrs Gregg?'

She looked flustered and Xander knew it had nothing to do with payment terms and conditions. He did love the way that Mrs Gregg tried so hard to be 100 per cent professional during working hours—but was actually enslaved to a little eavesdropping however hard she tried to defend against it. It hadn't been on the job description. She did everything he could ever ask of her, and often went beyond the call of duty. And she cared—for the company, for him. He knew that and he was grateful and he really shouldn't tease her so wryly.

'Everything is fine, Mr Fletcher,' she said officiously, but she scoured his face in much the same way as his mother was prone to do when she worried about him. 'Almost done,' she said, airily. 'Anything else I can help you with?'

'Like?' Xander was unable to resist.

'Oh, I don't know,' she breezed, rifling through papers and checking the desk diary. 'Wednesday night—did you want me to make a booking?' She appeared to be counting paper clips now. 'A reservation?' She was organizing a pile of compliment slips into a crenellated pattern. 'For—two?'

Xander thought quietly back to how kind Mrs Gregg had been to him when he finally broke up with Laura. How, every couple of days, she'd bring in Tupperware containing a stew, or a casserole—

284

which she feigned was leftovers. How she'd diverted calls when he needed a moment to stare deep at nothingness forlornly, how she'd talk tangentially about so-and-so whose son was to be married just nine months after some awful woman who was never worthy of him had left. Mrs Gregg had met Laura on a number of occasions and had been sweet and welcoming but when they split, she never mentioned her name again. Well, just the once. *I found her a little self-centred if truth be told*, she'd said to Xander. *The world seemed to revolve around Laura—whereas I'd like to see you with someone who thinks the world of you.*

'Thank you, Mrs Gregg,' Xander said, realizing he hadn't thought of Laura for some time. 'But the Black Ox is my local—and they don't take bookings.'

'You're taking her to a *pub*?' She bristled, as if he should think again.

'It's a gastro pub,' Xander said.

'Ah,' said Mrs Gregg, sorting envelopes by size and lining up the top-left corners. 'All the rage.'

'It's very nice,' said Xander.

'Lovely,' said Mrs Gregg, looking over her glasses and down her nose at an invoice she was sure had been paid. 'And her name is?'

'Her name's Stella,' said Xander evenly.

And then Mrs Gregg looked at him squarely and her voice changed. It was level and wise and tender too. It wasn't his PA speaking. 'Good for you, Xander. Good for you.'

*       *       *

Caroline phoned Xander on Tuesday, asking him if

285

he'd mind babysitting the following evening.

'Sorry, Cazza—I'm busy.' Then he thought, I really needn't say anything else at this point. And then he thought, but wouldn't it be nice for Caroline if I did. 'I'm—er—going out to dinner.'

'Oh?'

'Yes—with Stella.'

'Oh!'

'Yep.'

'Wow. Very good. Where are you taking her?'

'Black Ox.'

'Our Black Ox?'

'Yes.'

'That's brave!'

'Why?'

'I might call in, and stare at you both and fire questions at her.'

'God. Please don't.'

'I'm joking. Anyway, I won't need to—the rumour mill will swing into action and I'll hear all about it at various points the day after.'

Xander laughed. He hadn't thought about that. He'd simply wanted to take Stella to a place he really liked. And anyway, who cares who saw him or what was said. He certainly didn't—not this time.

\*        \*        \*

When Will asked Stella where she was going and what time she'd be back, she paused. She could very well say, I'm just going to have some supper with a friend. But he'd ask which friend. And if she said Jo, that would be a lie. And she never, ever, intended to lie to her boy. But if she said Xander, would Will wonder why she hadn't simply said so in

286

the first place? Because Will thought of Xander as being his pal as much as hers.

'Your friend Xander asked if I wanted to have some supper with him,' she said, wondering if Will's pyjamas had shrunk because surely they couldn't be above his ankles and wrists already.

'Oh!' said Will, as if a penny had just dropped. *'That's* what an off chance is. It's a supper invitation. I *see*.'

'I won't be back late—and I told Grandma you can read until eight o'clock.'

'And will I be awake when you get back?'

'You might be—or you might be asleep. But I'll come in anyway—you know I always do.'

'OK.'

'OK. Night, angel.'

'Night. Mummy—?'

'Yes?'

'You look nice.'

*     *     *

It was a beautiful evening. After a fine day, wisps of cloud sneaked across the sky and the slumbering sun spun them salmon pink. It was warm enough now just for short sleeves but Stella had taken the lavender-coloured ballerina wrap that Alistair and Juliet had bought her last Christmas. It went well with her white top and slate-grey trousers which her mother kept telling her were either called pedal-pushers or clam-diggers in her day but for the life of her she couldn't remember which. Stella thought they were called cigar pants—but then she thought perhaps it was cigarillo pants. So she and her mother had decided on calling them

287

Slim Fit Ankle Length. Her mother begged her to wear a Nice Pair of Heels—but Stella insisted on her black suede ballet pumps because she loved them. And Xander had said something about a stroll.

'But if you're in heels, you have every excuse to teeter and to take his arm for balance.'

'Mother!'

'OK. All right. What do I know. Just enjoy yourself.'

'Hope so.'

It was tingles of desire, a zip of anticipation and a heart running twenty to the dozen on hope, which propelled Stella down the garden path to Xander's front door.

'Hey,' he said, thinking she looked lovely, wondering if he could say it out loud but feeling strangely unconfident to do so. She felt thrilled by the sight of him, bit down on a grin and made that peculiar snort thing of hers.

'Hullo,' she said and they kissed quickly, clumsily, and said boring things about the weather. He was wearing a soft washed denim shirt and had either forgotten to tuck one side in or else had omitted to pull the other out. She wanted to do it for him, but she clasped her hands together and rocked on the spot.

'I'll just get my keys,' he said, with a scratch of his head.

'And your shoes,' said Stella.

'Hungry?'

'I think so,' she said. 'You should always untie laces before you put on your shoes.'

'Cheeky mare,' he muttered.

She put her hands on her hips and tutted and

288

thought to herself, oh my God I'm so happy to be here.

*     *     *

With its beams and flagstones and mismatched thick wooden tables and chairs, two inglenook fireplaces and also a secluded but sizeable beer garden, the Black Ox suited every season. Xander and Stella were seated at a table for two, by a window overlooking the garden. The staff referred to him by name and Stella liked that; flattered not to have been taken anywhere else. Eyeing another diner's fish and chips, both she and Xander ordered the dish and happily tolerated the slow service as it gave them the chance to linger over their drinks and privately delight in how smoothly conversation flowed.

'Are you going to get rip-roaringly drunk on me?' Xander asked.

Stella shook her head soberly. 'That's my modus operandi for blind dates only,' she said. 'Anyway, it's a school night.' She paused, looking around the pub, loving it all. 'Do you come here often, then?' She said it in a cockney accent.

'It's my lair,' he said. 'I take *all* the girls here.' It was obviously far from the truth and she felt chuffed.

'Well, I'm honoured.'

'How's Will?'

'He's fine—he got Gold Book at school so he's cock-a-hoop.'

Xander thought how much he liked her turn of phrase. It was quirky and old-fashioned and so much more descriptive than 'fantastic' or, God

289

forbid, 'awesome'.

'My mum's babysitting,' Stella told him.

'Are you close?'

She nodded. He wanted to know about her family so she told him about her brothers and their families—even made mention of her errant father. And she told him about Jo who, she said, was as close as she came to having a sister. He responded with talk of his own small family and both Xander and Stella thought to themselves, so many names to learn—and, in time hopefully, faces to put to names. The dinner arrived; the fish butter-flake-fresh encased in balloons of crispy fragrant batter, chips the size of kindling piled high and a gloss of peas obscuring any remaining white china.

'Mayo please,' Stella told the waiter, 'and ketchup too. Please.' She looked at Xander. 'It's Will's invention—you mix it together in precise proportions and you have mayonetchup.' She let him dip a chip into her concoction and it may as well have been the finest hollandaise for all his nodding. But he didn't mix it for himself, he stuck with tartare sauce. Chat was the most delicious accompaniment to the meal. Work. Hertford. Lydia. Friends. Family. They argued a little about Longbridge—Xander putting across his misgivings, Stella defending her position. It was an impasse but neither of them wanted it to be a barrier. They moved away from it.

In between the details asked for and the facts given, there was teasing and joshing and easy chatter interspersed every now and then with the heady contradiction of spontaneous yet lingering looks. Privately, they both hailed and cursed the setting—a public space, a table between them, food that really ought to be eaten hot. Undoubtedly, it prevented the privacy that his cottage might have afforded yet it also assisted in providing an ideal forum in which they could converse at length. He told her he half expected Caroline's face to press itself against the window. Stella admitted her phone was on silent because no doubt there'd be a barrage of texts from Jo.

'Will I have to fill in a questionnaire?' he asked her.

'No—but after the lie-detector test, she'll have you jump through a fair few hoops,' Stella told him. 'Oh—and she'll probably threaten you, too.'

'Protecting her pal?'

Stella nodded and, just for a moment, she stopped chewing and stared at something way beyond the melee of peas remaining on her plate.

Not yet, thought Xander. Not here. Not the time.

She glanced up at him and their eyes locked.

'Jo will ask you outright if you have any addictions,' Stella said, quietly.

He nodded at her. 'And I'll be able to tell her—no. Apart from running, I suppose.' Stella nodded and Xander tipped his head to one side and nodded back. He thought to himself, Christ—poor girl. And then he reminded himself, not here—not now.

It was practically dark outside now, the candle on the table casting caramel hues over his face—clean-shaven, the dip between cheekbones and jawline just perfect for her to run the backs of her fingers over. Her lips parted at the thought of how his skin would feel, a sudden recall of the taste of him, the sensation sending a bolt of desire so strong she looked away, as if lust was written all over

291

her face.

'Are you a pudding type of girl?' he asked her, half hoping she'd say no so he could just get her home to his.

'I am,' she said, wondering for a moment whether it was a deal-breaker or a trick question.

'That's refreshing,' he said. Even more so, he thought, when she scoffed the lot without offering him a mouthful and then helped herself to a spoonful of his baked Alaska.

When the bill came, Stella offered to go Dutch. 'Don't be daft,' Xander said, 'it's a date. It's my treat.'

'Thank you,' said Stella, feeling full and flush and pampered and just plain happy. A date. Nice to hear it out loud.

\*       \*       \*

Xander chatted briefly to the landlord and to one of the diners, exchanging pleasantries with a couple of others on their way out; introducing Stella to them all. Please don't let it be late, Stella said to herself as they left. She didn't wear a watch, she never had. She'd always been most adept at estimating the time—before the advent of mobile phones. Nowadays she was useless, but she really didn't want to check her phone, she didn't want to see all the larky missives from Jo, she didn't want to have to minimize her evening into abbreviated sentences. Fundamentally, though, she simply didn't want to see what the real time was. But it was dark. Cool, now. Very quiet, out in the village. She and Xander didn't speak, as if the air between them was loaded with messages so soft and scrambled

292

that silence was essential to decipher them. When they turned into Tramfield Lane, it was as if a notch on the night sky had been turned and the lane was velvety black and appeared to have a soft soundproofing of its own. And then Xander took her hand. And a surge of adrenalin stormed through her as she knitted her fingers against his and that's how they walked back to his cottage.

Inside, door shut on the outside world, they stood for just a moment before grabbing at each other, ravenous. As soundless as their first kisses had been at the weekend, now the room reverberated with them. Little gasps from Stella, a throatiness from Xander, their breathing audible and hastened, furniture knocked against, items clattering to the floor.

'Jesus Christ you taste good,' Xander whispered against Stella's lips before sucking them gently and slipping his tongue into her mouth. They stumbled, still locked in embrace, over his uneven flagstones to fall upon his sofa where their kisses came more slowly as they broke away now and then just to look at each other; smile, close eyes and open them again, stroke hair and arms and faces. Their legs were entwined and as they kissed, Stella instinctively rocked her hips against his thigh, sensing the bulge in his trousers, delighting in the charge it sent down to her groin. His hands, simultaneously gentle yet eager, burrowing up under her top, over her bra and at last to her bare skin.

When had anyone last felt her breasts? It would have been Charlie, of course, but his style was to maul them perfunctorily in a crude preamble to sex. Xander, it seemed, just wanted to touch and discover. And see her for his own eyes. He pulled her top over her head and slipped her bra straps down. And then he broke into a big open grin, smiling at her breasts as if they were the best sight in the world which far exceeded his imaginings.

'Aren't you gorgeous,' he said and she wasn't sure whether it was to her, or to them. With her fingers enmeshed in his hair she guided his face to them. God she was on fire, she was floating, sinking. With his tongue at her nipple, the graze of his teeth; with his hand travelling along her legs and adeptly in between them, Stella felt herself melt into orgasm and her head emptied as her body filled with feeling.

Xander kissed and kissed her face. Loving it that her eyes were closed yet willing them to open. And when they did, he saw how she was woozy with it all.

'Sorry—I—' she began.

'Sorry?' He looked at her as if she was mad. Actually, he looked triumphant. 'For what?' He was propped up on his arm, brushing her hair from her face. And then she winked and she said, what about you, boyo! And he said, you dirty cow and they laughed but they shifted around so that he was on his back, his erection visibly mapped out behind his trousers. She traced it coyly with her fingers, fiddled with his belt and his flies, suddenly desperate to see him. As his trousers were pushed down and his boxers were pulled away, Stella thought to herself, that's a really nice-looking cock. She floated her fingertips along the length, feathered her touch over his balls, judged by his shallow breathing, his eyes half closed but still boring into hers, that he liked what she was doing.

'I'm fit to burst,' he whispered, his hand at her

breast again. Eyes locked onto his, gently and deftly she pulled his orgasm in just a few minutes. Then, with her hand still around him, feeling the pulse and leap of his cock ebb away, she snuggled down next to him. Both of them sated, squished onto the sofa, tangled against each other, back in the present marvelling at what had just happened.

'Fuck!' he said quietly. Then he laughed. 'Fuck?' he said.

'Yes, please,' said Stella, as if he'd just suggested a cup of tea. 'Soon?'

She was in his arms. He kissed the top of her head. 'When can you arrange it?'

And Stella thought, oh god.

In Xander's cottage, time had done something strange, enabling her to be purely on her own with Xander. Not mum to Will, not daughter to Sandie who was currently sitting in Stella's front room. Not best friend to Jo, who'd gone to bed happily reading much into the fact that Stella hadn't replied to a single text. Stella had just been herself, thinking only of her own needs, not worrying about anyone else—it was a strange and liberating new world to explore. But the bastard bloody clock on Xander's DVD player goaded her: it's after half eleven! It's after half eleven! You won't be home till gone midnight! It's a school night! Your mum's babysitting! Get up! Get a move on! You have to go—now!

'Oh God, I have to go,' she moaned, burying her face in his neck. 'It's late—my mum!' She was soothed by his laughter, because over and above the sound of it was once again the feel of it, emanating from his chest just as she had felt it through her drunken haziness that night not so long ago. His

295

hand was in her hair, teasing out tangles, weaving locks between his fingers.

'Go,' he said. 'You need to go.' They unfurled from each other and stood. Xander pulled his shirt over his head to wipe at his stomach, Stella twanged her bra back into place and rushed into her top. Bare chested, Xander showed her to the door. She ran her fingers over his collar bone, sweeping her hands lightly over his chest.

'When?' she said.

'Soon as you can,' he said.

'Perhaps at the weekend?'

'Drive safe.'

\* \* \*

'Did you have a lovely time, darling?' asked her mum as if it were only half past nine, not gone midnight; as if Stella had popped over to Jo's and hadn't taken her ballerina cardigan anyway and had gone out with her mascara a little smudged in the first place.

'It was brilliant,' Stella beamed. 'Sorry I'm late. Sorry sorry sorry.'

Her mother brushed her apology away as if she was fussing over nothing. 'Any time,' she said to her daughter. 'I mean it—any time.'

Goody! Stella sang to herself as she waved her mum off, closed the front door and took the stairs three at a time.

Will! she whispered. It was brill!

# Chapter Twenty-Five

'Saturday?'

Stella stole a private moment behind the gazebo at Longbridge to phone Xander, which was slightly daft on account of it being open latticework with the clematis yet to break fully into bloom.

'Saturday,' Xander mused.

'Will's going for a sleepover at Jo's.'

'I see.'

'So I can come.'

'Phnar phnar,' said Xander and at the other end of the line, Stella giggled.

'Or you could come to me, perhaps?' said Stella.

'For a sleepover?'

'Yes,' she said, tingling. 'Yes—you can.'

\*       \*       \*

Stella didn't much like the people she was showing Longbridge to that afternoon. They were men in suits—a consortium—and they didn't really care for her guided tour. They'd dispensed with her quite quickly, having brought maps and aerial photographs with them. It seemed, for them, the devil wasn't in the details at all but in the potential for carving up the estate like a side of beef. They didn't care for secret bookcases or soft-water taps, they weren't bothered by fade-free wallpaper or a frayed piece of pipe that once carried messages from maid to chauffeur. They were, she decided, the type who'd stick two fingers up at the Prince Regent should he thrust his horse's arse at them—

297

but they didn't take any notice of the painting anyway. It was when she heard them say the apple store could come down to extend the lawn for something they called Lot 3a, that she excused herself and took refuge behind the gazebo to phone Xander. Now she didn't know whether she should go after them or wait for them to reappear—and she couldn't work out if she was pleased Lydia wasn't here or whether it would have been better had she been. Perhaps she'd have shooed them off the land. Or she might have sniffed out the ready cash which seeped from the fibres of their business suits like insidious air conditioning. Stella had already left a message for the Tompkins yesterday afternoon—why hadn't they replied? The Hakshimis were sticking at eleven which had made Lydia and Douglas Hutton tetchy with Stella.

*     *     *

What was that?

Over there—just flitting out of sight behind the summer house at the edge of the pond? Was someone there? Stella thought she heard a peel of laughter—but it could well have been skylarks or something rusty moving in the stables courtyard.

No! There!

Stella stared. Who *is* that? It was a woman skipping across the lawn like a child. Stella frowned, peered hard after her. Was she seeing things? Who gambols around in full-length peasanty kaftans anywhere—let alone Longbridge? The person had darted out of sight again, off in the direction of the tennis court. Stella looked around her—no sight or sound of the consortium honchos. No Mrs Biggins bashing mats on the lower steps. No Lydia peering haughtily from upper windows like an eagle in an eyrie. No sound of the creak and wince of Art's old wheelbarrow. No one around at all. Stella looked over her shoulder at Lord Freddie who was gazing intently in the very direction that the stranger had just headed.

'Do you know something I don't know?' Stella asked him.

'I know everything about this place,' he seemed to reply.

Stella came out from behind the gazebo, leaving her clipboard and mobile phone on the seat within it. She crossed the lawns, calling out a friendly but insistent hullo? every few strides. Something broke the surface of the pond as she walked past and she glanced at the concentric circles but saw only a fat frog sitting on a lily pad; so still, so glossy, so perfect, he looked as if he was made of the same plastic as a garden gnome.

That *was* laughter.

But there was nobody on the tennis courts.

'Hullo?' Stella called. She could hear something from beyond the yew hedge, over in the little orchard with the short, wizened old apple trees rising up from the ground like gnarled claws. It was laughter, unmistakably. She went through the arch, hewn from the hedge, and then she simply stood and gawped. There, with gay abandon, a woman not much older than Stella was swinging on the old tyre swing. Her hair was long, hitting against her back like a thick bead curtain as she swung to and from. Her long dress was tie-dyed in every imaginable shade of blue—bursts of purple and explosions of indigo, blooms of lilac, spatters

299

of sapphire, a sprinkling of aqua. She looked as though she'd been dipped in the clearest sea and the brightest sky. Barefoot. She was barefoot. And she was calling to Stella.

'Heidi! Heidi Girl!'

Stella automatically raised a hand in a bewildered wave.

'Come here, Heidi Girl!'

You look more like Heidi than me, thought Stella as, tentatively, she walked over. You with your twinkle toes and your peasanty frock.

'Heidi Girl—hullo.'

'Hullo,' said Stella who could see, close up, that the woman's hair was a mat of long golden dreadlocks varying in girth from snake skinny to great cords like those scooping away the curtains in Lydia's bedroom. 'I'm not Heidi,' said Stella. 'I'm Stella.'

Still the woman swung, quite vigorously, laughing—her head tipped back, legs extended, toes pointed, arms outstretched, body practically horizontal. Oh God—I know you're in a tyre, but don't let go. The woman soared back and forth like a benevolent angel. She let the tyre slow itself down and then, with a slither and a leap, she was standing on the grass next to Stella.

'Heidi Girl!' Her eyes danced. She was breathless.

'No,' said Stella. 'Stella.'

'I saw you!' her voice was sing-song. 'Behind the gazebo. Hiding. Hidey hidey girl!'

Stella thought, this woman is quite mad. But then she thought, who the Dickens *is* she?

'Love this swing! Haven't done that in *so* long.' She looked Stella up and down, then came in

300

close and whispered. 'Used to hide, myself. Badly as you!' Why wasn't she speaking in full sentences? 'Sneaked away to the greenhouse to smoke.' She giggled and ducked down behind Stella's shoulder as if someone had seen her. 'Very silly place to hide! Thought no one knew where I was or what I was doing. Till one day my mother offered me a cigarette.' She peered at Stella. She was standing very close, right up in Stella's personal space but oddly, it didn't feel as though she was encroaching. It felt to Stella as though she was in the presence of some life-size Longbridge sprite. Up close, she was older than Stella first thought—perhaps ten years older than Stella. Her skin was softly tanned, lines around her eyes from laughter and outdoors. Her eyebrows and the tips of her eyelashes were the colour of flax. In her nostril, a thin gold loop. 'Stella!' she said.

'Yes,' said Stella. 'But who are you?'

The woman tipped her head, as if surprised that Stella shouldn't know, as if this place was hers and it was peculiar that Stella hadn't come across her until now.

'Verity,' she said.

Not one single penny had dropped for Stella until then, because she would never have imagined that Lydia Fortescue's daughter would look or sound or act anything like the woman beside her.

'You're *Verity*?'

'Yes!'

'Of *Longbridge*,' Stella gesticulated in the air as if the estate might have disappeared.

'Yes! Verity Fortescue!' Her eyes were still glinting and flitting but her breathing was more even. 'But I haven't been Verity of Longbridge for

301

a long, long time.'

'You're Lydia's *daughter*?'

'Yes,' she laughed. 'Lydia's daughter!'

'*The one who lives with the Welsh*,' said Stella. Suddenly, the woman backed a step away and appeared timid, as though Stella's word had knocked her a little. After a moment, she nodded shyly before her beatific smile returned.

'It's so lovely to meet you,' Stella said, with genuine warmth and not a little curiosity.

'You too,' said Verity. 'Mother told me to look out for you. Told me not to scare you. Told me you are helping her to sell Longbridge.'

Stella nodded, wondering how Verity felt about it. Wondering too, when she'd arrived, how long she'd be here, what she was even doing here, and whether any of this would have any effect on anything else. Verity looked, to Stella, nothing like a Fortescue should—or was expected—to look. Instead, it was as if she'd walked barefoot all the way from the meadows of the first Woodstock festival, or had stepped off a Jimi Hendrix album cover, or had climbed through the bars of an Arlo Guthrie song and was totally unaware of the current year. Stella had an overriding urge to protect her from the navy suits and sharp talk of the consortium swaggering around Longbridge as though they owned it already.

'There are people looking around today,' Stella told Verity. 'That's why I'm here. They didn't want me, though.'

'Suity Sods!' said Verity. Then she thought about it. 'Not suited.' She shook her head vigorously.

'I know,' Stella said. 'But I had to show them around. They have money.'

302

Verity shrugged and nodded.

'Do you mind?' Stella asked tentatively. Verity tilted her head like a bird trying to locate a single seed. 'About your home being sold?'

Verity thought about it, tipping her head one way then the other and when she smiled at Stella she changed from artless and childlike, to sage and worldly. She shook her head whilst regarding Stella benevolently. 'Not a bit,' she smiled. 'Mother's decision and the right one for her. Haven't lived here for many many years—not my home. Lived With The Welsh—as Mother puts it—for longer than ever I lived here. That's my true home. I'll never leave.'

'Oh,' said Stella, panicking for a suitable response. 'I like the Welsh. My cousins used to live outside Crickhowell.'

Verity nodded then shook her head. 'Laugharne. Dylan Thomas country for me,' she said. 'So beautiful. Very peaceful.'

'Did you marry a Welshman, then?'

Verity giggled. Looked at Stella. Giggled again. 'You're funny and kind, aren't you, Stells Bells. No—not a Welshman. I don't even Live With The Welsh. I do live in Wales. But with other folk. My man is Brazilian.' Then she put her finger to her lips. 'Shh!' Stella was wide-eyed. 'He used to be French. Mother didn't mind him so much. But the Brazilian'll finish her off. So—shh!'

All Stella could do was nod earnestly because actually, she hadn't the faintest idea what any of it meant—living in Wales but not with the Welsh, a Frenchman who'd become Brazilian. How long had it taken for Verity's hair to do that? Had she not brushed it since she'd left Longbridge which,

303

Stella estimated, was two-thirds of her life ago? All she wanted to do was tuck down in the summer house with this woman and just listen to it all, ask her in what language were the tattoos on her foot and around both wrists, what they meant. Why had she left, why was she back? Her accent—a strange and seductive hybrid of upper-crust roundness enlivened by flourishes of South American, purrs of French and a twang that was transatlantic. And the chirruping staccato sentences. And Heidi Girl and Suity Sods and Stells Bells.

'I should go,' Stella said. She paused. 'I'd much rather stay and chat to you—but I'm meant to be working. I have to find the Suity Sods and wave my clipboard at them.'

'Peace, love and unity be yours,' said Verity, pressing her thumb gently on Stella's forehead.

Stella must have appeared alarmed by this because Verity instantly looked a little hurt.

'That's—very kind,' Stella rushed and smiled and squeezed her arm. 'Thank you. And peace, love and unity for you too, dear Verity.'

'Stells Bells,' Verity whispered.

'Are you staying for a while? How long will you be here?'

'Time!' Verity laughed, as if it was such a preposterous concept.

'Well, perhaps I'll see you again,' Stella said. And Verity nodded and smiled and pirouetted on the grass before walking away, the skirts of her dress all in a sway, like marsh grasses wafting in the breeze. As she made her way back to the gazebo, Stella looked over her shoulder but she saw no more of Verity. She could see the men standing on the gravel by their flash cars and she knew they wouldn't care if she went up to them or not but she would go over because it was her job to do so. She gathered her clipboard and mobile phone and walked towards them. Passing by the statue of Lord Frederick, there was just time for a quiet moment.

'You like her, your great-great-great—I don't know-how many greats—granddaughter, don't you.'

'She's one in a million and she's a dear,' he appeared to reply. 'Typical Fortescue,' he said, 'because a true Fortescue doesn't give a hoot what anyone thinks.'


## Chapter Twenty-Six

Will was confused and bad-tempered.

'I don't see why you can't clean and tidy up once I've actually *gone* to Jo's,' he said, observing his mother balancing on the table dusting absolutely nothing off the light fitting.

'Because.'

He hated that answer. It wasn't an answer. It was a rubbish sentence and he did not like the way that grown-ups were allowed to use it just because they were grown-ups.

'Cos what?'

'Will, don't wind me up. Please just help Mummy—OK?'

'I don't want to clean and tidy.'

'OK—so watch telly.'

'I thought I wasn't allowed to watch telly in the mornings.'

'Well, today's your lucky day because today you can!'

He switched on the TV but soon enough switched it off again because it was impossible to hear above the thrum of the Hoover. He watched his mother—she was hot and bothered and he just couldn't work out why she would choose to do something that put her in a bad mood and made her face red and her hair thatchy. Their home was always clean and tidy—all she was doing, as far as he could see, was making herself all messy.

'Mummy—*no*!' He leapt up from being the sorry lump in the corner of the sofa, becoming a small fireball of indignation. 'You've *broken* it!'

Stella turned off the Hoover and sat down heavily on the chair, hating herself for feeling cross with Will that his Lego space battle plane (his own design) had got under her feet—but hating herself more for wishing that Will had gone to Jo's already.

'Sorry, Will,' she said, genuinely contrite as she watched how tenderly he was examining the ruined model, as if it was a bird whose wing was broken. 'I'm really sorry.' She held her arms open and, a little begrudgingly, he shuffled towards her. 'Can you fix it? Can I help?'

'Of course I can fix it but it took me ages to make in the first place.'

'Does this bit go there?'

'No, that's the supercharge defender prong. It goes here.'

'And that bit?'

'That's not a *bit*—that's the turbo space-raid spear-shafter.'

'You could work for Lego when you grow up. You could invent amazing models.'

'I'd rather work in the Lego shop,' he said, brightening. 'Can we go to Legoland?'

306

'Definitely.'

'Tomorrow?'

'Not tomorrow—another time.'

That was another bad thing about grown-ups, Will thought. They say definitely when actually they mean maybe. So then you ask them again and they end up telling you off for nagging.

'Jo's going to take you all to the cinema this afternoon—then for a pizza. Yum! Lucky things!'

'What are you going to do?'

'Oh, nothing really.'

'So why don't you come too?'

'Because I'm busy.'

There—yet another annoying thing that grown-ups do. Say one thing one second and then the complete opposite a millisecond later and expect you, all the time, to accept that it makes perfect sense when, quite plainly, it doesn't. Will sighed and gave his mother a look of patient pity.

The doorbell rang.

'That'll be Jo,' said Stella softly, suddenly wanting to change all plans and just keep Will with her. Jo could read it on her face as soon as she came in.

'Softee,' she said, sotto voce. 'Don't think about Will, let alone worry about him—just think about yourself.' She placed her hands on Stella's shoulders. 'And give yourself enough time to tidy yourself up—you look shocking, girlfriend.'

'I feel—*guilty*,' Stella said, only just then deciphering her colliding emotions.

'Don't you dare!' Jo chastised. 'Just forget about us and indulge yourself. Disappear into your own little world for a change. You are allowed to, you know.'

After they'd gone, Stella decided against any more hoovering or tidying. Jo's calmly delivered assertion had quelled her need for frantic housework to make time pass quickly as well as to distract from the growing anticipation of Xander's impending arrival. She sat with a cup of tea, gazing at Will's special space vehicle, now fixed; content that it should remain on the kitchen table. Her heart, it appeared, had been repositioned in her throat while her stomach was relocated to somewhere behind her rib cage. She could only manage half a cup, though her mouth was dry and she could have done with drinking more. However, just holding the mug was stabilizing and a little while later, she went upstairs to shower, shave her legs and undertake a little selective tweezering here and there. She regarded her naked self and giggled—as if the concept that later on a handsome man would be ravishing her, was as thrilling as it was presently unbelievable.

*      *      *

Xander tore around the eight-mile loop in a personal best, went on the rowing machine for half an hour as if battling rip tides and then all but flooded the bathroom during a vigorous and scalding hot shower. Should he splash on some aftershave? He didn't usually—but he knew he had a bottle somewhere. He stared at his face in the mirror—silly git, just be yourself. He reached instead for the fragrance-free post-shave balm that he normally used and patted it into his skin as he went through to his bedroom. He had to laugh at himself. When do I ever—*ever*—procrastinate

308

about what to wear? And was he meant to take a change of clothes? Or just clean underwear for tomorrow? And what about a toothbrush? It all felt as protracted as packing for a holiday to a place where the weather was unpredictable.

Oh God—not the phone. He let it ring. But then his mobile trilled out with the ringtone he'd ascribed to his parents' number. Hi, Mum—fine thanks, and you? Dad? Cool. Cool. Busy—yep—flat out. Tomorrow—I'll call in tomorrow. No—don't cook lunch, I might be held up. I'll call you—tomorrow. Not sure what time—but I promise I'll call and come by.

His mobile rang again, almost immediately, and he automatically answered it.

'What you doing!'

Caroline.

'Hey, Cazza.'

'*What you doing*?'

It was her jaunty voice, the tone she used when she wasn't doing much and just felt like a chat.

'Nothing much.'

'Come on over, then.'

'Oh. Well. Actually I can't.'

'Oh?'

'I'm off out.'

'Yeah? For a run?'

'Done that.'

'So where are you off to?'

There was a pause.

'Hmm,' said Xander.

There was another pause.

'Ho!' said Caroline.

Xander wasn't sure what tiny word or noise he could make in reply, so into the hiatus Caroline leapt.

'You have *plans*!'

He hummed affirmatively, slightly distracted, the phone in the crook of his neck as he delved around a drawer deciding just to take fresh socks and boxers with him to Stella's. He'd leave them in his car with his wash bag and he went to the cupboard to stuff them all into a small rucksack.

Caroline had waited long enough. 'And do the *plans* concern a certain Stella?'

Shit. A direct bloody question.

'Are you seeing Stella, then, today?'

Caroline was tenacious—but always so bloody nice with it.

'Er—yep. I am.'

There was a strange squeak from Caroline's end of the phone before a torrent of questions tumbled down the line. None of them really needed answering, Xander thought. And then he thought, Christ, I feel so stupidly nervous.

'Xander?'

'Yes.'

'Well?'

He paused, sat on the edge of his bed, turned his back on his reflection in the mirror. 'If I tell you I'm so nervous my balls have shrunk, promise you won't take the piss?'

Caroline laughed—because Xander *was* funny. But no—she had no intention of taking the piss. 'You have a lovely time, mister.' She paused, continuing tenderly. 'Don't be nervous—you're a great guy. A really great guy. It's Stella's lucky day.'

'I'm going there—to hers,' he elaborated.

'And then?'

Xander was slightly affronted. What did Caroline want—a précis of all he'd spent the last couple of

310

days fantasizing about? 'I don't know—but, you know. Her son won't be there. So—you know—we'll have the place to ourselves.'

'I meant,' said Caroline measuredly, 'did you have plans, say, to go to the movies, or out for dinner?'

She knew he'd be reddening at the other end of the line.

'Oh. Ha!' And then he thought, fuck it, what the hell. 'I'm hoping we'll be making our entertainment, OK? And for your information, we kind of had hors d'oeuvres the other night. Back here. After the Black Ox.'

'So it's time for the main course, is it?' Caroline spoke with an audible grin. 'Well, bon appétit, Xander Fletcher.'

'Thank you,' said Xander, very sincerely.

'Oh—and make sure Stella has dessert, even if you've finished yours.'

'Phnar phnar,' said Xander, deadpan.

'Have fun, Xander. You're fab. Don't be nervous.'

But he was.

*　　　*　　　*

Xander was ready to go but his landline was ringing again. He glanced at the caller ID. Longbridge. His hand hovered. If Lydia was resorting to the telephone, it could be urgent. But there again, if it was really urgent, she'd track him down on his mobile too. He let the house phone ring out and then he stared at his mobile. Not now, Lydia. Please—not now. He gave it ample time to ring but it didn't. He switched it to silent mode, checked the back door was locked and nothing was on standby. Then he glanced around the room as if he was seeing it like this for the last time; as if tomorrow, when he came back, it would all seem very different—as if he'd be returning after ages away. He thought, next time I'm home, I'll be a changed man. And then he laughed out loud and swore at himself and thanked Jesus Effing Christ that no one heard that. Soppy git.

*     *     *

Half past three and time for tea. Stella had been reboiling the kettle every five minutes or so and suddenly thought how stupid it would look if she offered Xander a cuppa when he arrived and the kettle boiled in an instant. She poured the hot water down the sink, filled the kettle from the cold tap and left it. Then she thought how she shouldn't have made the cupcakes—he probably wouldn't remember the brief exchange when she gave him Mrs Biggins' rock cake initially destined for Will. And cupcakes suddenly seemed just too whimsical. Especially the way she iced them, which was the way Will liked. She piled them into a cake tin and put it away, then she assessed what shop-bought biscuits she had and decided that supermarket own-brand chocolate digestives were a good option. But she didn't want it to seem as though she'd opened a new packet in his honour, so she broke into the pack and stuffed the two broken biscuits which were topmost into her mouth. And, predictably, that's when the doorbell rang. Two minutes early—two all-important minutes in which she could have finished her mouthful and checked in the mirror for any stray crumbs. Instead, though she forced her mouth into concrete-mixer mode, she ended up spitting it all out into the bin before going straight to the door which was now being knocked upon.

'Not on the loo, were you?' Xander said, standing there with a grin; the sun behind him like prearranged stage lighting.

'No! Ha! Not this time.'

He looked a little puzzled, took his hand to the sides of her mouth and brushed away the drooping moustache of biscuit crumbs.

'Don't ask!' Stella groaned, resting her forehead lightly, quickly, against his chest.

'I might,' Xander said, sneaking a sniff of her hair.

'Come on in,' she said, her smile as wide as her door, her cheeks the same vermilion. 'Tea?'

'Please.'

'Biscuit?'

'If you haven't eaten them all.'

'Cheeky sod.'

'Stroppy mare.'

In the small kitchen, watching Stella make tea, Xander thought, I really want to kiss her. That awkward bash of lips when I came in doesn't count. He looked at her, she was turned away from him, her head hung low as she willed the kettle to boil. Her neck. The scoop of her pony-tail and the shaft of light revealing the downy hairs feathering their way close to her skin at the nape of her neck. He was only a step away. Now he was against her, his arms folded gently across her as his lips touched down lightly just behind her ear. And again—lower. And again—other side. Just perceptibly, she moved herself backwards so she was firm against him and tight in his grasp. And then the kettle boiled and they found they were standing a little too close to the scorch of its steam.

They took their mugs and a biscuit through to the sitting room, where the kitchen table was. Stella sat but Xander perused the room, asking about the photos, asking for recommendations amongst her paperbacks, taking the piss out of certain CDs in her collection, finding they liked the same films, offering to lend her his *Sopranos* boxed set. Then he came and sat next to her, eating another biscuit; crumbs on his face which she took great pleasure flicking away—archly at first, then tenderly. Xander admired Will's Lego creation. And then Stella said, no! you mustn't touch it! it's a one-off—hands off you dreadful man! And she smacked the back of Xander's hand and he caught it and kissed inside her palm and it sent such a shot of desire through her she thought, shall I ask you to come to bed right now?

'Shall we get some fresh air?'

\*　　　\*　　　\*

They strolled towards town, deciding to cook a meal later and reeling off a list of favourite ingredients that would make for a very eclectic spread indeed.

'Favourite dish in the world?' Xander asked her.

'Baked potato and butter,' Stella replied. 'You?'

'Frog's legs.'

'Seriously?'

'No. Not seriously. Roast chicken.'

'We could have roast chicken later?'

'But I liked the sound of your fish cakes.'

'OK—back to plan A then?'

'Yes. Bananas. I can make these really amazing caramelized bananas with toasted sesame seeds.'

'I *hate* sesame seeds.'

'Don't be ridiculous—how can you *hate* something so tiny and inoffensive.'

'You told me you hate alfalfa—and that's even less offensive.'

'Exactly. It's just a whole tangle of nothingness. It's like talking to yourself. Pointless.'

Stella laughed. 'Oh God—I talk to myself all the time.'

Xander laughed too. 'I'd never have guessed!' And he jogged across the road. Stella was a few strides behind and forgot to judge the traffic, too busy wondering what on earth Xander made of cottage cheese if he thought alfalfa was bland. A car tooted her, another screeched its brakes, then a cyclist came from nowhere and swore at her and Xander laughed because she was so flustered. And as soon as she reached the kerb he swept her up tight and kissed her. There they stood—to the outside world, a couple snogging most inappropriately right in the middle of the pavement.

'Let's not go shopping,' Stella murmured. 'Let's go back home.'

'By the way, what were they like—the consortium?' Xander wasn't sure where that came from when his mind had been gamely on returning directly to Stella's.

'Awful,' said Stella. 'I didn't like them at all.'

'It would be the worst outcome,' said Xander. He was walking fast, irritated. 'They'll just chop the estate up and sell it on as quickly as they can.'

'I figured that.' Stella stopped him a moment. Had she detected a hint of accusation in his voice? Please no. That's unfair. 'But if they make an offer, I can't do anything about it. You know that, don't you? I'd get sacked.'

Xander was silent. But then he sighed, and slowed down. 'I know.' He looked at her and the discontent which vexed the shine off his eyes had nothing to do with her.

'Do you still want to come back? Cook? And stuff?' she asked, a little unsure.

But he smiled and held out his hand to her and they walked back to her house, saying little and thinking no more about Longbridge.

*     *     *

Inside, Stella shut the front door and pressed her back against it. Xander stood a little in front of her and watched her thinking.

'You OK?' he asked.

She nodded. Didn't look up. 'It's been a while—for me.'

'That's OK,' he said quietly. 'We don't have to—if you don't want. If you don't feel ready.'

Stella regarded him. 'I've thought of little else,' she said. 'Actually.'

'Hussy,' he teased.

'Quite the opposite,' she said. 'I've probably forgotten how to do it.'

Xander touched her hand and her fingertips furled around his. 'For what it's worth,' he said, 'I'm nervous too.' Stella looked at him, surprised. 'It's true,' he shrugged. And he thought to himself how

316

true it was. 'It's been a long time for me too.'

Being with someone about whom he cared, someone who mattered—that it mattered to him what they thought. Sex was easy—with Siobhan it had been so easy it was facile, indelicate. Here, today—Stella right here, it all seemed portentous. Sex with someone he hadn't cared for had been a great way to end an evening. You come—they go. But now, about to make love with Stella for the first time, he anticipated a beginning—that something which had been germinating for a while, would now break through the surface and grow.

'What are you thinking?' Stella asked shyly.

'That I want you—that I'm really ready for this.' And his words carried her upstairs to her bedroom.

He let her see to her room, to close the curtains and take the scatter cushions from the bed, placing them in a little pile on the chair. She folded the throw and draped it over the top of the cushion stack, then she took the top two pillows and put them on the floor, revealing another two underneath. And Xander thought, I bet she does this every night, all methodical in her ways. Four pillows, plumped daily, though she sleeps with only one because she sleeps alone. And it's been a while for her.

She shrugged—as if there was no more faffing to be done and could he possibly remind her what came next. He went over to her, running his hands down her arms till he held her hands and drew her close to kiss, slipping one hand up under her T-shirt and along her back. God, her skin was whisper soft. She pulled her top off and Xander drank in the sight of her, thinking to himself how misguided all these lingerie manufacturers were

317

because, to him, a plain white bra was it. He sat on the edge of her bed and, with his hands at her hips, pulled Stella towards him and brought his lips to her skin. And Stella thought, I am well and truly ready for this. And then she thought how there was nothing else to think about.

Getting naked. At first, a gentle fumble with each other's zips and buttons but as more flesh was revealed, the greater the urgency and they resorted to undressing themselves and be done with it. Folding into each other for the first time, skin against skin, all the scents, every sense wired. Standing for a while, just tracing fingertips up and down each other while kissing gently. So far, so chaste. But as tongues probed, and Xander's fingers discovered Stella's nipples erect, and Stella felt him grow against her, their touch changed to eager fondling and delving and they fell on to the bed. The intoxicatingly perfect contradiction of the softness of a woman, the hardness of a man creating a heady impatience. So when Xander, tactfully, slowed the pace of his hand as his fingertips skimmed over her pubic hair, Stella parted her legs and pushed herself into his touch. Moist and warm, her mouth, her sex; fingers, tongues, deeper. His cock was straining for her, her grasp so tantalizing because as good as it felt, it served only to imply that her pussy would be even better.

It's been a long time for her.

Xander on his back, Stella on top, his hands in her hair, holding her face away, smiling at her. She dipped her face to his to kiss him awhile before locking eyes and lowering herself slowly until finding the tip of him. Pushing down just a little, a little more. Xander's hands—one cupping her

318

breast, the other fondling the curve of her buttocks, tracing the split in between them. His cock now deep inside her, the intensity of the sensation stilling them both for a caught moment, before releasing them into companionable writhing and shared desire. Her orgasm was soon building and he could sense it, not just from the familiar clues of hastened breathing but from the feeling of being sucked into her, a snugness enclosing him, pulling him deeper as the gasps she made correlated to the intense pulsing around his cock. Spent, she softened, her body fitting against his, her face buried in his neck, her heart still racing, her breathing fast. Her skin a-tingle and damp, every now and then a little involuntary squeeze from her sex.

As Stella lay there, in a small heaven of Xander's making, he ran his hands up and over her body, every dip and curve increasing the commotion charging a straight pathway from brain to heart to stomach to balls and back again. Jesus, he needed to come. Slowly at first, he began moving into her again, soon enough feeling Stella join him, both of them pushing and bucking, hands everywhere, lips and tongues and teeth. She could sense Xander's build-up, that his come was imminent. There hadn't been time for mention of condoms. Timing it instinctively, Stella exchanged her sex for her mouth and as Xander came he thought how his future did too.

'Good God, woman,' was his opening gambit, a while later, when the power of speech returned.

'Blimey,' Stella agreed, snuggling into the crook of his arm, stroking the dark hair which was lightly sprayed over his chest and tapered becomingly down his stomach. He encircled her wrist, his other hand enmeshed in her hair, his lips pressing gently against her forehead. He felt not simply replete physically but so comfortable. Sleepy and yet not sleepy—just a level of cosiness and comfort which was at once energizing and yet calming. Alert, alive, peaceful. Romantic, he thought, that's what I'm feeling. And then he thought, you soft bastard. And he smiled at himself and thought, so what.

'Beautiful arms,' he told her. She looked up at him, obviously chuffed. 'Nice tits, too,' he added and her laughter was joyous and contagious.

'It's not even six o'clock,' Stella marvelled. 'How decadent.'

'I know what you mean,' said Xander. 'Good planning, though—we can do it all over again later on.'

'You'll be up for that, will you?'

'Cheeky bitch. Feed me well, I might make it your lucky night.'

Stella laughed. 'Arrogant sod.'

'Stroppy cow.'

'You *always* say I'm stroppy.' Stella thought about it. 'And I'm not always stroppy.' She pouted becomingly and he kissed her nose. She settled against his chest and listened awhile to his heartbeat. 'You were bang out of order that day at Longbridge.' She recalled him belting towards her.

'I know,' he said. 'Looking back, I fancied you even then—though you infuriated me. Or possibly because you infuriated me.'

'It wasn't me infuriating you—just what you assumed I stood for.'

'I know. I'm sorry.'

'It's OK,' Stella said.

'Obviously,' said Xander, running his hand down

to her bottom and giving it a squeeze. 'Otherwise I doubt you'd have just let me do all those unmentionable things to you.'

She giggled. 'I have to admit, I felt like some self-possessed nympho in my eagerness to palm off my son to my best friend so I could leap into bed with you.'

'You were rather bloody good—for someone who claims to be out of practice.'

'You weren't too bad yourself,' said Stella.

And Xander thought, would I ever tell her about Siobhan? Would it be necessary? How utterly inconsequential all that now seemed to him. It almost bemused him how, at the time, he thought he had one up on all his conventionally married or shacked-up friends. Actually, thinking about Siobhan now—the situation they manufactured—it wasn't just unsavoury, it was a little sad too. He regretted it. He couldn't imagine Stella doing that. And, with her in his arms, he was pleased about this. Happy that it was this type of set-up he wanted most. He kissed her.

'What's in your fridge?' he asked.

'Is that a euphemism?'

He laughed. 'If memory serves me correctly, fridges are cold and you—' He ran his hand over her body, down between her legs. 'You are hot.'

'Why do you want to know what's in my fridge?'

'Because we were meant to be buying the ingredients for dinner—only you dragged me off to bed.'

'– with you protesting all the way.' She laughed. 'I'll rustle up something. Or we could call for a takeaway. Or go out if you like—though nowhere near here is as nice as the Black Ox.'

'For what it's worth, nowhere tonight would be as nice as simply staying here.'

Stella soared. 'Oh, I meant to tell you—when I was at Longbridge the other day, guess who I met! Verity!'

And in an instant, she felt Xander stiffen as if his blood had not just run cold, but had momentarily stopped flowing altogether.

'*What?*'

'I met Verity?' She felt suddenly uneasy. Xander had pulled away from her and was staring at her. 'She was at Longbridge,' said Stella. 'On the swing. I hadn't a clue who she was—no one else was around apart from this consortium who were viewing.'

'You only tell me this *now*?'

Stella was stumped. Xander practically leapt out of bed and was rushing into his clothes. What had she said to cause this reaction? 'What are you doing? Xander?' She sat up, gathering the sheets to her.

'I'm sorry,' he muttered, only glancing at her. He was distracted, irritated. There was a sense of unease, of urgency. He was going. He was missing a sock. 'I have to go.'

'I didn't—' Stella was audibly upset.

'I know,' Xander said, as he made for the door. 'I know. You wouldn't know. But I have to go. Sorry, Stella—I'll call you.'

And with Stella still in bed, in as much of a confused scramble as the sheets around her, Xander left her house. She was utterly bewildered, having absolutely no idea what any of it meant, whether any of it was her fault. Something was deeply amiss. She was on her own on the one night

322

she believed she wouldn't be and she felt wretched. After two years alone and a prolonged period of hell before that, the recent glimpse of what might now be her due had been nothing but a mirage. It had all gone belly up and she couldn't fathom why.

Fuck you, Xander! Don't you bloody dare dick me around.

## *Chapter Twenty-Seven*

For an hour, Stella kept her mobile phone to hand; checking the screen, checking that it wasn't on silent mode, that the volume was on max, that she hadn't somehow missed a call or a text. At half past eight, she switched it off in disgust. She toyed with the idea of not just phoning Jo but driving on over, knowing that her friend would be there for her, with Doritos and houmous, wine and wise words to say about all of this. But Stella stayed put. There was something humiliating about what had just happened—she'd misread a situation horribly. What an idiot. Told you so. But she also felt hurt, and dreaded telling all those who were in the wings, rooting for her. She didn't want their sympathy or their support because actually she'd rather they didn't know. What distressed her most was what she perceived to be her own inability to correctly read the situation. Truly—and slowly, sensibly— she'd allowed herself to acknowledge Xander as lovely, trustworthy, normal. It turned out she was wrong. All that nonsense her friends and family had spouted that, post-Charlie, she'd be older, wiser and more adept at telling princes from frogs. She was rubbish at it. Even now, sitting in on her own on a sorry Saturday evening, she just couldn't see where the warning signs might have been posted.

Feeling piqued was better than feeling blue. And, in a right old strop, she sat there thinking everything was crap. Apart from Xander: he wasn't just crap—he was a shit. Yet it just didn't feel cathartic, nor did it bring with it any empowerment because somewhere, deep down where she refused to look, something simply didn't add up. The Xander she'd come to know, whose company she enjoyed, whose personality she clicked with—and the intrinsic messages he'd given her through his own shyness, the tenderness of his kisses, the power of his lovemaking—just didn't sit well with the Xander who had bolted from her bedroom just over an hour ago. But there again, she chastised herself that she couldn't trust her own judgement so, for the time being, she was best left stomping around and muttering.

I could have fallen in love with Xander. Thank God I didn't.

But perhaps you already have—and that's why it feels as bad as it does.

*       *       *

When her doorbell rang at ten o'clock, she knew it was him but she remained on the sofa, determined to place a thick-skinned layer of stubborn defiance over the stupid scatter of deranged butterflies which had suddenly taken wing in her stomach.

The letter box flapped up.

'Stella. It's Xander.'

His voice tired, grave.

324

Don't answer! Don't you bloody dare!

She didn't hear the lid flap down.

Don't look, don't turn, don't even look to see if the front door is reflected in the television screen.

'Stella.'

He's still there. Stupid bastard man.

The lid flapped down.

Shit.

No! Don't let that be your reaction! Think, good! Think, good riddance. Think, sod off.

The doorbell rang again and up flapped the letter box.

'Stella, for God's sake. Your phone is off—I've been trying you for an hour.'

So what. Go away.

'Go away.' She wasn't sure she intended to say it out loud.

'I understand.' His voice was a little hoarse. 'I understand. Look, it's not simply that I can explain—and that of course I want to, for my own ends. It's that I want to share something with you because you, of all people, might just understand. And want to know.'

What is he going on about? *So* full of crap.

'Stella?'

She told herself, he has been trying to phone. She told herself: he has come all the way back. She thought, he is grovelling at my front door. She told herself, you ought to hear him out. Then she thought, no—done that before. It doesn't work, it's the first weave of what soon becomes an entire doormat to be walked all over. No. Never again. Go away.

'Jesus. Please. I've bought a curry.'

I'm not hungry. The saliva, the rumbling

stomach—it's Pavlovian, that's all. Because we mentioned a curry earlier on, that's why. That's what we were planning. Before he behaved like a bloody bastard sod.

'Stella. You might think I'm a bastard—but I'm not. Yes, I've brought curry—but the real peace offering I've brought is honesty.' A long pause. 'Stella?' And another. 'OK.' Resignedly.

The letter flap went down and all was quiet.

But Stella didn't move. She stayed still for quite a while longer; forbidding herself from wanting to hear the doorbell or for even thinking of turning on her phone. A good quarter of an hour she waited before she padded over to the front door, peeped through the spyhole and saw nothing but the compressed view of the street lamp and the plumber's van that for some annoying reason was always parked right outside her house. She told herself she was relieved but actually she was deflated too. Perhaps that was why she opened the front door. And Xander, who'd been sitting on the front step with his back heavy against the door, almost tipped right over onto the mat. In his lap, shards of pappadam and a foil container with half an onion bhaji left. He looked up and offered it to Stella, as if that alone might be the reason for her opening her door.

'I didn't know what you might like—so I've brought balti chicken, madras hot, and a few side dishes. Bombay potato. Saag. A mixed vegetable curry—dry. A plain naan. Pilau rice. Kingfisher beer.' He remained where he was, scuffling through the bag just as he shuffled over his words.

\*       \*       \*

326

Perhaps it had something to do with his obvious nervousness, or something to do with the fact that he remained sitting and she towered over him, something to do with an image of him analysing a menu and trying to phone her and then hoping he'd chosen well. And also it had something to do with the fact that he *was* still there, outside her door, not knowing whether or not she'd open it. Just sitting there, with his thoughts and a smear of mango chutney on his chin. Stella let one butterfly at a time float up through a hole she'd just made in the blanket of self-righteous anger she'd been swamping them with.

'Can I come in? Please?'

She nodded.

'Thank you.'

She walked into the house and once Xander had got to his feet and followed, Stella was already bringing plates and cutlery through to the table where Will's Lego space vehicle was still the centrepiece.

'Eat,' said Xander quietly, watching what she chose and feeling quietly proud that he'd been so right. 'I ate all the pappadams,' he admitted.

'Greedy pig,' Stella muttered but when she glanced up Xander was able to catch her eyes and hold them and pass her a tilted smile which she reciprocated, and it gave him a modicum of hope. Taking a swig from the bottle of Kingfisher beer, she pushed her plate to one side. 'OK,' she said. 'Shoot.'

'It's hard,' he said. Then he went quiet. 'It's like—the people who know, don't talk about it. And people who don't know—aren't told.' He

327

looked up: Stella appeared justifiably confused. Xander felt weighed down by responsibility—to Verity, to Lydia, to what had been entrusted to him since childhood. But he felt a responsibility to Stella too. He left the table and went over to the bookcase, absent-mindedly running his fingertips over the undulation of spines. 'I haven't even told Caroline the entire story—and she's my best friend. And I never told Laura.'

'Laura?'

'My ex.'

'Oh.'

He turned to face Stella. Though her face had softened, she was sitting rigid with anticipation. And he could hardly blame her.

'You've probably heard the way gossip and rumours flood the village as if facts trickle down the Longbridge driveway to become a torrent of fiction by the time they reach the shop, or the school playground, or the postbox?'

Stella raised her eyebrow and nodded.

Xander continued. 'But this is one thing, concerning the Fortescues, that you'll never hear a single rumour about. Because, at the time, ranks closed and protected those concerned.' He was talking quietly. 'It wasn't so much a secret to be guarded, but something that was simply very, very private—to be shared only by those who were there.' Then Stella watched as he winced at the memories.

'What is it?' she asked in the soothing voice she employed when Will cried. 'What happened?' She could see anguish on Xander's face and, just then, she could differentiate between his lovely laughter lines and harsher scratches around his eyes where

328

some long-carried pain was etched into his being the way acid eats into the copper of an engraving plate.

Xander stood with his back to the bookcase. Stella didn't know whether to stay put or go to him. But he returned to the table and sat down. Instinctively, she stretched her arm across to him. He let her take his hand and it helped.

'Lydia had a son,' he said.

'Edward,' said Stella.

'He died at just seven years old. Heir to Longbridge. Love of Lydia's life—she's very honest about that. Really, she wanted another son—desperately—in Edward's honour, to ease the pain, to help the marriage, I'm just guessing. I never really knew Jolyon, Lydia's husband. He was around—but very stern, very self-contained and seemingly not interested in his family or anyone connected with them. So Lydia wanted a son but instead, all she got was Verity.'

Stella frowned.

'I know,' said Xander. 'Hard to believe. But Lydia *really* wanted a son, and Verity was everything Edward wasn't—a difficult baby, an awful toddler and a troublesome child, by all accounts. And—a *girl*. Lydia didn't want a girl— she wanted Edward back. But she got Verity—and after that, bizarrely, no other boy would do. Which is why I held my breath when I saw Will that day. Because when Lydia first met me, when I was little—we came to Longbridge when I was four and Verity was nine—well, Lydia was pretty vile. Not monstrous—just withering and cold and rarely spoke to me. My mother was nanny to Verity and I loved Verity.'

Xander looked at Stella straight. 'I *really* loved her. Even now I can recall the pure wonder I felt. She was so—' It was impossible to put into words. He tried again. *'Floaty,'* he said. 'Like she wasn't wholly human. Like she was part fairy, part bird, like she'd seen so much and yet knew nothing— like she was snowflake or breeze, something you were blessed to have while being acutely aware of its fragility, its transitory nature. She'd take my hand and we'd literally spend all day running around Longbridge—the land, the house, our apartment. All weathers, in and out of years. Laughter, whispering, imagining. That's what filled my childhood—I mean, there was school, and mundanities, but my overriding memories are just of me and Verity *playing*, always in this fantastically detailed make-believe world of hers.' He paused momentarily, reliving a memory happily.

'My mum's very—nurturing,' he said. 'She's actually a bit of a hippy. It was amazing that Lydia employed her at all, really—they'd had nannies in starched uniforms before but they'd all resigned or been booted out. But Verity loved my mum from the start—was always calmer when with her. Anyway, when I was little, Verity was very much like an older sister, pulling me into her games, coaxing me up trees, fussing over me. And then at some point it shifted—I can't quite tell you when. Perhaps I was about nine and suddenly I just knew *I* had to look out for *her*. She was about fourteen, fifteen at the time. She'd been expelled from school and was being tutored at home. My mum still looked after her. Suddenly floaty changed into something *so* light, *so* flimsy it became frighteningly insubstantial, like the faint smear of water in

330

your hand where a snowflake has melted. I guess nowadays they'd happily fix a title on it, call her bipolar or manic depressive. I don't know.' He paused again.

'But if a dead child was a public tragedy—and I'm told the village rallied for the Fortescues at that time—a mad child brought a level of shame to the family that meant utter privacy was essential. People knew something wasn't right with Verity, but after the tragedy of Edward, they actually tempered any rumour-mongering. I believe it was more whispers—but with sympathy. Which of course, Lydia hated because she's proud and aloof and, whether rightly or wrongly, truly believes herself superior—at the top of the Long Dansbury pyramid. She said to me once—I'll never forget, *It isn't what they say about you, it's what they whisper.*'

Xander went quiet.

'What happened?' Stella whispered, now taking his hand in both of hers. 'To Verity?'

'Twice,' said Xander, looking at Stella as if asking, *what could any of us have done?*

Stella gave him some time before she asked. 'Twice? What happened twice?'

'The first time when I was ten—on her fifteenth birthday. We were up in the clock tower together. Playing. She was truly excellent at playing, especially up there. We loved the clock tower—you could look out from every side, it had its own air quality, its own on-a-level-with-birds'-nests quiet. We were hidden. We could see everything. We pretended it was the Four Corners of a Distant World. That day it was some convoluted make-believe game of Verity's—typical trapped damsels and dark lords. So—forgive me—but I just

331

didn't realize when it was no longer a game. When she made to jump.'

Stella gasped. 'Verity *jumped*? From the clock tower? But it's twenty feet high!'

'She didn't leap,' Xander continued, 'she sort of slithered off, partway. And time just ground to a halt. She stayed there—gripping on to the parapet. So I tried to hold on to her and raise the alarm and she said, don't shout, don't you dare shout you little shit. But I just held onto her hand as tight as I could. And then Lydia and Art were there and Verity just dropped. A crumple. So still. Knocked herself out. Broke near enough every bone in her foot.' Xander observed Stella, who was visibly shaken.

'Lydia came to our apartment later. I was ready for bed. I remember being shy about my pyjamas—I don't know why. Lydia was adamant. *Verity fell. She fell from the clock tower because she wasn't looking. An accident. A family matter.* And though I told my mum and dad that I dropped Verity, they said if Lydia says Verity fell, then Verity fell. I remember my mother telling me that the easiest way to keep a secret is without help.'

'That's a tall order for a ten-year-old boy,' said Stella. 'But Verity—do you really think—?'

Xander nodded. 'Because the next time was just a month later. And that was very serious. She cut her wrists. Mrs Biggins found her.'

Stella shuddered, stunned. She thought of the woman she'd met that week—all barefoot in nature, with flowing robes and laissez-faire hair and healthy nut-brown skin. Her poise and self-contentment; her funny, strange sing-songy voice, her childlike and playful demeanour. Heidi Girl. Happy woman.

'So—she was sent away,' said Xander, as if in conclusion. 'And she's rarely been back since.'

'Sent away—where?'

'Hidden, if you like. To a—you know. Lydia called it "somewhere safe". So I'll have to respect that and call it "somewhere safe"—not a loony bin, but a wholesome version of one. Whatever you'd call it. And it *was* a place of safety for Verity and it really did help.'

'Did you still get to see her?'

'She came back, for short periods. In between times, people would ask Lydia, how's Verity—as if she was simply away in some Swiss finishing school. Of course there were rumours by then—but you'll find people just don't gossip salaciously about something like that, however scant the known details, however much Lydia might rub people up the wrong way. It's a humbling, humiliating thing, isn't it? That title and riches cannot command health and happiness. That tragedy struck the privileged not once, but twice. That Lydia was too proud to accept sympathy or support—and how lonely a place that must be. I suppose, to the village, it's what made Lydia more *human*.'

'And Verity never came back to Longbridge?'

'Well, when she was eighteen, it was up to her and luckily she was in a position to finally make her own decisions and sensible ones. I like to think she was never really *deranged*—just delicate. Something chemical was amiss—but she had help and they were able to redress the balance.'

'With medication?'

'And the rest,' said Xander. 'Electroconvulsive therapy.'

'Jesus, poor kid,' said Stella.

'But you see, I don't think of Verity as "mad" because she categorically isn't. She's just unusual. Eccentric. Special. To the world, Lydia makes light of it, implies they're almost happily estranged— banters how her daughter *"lives with the Welsh"*. Appears not to worry, not to hurt. Doesn't give the gossip-mongers anything to grab, anything to run with. People haven't forgotten about Verity—but she's so seldom back and when she is, few know about it. So she's simply slipped from the memories of most. Which is how she'd want it and how Lydia likes it.'

'Verity told me that she doesn't actually live with the Welsh at all—she lives with a French man, who's now Brazilian. Or something,' said Stella. 'She didn't strike me as mad in the medical sense. She came across as endearingly, colourfully, *potty*. Slightly bonkers but in the *best* sense of the word. I use it as a compliment.'

Xander laughed. 'She had a French boyfriend for a few years—I'm guessing she's now with a Brazilian bloke.'

'In Wales?'

'It's absolutely perfect for her—she lives on a sort of commune. Not yurts and tree hugging and clothes knitted from mung beans—but just a few families living simply, quietly, unmaterialistically. It's home. Longbridge isn't.'

'Have you been there? Have you visited?'

'Yes—yes, I have But not for a while. I took Lydia once. And I've been a couple of times. But I could see our presence was not good for Verity. I understand. I understand how she can't have a crossover in her new life from her old. Not that she's reinvented herself—she's just comfortable

334

there, it's where she's at her most capable. Happy. Her independence from what was. Her belief in herself and the life she's chosen. She lives there *successfully*. So even for me—let alone Lydia—to go there, you can sense it's disruptive. Intrusive. Potentially destructive—like a self-sufficient tribe suddenly exposed to bacteria from the outside world. If that doesn't sound too extreme.'

'Some Eskimos had never had the common cold before they had contact with the likes of us,' said Stella, who'd recently learned so when watching *Blue Peter* with Will. 'She's made a life for herself, Xander—she has balance. How many of us can truly say we've achieved that?'

'Lydia *does* know that.'

'Ultimately, Verity chose life,' said Stella with not a little awe.

'Lydia knows that too,' said Xander. 'The tattoos.'

'On her foot—and on her wrists,' Stella recalled.

'They're very profound for Verity. Lydia hates them, of course—makes light and says her daughter is "*inked like a navvy*." But for Verity, they signify something positive and profound over something negative. Apparently they translate to *peace, life, hope*—in ancient something-or-other. They cover her scars.'

'Is she OK now? I mean—medically?'

Xander smiled. 'She seems absolutely fine. Has been for years. She's just—unusual. And for an unusual person to enjoy life, they have to gain the wisdom to choose a life that is as unconventional as they are. Otherwise it's forever square-peg-in-round-hole syndrome.'

'But it means they have to leave the round hole.'

Stella paused. 'Longbridge.'

Xander nodded. 'Longbridge was bad for her health. Wales is good.'

'Why was she back?' Stella asked. 'Why did you rush there?' She needed answers. 'Did you see her?'

Xander shook his head. 'She went after lunch.'

'Did you speak to Lydia? Mrs Biggins?'

'Lydia was there,' Xander said. 'She told me Verity had phoned me earlier. I didn't tell her I'd ignored the call thinking it was just Lydia.'

'What did she say?'

'Lydia said she wasn't sure whether Verity would be back before Longbridge is sold.'

'Was Lydia OK?'

'Yes. She seems tired though. She has her arm in a sling. Tripped.'

'You're very close,' said Stella. 'To Lydia.'

'Even when I was very young—even when I found Lydia really quite terrifying—I felt like a mediator between her and Verity. When Verity went—that's when Lydia reached for me. That's when I became her link with both Edward and Verity.'

'Dear Lydia,' Stella said softly.

'One thinks of her as this hard, aloof, upper-class harridan. But God she must have been through it. She doesn't hate her daughter, she doesn't resent her, she's no longer embarrassed by her. I think she's even happy for her—but I also think that alongside day-to-day Lydia who's a dreadful snob and terrorizes people, she runs a private parallel life in constant mourning for her children.'

'It's no one's fault,' Stella said. 'Edward could have lived—and Verity would still have been

336

Verity.'

Xander tipped his head and finally he smiled and his laughter lines superseded all others. 'I knew you'd see it that way,' he said. 'That's why I felt I could go—but also come back. And I'm going to sound like a soft bastard now but I don't care—I'm almost forty, fuck it! But I wanted to tell *you*, Stella, because I sensed you'd feel it, that you'd understand and not judge.'

Stella shrugged. 'You're not a soft bastard,' she said. 'You *can* be a moody git—but I suppose perhaps it takes a stroppy cow to handle one of those.' She went over to Xander, took his face in her hands and kissed him while he held on to her, tight.

He looked at her. 'You've gone all—pensive,' he said.

Stella took a moment. 'Xander,' she started, cautiously. 'Are you—were you?' She shrugged. 'In love—with Verity? Is there unfinished business? Baggage? It's cool—it's fine. But I'd rather know.' She was fiddling with a piece of Lego.

Xander put his hand over hers to still it. 'No,' he said. Then he laughed. 'Perhaps when I was six or seven. But no—not in reality.'

'It would be OK—' Stella started.

'This might sound pompous,' Xander said. 'But I suppose—like I think I've said to you—I feel responsible in some ways, for both Lydia and Verity. I sort of became the man of the house at Longbridge—for Lydia in lieu of Edward. For Verity as her rock. For Lydia again, when Verity went. For Lydia, as she's aged. And now, for all of them again. That's why I feel so strongly about the sale. Far more than Verity does. Possibly as much as Lydia does.'

Stella considered all that Xander was telling her. But actually, what she most wanted to contemplate was Verity herself. How Stella wished she'd known all this before she met her. Or perhaps it was good she hadn't—because she'd taken Verity simply as she'd found her, unprejudiced by anything known. Stella's overriding impression was that she'd been in the presence of someone extraordinary, someone who, at some point, had been kissed by a rainbow. Someone so integral to Longbridge Hall despite the fact that she had left so long ago. And then Stella thought, behind that banner Xander brandishes to Save Longbridge! Save the Village! Save the Aged Residents! is a whole other story—and it's *his* story.

'Verity *is* special to me,' Xander said. 'And Lydia is too. And most of all Longbridge is special to me. It's been the benevolent safe place in which all of this played out. Fundamental to my childhood—to my experiences, to shaping the person I became.' He paused. 'See, told you it would sound pompous!'

'Which is why, out of all of them, you so long for it not to be sold,' said Stella, putting her hand, now, over his.

All talked out.

They half watched a bit of a film on Channel 4; shoes off, Xander's feet on the coffee table, Stella curled on the sofa in a furl around him.

'Can I still stay for the sleepover?'

Stella laughed. 'I won't let you go.'

'Good.'

'Do you want to go to bed now?'

'Do you?'

'I don't understand what on earth is going on in this movie.'

'Don't you? But it's just so, like, post-modern sub-noir.'

'I think it's a pile of poo. Come on.' And Stella switched off the lights and led Xander back to her bedroom.

In her bathroom, he thought of his overnight stuff in the bag in the car. And then he saw the new toothbrush she'd left for him. He ran his finger over the bristles. What a gorgeous girl. What a night. What a day. He'd divested himself of so much and yet he felt far from empty, not remotely deflated. In fact, he felt replete, the same satisfying fullness of having eaten just the right amount of a perfect Sunday roast. He could love Stella. Perhaps he already did. He nodded at himself, welcoming the notion that he was potentially minutes away from a fine night's sleep in the arms of a beautiful woman. He was pleased she knew, pleased he'd found the courage to share. Pleased that Verity had met Stella and that Stella had met Verity. Pleased that Verity and Lydia had both coped without needing him there. That perhaps Verity had said her final goodbyes to Longbridge. That, actually, she'd made her peace with the place a long time ago.

When Stella and Xander's bodies folded into each other, however, it wasn't just emotions that were stirred. Making love for the second time was both gentler and somehow more adept. In the dark. Sensing what was wanted. Coming together. A physical and cerebral correspondence.

'You're a sexy minx,' said Xander, afterwards.

'Bet you say that to all the girls,' said Stella.

'I haven't yet met *all* the girls,' said Xander. 'Ow! Did you just *pinch* me?'

'Yes,' said Stella. She paused. 'Laura?'

'Laura?'

'She was your significant ex?'

'Yep.' Xander stroked Stella's hair as he spoke. 'We were together that all-important decade from our mid-twenties—when you think you can shape the world.' Stella trailed her fingertip over his lips. 'The long and the short of it is that classic phrase—when we grew up, we wanted different things from life.'

'Oh?'

'Laura wanted to travel and run a beach bar in Cambodia and do a ski season in Banff and crew a catamaran over the seven seas.'

'And you?'

'I just wanted to live in Long Dansbury. And have a family.'

'She didn't want that?' It seemed preposterous to Stella.

'No.'

'And you didn't want to see the world?'

'Not really—I'd done a fair bit of travelling in my student days.'

'You loved her?'

'Very much. But ultimately we were in that clichéd trap of staying together because we were a long-term couple and it was easier than splitting up.'

'But you did split up.'

'Ultimately, we weren't peas in a pod. We were poles apart. All the idealism of our twenties—it was transient. It was just the stuff of late-night deep-and-meaningful conversations behind curtains of spliff and a backdrop of Pink Floyd. Ultimately we didn't believe in the same things—and we didn't want each other. It was habit.'

340

'Do you see her?'

'She lives in New York, these days.'

'*New York*?'

'With a banker husband and two kids.'

'How bizarre! Does that hurt?'

'Nope. Not any more.'

'Blimey, Xander.'

'Blimey Xander what, Stella?'

'Been there, seen it, done it—you have.' He could feel Stella thinking. 'Verity—Laura. I'm afraid I'm horribly dull in comparison.'

Xander laughed. He kissed her forehead.

'I'll be the judge of that,' he said. Snuggled against her. Yawned. Yawned with the bliss and relief and comfort of discovering someone with whom he could be wide open, with whom he could also close off from the world. He yawned with the effort that had accompanied so much revelation. Yawned because he'd just made love to Stella and his body was wonderfully tired. Yawned because Stella's bedroom was all about soft darkness and cosiness and a lovely scent. Yawned because he was ready to surrender himself to sleep after a spectacularly big day in his life.

'What a life you've had,' Stella said, kissing him affectionately on the cheek as she nestled her head against his shoulder. A man in her bed. This Xander man.

'But I've never loved anyone enough to actually marry them,' he said, sleepily. '*Whereas you did.*'

Xander, however, was sound asleep by the time Stella thought, Christ, how on earth do I begin to tell you about Charlie?

# Chapter Twenty-Eight

'Yes, but how did he *know* Verity was here—if he didn't answer her telephone call and she left no message!' Mrs Biggins wasn't asking Lydia a question, she was stating something blindingly obvious which had bypassed Lydia. Mrs Biggins was literally rubbing her hands with glee. Stop it, thought Lydia, your paws are red enough already. 'Why come belting round on Saturday evening?'

'To see her!' Silly woman.

'But belting round?' Mrs Biggins cocked her head. 'He can only just've heard she was at Longbridge. If he'd've known earlier, he'd've been more refined, more formal about it all. Instead of which, he's hammering on your door past supper-time!'

Privately, Lydia reasoned it all out. Mrs Biggins had a point.

'Did you ask him?'

'What?'

'How he came to hear?'

'No.' Lydia thought back to Saturday night. It was only Monday morning but the new week made Saturday suddenly feel very distant. That was no bad thing. She'd felt pretty wretched on Saturday—with her arm in a sling, with Verity gone. It had been enough to tell Xander that Verity wasn't here—to then idle away half an hour with light and informal chit-chat about how she was, though her visit had privately disconcerted both of them.

'Interesting, though,' Mrs Biggins said, attempting to dust and then thinking she'd do it properly later. 'Interesting to wonder about Xander's Saturday night.'

It was. Lydia admitted it to herself once her housekeeper had left the room with promises of mid-morning coffee. A daughter Lydia ceased to have any plans for, over whom she had no control—and a man she'd known since a boy in whom she was investing hopes and plans and whom, it seemed, was ticking them off for her one by one.

Which left Lydia thinking about Miss Hutton—whose purpose was twofold. Stella might be fulfilling the obligation she knew nothing of—but she appeared to be failing in her objective to sell the bloody place. Irritated, Lydia walked to the hallway and made a phone call to Elmfield Estates.

'What *is* going on?'

'Good morning, Lady Lydia.'

'Miss Hutton—have you heard nothing?'

'I left messages for the Tompkins and the consortium. I have a Japanese gentleman keen to view on Wednesday.'

'Why don't I phone the Tompkins?'

'Because that's my job.'

Lydia harrumphed.

'And it's not the done thing.'

She harrumphed again.

'And you hate the telephone,' Stella said.

'So?'

'It shows.'

Impudent girl! But Lydia had to admit, Stella had a point.

'Lydia?'

'Yes?'

'How is your arm?'

'Much better. A little achy—still in this hideous

343

sling. Thank you for asking.'

And then Lydia thought, but I never told you about my arm. Lydia thought how she hadn't seen Stella since before Verity's visit. Lydia thought, how do you know about my arm? And then she simply thought, bugger this—I shall damn well ask you straight.

'Miss Hutton—how did you know about my arm? Some rumour in the village that I was swinging from the chandeliers, perhaps? Or that you'd twisted it, to have me part with Longbridge for a song, perhaps?' Lydia liked that. Very good. 'Well?'

And Stella thought, very good, Lydia, you've got me. And Stella thought, can it hurt? She wanted to sing it from the rooftops anyway—the presence in her life of a lovely new boyf, as she was already calling him. She cleared her voice. 'Xander told me.'

'And when did you see Xander?' Lydia's inference was that *surely* Xander and Stella were linked only by Longbridge matters.

Stella cleared her throat again. 'On Saturday.'

'Saturday?'

'Socially.'

'Socially!'

Stella waited. 'I owe you my gratitude, Lady Lydia.' She was utterly sincere.

'For what?' Lydia wasn't expecting such guilelessness.

'For Xander, of course,' said Stella.

And Lydia realized she couldn't play further with Stella's honesty and sincerity. She'd just have to be gracious. 'My pleasure.'

'Pardon?' Stella had heard her—but she wanted Lydia to repeat it, without the mumble.

344

'It's a pleasure,' said Lydia.

Neither woman mentioned Verity though they were aware how Verity had brought Xander to each of them on Saturday.

*      *      *

Geoff had the phone under the crook of his chin, gesturing to Stella while she was finishing her call to Lydia. *Tomp-kins*, he mouthed and Stella beckoned furiously for him to put the call through.

Please please please.

'Mr Tompkins! Good morning!'

'Morning, Stells.'

That's fine. You can call me Stells.

'Did you have a lovely weekend? Is Mrs Tompkins well?'

'Thank you—yes to both.'

'Good!'

Tone it down.

'Good. Mr Tompkins, I'm so glad you've called. Any thoughts about Longbridge Hall?'

There was silence.

Oh please oh please oh please.

'Been thinking of little else, Stells. I love it, love the place. We both do. Can see it—you know—as the seat for Tompkins past and Tompkins future.'

And Stella thought, so why can I sense the "but".

'But the problem is, it scares the wife. It's too much to take on.'

'If it's the guide price—' Stella butted in, desperate to head off the worst.

'Not the price, darlin'. It's got all them bedrooms—but only three baths. And a grand dining room—but a rubbish kitchen. And it's listed,

345

so it's non-stop hassle, Stells, hassle all the way.'

'But you could live in the dower house—while having the main house renovated? We could factor that into any offer you might make?'

'No, Stells. Not just the house—all that farmland. I mean, I like a garden. I've got a huge one, myself, right now. And Longbridge has *grounds*—which is a rung up on a garden and I like that. But not the farm. We're not farming people, Miss Hutton. No, Stells. I am sorry. Please pass me regards on to the Lady, won't you? And you keep your eyes open, will you? For something big—with nice bathrooms, en-suite, you know? And a killer kitchen.'

Stella was nodding. Mr Tompkins couldn't hear it.

'Hullo?'

'Of course, Mr Tompkins, of course.'

She sat with her head in her hands until Geoff came over and gave her shoulder a gentle pat, partly to block the snidely triumphant look on Gill's face.

'All's not lost,' he said. 'You have yet to phone back Mr Murdley.'

'Mr Murdley?'

'From the consortium,' Geoff pointed to the Post-it he'd placed on the edge of Stella's monitor.

'How can I sell Longbridge to someone called Murdley? Isn't there a Dickens character called Murdley? In a draughty house with secrets in the cellar and rumours floating out of the rotten rafters?'

Geoff smiled benevolently. 'You're really not an estate agent, Stella, are you? You need to get out of this trade—just as soon as you've sold Longbridge and you can afford to.'

'I can't sell Longbridge to a consortium,' she whispered.

'That's not for you to decide,' Geoff said, quite sternly. He removed the Post-it, dialled the number on Stella's phone and handed her the receiver when he heard the ringing tone. 'And it was Murdstone,' Geoff said.

'*David Copperfield*,' Stella said sadly.

Mr Murdley was syrupy smooth on the phone. The offer was eleven, with exchange of contracts in two months, completion by the end of the year.

'I will present this to Lady Lydia Fortescue,' Stella said, 'and report back to you.'

Geoff tutted at Stella ten minutes later, as she'd remained at her desk staring into space.

'What!' she protested, to which he raised his eyebrows towards the phone. 'Lydia hates the phone!' His eyebrows inched higher. 'I'm going there on Wednesday—the day after tomorrow. With a Japanese client. I'll tell her then.' His eyebrows stayed as they were. 'Geoff,' Stella remonstrated. 'Let me do this my way.' But she knew there was a right way to do things, and her proposed method was wrong. However, there was nothing wrong with waiting until later this afternoon—Lydia tended to nap, intentionally or otherwise, after lunch.

Walking up St Andrew Street, Stella saw two commercial properties to let and as able as she was to imagine her gallery in either, the thought simply depressed her because it wasn't remotely plausible. She mooched off to walk down to the river and sat there, picking at a sandwich and ignoring the swan and the geese and a couple of youths loitering on BMXs. Her mother called but Stella didn't answer it. And then she thought of how her mother always said, if you're feeling upset, do something to make yourself feel not so. She stared at Xander's contact details. And sent a text.

Having a rotten day ☹

Then she wondered if Xander hadn't yet ascribed an ID to her number. So she sent another.

This is Stella

Xander was mid-conversation with Mrs Gregg when his phone bleeped through two messages close together. Mrs Gregg observed him grinning inanely at his phone and realized he wasn't going to finish his sentence. She watched him stare at the ceiling before tapping out a message.

This is Xander. A rotten day deserves a nice evening. You free? Xx

She liked it that he didn't abbreviate. She thought she ought to go easy on the Emojis.

Would love to—but it's a school night.

Mrs Gregg noted that, after that bleep, Xander responded quicker.

Does Will like fish & chips? Do you?

Stella regarded her limp sandwich and thought about fish and chips for tea. With the best delivery man in town. She couldn't think of a larky reply. So she just wrote yes please—thanks ever so. And after she'd sent it, she thought, my mum's right. So she phoned her as she walked back to the office.

Let the afternoon fly by! Let Lydia not be in.

But the afternoon dragged. And Lydia was in.

'Yes?'

'Hullo—it's Stella again.'

'Couldn't this wait until Wednesday when you bring Japan?'

'I have news—from the Tompkins and Mr

Murdley.'

'Murdley?'

'From the consortium.'

'And?'

'The consortium are offering eleven.'

'Yes, yes. But what about my friend Mr Tompkins?'

'Your friend Mr Tompkins sends his regards—' Stella closed her eyes. 'But I'm afraid Longbridge isn't for him.'

There was a long pause. Lydia's voice, when it came, was brittle. 'But it *is*,' she said. 'It *is* for him.'

'But not for his wife.'

'No?'

'No,' said Stella softly. 'People want en-suites and dressing rooms and snazzy kitchens. It's what they expect.'

'Has the woman no vision!'

Stella knew Lydia was just frustrated. 'They wished Longbridge was as they can picture—but they just don't want the undertaking themselves. Or the farmland.'

Silence again. 'I see.'

'So we have the consortium and the Hakshimis, both on eleven. I suggest we let them each know we have another offer—plus a viewing on Wednesday.'

'As you see best,' said Lydia. And she hung up.

*        *        *

Will was delighted with his fish supper—not least because his friend Xander insisted they ate straight off the paper, ignoring the way his mum put her hands on her hips in disgust. Xander didn't even want his mum's knives and forks—telling her that it was a travesty (whatever that was—but Will could guess) not to use the wooden *spork*, as Xander called it. Spork, thought Will—what an ace word! He would call horrid Benji at school a spork from now on. So they all sat at the table, with hills and valleys of paper between them, piles of big fat chips and fish that fell from the batter in landslides of glossy white flakes. And his mum was a bit giggly which sounded nice. *And* she let him stay up fifteen whole minutes later to allow Xander to play in a Lego space battle. Will thought how his mum was double-nice when their friend Xander was about.

Ready for bed in R2D2 pyjamas, he looked Xander up and down. 'Do you want to come again? You can be Anakin next time. I don't mind.'

'Brill,' said Xander.

'Just go and ask my mum—she'll definitely say yes.'

'OK,' said Xander. 'Night then, Will.'

Xander came downstairs and into the kitchen, his finger to his lip to hush her until he was close next to her, kissing her silently. Her arms about his neck, his hands in her hair, tugging out her pony-tail to weave his fingers in and out. His hands sweeping over her body, cupping a breast, taking a squeeze between her legs, leading her hand to the thick cord of hardness trapped tormentingly behind his trousers.

Stella pulled away. 'We can't—not yet. Not with Will—'

'I completely understand.'

Then he pulled Stella close again, running his hands over her, whispering into the top of her head. 'When I get home, I'll have to have an almighty wank.'

350

Stella giggled. It sounded so licentious—yet actually, the thought of it turned her on.

'And while you're hard at it,' she said, tracing the shape of his straining cock, 'know that I'll be doing the same.'

## Chapter Twenty-Nine

The Japanese couple said no to everything Stella showed them at Longbridge but nodded so much and smiled so politely all the while, that she wondered whether no meant yes. However, it was clear they didn't like Longbridge for exactly the same reasons as the Tompkins—they expected modern fittings, dressing rooms and a degree of luxury that Longbridge, currently, could not offer. Lydia was growing impatient, Stella increasingly anxious that if the property didn't sell soon, they'd be faced with the lull over the summer months before trade picked up again in the autumn.

'I just want it sold,' Lydia said. 'I told you that. And *you* told me it would go like hot cakes.'

'I can't force people to buy,' said Stella. They were standing by the tennis court which, in the clean light of a summer's mid-morning, looked mossy and unkempt, the surface scuffed, raised here and there by a tree root, the net in need of repair, the lines wanting a fresh lick of paint. It was the same with the swimming pool. Leaves on the surface and debris on the base, and when the breeze rippled the water green tidemarks on the tiles slugged into view.

'So we're on eleven. With two offers?'

'That's right,' said Stella.

'Well—play them off against each other!' Lydia barked as if Stella was an idiot for not having done so already. Stella watched her walk away, arm still in a sling, the precise reason for it still concealed. Taking a seat on the low wall by the rose bushes, Stella phoned both potential buyers, compromising her integrity in service to her client's instructions. Then she headed back to her car, waving apologetically at Art as she went. She enjoyed their little chats but today she didn't feel like talking. In the five minutes it took to drive through the village, Mr Murdley had called her back. The consortium would up their offer to twelve. But it was on the table for twenty-four hours only. Stella drove back to Longbridge. By the time she parked, the Hakshimis' representative had called her back with a final offer of eleven and a half. Progress and potential felt like the sword of Damocles poised over Stella's shoulders. But she had a job to do. She ignored the scent of early honeysuckle and she looked the other way from the clamber of wisteria adorning the side of the house, marching up the stone steps and telling the lions not to look at her so reproachfully.

Mrs Biggins opened the door with a theatrical *shh!* to her lips—Lydia was listening to the afternoon play and was not to be disturbed. Though, at the volume she had it at, Stella and Mrs Biggins could easily have sung 'Rule Britannia' at the tops of their voices and Lydia wouldn't have heard them.

'May I wait?'

'Come into the kitchen—kettle's just boiled,' said Mrs Biggins. She made Stella tea and brought to the table two trays laden with individual pastry

352

cases just out of the oven. 'Get dolloping,' she said, handing Stella a teaspoon and a jar of home-made damson jam. 'Nothing like a jam tart.'

Stella was glad of the task and the company. She had sensed for a long time that there was something wily about Mrs Biggins, an all-seeing eye, ears always peeled. She liked her loyalty to Lydia—but also the growing camaraderie she now extended to Stella. Always at her ladyship's behest—and yet never not her own woman too.

'Hear you met Verity,' Mrs Biggins said, casually.

'I did,' said Stella, adding a little more jam to her first two tarts, estimating that a spoon and a half was the right amount. 'She's extraordinary.'

'Bless her,' said Mrs Biggins. And then Stella thought, crafty old thing—that was an opening, not a closed statement. It reminded her of the way her mother saw to splinters during Stella's childhood— diverting her attention while she quietly and deftly drew it out. 'Shame Verity didn't get to see Xander.' Mrs Biggins let that lie long enough for Stella to fill another two tarts. 'He was out, Saturday, when she called him.'

Stella filled another case, then licked the spoon thoughtfully. 'He was with me,' she said evenly. 'But I think you know that.' Certainly the smile that Mrs Biggins bit into attested to it.

'You'll need to use a fresh spoon, love—can't be poisoning the WI with your germs.' Mrs Biggins passed Stella a clean spoon. It was the same as the one at Xander's. She turned it over and over between her fingers, dipped it into the jam and, absent-mindedly, put it directly into her mouth. Mrs Biggins chuckled.

'Sorry,' said Stella. 'I was miles away.'

'Cavorting with Mr Fletcher, no doubt.'

'Mrs Biggins!' Stella remonstrated. 'Actually, I was thinking of the two raised offers that have come in for Longbridge.'

'Of course you were,' said Mrs Biggins. 'Well, the play'll be done with in ten minutes. Then you can see Lady Lydia. And the first batch'll be ready,' she added, placing a tray of jam tarts in the oven.

'Will you still bake—when Longbridge is gone?'

'Longbridge'll never be gone—it's just that I won't be here. But I can bake anywhere. It's what I am,' said Mrs Biggins. And just then, Stella really worried about her. 'I'll be fine,' said Mrs Biggins, as if reading her mind. 'I have plans.'

'Can I keep the spoon?'

'If it happens to find its way into your bag, I won't know about it,' said Mrs Biggins.

'It's just EPNS,' said Stella. She paused. 'Like the one Xander has.'

Mrs Biggins cast her eye over Stella's jam tarts. 'You been into his drawers already?'

And just then, Stella was reminded of her late grandma, who always referred to knickers as drawers. She screwed the lid back down onto the jam and regarded Mrs Biggins levelly. 'Well—Xander's certainly been into mine.'

Like a waft of fine sauce, Stella's words rose into the air.

Sauce indeed. Mrs Biggins threw back her head and laughed until the tears were squeezed from her eyes and she was patting her chest furiously. And that was when Lydia appeared, to see what all the fuss was about.

\*　　　\*　　　\*

'Please go with the Hakshimis.'

'And forego half a million pounds?'

'But Longbridge will stay as a family home.'

'Don't whine. I don't care what happens to Longbridge, I only care about the money.'

'Do I phone Mr Murdley?'

'Do you really need me to tell you how to do your job, Stella?'

'Say I can get more out of the Hakshimis—say they offer the same—will you go with them?'

'That's conjecture,' said Lydia, 'and it won't pay the bills. Just sell the damned place, will you. Now take some jam tarts and go, would you. I have a headache.'


## Chapter Thirty

'I'm afraid you are to be put on display,' Stella told Xander apologetically, when she phoned him to extend Robbie and Sara's invitation to the BBQ that coming Sunday. 'My brothers will interrogate you, my sisters-in-law will stare at you and their offspring might very well poke you.'

'And your mother?'

Stella thought about it. 'My mum will be nervous.'

'And you?'

'I'll be nervous too.'

'I'll behave myself.'

Stella liked his response. 'If you promise to behave yourself—I'll let you be naughty later on.'

'How naughty?'

'*Very* naughty.' She giggled. Though they'd slept together the night through only twice, that wasn't to say that the lusty fumbles they snuck once Will was asleep on the weekday evenings Xander visited, hadn't left them furiously tantalized.

'You do know,' said Xander, 'that this will pave the way for me to parade you in front of my friends and family?'

'The Spanish Inquisition comes to Long Dansbury?'

'It'll be a Geordie interrogation, if I know Caroline.'

'And your folks?'

Xander thought about his parents. His mother would love Stella—relieved at how different she was from Laura. And his dad—his dad might well give up dominoes to meet her. Whatever Xander brought to their house—a bag of shopping from M&S, messages from Lydia—were always gratefully received. He knew Stella would be no different. They'd be simply thrilled.

Out in the open. A relationship. A couple.

But that left just one person.

'Stella,' Xander fell quiet. Stella didn't prompt—at the other end of the phone line, she was double-checking Will's school bag for the next day. 'Will.'

'Will I what?'

'No—*your* Will. Are you going to tell him?'

'Will's sold on you already,' Stella laughed. 'You're his buddy.'

'I know,' said Xander quietly, 'but I mean—as delighted as I am that he thinks of me as his buddy—how will he be about sharing his mum?' There was no response from Stella. 'That his bud can also be his mum's boyf? Will he be OK with

356

that? It'll save skulking around. It'll mean more sleepovers.' He liked Stella's terminology. He liked being her boyf. He wanted more sleepovers. 'Stella?'

Stella thought about it. 'Soon enough,' she said at length. 'If that's OK with you.'

'Of course,' said Xander. 'When you think he's ready.'

And Stella just said yes. Thanks. But she thought how actually her reticence wasn't really for Will. It was all about her. As she'd often said to Jo, the world had to be a very safe place for her finally to come out of hiding.

*       *       *

Though the Stickies stuck to Xander, he ably conducted conversations with Robbie and Alistair, Sara, Juliet and Sandie while the toddlers clung to his legs and tugged at his clothing and left paw-prints of goop as if marking him as approved. Initially, the teenage twins, Pauly and Tom, weren't that interested, giving him a casual nod before shuffling to the sofa with their iPods on. That changed when it transpired that Xander was an alumnus of St Alban's Boys School—where Pauly and Tom attended—and the twins then went through the entire staff hoping to find relics from Xander's days. He'd been in the rugby and hockey first teams—cool! All the while, Sandie Hutton quietly watched—noting how Xander reacted to her family, the details they drew out of him, the way he glanced over to her daughter, his ease and his unease, his natural good manners and his occasional shyness. It wasn't so much a devil in the details, but a nice man heading for forty whom Sandie reckoned suited her daughter pretty well.

Everyone sought out a private moment with Stella.

'Bloody hell—he's not ugly is he!' Juliet whispered approvingly when giving Stella a bowl of peas to take through.

'He's a keeper,' Sara said, sotto voce, swapping peas for baby wipes, for Stella to mop Ruby's face which was a ketchup battleground.

'So,' Alistair said to Stella. 'Xander's the reason poor Rupert didn't get a look-in.' His sister shrugged and waited, her eyes travelling fast over Alistair's face for a hint of his opinion. He offered her an After Eight. 'He's a nice guy,' he told her soberly. 'You can tell.'

Stella nodded; relieved, heartened. 'He is.' She paused. 'I really like him—I mean, *really*.' Alistair nodded. Stella's face dropped. 'I'm late with the rent, Al,' she said. 'I'm sorry. Can it wait a week?'

Alistair brushed the subject away as if it was a bad smell.

'I think I've sold Longbridge,' she said.

'So I heard.'

'It's with the lawyers now.'

'Why do you look so glum?'

'It didn't go to the right people.'

'I'd say anyone with fifteen million quid can't be wrong.'

'It was twelve.'

'Oh. I heard fifteen.'

'Where?'

'I don't know—some grapevine or other.'

'No. Twelve. Anyway—when the commission is through I want to pay you the proper rent. A year

358

in advance. I've done my sums. It adds up.'

'Oh shut up, Stella.'

'Please. It's important to me.'

'We'll talk about it, as and when. Now, does your bloke take milk and sugar?'

*      *      *

Sandie and Xander were sitting next to each other on the sofa, companionably watching the Stickies attempting to eat their toys.

'Do you have children, Xander?' Sandie asked.

'No,' he said, openly.

'Do you like them?'

And Xander thought, shall I say, oh yes, with clotted cream and jam? 'I couldn't eat a whole one.'

Sandie looked at him sharply then looked away, smiling.

'I do like them.'

'But you don't have any?' She'd turned to him again.

'No.' He paused. 'No children.' He paused again. 'And no skeletons in my closet.' He shrugged. 'There was a time when I hoped to have them—children, that is, not skeletons. Not that I'd keep a child in a closet, obviously. But yes, I did want them.'

'You talk decisively in the past tense?'

'Sort of.' He saw from her aghast expression that he needed to clarify this. 'What I mean is—the time of which I spoke, yes—that's firmly in the past. But yes, I'd like kids, some day.' He paused again. 'My mother would make an excellent grandma.' He shrugged at Sandie. 'Family is important to me.'

Sandie looked at him. Can't be easy, being

359

thrown into a melee of three generations of Huttons when all the poor man probably wanted to do was to have a quiet Sunday with just the one family member. Two, possibly. Sandie thought about it and the more she thought about it, the clearer and more plausible the image became. Xander simply and quietly sharing the Sunday papers with Stella, being happily distracted by Will every now and then, with some Lego conundrum or other. And Sandie thought, enough with the third degree. She thought, we need to assist these two. We need to let this chap know that.

'Do you watch *Downton Abbey*?' Xander asked, imagining that she did.

'Always a pleasure to babysit,' Sandie said, tapping his knee and smiling at him.

\*     \*     \*

Robbie asked Alistair and Xander to give him a hand with the flatpack climbing frame that had been delivered the day before.

'It's like that scene in that movie *Witness*—when the Amish gather to build a barn,' Juliet said dryly, standing alongside Stella and Sara, watching from the window as the men toiled.

'Has your Jo met him yet, by the way?' Sandie asked.

'Not yet,' said Stella. 'Hopefully this week.' She paused; grinning at no one in particular. '*If* I can find a babysitter.' And as they all observed Xander scoop up Ruby and plonk her in the paddling pool, before whacking his thumb with a hammer and receiving a friendly pat on the back from Alistair, three offers to babysit flooded in.

360

Ruby came back to Xander for more. Finn too. Xander obliged, now wet as well as sticky and with a thumb that throbbed.

'Well—if my children give you their seal of approval,' Robbie said to him, 'who am I to disagree. You've passed the test—welcome to the Hutton fold.'

Xander laughed. They chinked beer bottles.

'I take it you know about Charlie,' Robbie said.

'I know about Charlie,' Xander said.

'About what happened?' Robbie glanced over his shoulder, as if to check Alistair was out of earshot.

'I'm trusting Stella to tell me on a need-to-know basis,' Xander said, feeling somewhat off his guard.

Robbie sipped his beer thoughtfully. 'You do need to know,' he told Xander. 'Seriously.'

*        *        *

Will begged Stella to allow him to be dropped back home later—that she was to listen to Grandma and to Aunty Juliet, both of whom had readily offered. When she agreed, he hugged her and told her that she was The Best. The goodbyes were cheery, the come-again-soons were genuine. Xander's gratitude was sincere—going beyond his full stomach and in spite of his stained, wet clothing.

'I'm exhausted!' Stella said. 'Was that OK? Did you like my family?'

'It was very OK,' said Xander, flicking on Stella's indicator. 'You're a great gang. I liked the noise.'

'Good.' She glanced at him as she drove off. 'I didn't know you went to St Alban's Boys.'

Xander smiled out of the window. 'Funny, isn't it,' he said. 'Sleeping with someone gives you this incredible sense of intimacy—like poring over an autobiography in 3D and yet there are still all these unknown mundane details.' He looked at her bare arms, her profile—her lips parted as she negotiated a roundabout, a slight smudge of mascara.

They were stopped at traffic lights.

'Trouble is,' Xander mused, 'whenever I see you, I'm torn between wanting to talk and talk and discover everything about you—and just simply fucking your brains out. The light's green. Stella. Green light.' And Xander raised his hand for the cars behind them, as if asking for pity for the driver.

'Where am I going?' Stella asked, having told Xander he was a filthy pig. *Filthy*.

'Back to mine,' said Xander, 'I'm wet.'

'That's my line,' Stella said.

*     *     *

Later, lying in Xander's bed, both woozy from lovemaking, him tracing his fingertips along her arms, Stella looked up at him.

'It's summer,' she said, 'and yet still your bedroom is cold.'

'Is it?' He put his arms around her and brought her close. 'I don't notice it.'

'But the whole room—it feels cold and it *looks* cold.' She glanced around. 'It's like it belongs to a different house.'

'Take your estate agent's hat off—it's Sunday.'

'No—I don't mean in an objective way, but

362

subjectively. The rest of your cottage—you've done it so nicely. It's really lovely—homey and bright and everything suits the proportions and the light. The furniture, the colours, the layout. But this room—' She propped herself up on her arm and looked around again. 'It's a bit *miz*, Xander.'

He sighed and pulled her down again. 'You girls and your obsession with bloody cushions and throws. Look—I'll buy a pair of curtains.'

She laughed. 'It would take a lot more than that,' she said and then did a theatrical shiver and nestled in close. 'I have to go,' she moaned, picking up his wrist to look at his watch, kissing his chest. 'I really have to go.'

'I really want you to stay,' he said. His bed smelled of sex and the notion of sleeping alone that night seemed to cruelly contradict the togetherness they created.

'I can't. Not tonight.'

'Next weekend?'

'Maybe. Hopefully. I'll try and arrange babysitting.'

'If you can't—you could bring Will, you know. I understand. I don't mind—I have the futon.'

'I think I'll be craving grown-up time,' said Stella.

'Well—I wanted to offer.'

'And I'm grateful you asked.'

'Remember, the village fete is next weekend. Lydia lets the lower pastures be used for car parking—either side of the driveway, when you first turn in. She lords it up on the day—but has kittens leading up to it and a nervous breakdown afterwards. It'll be strange this year. But stranger still, next year.'

'So much change in the air—it'll be poignant. I

don't even know which "lot" the consortium have plonked on that part of the estate. Whether there'll be parking on offer next year—'

'– and if there is, whether the proceeds will be given to the community—which is what Lydia does. Tell me about Charlie.'

It came from nowhere.

Stella wasn't expecting it and Xander was unaware he was to say it. Instantly, he felt Stella deflate a little.

'Some other time,' he added quickly. 'I know you have to go now.'

'There's not much to say,' Stella said, pulling carefully cultivated brightness around her along with Xander's duvet. 'It went wrong a long time ago. We divorced. It's history.'

'But Will—does he see his father?'

Stella had left the bed and was now walking around the room, dressing. 'No,' she said conversationally. 'Not in ages.'

'Define *ages*.'

'Years,' said Stella, bluntly.

Xander watched her. She's faffing, he thought to himself. She's having trouble with her buttons. She's put her knickers on inside out. She's humming tunelessly, blithely. Her awkwardness was palpable, not least because she was so desperate to hide it. OK, thought Xander, that's OK. It is history—but it's her story and I guess it's her prerogative as to when she tells it.

She came back over to him, sat on the edge of the bed, her eyes skittering here and there, before she smiled at him and kissed him on the lips, eyes closed.

'Speak soon, you,' she said and though Xander

364

couldn't fault the tenderness with which she said it, when she left he lay in bed a while longer, pondering her reticence to share.

## *Chapter Thirty-One*

What Bert Hutton liked immediately about Stella was that she didn't alter the pace of his life in any way. Xander brought her in, Audrey offered her tea and Bert said, sit yourself down, love. She brought no fuss with her. Bert knew how, after Xander and Stella left, Audrey would assess the girl's 'energy'. No doubt she'd say something about her bringing fresh air without a breeze. In comparison, Laura had always been something of a whirlwind—very jolly, very chatty but just a bit overpowering for Bert. After Laura's visits, Bert always felt exhausted and Audrey was visibly ruffled; picking things up to put them down again—ornaments, photo frames, a vase of flowers, a pile of letters—as if Laura's energy had blown everything in their home slightly off kilter. This Stella—she had a quiet softness about her. Yet she wasn't shy. Shy people unnerved Bert; putting him on his guard, making him feel as awkward as they were. This Stella wasn't shy, she was just—calm. Smiley. Refreshing. He could see what his son saw in her; Bert liked the way she simply sat, waiting for the cup of tea, listening to Xander chat, taking in the room and the details of their lives, all the while stroking the arm of the sofa.

'Xander'll say scones are an afternoon

institution,' Audrey said, offering one already loaded with cream and jam to Stella. 'But I think that's a nonsense.' It was elevenses. 'It's a Lydia-ism,' she said and Stella grinned, knowing just what Audrey meant.

Stella took a bite. Delicious. 'This is Longbridge jam,' she said.

Audrey glanced at her, surprised.

'I did the jam tarts with Mrs Biggins last week,' Stella explained. 'Impossible not to lick the spoon accidentally-on-purpose.'

'Xander tells us that you've sold Longbridge,' said Bert. Stella noted a tone of admiration in Bert's voice, as if it was an achievement of which she should be proud. She was touched, though she did wonder, just then, what inflection Xander had used when he told his parents what she'd done.

She munched pensively, picking crumbs from the sofa before she answered. 'Well, Lydia has sold Longbridge really,' she said, 'but yes, I brought the client to her.'

'Well done!' said Audrey.

'Thank you,' Stella said, somewhat lacklustre. She could see that Xander's facial expression echoed her tone of voice.

'An estate agent!' said Bert, as if his son had brought home a brain surgeon.

It made Stella wince. That this reputation should precede her was at odds with whom she felt herself to be. 'Not really,' she said.

They all looked at her, expectant. 'My heart— is in art.' She giggled almost immediately, having neither intended it to sound so pompous—nor to rhyme. Audrey and Bert glanced at Xander with fleeting confusion.

366

'My background is art,' Stella elaborated. 'This is a relatively new thing for me—property.' She didn't want to call it a career. It sounded too permanent.

'A sideline?' Bert asked.

'A side*step*,' Stella clarified. 'Needs must—and all that. I'd like to return to art one day, though.'

'An artist!' Audrey was delighted.

'Well—not really,' Stella all but apologized. 'Just an art historian and erstwhile gallery owner—but, in a recession, there's not much call for either. Which is a shame, because I believe art gladdens the heart—and in a recession, we all need a bit of that.'

Bert thought, Audrey is going to love this one— all principled and appreciative. Bert thought, this one will help Audrey to stop worrying about Xander. Bert thought, Xander looks made up with this one. He looked at his son, sitting at ease in a chair next to him, opposite the sofa on which his mother and his new lady were busy forming their mutual appreciation society. He looked at his son, all relaxed and bright about the eyes, clean-shaven, already staying longer than he had in ages. Bert had a little nod to himself. This one'll do nicely.

'And Xander says you have a super little boy?' said Audrey.

'Called Will,' Bert felt he should add, so that Stella could infer that Xander spoke of the child as more than a passing comment connected to her.

'Yes,' she said. 'He's almost eight.' She beamed. 'He's with my mum, at the mo'.'

'Wouldn't he like to go to the Dansbury fete today?'

'Oh yes—he's coming. They both are.'

Xander felt his parents glance at him. He hoped

the look he returned said, no offence, folks—I'll introduce you one at a time.'

'He wants to help Lydia park the cars—I think he envisages her turfing out the drivers so she can ride the cars roughshod over her lawn.' Stella laughed. 'Can you imagine!'

'She's a dreadful driver,' Audrey said. 'Art won't even let her near the ride-on mower.'

Stella helped Audrey take the plates through to the kitchen as Xander was letting his father show him what was doing well in the vegetable patch. The women watched the men standing at the back of the garden with their hands on their hips, while Bert nodded in the direction of this vegetable or that herb. Audrey stole a glance at Stella who was now dabbing at scone crumbs and licking them off her fingertip. 'You can have another, love, if you're still hungry.'

'I imagine the cake stall will be loaded with them,' Stella said. 'Xander said the week before the fete, you're in a baking frenzy.' She paused. 'That's nice—even though you don't live in the village any more.'

'Once you've been part of Longbridge, your connection with the village is permanent.'

Audrey observed Stella looking suddenly crestfallen. 'I think I've fallen a bit in love with that place,' Stella said quietly, 'and I feel guilty that it's going. I wish I could have either prevented it—or else found people better suited to it.'

'You were following orders,' Audrey said kindly. 'And no doubt, they were given with a bark and a bite and not much in the way of a please or a thank-you.' She paused. 'Dear Lydia,' she chuckled.

'I'll miss her too,' said Stella. 'Even though she's

368

frequently pretty vile to me. It's crazy—I'm not ready to let any of it go.'

'Well,' said Audrey at length, 'you've picked yourself a very fine souvenir, haven't you.'

For a split second, Stella thought that somehow Audrey knew about the spoon she'd pocketed. But then she realized Audrey was referring to Xander. And Audrey saw the blush creep up Stella's neck and over her cheeks. And then Audrey saw Bert put his hand on Xander's shoulder and let it lie there for longer than his usual prosaic pat. And Audrey thought to herself, all is well with my world. At long last.

*     *     *

Lydia didn't take much notice of the drivers—in the main, she simply pointed them to one TA cadet or other whom she roped in on the day of the fete to guide the vehicles along the appropriate parking lines. Lydia just liked being there, at the helm, in control. Privately, she was acutely aware this would be her last fete and she was adamant that she wouldn't let the sudden wash of emotion show in any way. So she barracked drivers for veering off the tarmac too early, and she whacked her bamboo cane over the windscreens of others she deemed to be travelling too fast and she absolutely refused to converse with anyone who wound down their window and called to her from afar. Everyone had to slow down to a reverential crawl, if not a complete standstill, right beside her before she would deign to direct them left or right. She also charged them £5 per car which she'd later make much of donating to the community—but for now,

369

the money went into a leather hunting pouch that had belonged to her grandfather. Thus, when Lydia heard distant squawking of 'My Lady! My Lady!' she steadfastly ignored it.

'She's elderly—like me. She probably can't hear you. Why don't you pop out here, and run along and say hullo,' Sandie told Will, having little idea of Longbridge protocol or Lady Lydia's obsession with etiquette. All Will knew was that his grandma often had top ideas, so he happily scrambled from the car and careened the few yards up the driveway to where Lydia was standing. It did cross Sandie's mind that the woman looked as if she was holding some kind of retributional cane, rather than a stick—but then Sandie thought, who on earth could object to Will?

'My Lady! My Lady!'

Oh dear God, thought Lydia. But the nearer Will came, and the more gold the sunlight spun into his hair, and the clearer the absolute delight on his face at seeing her, the softer she felt.

Dear darling Edward. Is it you?

'My Lady!' Will was effervescent and absolutely out of breath. First he saluted. And then he bowed. And Lydia tapped him on the shoulder with the cane as if she was knighting him.

'Yes, yes, that's quite enough.'

'I've come to help!'

'Help?'

'My mum said if I saw you I was to be helpful about not letting things get in the way.' He paused. For a horrible moment, it struck him that maybe his mum had said he was to be helpful and not get in the way. But he thought better of it; his teacher was always telling him how helpful he was, it was obviously a skill and today he intended to employ it to the best of his ability to assist Her Ladyship Lydia of Fortescue. He beamed up at Lydia, the sunlight causing him to squint with one eye, then the other.

'Your nose,' she said distastefully, 'it's running.'

He wiped it on his arm and stood again to attention. 'What do I do! Where do I point!'

Lydia stared at him. She had an overwhelming desire to touch him; just to hover her hand so it caught the tips of his hair, to feel how his small bony shoulder might nestle into her palm, how his chin might feel like a plump little plum between her thumb and finger.

A car tooted. Some one called out, 'Come on, love!' Will gasped. You must never, *ever*, refer to this lady as anything other than Lady!

'Did you hear that?' Will was aghast. 'Shall we banish that car from your kingdom? It's the red one.'

'Peasant,' Lydia said. 'We'll send him over that way—hopefully he'll step in cow shit.'

Will almost fell over. Not just an adult—but *royalty*—using the *S* word! This was the best day in his entire life. Standing to attention next to Lydia, who said disparaging things under her breath to him about all the approaching motorists, Will copied her arm gestures, pointing the cars this way and that.

'We'll send this old bird over that way,' Lydia chortled.

'That old bird is actually my grandma,' said Will casually, 'and I think she'd probably prefer it if you called her Sandie—if that's OK with you.'

\*       \*       \*

371

Stella and Xander were waiting at the cake stall for Will and Sandie but, half an hour after they'd arranged to meet, there was still no sign of them and Sandie's phone was off. Just as Xander and Stella were discussing what on earth to do, and whether Will would be mortified by a message over the tannoy, they saw them. A veritable procession. Lydia walking demurely, nodding to all and sundry, her hand on Will's shoulder as if he were part pageboy, part walking stick. Will walking in a peculiar gait to fall in line with Lydia; behind them, Sandie like a lady in waiting, desperate to look around her but compelled to keep her eyes fixed low and ahead, as if in service to Lady Lydia. They stopped a few yards short of Stella, who felt a bizarre impulse to curtsey which, if Will hadn't then scampered over to her, she might well have done.

Lydia looked slowly from Stella to Xander and then back again, as if all that Stella had said might have been little more than joshing rumours and that only her own eyes could calculate the truth of it. As if sensing this, Xander slipped his hand around Stella's waist for a moment—long enough for Lydia to see, but for Will not to notice.

'Good afternoon,' Lydia said. 'A wonderful turnout, don't you think?'

The three of them shared a silent moment reflecting that this was Lydia's last time promenading as lady of the manor. Walking with Will from her fields to the fete, it had crossed her mind whether she'd be able to insert some sort of covenant into the contract—that all future owners of Longbridge had a duty to the village at such times as the fete or Christmas. Wondering about this, in a businesslike way, overruled any sentimentalism creeping in on such fine and jolly proceedings.

'I hope Will didn't make a nuisance of himself,' Stella was saying.

'On the contrary,' Lydia said in a voice new to Stella and which Xander hadn't heard for many years, 'he was most helpful.' The timbre was soft— as though her vocal chords were bouncing on a feather bed. She looked at the boy. 'And a lot of fun.' And she reached for Stella's wrist and, as she squeezed it, she made a sound the closest to a giggle that she was capable of. 'I taught him to swear,' Lydia said. 'I do hope you won't object.'

'It's for best only,' Will told his mother, as if Lydia's ripe language was a suit of the finest worsted wool to be worn on only the most special of occasions.

Stella didn't know what to say and by the time she was about ready to reply, Lydia was already telling Will to come along—that they had rounds to make. This was not what Stella had envisaged—she'd thought she'd be strolling around the fete with her mum, her lad and her boyf. Her mum was now deep in conversation with the man on the honey stall, her little lad had been commandeered by aspirant monarchy and her boyf was suddenly nowhere to be seen. Stella picked at the free samples on the cake stall and, recognizing Audrey's scones, bought one.

'Greedy pig.'

Xander's back, thought Stella and before she turned to face him, she wondered if it was peculiar that the disparaging pet names he already had for her should swell her heart so. Stroppy mare.

Moody cow. Greedy pig. He'd called her a Dirty Bitch too last week, after she'd bustled him into her downstairs loo and surprised him with a particularly artful blowjob.

'Do you speak to Stella's mother with that mouth?' It was Caroline, standing alongside Xander and jabbing him in the ribs.

'Where *is* your mum?' Xander asked.

'Talking to the honey man,' said Stella.

Caroline and Xander groaned. 'She'll never get away,' Caroline said. 'Go and rescue her,' she told Xander. They watched him saunter off.

'Hullo,' Caroline said to Stella, 'again.'

'Hullo,' said Stella.

'Have you been stared at an awful lot?'

Stella looked confused.

'You're the toast of the fete,' Caroline laughed. 'You've rained on Lady Lydia Fortescue's parade. You would've thought everyone would be whispering about her—about this being her last as lady of the manor. If she comes next year, she'll have to pay entry. But no—as soon as we got here, all the talk has been "Ooh er! Xander's here *with a woman*." Although Bob referred to you as "a bit of skirt" and Mrs Patek, from the shop, called you a *"Young lady".*' Caroline paused. 'Obviously, she hasn't seen you after a night out in Hertford.'

Stella laughed. 'Oi!' she said. 'You told me I could forget all that!'

Caroline held her hands up in surrender. 'You're right. I apologize.'

They paused, glancing over to observe Xander trying to extricate Sandie from the non-stop conversation of the bee man so as to introduce her to Audrey who'd just arrived for her stint on the cake stall.

'So!' said Caroline.

And Stella knew what she meant. She nodded, shrugged and beamed at the same time. Caroline clicked her tongue and grinned. 'Really pleased,' she said. 'For both of you—match made in heaven and all that. By the way, I saw your little lad with Lady Lydia. He was all but shooing us peasants out of her way.'

'They rub along fine,' Stella said. 'It's funny.'

'Congratulations, by the way, on flogging the old place.'

'Well, I hope I've done the right thing,' said Stella.

Xander and Sandie were back and Caroline was introduced. The four stood and batted chit-chat between them like an impromptu game of badminton.

'Xander, are you still coming for dinner tonight?'

'Yep.'

'Stella?' Caroline asked. 'Would you like to come too? You're most welcome.'

'Oh! Thank you. But another time, perhaps. Babysitting—you know!'

Sandie overheard this. 'But darling, I can babysit.' She looked at her daughter. 'Will can come to me.'

'Tonight?'

'Yes, tonight.'

She thought about it. 'But Will has an early start tomorrow—it's a cricket match.'

'Well, I can stay at yours then.'

'No—I mean, I'll come back. But yes, if you could babysit at mine, that would be perfect.'

'No—and *I* mean, *I'll* stay at yours,' her mother

said, unequivocally. 'You needn't worry about what time you get in, then.' She paused and looked from Caroline to Xander to Stella. 'In fact, you needn't come back tonight. I'll meet you at cricket tomorrow. I know where it is.'

It was as though her mother was facilitating a night of fornication for her daughter and, to Stella, it felt not just embarrassing, but really rather wrong.

'You can stay on my futon!' Xander said, assessing the situation and employing an appropriately theatrical tone as if the marvellous idea had just come to him.

'There you are!' said Sandie, winking at Xander.

'Sorted!' said Caroline, winking at Sandie.

'Well—thanks very much,' said Stella, regarding them all with wry suspicion.

\*      \*      \*

They strolled through the fete together, with expensive stop-offs for Sandie at the home produce stand, the plant area and the greetings cards stall where the breeze caused the wares to flutter like caught paper birds. All the while, they kept an eye open for Lydia and Will. Ultimately, it was the PA system which alerted them to their whereabouts.

'Ladies, gentlemen, girls and boys!'

'That's Will!' Stella exclaimed.

'Come to the dog show *now*! Lady Lydia of Fortescue is going to judge the dog show. *Now!* Roll up and come along. *Now!*'

'Oh God, you don't want him getting a taste for a public address system,' said Caroline.

'Too late,' said Stella.

376

'And he's already got a taste for minor aristocracy,' said Sandie.

'A lethal combo,' Caroline said.

They laughed and headed over to the dog show. Lydia, assisted by Will, stood in the middle while the very serious business of judging '*Owner Who Looks Most Like Dog*' took place. In the end, after much whispering and pointing, Lydia and Will gave first place to a small girl dressed top to toe in black and white who'd been pulled around the ring by a black-and-white English pointer. Second prize went to a gruff old boy whose whiskers matched his schnauzer's and third prize went to a flame-haired girl and her red setter. Next, Will and Lydia judged the obstacle race and gave the prizes on a completely subjective basis. Finally, the obedience competition which was such chaos that Lydia, who took this very seriously, was tempted not to give any prizes. Will, it appeared, managed to make her see otherwise.

'I've had the best time,' he said to his mum and her group. 'I've been a *judge*.'

'Five minutes,' said his grandma, 'then we ought to make a move.'

Will looked at his mother and tried to ask 'Ten?' His mum just gave him that annoying raised-eyebrow look which translated to don't-argue-with-your-elders-and-betters.

Five minutes came and went. And then it really was time to go.

'Sweetheart, Grandma's going to take you home. And stay the night. And take you to the cricket match,' said Stella.

Will looked perplexed. 'What about you?'

'I've been invited to a party,' said Stella.

'Whose party?'

'My party,' said Caroline. She assessed Will's displeasure. 'Sometimes I have parties for children, sometimes for children and adults. Very occasionally—like tonight—just for adults where we sit around and talk about the news and weather. You can come if you like.'

Will tried to be as polite as possible when turning that one down. 'Why is Grandma taking me to cricket though? Where will you be in the morning?'

'I—' Stella wasn't sure how to answer.

'I said she could have a sleepover at my house as it might be a late night,' said Xander.

This made sense to Will. He wasn't entirely happy about it, but it did make sense. 'Oh, all right,' he said. 'Bye.'

Caroline, Xander and Stella waved them off. Once or twice, Will looked over his shoulder and though Xander and his friend were strolling off, his mum was still looking his way and waved as soon as he turned. She was still standing there, waiting to wave, waiting for him to turn, after he'd made his grandma take the detour so he could bow goodbye to Lady Lydia (who assured him that getting the cars off her land was far easier than parking them there in the first place, so thank you for asking, young man, but no—we won't require your assistance).

'I'll just say bye to Mum,' said Xander when a couple of Caroline's friends came over and Stella was being welcomed into their coven.

Audrey was doing a fine job rearranging what was left on the cake stall so that it still looked abundant. 'You off?' she said.

Xander sniffed his armpits and they both

laughed at their oft-repeated skit. 'I'll drop by during the week,' he told her. 'Tell Dad.'

Audrey looked around her, wistfully. 'It's been a lovely day—a much better fete than last year's.'

'Strange though—isn't it?' They both watched Lydia, lording it over a gaggle of villagers. 'End of an era,' Xander said.

'I'll bet that phrase is doing the rounds at the moment!' She regarded Xander. 'But it is also the start of a new one—which needn't be a bad thing, love. You do know that?'

He shrugged, nodded and, a little reluctantly, smiled.

'Verity wrote to me last week—said she'd missed you when she was here,' said Audrey.

'I dropped her a line.'

'I know,' said Audrey. 'She wrote that you'd told her about Stella.'

Xander looked surprised but his mother raised an eyebrow. 'Verity tells me most things,' she said. 'She always has, remember. And she said how happy she was for you. Her very words were: *He needs someone else to look after. I'm all grown up, after all. He seems to forget that. And I'm just fine.*' She looked at her son intently.

Xander placed his arm around her shoulders. 'Mum—I'm not doing too badly myself.'

'Finally, no one need worry about anyone.'

'Apart from the fact that you leave your car and front doors unlocked.'

Audrey lightly scolded her son and busied herself with the cake display, making him pay full price for a scone.

'You OK?' Xander was at Stella's side, running the back of his hand up her arm.

Will was gone from view now. Stella turned. 'Yup,' she said. Pure grown-up time until tomorrow morning. How luxurious. How—illicit!

'Do you fancy building up an appetite before dinner?' he asked.

And Stella replied that he was a dirty dog and Xander said he'd take that as a yes, then.

## *Chapter Thirty-Two*

As they walked back from dinner at the Rowlands', Stella thought to herself how lovely it had all been. A warm and welcoming home, meeting people she had much in common with—and the surge of excitement from catching eyes with the man she was falling in love with, matched by the buzz derived from the approving looks from those closest to him. She felt proud of herself, as if newly aware of her merits. It was a heartening boost to a self-esteem that had been depleted over the years. She squeezed Xander's hand as they strolled.

'What's that for?'

She shrugged. 'For a lovely evening.'

He squeezed her hand back. They were passing the entrance gates to Longbridge.

'God, it looks dark up there,' said Stella.

'Lydia's plain mean when it comes to lights and heating. Lights are only allowed on at dusk—and heating only in October. Late October,' said Xander.

'But she's always cold,' said Stella. 'She's always standing with her back to one of those ancient electric bar heaters placed in the fireplaces. And she always has a cardi around her shoulders.'

'*Cardi*,' Xander laughed softly.

'What?'

'Nothing.'

'She's all on her own up there, Lydia is. I'm not sure I'd like to sleep alone at Longbridge.'

'It's not haunted,' Xander told her, 'despite seeing its share of sadness.' He paused. This could get maudlin. There was no point, not any more. 'But as for my place—' He regarded the fleeting concern on Stella's face before laughing. 'Come on, let's get home and play ghosts and ghoulies.'

'Is that a euphemism?' Stella asked.

'Ghoulies, not—'

'Yes, yes—I get it.'

Back at the cottage, after a cup of tea, they went to bed. They couldn't wait to go. They cuddled and kissed and smiled and chatted. Sex was not on the agenda—they'd made love energetically before leaving for dinner. It was sleep. It was the notion of sharing their slumber at Xander's place for the first time. It felt such a treat, such liberation for Stella to be away from home. And it felt simultaneously new, exciting, comforting, for Xander.

'Are you warm enough?' he asked, woozily.

She snuggled closer still. 'Toasty,' she said.

'Night.'

'Night.'

\*      \*      \*

Stella woke in the small hours. Waves of adrenalin washed all vestiges of sleep away. She lay there awhile, telling herself not to be silly, to look where she was (she turned and gazed at Xander, sleeping soundly). She told herself everything was fine—reached for her mobile, checked she had a signal, checked there were no further messages than the one from her mum saying all was fine and not to worry. But it was no good. It was of little comfort. In the hazy shadows of a night-drenched room, it all seemed startlingly clear. It felt fundamentally wrong.

Though she left the bed as soundlessly as she could, in that perpetually cold room the absence of her body heat filtered through Xander's dreams like an ill wind and woke him.

'Stella?'

'Oh. It's fine. Ssh,' she said, 'go back to sleep.'

'What are you doing?'

There was no reply. The room was curtainless but there was no moon and all he could see was the basic shape of her. 'What are you doing?' Xander reached for the bedside lamp. Flicked it on, squinted against the sudden harshness and was shocked to see Stella fully clothed. 'What are you *doing*?'

'Going,' she said, quietly.

He sat up. '*Going*?' He fumbled for the clock. 'It's three in the morning! What's happened? Is everything OK?'

'I just need to go.'

'Go? Why?'

She looked down and then over to him. 'It doesn't feel right. I should be at home—be there when my little boy wakes up.'

Xander scratched his head. Just then, Stella reminded him of Verity's childhood pony—a pretty little thing that seemed to like affection but if you approached too quickly was prone to bolt away. He waited, looking at her, his head tipped. 'Will you talk?' he asked. 'Only—Will seemed cool about his grandma staying. About you staying.'

'I know, I know!'

'And your mum seemed happy to, er, facilitate your sleepover?'

'I *know*!' She was fretting.

'Stella?'

'It's just—I've broken a very solemn vow I made to myself.' The silence that ensued told her that Xander expected to be told what that was. And she thought about it. There was every reason for him to feel he deserved an explanation. 'I just promised myself that I'd always be there for Will.' She paused. 'That I wouldn't abandon him.'

Hard not to laugh a little. 'You're not abandoning him—you're just with me, overnight. He's snuggled up in bed, safe and sound. With your ma. You'll see him first thing.'

'It's difficult,' Stella croaked. 'To explain.'

'Do you want to try?'

His voice was so gentle and it just made her feel worse. She shook her head and Xander sighed, exasperated as she made for the door.

'For God's sake,' she heard him mutter under his breath. Then the click of the light, the irritated scrunching of the duvet. Then nothing. She walked downstairs, cursing the old cottage for the squeaks and groans that accompanied her footfalls. Hovering momentarily by the front door, she then left, closing it as quietly as she could. With tears streaming down her face, she headed for her car. Sitting behind the wheel, she cried her eyes out. What was she doing there, at stupid o'clock? Why wasn't she at home? Why wasn't she back in bed with Xander? Why could she only be a good girlfriend if she was being a bad mum—or a proper mum and a crap girlfriend? Why was it so complicated? And then she yelled out into the private space of her car. 'Why are you complicating things? I divorced you! I don't even know where you are, you bastard! Why are you *still* complicating things?'

Abruptly, she stopped crying and stared at the shadowy curve of Tramfield Lane snaking its way into the night. Then she laughed, almost maniacally, before settling her breathing and cupping her face in her hands.

'Why am I letting Charlie complicate things!'

It wasn't a question. It was ridiculous. Ridiculous! She left the car, gave the door a hearty slam and chanted, ridiculous! bastard! fuck off! all the way back to Xander's front door.

He heard the knock. Actually, it was a veritable drum roll of banging. He hadn't been asleep, he'd been lying there, miffed, let down—and, truthfully, upset. It didn't take long for him to slip on a pair of boxers, but still she hammered at the door. OK, OK. He pulled on a T-shirt as he took the stairs. Still she rapped. Her knuckles must be raw, he thought.

There on his doorstep, Stella looked both terrible and triumphant with her bed-mussed hair, tear-streaked face; shivering, smiling, wincing at herself.

'Sorry,' she mumbled. 'Sorry.' She shuffled a bit. 'Can I come in?' She started crying again, looking at her shoes, shoulders heaving. Like she did that night when he rescued her from her drunkenness and the blind date man called Blimey O'Riley.

384

'Please?' She looked up at him. He ushered her in, not sure what to say and what he'd be hearing. 'Can I have a cup of tea, please?'

'I was going to suggest cocoa—but if you'd like tea?'

'Cocoa!' It was as if it was the most extravagant offer she'd ever been made.

She hovered nearby while he made it. He could sense it, but kept his back turned to her, unsure of why she was here, what had caused the hysterics, what he was about to hear. Was this to be a face-to-face Dear John moment? Or something else? He had no idea. He brought over the two mugs and sat down in the chair. Stella curled herself into the edge of the sofa closest to him, hands encircling the mug of cocoa as if she'd been out in the cold for ages.

'You came back,' he said evenly, taking a sip.

'I did,' she said.

Oh, how to say all of this! How to say it so that it didn't scare Xander off, repel him.

'I—' she began. 'It's difficult.' They sipped thoughtfully. He'd made the cocoa just right—not ready-made hot chocolate, but bitter cocoa powder made into a paste with a smidgen of milk, lots of sugar and then stirred to perfection with milk heated to frothing. She looked at him over the edge of the mug. She loved him. That she knew. She'd tell him so. But first she'd tell him what she felt he deserved to know.

'I married Charlie,' she said. 'Whom I loved in a passionate us-against-the-world kind of way. Swept off my feet. Charmed by him—all of that.'

'Been there, done that,' Xander said helpfully. 'Laura.'

It did help. Stella nodded. 'In the early days, it was fun, carefree—crazy. We'd gad off here and there, live the high life. He was charismatic, full of life, full of himself. I was sold. And then we married.' She paused. 'I was pregnant already.' She paused again. 'I didn't mind that he didn't seem enamoured with that, nor that he just said "*Sure, why not*" when I suggested marriage. I assumed it was a timing, planning thing—as Will was, well, unexpected.' She broke off. 'I don't know how to tell you this.' She broke off again. 'It's so awful.' She wondered if she'd be able to see it through. She sipped, sipped again. If she kept sipping at this rate, there'd be nothing left—but mightn't she need to take refuge in her mug later on? What to do. What to do.

'Go on,' said Xander.

'Charlie. Had. Addictions.' She paced the three words slowly, quietly, whilst staring fixedly at her lap. Eventually, she looked at Xander who was frowning.

'What sort of addictions?'

'In the main—gambling.' She had to look at her lap again. 'Though I guess you could say he did everything to excess. Drinking. Oh—I can't.'

'Christ.'

She took a deep breath. 'And other stuff.'

'Oh?'

'Escorts.'

'*What*?'

'I haven't told anyone about that. Please don't tell anyone. I just told them about the gambling.'

'As if that wasn't bad enough.'

'I—knew something was wrong. I *knew* something was wrong. But he kept saying I was

386

paranoid and to get over myself and not to be so stupid and for fuck's sake to stop spying on him.' She paused. 'Making out it was me who was in the wrong. I hated that. But what option did I have?'

'Go on?'

Her grammar was clunkingly awkward—it was redolent of how she was feeling, how deep-seated her angst—but Xander had a handle on all she was saying.

'The long and the short of it was that he gambled his money away.' She said it very quickly. And then she speeded up again. 'And mine. And some of my mum's. Not in that order.'

'Your mum's?'

'It all sounded so plausible. Some fab new business worth buying into—and could she invest twenty grand as a short-term loan.'

'Christ. Has he paid it back?'

Stella shook her head.

'Christ, Stella.'

'He'd bet on anything. Mostly, he just liked backing horses—which was weird, because he didn't like animals. But casinos too. And online. That was the worst.'

'How did you find out?'

Stella looked embarrassed. 'I snooped. He was right about that—I did spy. I was desperate. I couldn't understand it—if he had a good job, why was the joint account always plundered? Why was it me topping it up to pay the mortgage, the bills? Where was the hundred pounds my mum gave me for my birthday? Then the phone calls came—from credit collection agencies, who were polite and evasive and only wanted to talk to him. And then there were calls from debt collectors who were rude

387

and threatening and told me to tell him they'd called, that they'd call back, that they'd be calling around.

'I'm afraid to admit I resorted to steaming open his bank statements, his credit card statements. I can't describe the shock, the dismay, the disbelief. So much cash going out. Really bizarre activity— you know, between ten and eleven in the morning, let's say, four or five different withdrawals from ATMs of a hundred and fifty quid a time. Day after day. Why wasn't he in the office? What was he doing, that time of day, plundering ATMs within streets of each other? God—this is so long ago. But when I think back, I relive it all.'

'If you don't want to, it's—'

'No,' said Stella. 'No. I want to.' She nodded at Xander. 'Then Charlie lost his job. He made it sound like he was the victim—and he was so compelling. Why wouldn't I believe him? I was his wife. He had a child with me. Why wouldn't my family believe him? He was so—nice—charming to them. Poor Charlie, we said. Don't worry, we said. It's not your fault, Charlie. It's my bastard boss, he'd say. Or he'd say, it's the sodding bank. At that time, we didn't know he'd actually been sacked. Anyway, he found other work—in which my mum invested twenty grand. But it was some left-field new company. And before long, I was paying all the bills again because he told me they'd all agreed to slash their pay to keep the company afloat. Soon enough, he told me he'd offered to work without pay. It bugged me that I had this gut-curdling, creeping sense of doubt. I hated myself for it. I was a *wife*—I should be supporting and trusting my husband. Wasn't my husband simply being magnanimous? I hated myself for simply not

388

trusting him. I should be proud—not suspicious. But with my heart in my mouth and with my head pounding, I steamed open his bank statements again.'

'And he *was* being paid.'

'Yes!' said Stella, amazed that Xander should guess which, in turn, made Xander feel so sad for her.

'Lie after lie—I'd ask him things to which I knew the answer, just so I could catch him out. But I found it so difficult to confront him. Because when someone behaves like that, and you're the closest person to them, they somehow draw you in, you start to shoulder their secret for them. You put on a brave mask over the worry lines on your face. You feel compelled to tell the outside world that all is well. You keep plugging the holes with your money. Throwing good money after bad.'

'Well, you're hardly going to tell your mum, hey, your son-in-law has squandered your twenty grand but I don't want my marriage to end.'

Stella reached her hand for Xander. And continued. 'You don't want anyone to know. You don't want the *Poor Old Stella* rumours doing the rounds—however well meaning and empathetic the intention. It was mortifying. The straws I clutched at—pathetic! Perhaps it'll change. Hopefully it's just a blip. He'll see the error of his ways. He'll shape up. He'll make good.

'But no. The calls, the letters, they kept coming. And any time I wanted to talk about them, he'd give me short shrift. He'd tell me I didn't understand "business". That I was being unhelpful. That a certain amount of debt could be a savvy thing, sometimes. That he needed my support,

389

my love—that to confront him and doubt him was simply telling him I didn't love him.' Her voice lowered, cracked, disappeared behind fresh tears. 'Truth be told, he was always a bit remote from Will. He wasn't particularly—*connected*—with my pregnancy. Fair enough—some blokes aren't. But, if I'm honest, he was ambivalent when I found out I was pregnant; almost embarrassed to tell people.

'I don't doubt that he loved Will—I have to allow Charlie his way of showing it, I suppose. We can't all be tactile, demonstrative people. That shouldn't belittle the love that some people feel—even if they have a weird way of showing it. But.' She didn't know how to continue. She looked to Xander.

'It's OK,' he said, 'I know what "but" means.'

'Always putting his own needs, desires, first. Quite absent, really. Always off somewhere or other—two or three nights a week. Business, apparently. Or a late-night drinking session because he was "stressed". Made me feel I was thick, or interfering; that didn't I know it was a "start-up company" and he was putting in all the hours God sent. And couldn't I allow him some let-up with his mates. So many nights when, with no warning, he simply didn't come home. Uncontactable. It was grim.'

'What happened?'

'Broke. Suddenly horribly, seriously, broke. Too humiliating and scary to tell a soul. Had already remortgaged. Had to take out a secured loan against the house—at a ridiculous rate of interest. Told me to get the house into my name or the bailiffs would get it.'

'So he admitted it?'

'By that stage he was really scared.'

'Did he stop?' Stella didn't answer. 'Tell me he stopped,' said Xander.

'No.'

'What a jerk.'

'I took myself off to this help group for families of gamblers. It was so bloody depressing—all these people desperately trying to love the perpetrators who were single-handedly and self-centredly fucking over their lives. They were desperate, it seemed to me, to accept it as an illness—to forgive them, to forgive themselves, to understand, justify, support. I walked out of there livid. I heard all these stories—and all I wanted to do was to yell at these poor twits and tell them to leave! Leave him! What a bastard! It's not illness—it's *weakness*! Then it struck me their stories were *my* story—but I hadn't left.'

'So you did?'

'It took another year. You just don't want to believe there isn't a solution. You just want to believe that you and your beautiful little boy can inspire someone to change their ways. You want to believe in good, not bad.

'I went to see a therapist—to try and understand. And she said that, for gamblers, the intoxicating reverberation to which they're addicted is the dichotomy between high self-regard and low self-esteem. I just sat and nodded and paid fifty quid a session to try and understand what the fuck that meant. The way she explained it is that the gambler always believes that they'll win, but simultaneously they taunt themselves that they'll lose. It's the hedonism of it all that's so addictive, the thrill of danger, of teetering on a precipice with a million bucks just beyond reach and the perverse exhilaration of what it might be like to fall all the way down.

'But when they have someone like you—and your family—supportive and close-knit, you bail them out because it's natural to your nature to do so. But thereby your propensity for goodness simply increases their appetite for bad behaviour. They never hit rock bottom because you send them that lifeline. Because you're essentially good and you believe in hope and in *amor vincit omnia*.'

Stella nodded as if convincing herself all over again.

'Whoa!' said Xander. 'They might not hit rock bottom, but that's not to say they're not detritus feeders scumming along the bloody sea floor eating shit.' His passionate concern was beautiful to Stella. 'But you left.'

'I did.'

'When?'

'When Will was three. But I took Charlie back because he made all the right noises. But a year after that, something happened and that was that. It was over. I had no trust, no belief left, no more forgiveness in me. That was just gone three years ago.'

'What happened?'

Stella looked into the mug.

It's time, she said to herself, it's time to sip the last of the cocoa and finish it all off. The lovely, comforting, ultra-sweet last sip.

'The car broke down,' she told Xander quietly. 'It was a flat tyre. But I had Will in the back and—ashamed to admit it, I didn't know how to change the wheel. So I called out the AA. And the chap came. And lifted the base of the boot to access the spare wheel. And there, stuffed into it, in a plastic bag, were handfuls of condoms and tubes of lube.'

This, Xander was not expecting and suddenly he had no words.

'I spent another small fortune I couldn't afford back with that therapist,' Stella said flatly, 'until she drummed into me that it was simply the other side of the same coin.'

'Jesus Christ, Stella.' Xander left the armchair and came to sit close to her.

'On that day, though, the AA man was so lovely. He really was. Older chap. He said nothing. But once he'd fixed the tyre, he told me I was a good girl and to take care of myself and my little 'un.' Stella sobbed a little, then visibly shook herself straight. 'He gave me the rest of his pack of Werther's Originals. I never ate them. I'd hold one in my hand, as a lucky talisman. I still have them.'

'What did you do, baby?'

'I checked the computer. I'm not very savvy when it comes to computers—which Charlie well knew. But I checked the thingy—you know—the Internet list bit.'

'Search History?'

'That's the one. And there were—sites.'

'OK.'

'For—escorts. Saunas.' She shook her head violently. 'I don't want to talk about it. Sapphire in Leeds. Aimee in Doncaster. Check the dates, Stella—wasn't he in Leeds on business last Wednesday? Doncaster the week before?'

'It's OK, beautiful. You don't need to.' Xander pulled her into his arms. 'It's OK. Enough. It's gone.'

She rested there awhile. 'I know—but I want to.

393

I want you to know. Anyway, that day I took Will and went to my brother's. I saw Charlie again only twice. Once when he was all tears, once when he was a seething mass of indignation.'

'You had to sell the house?'

'Negative equity.'

'And your business?'

'It wasn't making any money—dream career at a nightmare time. My brother—Al. I live in his house. He owns a couple of others which he rents out.'

'You've made it a home.'

'For me and Will.'

'But—Will. Does he not see his father?'

Stella shook her head. 'He barely remembers him. He was only just four when I finally left.'

'But does he keep in touch?'

'Hardly at all.'

'Where is he?'

Stella shrugged. 'France, I think. Bankrupt, I heard.'

'OK.' Xander paused. 'But tell me you get at least some support from him?'

Stella paused and then, reluctantly, shook her head and shrugged again. 'Not a penny.'

Xander was appalled, furious. 'What self-respecting father wouldn't support their own child?'

'It's OK,' Stella said. 'It's me and Will. And Will and me. As it's always been. We're not dependent on Charlie. We're a tight little unit, me and my boy.'

'But he's obliged to support you, isn't he? Legally? Morally?'

'On paper, yes,' said Stella. 'But it was so stressful—every month checking to see if the money had gone in. Phoning him to chase it up. Spending

394

money with lawyers. Forms. Declarations. The divorce. In the end, I just made a decision to lessen my anxiety, to shift the stress. To go it alone— completely alone. To bring up Will by myself. Sole custody.'

'And Will? He's such a great little chap.'

'I'm very close with my family—he adores my brothers. He's at a lovely school—loves his male teachers. He doesn't pine, because there wasn't truly much to pine for. It kicked off over half his life ago. He asks me stuff—and I answer honestly but temper the level of detail. He thinks he's rather special—but I suppose, I do tell him he is, the whole time.'

Xander had to stop himself from ripping into Charlie. Then he thought of Will—always Stella's primary thought. It clicked. 'And that's why you don't want Will to wake up in your house without you?'

Stella nodded. 'Not after those nights I'd wake up and Charlie wasn't back and I'd lie to Will, whatever his age, to say Daddy had to stay late at work. Daddy went in to work really really early.'

'He's a happy little lad,' Xander said gently, 'your Will.'

'I know.' She paused. 'It's just me. I don't want to sound unhinged—but my own self-esteem took a bit of a bashing.'

'I can imagine.'

'You wonder if it's something you did—that you didn't do—that might make someone behave like that towards you. You wonder what more you can do. You try this, that—anything. You cry. Shout. Beg. Threaten. Plead. Tough love. Soft touch. You hold out olive branches. You give ultimatums.

Chance after chance after chance.'

'You do know that actually it has nothing to do with you? That you're not remotely culpable? That some people are simply bad eggs?'

'I know,' Stella said quietly. 'It's taken a while. But I know.'

'What a loser.' Xander looked at Stella, touched her cheek. 'Just look at what he's lost!' He thought about it, quietly, for a moment or two. 'I love you,' he told her, quietly assured. 'Though I have to admit, it excites me *and* terrifies me, in equal measures. But I love you, Stella. So there.'

Stella smiled shyly.

'I *also* have to admit I do have a flutter every year on the Grand National,' Xander said. 'A tenner. Never more. Never won.'

Stella's smile turned into a giggle.

'And on my twenty-first birthday, bloody Caroline organized a strippergram.' He paused. 'I had to lick cream off her tits. The stripper—not Caroline, obviously.'

This time, Stella laughed. She sighed, gazed at Xander. 'Love you too, boyo,' she said.

'I might like to lick cream off your tits, at some point,' Xander said, very gravely. 'But I wouldn't pay for the privilege.'

'You can have me for free, matey,' Stella said. She lay against his chest, soothed once more by his heartbeat while he wove strands of her hair through his fingers.

'Thank you,' Stella said. 'For letting me be a bit mad upstairs. For letting me tell you all this—stuff. For loving me still, in spite of it all.'

'Do you feel OK, now, about staying here? If you need to go—at four thirty in the morning—

that's OK.'

'I want to stay—but I'd like to be home first thing.'

'That's OK.'

Stella fell quiet again. 'At some point, I'd like Will to know—about you. And Us. But I don't know when that might be, and how I tell him.'

Xander thought about it too. Love Stella, love her Will. Wouldn't be hard. 'I'd like him to know too,' he said. 'But it's entirely up to you. All in good time. But for now—come back to bed.'

''Kay,' she said and she looked absolutely exhausted.

In his bed, Xander brought her into his arms, tight against his chest. He thought of Will, imagined the little lad tucked up in bed in *Star Wars* jimjams, safe as houses, unaware of the strong warrior, the lioness that his mother was, prowling the night in her constant quest to ensure the best and most secure life for him. Stella. Mother, father, good cop, bad cop, supporting Will single-handedly— emotionally, practically, financially.

'Now I see why the sale of Longbridge is so important to you,' he said. 'That level of commission will make a world of difference to you.'

Stella traced patterns into his chest hair. She looked up at his silhouette, nestled back into his arms. 'But I don't want Longbridge to sell,' she said and that's all she was capable of before falling asleep fast.

\*      \*      \*

Xander was in the shower the next morning and Stella was getting ready to go when there was a

397

knock at his front door.

'Xander?' she called up.

She could hear him singing. She went to the door and opened it. It was Caroline.

'Hullo, pet.'

'Hey, Caroline.'

'You look crap.'

'Cheers!' Stella laughed. 'Didn't sleep much.'

'Spare me the details, missy—it's way too early and my stomach's all over the place!'

'Not *that*.' Stella paused. She liked Caroline, she was a good friend in the making—and she also liked her closeness to Xander. 'Late-night heart-to-heart,' she confided.

'Aha! Good for the soul,' said Caroline. 'Crap for the skin, though.'

'Cheers!' said Stella again. She might look ropey but inside she was aglow.

'Xander left these—the idiot.' They were his car keys. 'I don't even know why he brought them— you walked, didn't you? Hand in hand, head in the clouds, feet not touching the floor—that kind of walking?' Stella laughed and nodded. 'That's why his head's not screwed on at the mo'.'

'He's in the shower. Do you want to wait?'

'No, you're all right. I'll go. I'll call you—did my number come up on your phone?'

'It did—I've added you to contacts already.'

'Excellent. Oh, what an idiot. No taste. Whatso-bloody-ever.'

Stella was somewhat startled. 'Sorry?'

'Not you, pet, *him*.' Caroline was glowering around the room. 'If he knows I'm coming, he hides it.'

'Hides what?'

'That hideous bloody pouffe.'

At first, Stella thought Caroline was directing another insult at Xander. Then her gaze followed Caroline's and alighted on the pouffe. It was multicoloured patches of sagging leather. And pretty monstrous.

'I told him—I said to him, *if I'm redesigning your living space, you have to kowtow to one or two absolute rules*. One of which is—the pouffe goes.'

'Hang on—you designed it? Here?'

'In a former life, I was a designer—sets, actually, but interiors too.' She paused and looked at Stella, continued in a quieter voice, lest Xander should hear. 'When he split up with Laura, this place needed, I don't know, *restoring*. It was tasteful but it was very Laura. Xander needed to reclaim the space—if that doesn't sound too new-agey. She had a particular style, did Laura and, as was her wont, her taste dominated—though she was kinder than me, she let him have his pouffe. But that was about it. So it took a while—first for him to say yes, then for him to approve what I wanted to do in here, finally for him to actually give me the go-ahead to start.'

Stella looked around her. 'Well—I love it.'

'It's pretty good,' said Caroline, then she gave the pouffe a hearty kick.

But something wasn't quite right. Then Stella knew what. 'But Caroline—why did you do *that* to his bedroom?' Caroline frowned. 'Forgive me for saying this,' Stella continued, 'but couldn't you have carried on the downstairs theme upstairs too? It's so—cold. And bleak. And unwelcoming. Am I missing something?'

Caroline laughed and looked puzzled and

laughed some more. 'Did he not tell you? That I did the downstairs?' Stella shook her head. 'So he won't have told you that he didn't let me do anything upstairs?' From the look on Stella's face, the answer was obvious. 'He forbade it!' Caroline proclaimed darkly, but with a sparkle. 'I was hard at work down here—with my quality tins of limewash and Pavilion Gray and Skimming Stone. Meanwhile, upstairs, he blanked out all vestiges of Laura with the world's cheapest, harshest, completely unbrilliant white.'

'Why did he do that?'

Caroline did some split-second assessing of the situation. She really liked Stella—and she could see how much Xander meant to her, how much she meant to him. If this girl deserved one thing, it was honesty—and it would be the key ingredient to her relationship with Xander strengthening and her friendship with Caroline developing. Caroline thought if she could assist, then it was her duty to both of them to do so.

'Because, monkey, he said to me that he wasn't going to fall in love ever again. That his bedroom was neutral ground in which no feelings would take root. It was, he said, a place to keep clothes, to sleep and to have a quick shag every now and then with someone who meant nothing.'

Stella thought about that. She thought how there came a point in a relationship where details of past history should no longer be dragged up and picked over and that she and Xander had now gone past that. They'd talked honestly and at length; their previous lives and significant others had been discussed in detail—and should now be left. But still, she had to admit, she was a girl and, naturally, she was curious. She looked at Caroline and she thought, that's where her girlfriends were allies. 'Were there many of those?' she asked. 'Post Laura, pre me?'

Caroline felt she could answer directly. 'No, pet, I don't think there were. Not many. Certainly not recently. It's not very Xander—casual ding-dongs—however much he might have thought it could have been.' Then she kicked the pouffe again and started laughing. 'You never know, next time he entices you to his boudoir, you might find it all the colours of the rainbow.'

## Chapter Thirty-Three

Late July and school was out for the summer and the peal of children's laughter rang out with the skylarks. Stella turned juggling work and motherhood from a headache into a fine art. She planned Will's weeks meticulously, well in advance, so he knew what he was doing, where he'd be and what time she'd be collecting him, thus he never felt fobbed off. He'd ask her each morning where she'd be, what she'd be doing and she quickly learned not to mention if she was going to Longbridge—because Will had taken ownership of Lydia and felt that if his mum was going there, he really ought to accompany her, now that he was the Lady's right-hand lad and all.

She was summoned to Longbridge on the day Will was taking a dinosaur pottery course at Courtyard Arts, not too far from the office. The consortium's surveyor needed access to various

401

buildings and Lydia was not going to be there. Dear Barnaby's time had come and Lydia was taking him to the vets.

'Everything's unlocked,' Lydia told her, 'but I'll leave keys with Lord Freddie as well.'

'I'm so sorry, Lydia—for Barnaby.' Stella paused. 'For you.'

'He's a dog,' Lydia started brusquely. 'Thank you.' She softened. 'Dear old thing he is.'

'He'd be lost without Longbridge,' Stella said.

'You're right,' said Lydia. 'And he'll stay at Longbridge. I'll bring him home. He'll be with all the others—in the garden.'

Stella arrived well before the surveyors and Mr Murdley. She loved having Longbridge to herself and took her sandwiches to the pond, searching in vain for Mr Frog. How she hoped the consortium would somehow insist to whomever they sold this particular lot to, that the gardens had to be maintained just as they were—scraggly in areas, faded and formal in places, lush everywhere. The scent of rose and honeysuckle, the orchard branches laden, the lawn coiffured to perfection by Art. Perhaps Art would be kept on. Surely he was an asset to the place. She'd tried to ask him what his plans were, unobtrusively, but he just looked at the sky as if wanting the breeze to tell him which way he'd blow. It was the same with Xander. He was resolutely refusing even to think about it, let alone talk about it until, he said, contracts had been exchanged. Well, that appeared to be only a month off, if all progressed smoothly. Which would leave Longbridge folk only the autumn to find new homes by Christmas. Lydia still would not talk to Stella about her plans and would not entertain any

suggestions of properties on the market nearby—
not on paper, and certainly not to view.

Plop.

Just a fish.

She left her patch and walked up to Lord
Frederick.

'You must be hot in all that,' she said, looking
at his bronze knickerbockers and fancy tights,
waistcoat, frock jacket and flouncy cravat.

'One is trained to deport oneself correctly at all
times, whatever the weather and the attire,' he said.
'It's called breeding.'

'Well, I've come to collect the keys,' said Stella,
searching around the base of the statue, under
stones, without luck. 'Where's she put them?'

'Where do you think!'

Stella looked at him and burst out laughing. The
keys—a whole jangle of them—were threaded onto
a large ring which was looped over Lord Freddie's
outstretched hand. She thought of Rodin's *Burghers
of Calais*, but then she thought Lord Freddie
looked more like a pantomime gaoler.

'Thank you,' she said, reaching up to take them.
And she thought how Lydia most probably had a
relationship with this statue much like hers. Had
she chatted to him when she placed the keys there
that morning? Had Lord Freddie been an ally to
her throughout her life at Longbridge? Was she
really going to leave him here, not take him with
her?

'Did she tie ribbons about you when she was a
girl?' Stella wondered. 'Did she put a scarf around
you in winter? A pair of spectacles, perhaps? A
cummerbund? A straw boater?'

'I humoured her,' he appeared to answer. 'She's

kin.'

'Thanks for the keys,' said Stella.

'Come back in November—I'll be holding a brace of pheasants, no doubt.'

She sincerely hoped he would be doing precisely that, for many Novembers yet to come. The crunch of fat tyres on shingle caused her to hastily take her leave of Lord Freddie and make her way to the car park where Mr Murdley and a beanpole-tall surveyor were waiting for her. They wanted to see the stable wing—Art and Mr Tringle's apartments. And Xander's childhood home above the coach bays. She heard them muttering something about holiday lets and at that point, she decided that, for her sanity, it was best not to eavesdrop. Art and Mr Tringle were in and Stella waited outside with each of them while Murdley and Beanpole nosed around their homes. It was a little like watching cack-handed comedy surgeons delving into someone's guts. Both times, they came out swiping their hands over their jackets, as if the interiors had in some way displeased them.

'This way, please,' she said, taking them up the worn stone steps to Xander's old front door. She went ahead of them and, as soon as she entered, she became at once blissfully unaware of their presence as she relived that Saturday morning when she'd squeezed past Xander, so close as to feel the heat of him, to see his neck, to glance up and find his eyes momentarily locked onto hers. She was going to tell the men about the partitions, refer to the space as a moveable feast. She was going to say, through there is the clock tower section. Where Xander played with Verity. Where Verity—

No.

There were secrets to Longbridge that would stay that way.

*    *    *

'We would like to see the workshops next.'

'Haven't you already seen them?'

Mr Murdley regarded her as if she was the most impudent thing he'd come across. 'The workshops—Miss Hutton?'

'Of course.'

'Mr Richards is a cabinetmaker,' Stella said, before knocking. 'I'm so sorry,' she said to him, 'would you mind very much if these people just had a quick look in?' Resignedly, Mr Richards stepped outside and disappeared off to a favoured tree stump where he had one of his two daily cigarettes. The tree surgeon was out, but he'd told Stella where to find the key so she creaked open his barn and the sunlight streamed in, making all the logs look as though they were of gold. The last space was occupied by the pair of nerdy computer geeks, who sat with their backs to the glorious view and the beautiful day. They too felt compelled to leave while Murdley and Beanpole went in, and Stella found herself feeling quite tense, as if witnessing some kind of unlawful raid. She shrugged at the tenants and they nodded back at her.

'Thank you,' said the surveyor. 'And now—finally—this byre place.'

'Sorry?'

'Where Mr Clarence lives?'

Oh. Clarence. Yes, well, you can bloody well call him Mr Clarence.

'He may not be in,' Stella said.

405

'But Lady Lydia assured us she'd given you keys.'

Stella led the way, through the grounds of the house, over two paddocks and along a cornfield to where, nestled harmlessly and quietly, the old stone building stood.

'Did you know his father was a dustman—from the East End? And became a cattle specialist—though he'd never seen a cow before coming here, during the War?'

But they took little notice of Stella. They were too preoccupied negotiating the rutted ground underfoot. Stella knocked gently on the door, gave a dignified wait before knocking again. She was sifting through the various keys, all unnamed, for one which looked most likely to fit the large old-fashioned lock, when the door opened.

'Hullo, Miss Stella,' said Clarence.

'Hullo.' Stella felt wretched. He looked so tired and old but today he was dressed so smartly. He must be sweltering. 'Did Lady Lydia—?'

'Yes,' he said. He peered over Stella's head to the be-suited men beyond. 'Please,' he said, 'won't you come in?'

Dear Clarence—wouldn't you feel more comfortable if you were to come out while they're in there? I'll stand with you. We can look at the landscape while they pick their way over your home.

'Please,' he said again, 'I have made a brew.'

Oh, Lydia! Could you not have explained?

Stella went in, followed by the men. Clarence had laid his table with teacups, a teapot stood in a knitted cosy on a trivet. There were fig rolls on a plate.

'Sit yourselves down,' he said. 'Please.'

406

And they all sat down.

He poured tea. He offered sugar lumps in a bowl with tongs shaped like a miniature pair of hands. And insisted everyone took a biscuit.

'What would you care to see?' he asked the men. 'What would you like to know?'

And while they explained about measurements and building regs and planning, Stella quietly looked about. From the outside, she'd thought the interior would be gloomy, but it was not so. Though not bright, there was a softness to the light that filtered in, bathing the interior in golden notes and gentle sepia shadows. She noticed the curtains first—Miss Gilbey must have run them up when she made her own from the offcuts of the Fortescues' fabrics. Then she looked at the furniture, much of which were cast-offs from Longbridge. And then she observed the lights, with their shades fringed with glass beads, delicate, feminine, at odds with the building. And then she saw the Rembrandt.

Everything else melted away. She heard no sound. She saw nothing else. It was as if she'd been transported into a bare white space at the end of which hung the sketch. She hadn't done a masters at the Courtauld Institute not to recognize a genuine Rembrandt when she saw one. She'd spent most of her student grant on amassing all the gloriously illustrated tomes she could find on the Old Master. She'd been to the Netherlands frequently, and to galleries all over Europe to find Rembrandt van Rijn. And here he was, waiting for her all this time, in a glorified byre in the middle of Hertfordshire.

Circa 1659. Definitely. The beret!

Same period as the self-portraits with the

beret, in the national galleries in Washington and Edinburgh—and the unfinished one that Stella had travelled by train all the way to Aix-en-Provence to see when she was a student.

Now here. Not big. A simple frame—badly framed, even. A drawing—pen and black ink, brown wash, oatmeal paper. Little more than a sketch, really, yet in some ways so complete. The eyes soft, knowing, penetrating. Curls of hair licked with gold, the delicate furl of moustache, the warmth of skin, the pervasive sadness of the furrowed brow of a man just fifty-three years old, bankrupt, who'd be dead a decade later.

Think!

Think!

Think!

*      *      *

Do not say a word.

Do not raise any attention.

Just leave your seat, without fuss, and wander over to the sideboard and peruse the photos. Look at it from the corner of your eye, drink it in. Turn, smile to Clarence. Go to the curtains and touch them lightly. Look at it askance again—gather more detail. Turn again to Clarence. And smile. Now take your time looking at the toby jug collection and turn to Clarence every now and then. Stare long and hard at the little water colour of Saffron Walden high street. Have a longer look at the tiny tinted etching of some woodland somewhere. Smile at Clarence. Nod at the men. Now. Only now. Turn and face it full on. Look at the Rembrandt. Look away, regard something else,

408

anything. Now look back at the drawing. Scour every tiny surface detail, look beyond the surface, to the world within it, the compelling realism by the genius's hand. The chiaroscuro, the play of light against dark. The depth of the gaze. The profound beauty of a portrait created over three hundred and fifty years ago, whose sitter appears alive today and all-seeing. Now turn and smile at Clarence. Just the same smile as you've been doing.

Only Clarence was busy offering the fig rolls and the men were busy trying to extricate themselves and no one was looking at Stella. So she sneaked more time with her hero. She took measurements in her head. Gazed and gazed at the face and asked silently, what are you doing here? How on earth did you end up here? How long have you been here? Can you help me?

The men had seen enough—and they hadn't even looked at the curtains. They'd drunk enough tea and had managed to eat a polite section of slightly stale fig roll but they hadn't acknowledged the toby jugs. They hadn't hurried Clarence, who talked in a slow, formal way, but they hadn't noticed the Rembrandt in that time. Clarence looked even more tired, as if the company had been much anticipated, specially prepared for but was, in truth, an ordeal from which he'd need time to recover.

'Gentlemen?' Stella said. 'I think we should go.'

They nodded, shook hands with Clarence and left. They stood awhile in the cornfield feeling just a little more humble as if it was slowly dawning on them that there was a human element to Longbridge Hall. Stella watched them, saw how for once they properly took in the view, that they were seeing at last the buildings connected with Longbridge as so much more than bricks and mortar; understanding them to be synonymous with the folk who'd lived in them for a lifetime and, in the case of Clarence, for more than one generation.

Stella thought to herself, you two have no idea whatsoever how everything at Longbridge is going to be fine. She thought, you think you just took tea in a cow barn. You have no idea of the secret it holds and the fact that the future of Longbridge as a Fortescue residence hangs quietly on the back wall.

*     *     *

She showed them to the car park and, as ever, Mr Murdley told her he'd be in touch as if it was something she should wake up each morning to eagerly await. After they'd gone, she hammered on the front door, clanked the bell, ran round to the side door, peered in through the drawing-room French windows. But no one was home. She jogged over to Lord Freddie.

'You'll never guess what!'

'Surprise me.'

'Rembrandt!'

'But it was I who surprised you—I bought it, girl. Before he was fashionable.'

She had to speak to Lydia. It couldn't wait. It wasn't for the telephone and it wasn't for tomorrow. She glanced at her watch. God! Time had stopped still for her at Clarence's but now it was racing away. She'd have to leave in half an hour to make it back to Hertford in time to collect Will. She paced the gardens. Come on, Lydia, come *on*! She circumnavigated the house, twice. Where *are* you!

410

She went in through the tradesmen's entrance and called through the house. Finally, she sat on one front doorstep, then another, then hovered by the lions. She really had to go. She'd be late. But she couldn't leave. So what could she do?

*     *     *

Xander's mobile was busy. She phoned his office, for the first time. She knew the lady who took the call must be Mrs Gregg.

'Oh, hullo,' said Stella. 'Please could I speak to Xander? Fletcher.'

'He's on a call,' Mrs Gregg said.

Stella could hear his voice, faintly, elsewhere in the office. 'I know,' she said, 'I tried his mobile but it's engaged.'

'If you care to leave a message, I shall ask him to return your call.' There was no cause for Mrs Gregg to deduce who this was.

'Actually, can you just tell him it's me—it's Stella?'

Mrs Gregg was quiet. So this is what she sounded like, the Stella girl. 'As I said, Mr Fletcher is on another call, I'm afraid.'

'Please, Mrs Gregg,' said Stella, and she really was pleading. 'Xander speaks of you so highly—tells me how he couldn't do his job without you, how frequently you go beyond the call of duty. Please could you just poke him for me—or hiss at him, or write it on a Post-it and slap it on his head?'

Mrs Gregg thought to herself that none of those things befitted a woman of her training or experience. Modern office managers might lark about but not her. Nevertheless she couldn't help

411

smiling.

'Please?' said Stella. 'Could you just perhaps alert him that there's a far more urgent call on the line—mouth *Stella* at him?' She paused. 'It's about the Fortescues,' she said. 'I'm at Longbridge. It's ever so urgent.'

Mrs Gregg cleared her throat. And then, for the first time in her working life, she snapped her fingers at Xander. He looked up at once, startled.

'Stella,' Mrs Gregg announced, 'on line one. At Longbridge. Urgent.'

'I'll call you back,' said Xander and he quit the call on his mobile and picked up the desk phone. 'Stella?'

'I can't talk now—Rembrandt's here and I've just seen Lydia driving up and I have to speak to her right away! It means I'm delayed. For the best possible reasons. But I'm going to be late to collect Will. And I was just wondering—I know it's a tall order. But is it at all possible for you to pick him up? Just bring him back to the office? Just for say, an hour? He'll be good as gold.'

It didn't matter that she was gabbling and what she said made little sense. It didn't matter that he was frantically busy. Suddenly he was far more flattered than he was put out. He was needed. He'd love to help. 'Where is Will?'

'Courtyard Arts—it's just before Port Hill. I'll phone them first.'

'I know where it is. No problem. Stella—are you OK?'

'Very OK!' she sang out. 'Everything is going to be just fine!'

\* \* \*

412

'Lydia!'

'Why are you still here?'

'Lydia!'

'What is it? What's happened?'

'Lydia!'

'For goodness' sake, Miss Hutton. He was an old dog and he'd had a good innings.'

'No! Not Barnaby—but *dear* Barnaby. But no! Lydia!'

'Good God girl, *what*? You're bright red.'

'The Rembrandt!'

'The *what*?'

'I was at Clarence's. He has a Rembrandt sketch—on his back wall!'

'And?'

'Last year, the Rembrandt self-portrait I'm pretty sure this was a sketch for, made millions at auction.'

'I beg your pardon?'

'This wouldn't reach that—but we are talking enough money to mean you don't have to sell Longbridge! You can sell the Rembrandt instead!'

'What on earth?'

'Your problems are practically solved—everyone's problems could be solved. Longbridge is saved. Everyone is safe—in the village, in the barns, Clarence, Art, Miss Gilbey. Rembrandt saves the day! I've always loved him—*always*!'

It wouldn't be until later that evening that Lydia would be charmed by all of this. Just then, she felt supremely irritated. She just wanted to get inside, have a Scotch and put her feet up.

'Lydia! Trust me! I *know* Rembrandt!'

'He's dead,' she said sharply.

413

Stella laughed joyously. 'I mean—my MA thesis. He's my hero!'

'He's not for sale.'

'Everything has a price—and the money you could raise at auction would sweep all your financial troubles away. I promise you.'

'He's *not* for sale, girl.'

Stella did not think before she spoke. 'Are you mad?'

Lydia was incandescent with rage and couldn't speak.

'You're broke—so sell Rembrandt! Simple!' Stella couldn't help but look at Lydia as though she was dense. Lydia had to swallow down splutters of fury.

'Stella Hutton!'

'But Lydia?'

'The bloody thing is not for bloody sale. Now for goodness' sake will you just bugger off and leave me alone.'

'But you said—'

Lydia growled, utterly exasperated. 'It belongs to Clarence. He always liked it. I gave it to him when he retired. He said he couldn't possibly—retire as well as take it. But I insisted he did both. There.'

'But it's worth a fortune!'

'It *belongs* to Clarence.'

'But you're on the verge of being homeless! You must take it back and sell it—I don't know— give some money to Clarence. Let him choose a different painting or something. He strikes me as being as happy with a new toby jug as with an old Rembrandt. This is your last chance to save Longbridge!'

Lydia looked at Stella, who was wild about the

414

eyes, her hair escaping from her pony-tail like a gorgon, her cheeks flushed, her chest rising and falling fast. And suddenly it hit Lydia. Dear Stella, she thought. She felt her strict and steely exterior, of which she was fiercely proud, bend and soften a little with warmth.

'Stella—I have money.' Lydia could see that this sentence alone held little meaning for the girl. 'I wasn't entirely—straight—with you. I *am* selling Longbridge. But *not* because I need the money. I want rid of the place purely and simply because I'm old. And I want to be able to make the decision of where I go next, while I still can.'

This was too much for Stella to take in—the true fact, the honest reason. She sank down to sit next to one of the stone lions, her arm about its back. 'What do you mean?' She sounded tearful.

Creakily, Lydia sat down too, her knees as neatly together as Stella's were akimbo; the older woman as controlled and steady as the younger woman was in pieces. She tapped Stella's knee. 'My dear—I am *old*. And frailer by the day. And that's why I don't want to live here any more. It depresses me. I can't turn the handles. I can't bolt the back door. I trip up and down the stone steps. My sight isn't as good as it was. And I feel the cold—dreadfully. The radiators—they're my enemy with their dastardly lukewarmness. I don't like being here on my own. I really don't. I am at a stage in my life when my distant memories are daisy fresh these days—they haunt me, taunt me with vivid times when the house was full and thriving.' Lydia left unsaid the words *with my children*. Her hand was back on Stella's knee. 'I have made my decision, Stella dear. I don't want to feel cold in the summer. I don't want to take a tumble and not be found until the morning. I do not want to die here. I want to be the first Fortescue who *doesn't* die here.'

'The bruised eye. Your arm,' said Stella vaguely, 'the sling.'

Lydia nodded. 'I have let this rambling old place go—and now you must do the same. Out of the two of us, it is you who needs to sell it for the money, not me. I'm selling it because it's time.' She paused. 'I am out of love with the place. And that's a very tiring emotion for a woman of my age to deal with.'

Stella looked at Lydia beseechingly. 'Couldn't Verity come back here—with her funny little tribe? They'd look after you.'

Lydia correctly judged Stella's tone and answered her with the same sensitivity. 'What— for me to spend my twilight years watching women knit things with alfalfa while men with pony-tails and plaited beards play pan pipes? It would drive me absolutely bonkers.' Lydia shook her head. 'It's not what they want and it would be as much of a millstone for them as for me. I am old enough to do as I please. One must never sully good memories. One must not allow memories of halcyon times to be overridden by newer ones of bad experiences. One owes it to the people, whether long gone or still here, who formed those memories.'

Stella looked down to see that Lydia's hand rested softly upon her knee. Gently, she put her own hand over Lydia's and let it lie there. It transpired that Lydia was the most modern of all of them.

'There's a good girl,' said Lydia, audibly tired. She looked at Stella, kindly. 'You wanted to do so

416

much more than your job—but really, dear Stella, your job is to look after me. And my wishes are that this old heap is sold and that this bony scrag—' she jabbed at herself—'enjoys her last years in warmth, comfort and without anxiety.'

Stella spoke, her voice compromised by the lump in her throat. She was holding hands with Lydia now. 'But where will you *go*?'

Lydia began to chuckle. She sighed. 'I'm going to that nice place where Mercy Benton lives. Summerhill Place. Of course, I remember it when it was the Duggen-Fanshaws' estate. Mrs Biggins is coming with me. We're to have neighbouring apartments. Mine's larger, of course—actually, it's the largest there. Two bedrooms, two bathrooms. A lounge and a study. My own French doors onto my own private patio and marvellous views over the Duggen-Fanshaws' parkland. Oh! And a proper sit-in kitchen. Mrs Biggins only has a galley kitchen and she will still be at my beck and call.'

*'You're checking yourself into an old folks' home?'* Stella was utterly aghast and not a little mortified.

'How very impudent! If you are to call it anything, you can call it Retirement Apartments.'

Stella looked appalled.

'And it does *not* smell of pee,' Lydia laughed. 'It's rather jolly—a lovely place. With elevenses and afternoon tea and all sorts of shenanigans laid on for residents. And there's a buzzer, you see, in the apartment. You press it if you need someone, quickly. And Mrs Biggins—she's prone to turn a deaf ear to me, wretched woman.'

Stella rested her head against the lion's shoulder, then she turned to Lydia and, reluctantly, she nodded.

417

Lydia looked at Stella. The girl was quite pale. 'I should like to take you there,' Lydia said. 'Show you how gay it is.' While her words reached Stella, Lydia quietly wondered why it was so important to her that her choice should meet with Stella's seal of approval.

'I hope you will be one of my most frequent visitors,' said Lydia. 'You. Xander. And Will. There will be shortbread for tea, you know.'

## Chapter Thirty-Four

Stella felt utterly dazed when she went to Xander's office. Any other day, she'd be excited, all eyes, keen to ingratiate herself with the infamous Mrs Gregg. But that afternoon she felt drained and her head so full of unbelievable facts that there was room in there for little else. Rembrandt and Summerhill Place in one fell swoop. It had knocked her sideways, all of it. She rang the buzzer to Xander's office and all Mrs Gregg could see in the entryphone screen was the top of Stella's bowed head. As she climbed the stairs, Stella tried to shrug off the bewilderments of the day with each footfall.

'Mummy!'

'Hullo, poppet.'

'I made this for you—Mrs Gregg showed me how.' It was a necklace made out of paper clips.

'It's beautiful.' It sparkled and, as Will placed it over her head, it lit Stella a little from the inside. She turned to Mrs Gregg. 'Thank you,' she said. 'For everything. I'm Stella.' She offered her hand and Mrs Gregg took it.

418

'Pauline Gregg,' she said in her bright, telephone voice. 'And it was no trouble. And young master Will—well, I've told him he can come by any time he likes, now that he's mastered the franking machine.'

'I'm going to work here, when I'm older,' Will said.

Stella glanced around. 'Where's Xander?'

'He has gone to a meeting with some fish and a cow,' said Will.

'At Fishers and Co.,' Mrs Gregg interjected, smiling at Will.

'He says he'll see us at home,' said Will.

'He said not to cook, that he'll bring fish and chips,' said Mrs Gregg.

'Thank you so much, Mrs Gregg,' said Stella. 'Really. You're an absolute brick.'

Mrs Gregg liked that very much. It was the sort of terminology she herself employed.

'Can we give you a lift anywhere?' Stella offered.

'Thank you but no—I'm partial to walking to and from the office.'

'Good for you,' said Stella. 'Well—if you're sure? We'll say goodbye. Come on, Will.'

Will went over and shook Mrs Gregg's hand. 'Remember,' he said, 'call me any time you need help. But most weekends I play cricket and during the week I'm usually at school.'

Mrs Gregg nodded most formally. 'I will certainly do that—most useful.' She looked at the Stella girl, watching her smoothing her son's hair, seeing the way she looked at him. Nice hands—clean nails kept sensibly short. A tidy way about her. Polite—and warm. Mrs Gregg felt pleased. Absolutely spot on, Mr Fletcher—very good choice.

'Any time you want me to snap my fingers at Xander, you just let me know.'

Stella grinned. Another ally in her life, another new person rooting for her and Xander. How lovely. 'Thank you. I'll try not to make a habit of it.'

'Come on, Mummy.'

'I'm coming.'

'By the way, Mrs Gregg let her children call her Mum when they were twenty-one, when she gave them the key of the door.'

*       *       *

'I'm not allowed to tell you that I'm better than you at reading *Beast Quest*,' Xander said, coming downstairs having just read to Will for twenty minutes. 'Will said, *don't tell my Mum*.'

'He says that to all my boyfriends,' Stella laughed. Fish and chips and a mug of tea had made her feel so much better. 'I'm sure it's just because my voice isn't low enough to do a proper scary beast.'

'Has he met many?'

'Beasts?'

'Boyfriends, silly.'

Stella put her arms around Xander's waist. 'There's only been you. Since Charlie.'

Xander knew that already, but for some reason it was nice to hear it again. Just so stabilizing not to play games, to simply embrace good fortune and get on with life.

'Don't go,' said Stella.

'I have no intention of leaving,' said Xander. And he really meant it.

'I have had the most bizarre day,' said Stella.

420

'You really couldn't make it up.' She poured a glass of wine for each of them and motioned for Xander to snuggle up close to her on the sofa while she told him all that had come to pass at Longbridge that afternoon. He knew about the Rembrandt—he told her how, when they were young and it hung in the nursery, he and Verity would move around the room mesmerized by how the eyes appeared to follow them. He didn't know about Summerhill Place. At first, it shocked him deeply. It seemed so undignified. But then he laughed and laughed and helped Stella see how Lydia really was having the last laugh of all.

'But we must keep a tight rein on the rumours that will abound from this,' Stella said. 'I know Lydia professes not to give a hoot what people think of her—but I do.'

Xander chinked wineglasses with her.

Stella sipped thoughtfully. 'Would you like to stay, Xander? I mean—the night?'

Xander tucked her hair behind her ears and thought to himself, that wasn't two monumental things that happened to Stella today—that's three.

\*       \*       \*

In the small hours, Stella woke Xander and asked if he'd mind very much sleeping the rest of the night on the sofa downstairs.

'But you're so toasty,' he mumbled, spooning close. 'And you smell so good and I was having such a great sleep.'

'Please? For me?'

He yawned. 'And your room is so—I don't know—calming, warm. Lovely.'

421

Stella chuckled. 'Yours could be too—if you bloody well let Caroline weave her magic up there.'

Xander groaned. 'God—is nothing sacred?'

'Not between two women who get on like a house on fire.'

They talked in the darkness, Xander quietly dissecting himself; working it all out, out loud, how after Laura he didn't want to be doing with love and all its panoply.

'I guess I claimed self-sufficiency,' he said. 'It was easier than being glum. And it warded off Caroline from wanting me to workshop my feelings the whole time.'

Stella laughed. 'My poor friends—the hours and hours they politely spent patiently listening to me analysing exactly the same issues over and over again.'

'For a while, though, I believed the myth I put out about myself,' Xander mused. 'That relationships weren't my thing. That love wasn't to come into my life because it was hassle I didn't need.'

'Well, I'll bet you gave the village something to talk about. That grouchy bachelor up Tramfield Lane, you know the one—the one who likes jogging.'

At this Xander launched at Stella, tickling her furiously and calling her a cheeky cow.

'Then I came along and turned your world topsy-turvy,' Stella said with mock self-importance.

To Xander it didn't seem appropriate to bat the truth away with some larky quip or ironic insult. So he said nothing, just spiralled her hair through his fingers as she lay against his chest.

'Well—you literally knocked me sideways,' said

Stella, thinking back to the first time she'd seen him on her very first visit to Long Dansbury. Then talk turned to the coming weekend and plans they could make that would fit around and include offers already made to one, the other, to both of them by their own friends and families.

'Proper relationship this, innit,' Xander joshed. 'Sweet!'

'You're such a dick,' Stella laughed, 'and I love you.'

'You love me enough to boot me out of bed, with a hard-on, to kip on your sofa instead?'

'Yes,' said Stella. 'Fuck off.'

But when Xander made to leave the bed, she reached for him, pulled him back, found his face and kissed him, encircled her hand around his cock.

'I don't have any more condoms,' he whispered at her nipple, his breath hot and feeling so good against her skin.

'I don't mind.' Her hands ran over the landscape of his back.

'You sure?' He brushed inquisitive fingers over her bush, probing for the delicious moistness concealed within.

'I'm sure.' She was moving herself against him.

'But what if—'

'What if what?' She'd pushed him onto his back and was inching herself down onto him.

'Christ, I want you.'

Want you too, thought Stella. Want you in my life. And Will's. Want to be a family.

And then neither of them could speak.

*　　　*　　　*

Stella sat up in bed when she heard Will going downstairs for his early-morning drink of water. She tiptoed to the door and listened. His little footsteps, suddenly stopping. Starting again. The tap running. Off again. On again. Off again.

'Hullo.'

Nothing.

'Said—*hullo, Xander*.'

'Hmmm?'

'You are asleep on the sofa.'

'Oh. Hmmm.'

'Here. I like water at this time in the morning.'

'Thanks, mate.'

'See you at breakfast. Did my mum say you can stay for breakfast?'

\*     \*     \*

You can stay for breakfast, Xander.

## *Chapter Thirty-Five*

Stella thought, I have to get to Lydia before the solicitor phones her. And then she thought there was simply no time for further thinking. She ran from the office, phoning Xander as she went.

'Do you have a number for Mrs Biggins?'

'Mrs Biggins?'

'Or is she like Lydia and doesn't have a mobile?'

'She doesn't have a mobile. What's up? Is everything OK?'

'No, it bloody isn't. It's mid-August! They've waited till now!'

'Stella, you're not making sense.'

'Sorry, it's just the Longbridge sale has collapsed and we were days away from exchanging contracts. I need to get to Lydia. I have to be there when Lydia hears. I don't want her answering the phone at Longbridge. I want to be the one who tells her. She needs to hear it from me.'

'I'll phone. I'll ask for Mrs Biggins, I'll tell her to intercept the phone if it rings.'

'Would you?'

'Not a problem. But Stella—drive carefully, hey?'

\*　　　\*　　　\*

Stella's journey to Longbridge was fuelled on all the expletives she could think of, strung into sentences that made no sense but were comforting to hiss out loud as she took the blind bends and undulating roads to the village. Up the drive, feeling like a doctor about to deliver a death sentence. She stilled the engine and sat for a suspended moment, knowing it did not fall upon her to tell Lydia—but knowing that, apart from Xander, she wouldn't have Lydia hear it from anyone else.

The lions looked forlorn today, as though there was something terribly undignified about trying to guard a house that would soon have no one in it to protect. They couldn't do their job. What was the point? Might as well allow the lichen to creep over them, to work in tandem with the centuries of frost that had already begun to erode their features.

Stella rang the doorbell. Please let it be Mrs Biggins.

It was Lydia.

'Miss Hutton.'

Does she know?

'To what do I owe this—unscheduled—pleasure?' Her sarcasm—so Lydia, so inappropriate for today.

She doesn't know. Shit. Fuck. The phone! Don't answer the bastard phone!

'May I come in?'

'You may.'

Lydia was heading towards the phone on the table at the end of the entrance hall.

Oh God! Don't!

Mrs Biggins reached it first.

'Longbridge Hall, hullo?'

Please let it be a wrong number; a call centre in Bombay offering some fantastic telecom deal, let it be John Lewis to say the electric blanket has arrived for collection, or Mrs Biggins' daughter in Bishop's Stortford telling her mum she'd forgotten her glasses.

'One moment, please.' Mrs Biggins clasped the handset to her ample bosom. 'It's Mr Michaels, the solicitor.'

All thoughts left Stella. All she could do was wait, the pounding of her heart reverberating around the entrance hall.

Lydia sighed and took a step nearer to Mrs Biggins. Then she stopped. 'Tell him I'll phone him in a little while.' Stella had to stop herself falling into Lydia's arms and hugging her with all her might.

'She'll phone you in a little while.' Mrs Biggins listened, then buried the phone in her cleavage again. 'Says it's urgent.'

426

'Preposterous!' Lydia took the phone from Mrs Biggins.

'No!'

But the women merely glanced at Stella, as if by now well aware of her peculiarities.

Lydia cleared her throat. 'I said—Mr Michaels—that I will call you in a little while. Good day!' And she slammed the handset down into the cradle. She turned to Stella. 'Come along, Miss Hutton. Mrs Biggins, we'll have elevenses in the conservatory, I think.'

\*     \*     \*

Lydia observed Stella closely. The girl looked awful. Pale and fidgety. She really ought to do something with her hair. Her forehead was misted with perspiration.

'Are you all right?'

Stella shook her head.

'What on earth's the matter?'

Stella was visibly shaking. 'I have bad news.'

And the first thought that came to mind for Lydia was Xander. Specifically, that something wasn't right between them and that Stella wanted to tell her so, before the rumour mill cranked into action, sending out husks of misinformation as it ground the true facts into a fiction of dust. In that moment, it seemed logical. Lydia braced herself.

'Longbridge,' Stella whispered, her head dropping, her shoulders slumping and an effortful sigh seeping out of her and filling the room.

'Longbridge what?'

Stella looked up. 'There's no easy way to tell you this, Lydia.' She shrugged—a gesture she knew

Lydia thought to be most uncouth but which, today, she just could not counter. 'The consortium—it's fallen apart. It's over. The sale has fallen through.'

Lydia bristled and her face, majestically aquiline at the best of times, resembled now an eagle poised to swoop for the kill. 'I've never heard anything so ridiculous in all my life!'

'It happens,' said Stella.

'But we're about to exchange! Any day! Just before the August bank holiday!'

Stella nodded. 'I know.'

'Is that why Mr Michaels was phoning me?'

Stella nodded. Then she looked up at Lydia. 'I didn't want you to hear it from him. I wanted to be the one to tell you—and I wanted to be here with you, when you heard.'

Lydia was speechless, staring at Stella unblinkingly as if trying rapidly to translate a language alien to her. 'Is it beyond repair? Can a consortium be patched up again? Can't they find new threads of money elsewhere, to hold it all together?'

Stella shook her head. 'No, Lydia.'

There was a hideous, heavy silence.

'What bastards!' Lydia hissed. 'And that's being polite.'

They fell silent again, regarding the elevenses tray that Mrs Biggins had brought in. Just then, the divine shortbread looked about as edible as concrete slabs dusted with asbestos powder, the tea as undrinkable as bilge water. They sat and privately panicked.

'Can you sell it?' Lydia asked at length, her voice low, her eyes ice blue, slicing into Stella like a blade.

428

'The market is dead at the moment, Lydia,' Stella said. 'It might pick up once people are back from their summer breaks. But the predictions are not good. Prices are low and sales figures are dropping and nothing's coming on to the market. I will try my absolute hardest—you know I will.'

'I wanted to be out of here by Christmas.' Her voice was broken.

'I know,' Stella tried to soothe. It disturbed her greatly to see Lydia so ruffled, so deflated—like seeing a once-imperial eagle previously so in control of its territory, now moth-eaten and crushed in a cage in a run-down zoo.

'Thank you for coming, dear.' Lydia tried to straighten, tried to broaden her shoulders, but she looked hunched, winded. Visibly, she summoned her strength to bring a vestige of elegance and control to her demeanour. 'I do appreciate it. Please—see yourself out. And do ask Mrs Biggins to come to me.'

\*       \*       \*

Everyone was knocked sideways by the news and it reverberated around the village like the ball in a bagatelle. No one took any satisfaction from Lydia's misfortune. They felt for her. And, all over again, they worried what it might mean for the rest of them. Mr Tringle had already packed up his apartment to move that coming weekend to the south coast and live with his brother, hoping for cat-friendly sheltered accommodation down there at some point. The workshops were now empty, apart from the stock of logs belonging to the tree surgeon. Just a few retired ponies remained at the livery yard, living out in the paddocks blissfully unaware while their owners were trying to find pastures new. Only Art carried on regardless, busy as ever—especially this time of year with the raspberries and sweet peas. When he was given his final marching orders, then he'd go. No use worrying about things till then—can't let standards around the place slip. Prettiest time of year, in many ways, certainly the most fragrant. Roses need his once-over, daily. Orchard is heavy.

Xander's neighbours, the Georges, had vacated number 2 Lime Grove Cottages; renting elsewhere in the village, hoping a family property might come on the market and they'd be in the best position to secure it. It was strange for Miss Gilbey and Xander. Where once the little terrace of three had interchanged the warmth from dwelling to dwelling, it felt now that there was a cold space between them. Stella took Miss Gilbey a casserole last week. And Xander had been checking in every evening when he was home from work.

Xander was particularly irked by the news, worrying about Lydia, about Stella too who was mistakenly blaming herself more than the consortium. Privately and resignedly, he'd started looking online at properties nearby—a depressing, time-consuming undertaking and one that now seemed to have been a criminal waste of energy and effort.

Douglas Hutton was livid, hitting the phones to blacklist Murdley amongst all the other agents he knew. Geoff was most concerned for Stella, who looked absolutely terrible. Even Belinda derived no pleasure from the misfortune of her nemesis. Although it had been both depressing

430

and humiliating for Stella to tell Alistair, her lovely brother simply told her not to worry, never to worry and he rubbished her desperation to pay more rent and on time. Predominantly though, Stella's thoughts were for Lydia alone, about how the news would affect her in the short term and beyond. Deep down, Stella was pessimistic about Longbridge—it was categorically not the time to be selling a property like that.

*     *     *

However, there were children and friends and love and careers to be considered and life just had to roll on regardless, like the wheat fields at Longbridge. On the August bank holiday, Stella, Xander and Will gathered for a long-planned picnic in the grounds of Hatfield House with Caroline, Andrew, Robbie, Sara and the various children. Will felt most grown-up, bossing the little ones around, and was charmed to discover that not all toddlers are necessarily sticky. Andrew and Xander were explaining strange numbers to Robbie, connected with pedometer readings and resting heart rates. Sara, Caroline and Stella lounged on the picnic blankets and picked at the olives and cornichons.

'Glorious day,' said Stella.

'Isn't it,' said Caroline.

'This place is so beautiful,' said Sara.

'Positively verdant,' said Stella.

'A cacophony of colour,' said Sara.

'Kids are having fun!' said Caroline.

They watched the children exploring a cavernous ancient oak as if it was a mysterious land better than Narnia.

'I love the colour of bark,' Caroline mused. 'It inspired a paint I once mixed, for a set I was dressing—took me ages to perfect the precise tone, the weight of the colour. But it was perfect. I called it "Bleached Bark Buff". Can't remember for the life of me what combination I used.'

Stella laughed. 'That's what Farrow and Ball are for, these days!'

Caroline passed the mini pimentos stuffed with feta over to Stella. 'Shame, as it would really suit my kitchen. That's my next project.'

'Your kitchen is immaculate,' Stella protested. She turned to Sara. 'You should see it—it's gorgeous as it is. Uber *Homes and Gardens*.'

'See,' said Caroline, self-deprecating as ever, 'I've too much time on my hands, me.'

\* \* \*

Slightly sunburnt, Xander, Stella and Will returned home.

'That was a great day—can we do it again? I like being a hero,' said Will. 'Xander—are you staying for a sleepover?'

Xander glanced at Stella who'd turned away, smiling.

'Er—yes,' said Xander. 'If that's OK with you and your mum?'

'It's fine by me,' said Will. Then the boy looked hard at Xander and looked hard at his mum who had just brought him a carton of smoothie.

'You OK, pumpkin?' Stella asked him.

'I was just trying to work out stuff,' said Will. 'About sleepovers.'

'Oh?'

'Grown-ups are *weird*,' he said. 'Really weird.'

'Charming!' said Xander.

'What I mean is—you send me up to bed and you say, don't get out of bed! You go on *and on* about Sleep Is Important. You say, tuck down! You say, night-night! You say, Snug as a Bug in a Rug.' Will looked at the grown-ups who were gawping at him because they so obviously just didn't get it. Gosh, they could be annoying—their habit of saying stuff that didn't make sense, of telling kids one thing because it was 'setting an example', then doing the complete opposite themselves. 'You always tell me all of that,' said Will. 'Don't you?'

'Er—yes?' said Stella, glancing at Xander who looked equally confused.

'Well then,' said Will. 'When Xander comes over for a sleepover, a million times a week, why does he spend half the night in your bed, Mummy, and half downstairs on the sofa?' Will thought about it. 'If staying in bed is so important and if a good night's sleep is so special?'

Why had the grown-ups gone bright red? Why couldn't they speak? They didn't honestly think he didn't know, did they?

\*       \*       \*

Together, Stella and Xander went into Will's room at bedtime. Xander read to him with Stella between them, Will somewhat squashed to accommodate two adults sitting beside him on the bed.

'Well!' said Xander, clapping the book shut. 'What an exciting chapter to leave it at tonight.'

And Stella thought, what an exciting chapter

433

to start.

'Will,' she said. She smiled at Xander who nodded, just perceptibly. 'Xander and I wanted to ask you something. We wanted to ask you if you thought it would be a better idea if he sleeps all the night in my bed.'

'Of course it is!' said Will. 'Der!'

'And I wanted to ask you something, Will,' said Xander. 'I wanted to ask you how you felt if I told you I love your mummy very much.'

'Der!' said Will again. 'I know *that*! You're best friends!'

'And that I love Xander too,' Stella said. 'Love him as a best friend—and in a grown-up way as well. Beyond best friends.'

'What's that?' asked Will.

'Like a couple,' said Stella.

'Like married people?' asked Will.

Stella looked at her lap, looked at her baby boy, and nodded.

'Maybe,' said Xander. 'One day. Hopefully.'

Will sighed and tugged at his mother's sleeve. 'But you did that,' he whispered.

'I know,' said Stella softly.

'Xander won't make you sad, will he? If you get married as well as be best friends?'

A tear edged out of Stella's eye and she tried to brush it away before Will saw it.

'I want only to make you and your mum happy,' said Xander. 'Because it seems really right to me— after the happiness you both bring me.'

'Right,' said Will, wondering where this was going. Did that make Xander his dad? And would he be a proper dad, in that case—like Luca's and Jakey's at school? That would be very cool. And

434

could he keep calling him Xander? And his mum was sitting there pretending she wasn't crying, so perhaps tonight wasn't the best time to ask about stuff like that.

'I've been looking a long time,' said Xander, 'hoping to find people as wonderful as you two.'

And, having been kissed and kissed again by both of them, Will went to sleep after a fantastic day, feeling really great.

## Chapter Thirty-Six

Although only a fortnight later, with Will now back at school and a sudden dip in the temperature, it felt indisputably like autumn and as if Longbridge had been back on the market for ages. Heading for the end of the month, there still hadn't been a single viewing. Stella was demoralized, it was affecting her ability to sell the properties she did have on her books and she told her uncle and Lydia that they ought to be pragmatic and consider relinquishing their sole-agency status at Longbridge. Dougie tended to agree with his niece. Lydia wouldn't hear of it.

As with the best ideas, it confronted Stella unexpectedly and apropos of nothing, really. She was having lunch at her desk, picking out the cucumber from the sandwich and slipping ready-salted crisps in its place. Outside, a shopper had tied their dog to a lamp post and it was barking. It was having a good old yap. Bark.

Bark.

Bleached Bark Buff.

With a mouthful of sandwich, Stella's jaw dropped.

'Stella?'

'Stella?'

Geoff and Belinda were concerned. She appeared paralysed, a gob full of tuna mayo. She looked like a broken concrete mixer. Suddenly, she sprang from her seat, grabbed her car keys and bolted from the office, leaving the rest of her sandwich, her phone, her bag. Her desk looked as if Mrs Invisible was busy at work there.

\*　　　\*　　　\*

In a daze, Stella drove much too fast to Long Dansbury. Didn't slow down to acknowledge Tramfield Lane on the left. Turned right two streets after the school and headed down Beane End Lane to the houses whose gardens gambolled down to the river. She parked, but left the engine on. Ran to the front door of Ford House, rang the bell and hammered her fists against the wood.

'Stella! Jesus, pet—what's up?'

'You're coming with me,' Stella said, pulling Caroline's arm. 'Where's Sonny?'

'I've just dropped him off at school—he's doing afternoons only on Tuesdays and Thursdays, full days on the others.' Caroline suddenly panicked. 'Is he OK?'

'Yes, yes of course. Come on. It's you I need. *Now!*'

'I'll—er—get my keys?' Caroline disappeared into the house to find her keys, gone from view only a moment or two but Stella was already ringing the bell again as if Caroline might have forgotten she was there.

'What is it?' Caroline asked, having to jog to keep up with Stella who was already at her car. 'What's going on?' She jumped into the passenger seat, having no time to fix the seat belt before Stella stamped her foot down and sent the car shooting off. 'Stella! Where are we going?'

Stella looked at her. 'Longbridge.'

'*Longbridge*?'

'Yes.' Her voice was both calm and buoyant, similarly she looked wild about the eye and yet determined. She glanced at Caroline just before she turned right on to the high street before turning left into the driveway of Longbridge. When she stopped the car near to the house, she turned to face her. 'You said you have too much time on your hands—that you need another project.'

'Yes?' said Caroline. 'And?'

'Come on!' Stella laughed. 'Come with me!'

*    *    *

Nothing much surprised Lydia these days so when she opened the door to see Stella standing there, breathless and unkempt, and next to her, Xander's willowy blonde friend from Up North Somewhere, she simply said, come on in. Mrs Biggins! Tea for three, please. In the library, thank you. *Today*, thank you!

Lydia and Caroline sat, Stella jigged around the room. Then she stopped in front of Lydia, as if she was about to break into song.

'I'm going to sell your house!' she giggled, with an unintentional snort at the end which made Lydia baulk.

'Well, that's good,' said Lydia flatly, 'because I've sold the land.'

For Caroline, it was like being in a verbal dual.

'What!' said Stella.

'I *beg* your pardon!' said Lydia.

'You've sold the land?'

'Yes,' said Lydia, 'this morning. I've sold it to Mr Rethington.'

'Mr Rethington? Your neighbour and nemesis?'

'Nonsense! You know me—I'm rude about everyone. Rethington has farmed my land for donkey's years,' said Lydia. 'He's always wanted to buy it, to double his own acreage. But I've always been too stubborn to let him have it. Well—now it's his.'

Trying to digest the fact was like trying to swallow the lump of sandwich which had stuck in her throat most of the journey from Hertford to Long Dansbury.

'But Clarence?' Stella spluttered.

'He's part of the cornfield. He's being bought too!' And Lydia laughed like a drain. Wiping the tears from her eyes, she turned to Stella. 'Now—what were you saying about selling the house?' She glanced at the Northern Woman. 'And you,' she said, 'what business is this of yours?'

'I have no idea, pet,' Caroline said and Lydia was so taken with the woman's bluntness she quite overlooked the impudence of such informality.

'But I *do*,' said Stella, 'I have a cracking idea—but there's no time to lose.'

\*     \*     \*

On 14 October, Stella made the call. She asked

438

her uncle to leave his office and as she shut the door, she pushed her back against it and stood still for a moment, eyes closed, in supplication to any God of any creed who might look kindly upon her and all those about for whom she cared so very much. Slowly she walked to her uncle's desk. Sat in the chair and swivelled once to each side. She took a deep breath, lifted his desk phone and dialled. If it went through to answerphone, she'd leave no message. She'd simply try again. And again. Until it was answered.

She took it as a very good omen that it was answered on the second ring.

'Hullo, Mr Tompkins—it's Stella Hutton here. How are you?'

'Stells!'

'How are you, how is Mrs Tompkins?'

'We're bloomin' great, darlin'. How are you?'

'I am very well. Mr Tompkins—are you still looking?'

'Looking? I'm good-looking!'

'Ha! I mean—for a house. A beautiful house— an heirloom? A status symbol?'

'Why?'

'I have something for you.'

'Oh?'

'But you can't see it until next Thursday.'

'We're going to Dubai next Friday.'

'Good—then you'll come with me to see it next Thursday.'

'Tell me more?'

'I can't.'

'You can't?'

'No.'

'Well, where is it?'

439

'I can't tell you that either.'

'Lummy.'

'No one else knows, Mr Tompkins—only you.'

'If you won't tell me what it is and where it is, how will we find it?'

'You'll come to me—here at Elmfield Estates— at nine thirty prompt next Thursday. With Mrs Tompkins. It is essential she comes too.'

\* \* \*

A week later, Xander tried to wrestle Stella into staying in bed for just another five minutes.

'I can't.'

'I know,' he said, nuzzling her neck, 'it's a school day.'

'It's D-Day,' she said.

'I know,' Xander said. He too had thought of little else. Gossip had flitted around Long Dansbury like the eddies of autumn leaves. What's with all the vans going up to Longbridge? I've heard it's falling down. I was told Her Ladyship's making it into apartments. Perhaps Rethington has something to do with it. But all those vans—every day—in at dawn, out at dusk. What's in those vans? What's going on up there? No one's seen Lady Lydia for days. Perhaps she's not up there at all. I heard it's become a film set. Tom Cruise. No, not him—the other one, George Loony. Apparently, Mercy Benton was seen going up there the other day. Mercy!

Xander watched Stella dress, a little swoop in his groin as she encased her bottom in nice white M&S knickers. 'I'll take Will to school for you, if you like? Give yourself enough time to psyche

440

yourself up.'

'I feel wired already,' said Stella. She patted her stomach. 'I feel like I developed an ulcer overnight.'

'Babe,' he said. 'You'll let me know, won't you? Soon as—anything?'

She nodded. 'Will do. Will!' she called. 'Are you dressed?'

'Nearly!' came the reply.

'*Nearly*,' Xander laughed. 'That means jimjams and crazy hair.' He looked at Stella. She looked neat. She looked ever so nervous. 'Come here.'

She sat on the bed. Gently, Xander released her hair from the pony-tail. 'There,' he said. 'You be Rapunzel today—just let your hair down a little and rescue Longbridge.'

Stella regarded him. He looked very grave. She laughed.

'You silly arse,' she said, kissing him and hollering for Will as she left the room to go downstairs and make breakfast for the three of them.

\*       \*       \*

At 9.30, the Tompkins' Bentley rolled up outside Elmfield Estates.

'Bye,' Stella said distractedly to her colleagues and she hurried from the office.

'Morning!' Mr Tompkins still looked as though he'd just stepped off a Mediterranean golf course.

'Morning!' Mrs Tompkins had gone blonde. She looked as though she'd stepped off the set of *Dynasty*. She looked rather fabulous. She was wearing half an alpaca inside out, it seemed, but it suited her. Especially with the high-heeled

441

shoe-boots and violet lipstick.

'Morning!' Stella called. 'Please park around the back—we're taking my car.'

Mr Tompkins began to splutter but a dig in the ribs from his wife soon stopped that.

Off Stella drove, Mrs Tompkins next to her, Mr Tompkins in the back with his knees unnecessarily close to his chin. Ignore him, Mrs Tompkins had whispered to Stella. He's a terrible snob—he don't like being a passenger in the front, never mind in the back—and he don't believe women can drive.

Stella resolutely refused to give any details of the property they were to view, apart from saying it had a few outbuildings and stood in thirty acres. When they reached Long Dansbury, the Tompkins' silence spoke volumes but she drove on blithely. When Stella turned the car up the driveway to Longbridge, Mrs Tompkins didn't prevent her husband spluttering out his indignation.

'What you playing at, Stells?'

'Just wait and see.'

'But—'

'No, Mr Tompkins. Don't say anything. I think of you—and your wife—as amongst the most sensible and open-minded people I've ever met. Please. Just wait and see. Keep your eyes and ears open.'

Nonplussed, they followed Stella up the stone steps—at the top of which she paused, looked to her right hoping to catch sight of Lord Freddie for a fortifying wink or something, but he was staring out over the lawns fixated by a quarrel of fat pigeons. Mrs Biggins opened the door. Into the hallway they went. So far—so the same. Mrs Tompkins looked around her. So did Mr Tompkins. Stella could see, from the briefest glance, that they

442

really did love the old place. They were shown into the drawing room, the autumnal light bathing the interior with kisses of caramel hues. Lady Lydia rose from her chair, elegant, composed. Her hair in an immaculate chignon, dressed demurely in navy slacks, a cream silk shirt under a cashmere cardigan a tone deeper, over which two strings of pearls clicketted expensively as she walked over to greet them.

'How lovely to see you both,' said Lydia. But she didn't offer them a seat. And there was no tea or delicious baked goods from Mrs Biggins. Lydia turned to Stella. 'Shall we?'

Stella nodded. 'Please, Lady Lydia—after you.'

So Lydia led the little party out of the drawing room and up to the first floor.

'I don't believe you saw the master bedroom?' Lydia said as if, silly her! she'd quite forgotten to show it to the Tompkins on their previous visits! She opened the door and let the Tompkins go in first. Soon enough, she and Stella had to push them in further because they'd all but stopped dead, relegating Lydia and Stella to the corridor.

'Blimey,' Mr Tompkins eventually managed. But Mrs Tompkins remained speechless. Stella winked at Lydia who surprised her by slipping her arm around her waist and giving her a little squeeze.

Gone was the chintz and the chill. There was no sign of the faded carpet in sickly raspberry. Instead, the floor was dark oak, in extravagantly wide boards. Inlaid in the middle, a section of carpet of the finest, thickest cream wool. Roman blinds in silk the colour of mercury were folded up high in the window bays, both of which were flanked by softly pleated curtains in heavy silk columns the colour of gunmetal which

443

ended in a blowsy swirl over the floor. The bed was super kingsize, a mahogany *bateau lit*, made up with crisp linen and a selection of cushions running the tonal gamut from black, through all the greys, to white. Elsewhere, the chairs, the chaise longue, were elegant in their design and upholstery. As if the natural light wasn't enough, a contemporary take on a classical chandelier descended from the magnificent plaster ceiling rose, as if the room had been designed around it centuries ago.

Mrs Tompkins looked at Stella.

'Don't look at me,' said Stella, stepping back. 'Lydia's your Lady.'

Gravely, Lydia nodded at the doorway at the end of the room. With great trepidation, the Tompkins approached. They had a hunch that the awfulness of avocado which had so disappointed them on their previous visits, would be gone. But they had no idea what they'd find instead. They opened the door and gasped. The room seemed so much bigger! The floor tiled in huge travertine slabs, a free-standing bath, traditional yet modern in the middle of the room. His and hers sinks, hewn out of travertine behind which the entire wall was one mirror, curiously and brilliantly lit from behind. A wall of glass demarcating the wet-room area. A vast chrome ladder of a heated towel rail heaped with thick white towels. On the back of the door, two robes, black, and embroidered in gold on the pocket of each, a curlicue T in thick gold embroidery.

'I—' Mr Tompkins was stroking his pate as if he'd very probably hit his head and was currently concussed.

'It's—' Mrs Tompkins was caressing the robe as

444

if in a dream from which she dreaded waking.

'Look, let's go downstairs and have a nice cup of tea,' said Lydia and they followed her down to the kitchen. Only, she didn't go through that door. She carried along that section of house and pushed open another door—the Tompkins couldn't remember what had been there and Stella wasn't going to tell them it had been that vast, dank, dumping ground that, just a month ago, had stored a clatter of bikes, a parade of prams and generations of Fortescue junk. If they had recalled it as such, then today's transformation would seem all the more miraculous.

They were standing in a divine kitchen—again, traditional and yet elegantly modern. Curved units in American walnut topped with creamy white Corian. An oval island in the same. A vast Aga uniting contemporary elements with timeless charm. The walls in a beautiful colour—a sort of bleached, bark buff. Floor in warm Cotswold stone.

'What did you *do*?' Mrs Tompkins whispered.

'And how did you do it?' Mr Tompkins asked.

Mrs Tompkins walked over to one of the two sinks—the one in the island. She made to turn the tap on. No water came out and the whole thing wobbled. She turned to Stella, confused.

Stella gulped. 'It's not plumbed in yet,' she explained. 'Nothing is,' she added with a nervous smile.

'But it *could* be,' said Lydia. In fact, everything was a facade—and yet, far from being fake, it was a hint, a taster, a helpful leg-up to these sweet-natured folk who wanted to climb right to the top of the property ladder, who had the wherewithal but not the know-how.

445

'My friend, Caroline Rowland—you'll be wanting her number,' said Stella, regaining her composure. 'She's been working flat out on this, for the past month.'

'I need to sit down,' Mr Tompkins said.

'Crunching figures is so much easier when one's seated, don't you think?' said Lydia, to which Mr Tompkins simply nodded. 'Now—time's moved on, since we saw you last,' Lydia said, quite sternly while the Tompkins sat to attention and hung on her every word. 'And I'm afraid the acreage is vastly diminished. There's no longer any farmland at Longbridge Hall—though, of course, it still provides the uninterrupted views. There's just the Hall now—and the thirty acres of parkland it sits in. The dower house too, and the stables courtyard—with the first apartment remaining in the tenancy of Mr Arthur Jonston for his lifetime. Not that you'd want to kick him out—what he doesn't know about the grounds isn't worth knowing. It's testimony to his experience and longevity here that the gardens are as lovely as they are.

'The livery yard—it's empty. But it used to bring in enough income to wash its face and it's too far away for you to hear, see or smell. The workshops—they're empty too. But I have to say, I quite liked having people in the buildings.'

The Tompkins were taking mental notes, as if all of this would be told to them just the once. Lydia cleared her throat.

'And the cottages on Tramfield Lane are no longer part of the sale,' she said. Stella whipped around from gazing out the window where she'd been having a private chat with Lord Freddie. She caught Lydia's eye. They hadn't talked about this.

446

Lydia was just slightly flushed, as if perhaps the idea had only just come to her, taking root immediately and was not open for further discussion.

Mr Tompkins looked from Lydia to his wife. 'Well, your Lady Lady Fortescue,' he stumbled. Looked at his wife. 'We have a lot to think about.'

Lydia chortled. 'Nonsense,' she laughed. 'No, you don't—not at ten million you don't!' She shook her head and laughed again. 'Silly man!' She tapped Mr Tompkins on the wrist. 'Silly man!' she repeated.

'You silly old sod,' Mrs Tompkins said to her husband, 'course we'll 'ave it.'

*　　　*　　　*

Stella came over to join them.

'There are two things,' she said, 'about the sale.'

Lydia winked at her. The Tompkins were all ears.

'Firstly,' said Stella, 'the apple store stays.' They shrugged and nodded and it hadn't crossed their minds not to keep it. Stella took a deep breath. 'Secondly—Mr and Mrs Tompkins—if you are to sell your current house, the condition is that you place it in the hands of Geoffrey Mumford, my lovely colleague at Elmfield Estates.'

Mr Tompkins frowned. 'Why wouldn't I give it to you to shift, love? Good commission you'd make— last valuation was three mill.'

'Because,' Lydia interrupted, 'it's time for Miss Hutton to return to her roots. She's an art historian, you know. And her first role is to be finding purchasers for the art here at Longbridge which I shan't be taking with me.'

'I love that painting of the big horse,' Mr Tompkins said. 'Nice round arse—reminds me of someone.' He winked at his wife who simply turned to Lydia and Stella with an expression of theatrical exasperation.

'You can have first refusal on it all,' said Lydia. 'Furniture, art—and I'm throwing in all the curtains. For free.'

'Can't say fairer than that,' said Mr Tompkins.

'I like a nice big painting,' said Mrs Tompkins. 'I don't know about art.' She turned to Stella. 'But you do, then?'

Stella nodded. They could see she couldn't talk and they chose not to comment on the fact that a tear had just fallen audibly onto the plate in front of her.

'Best in her field,' said Lydia. 'Especially Rembrandt but unfortunately, we don't have one of those. We do have a Reynolds, though. Come and see.'

* * *

That evening, Xander returned home to find a hand-delivered letter waiting for him on the doormat.

Thursday 28th October

My dear Xander
Would you come to Longbridge tomorrow evening? Join me in a glass of sherry? 6.30 prompt.
Lydia F

'I've been summoned,' he phoned Stella. Stella thought, it's something to do with the cottages on Tramfield Lane. But though she didn't know what, she sensed not to even mention it to him.

*     *     *

Mrs Biggins was on her way home when Xander arrived.

'She's in the library,' she told him.

'How are you, Mrs Biggins?'

'I'm jolly,' she said. 'As always.'

'You always are,' said Xander, 'unless you're crotchety with Lady Lydia.'

'That's when I'm at my most jolly,' Mrs Biggins said and Xander knew exactly what she meant.

He shut the great doors behind him, knocked gently at the library door and entered on Lydia's say-so.

'Good evening, Xander.' She looked tired yet radiant—the sort of heady exhaustion that comes from supreme effort, hard graft and ultimate triumph. A bit like running a marathon.

'Good evening, Lydia.'

'Have a seat—no, next to me. There's a boy.'

He sat. She passed him an envelope. It had his name and address on the front. He was about to open it when she stilled his hand. 'Longbridge has been sold,' she said.

'I'm so pleased,' said Xander. It was that marathon feeling again.

'Very good people,' said Lydia. 'Who want to buy my taste. I have come to see that in this day and age, the big money is found where you'd least expect it. And one is not to judge on background—

449

but the quality of the person alone.'

'Well done you,' said Xander.

'Well—I had a little help from Caroline and Stella,' she said. 'We will exchange contracts by Christmas, with completion planned for next spring.'

'Very good,' said Xander, 'that's a decent run of time for you. And we'll all help in any way we can.'

'I know.'

'I heard about Art,' Xander said. 'That's great. I'm so happy for him—and I know how much it must mean to you.'

'Yes, yes,' said Lydia. 'And we need to talk about you.'

'Me?' He laughed. 'I'll be fine—I'm a grown man, you know.'

Lydia couldn't find her voice. She swallowed hard. Drew herself up nice and straight. 'You're a Longbridge Boy,' she said.

He took her hand. 'And I'll never forget it.'

'I'll say,' and Lydia laughed. She looked at him. 'Dear Xander.' She paused. 'In this envelope are the title deeds for number one, number two and number three Lime Grove Cottages, Tramfield Lane, Long Dansbury.' She felt Xander pull away but she grabbed his arm and steadied them both. 'I know what you are like—how proud you are. I'm not giving them to you, but you will buy them at a peppercorn price. I was in that wretched place, Tesco, the other day. Mrs Biggins wanted to show me *clothing*. Can you believe that? But it gave me an idea. *Three for Two*, they call it. Apparently, it's everywhere these days. So—you can have the three cottages for the price of two, Xander. At their value on the day you were born.'

450

He couldn't speak.

'However, there's a great big But,' she said and, automatically, they both glanced through the open door to the enormous horse's arse facing them from the canvas on the stairwell. 'And the caveat is that you look after Miss Gilbey—just as you do now. You will be her landlord. She's independent—but she's old. Almost as old as me. And we all need a watchful eye in our dotage.'

'I don't know what to say. I—'

'I haven't finished!' Lydia snapped.

'Sorry,' said Xander, 'please.' Half thoughts churned with a barrage of emotions.

'The final condition of this deal is that you knock number two and number three into one.'

Xander looked at her. Tipped his head. Knock them into one? He looked at Lydia, who appeared to be wanting to say something, but was unable. He wondered if he should offer her a tissue to wipe away the tears that wouldn't stay put. Wondered if she even realized she was weeping.

But Lydia did speak. 'You knock the two cottages into one and you make it into a family home, Xander. You make it into a little Longbridge of your own.'

# Epilogue

'Here, Will, you can have this.' Xander plonked a fleece beanie that had been a freebie from a client onto Will's head.

'How much will My Lady Lydia pay me?'

'Well,' said Xander, as if doing advanced maths by staring hard at the sky, 'it depends. She tends to change the going rate from year to year.'

Though all the airports were shut with the snow, the day was bright and the road to Long Dansbury from Hertford was surprisingly clear and very beautiful. It really was like driving through a Christmas card depicting a classic winter scene of yesteryear.

'Are you sure this is a good idea?' Stella asked. 'Sounds pretty dangerous to me.'

'Is your mother being rude about my driving?' Xander asked Will, glancing at him from the rear-view mirror. Will just laughed.

'You know what I mean,' Stella gently scolded.

'It's a *terrible* idea,' Xander laughed, 'but it's a tradition.'

'Is that why she's asked the Tompkins? To hand it down?'

Xander smiled. 'I reckon so. Come on! There she is.'

Lydia was a strange sight indeed, top to toe in tweed with enormous ancient mittens—the type that Scott would have packed for the Antarctic—and strange old gumboots from which froths of insulating newspaper puffed out of the tops.

'Welcome!' Lydia called. 'Come on!' Will

scampered over to her and she patted at him as if he was a Labrador puppy mid-training. 'Come on!'

Arms linked, Xander and Stella strolled over.

'I haven't all day, you know—there's Christmas carols at Summerhill Place this afternoon. Mercy has arranged for Mrs Biggins and I to attend. Guests of Honour.'

Will looked expectantly at his mother—and Stella said 'maybe' under her breath.

'Right,' said Xander, 'which tree?'

They followed Lydia. A path had been neatly cut into the snow, and the grass crunched underfoot as if it had been iced by Mrs Biggins. Through the gardens they went, to the little copse behind.

'That one,' Lydia decreed. They looked up the tall straight trunk to the bare branches. High up, like a puff of green candyfloss, the mistletoe gathered in a great thatchy ball. Art was already there. With a ladder. And Clarence, just watching. Art held the ladder, and with a hearty slap across his shoulder blades from Lydia, Xander climbed.

'Lydia!' Stella gasped.

'Oh hush, girl,' said Lydia. 'We've done it this way for ever.'

Xander scaled the tree nimbly at first, then cautiously, and then just an inch at a time. Suddenly, mistletoe rained down on them in clumps and Xander was making his passage back down the tree. There were two baskets nearby and Will was gathering the sprigs and sprays into one of them.

'Not bad,' Lydia assessed the basket. 'A little paltry.' She seemed irritated and looked about her, suddenly brightening. 'There! Look at that lot up there!' The mistletoe in a neighbouring tree was twice as high.

454

'Lydia—absolutely not,' said Stella. Lydia turned to Xander as if to say, you're not going to let her talk to me like that, are you?

Xander shrugged. 'She's the boss,' he said and, after a moment, Lydia thought, that's no bad thing.

'I'll be back in a jiff,' she said, and disappeared.

In the meantime, the Tompkins arrived, kitted out from top to toe in brand new attire befitting the nouveau landed gentry in a style that was seen last in the nineteenth century. They'd added modern snowboots and ski gloves, and fluffy white ear muffs for Mrs Tompkins. They looked as if they were half in, half out of a time warp but it was rather touching and they looked very chuffed. Everyone chatted amiably as they waited for Lydia. Will went through his Christmas wish list for the umpteenth time, should anyone happen to be listening.

And then Mrs Tompkins screamed.

And Stella said, oh Jesus.

Mr Tompkins said, flippin' Nora.

And Will screeched with delight, *she has a gun!*

But Xander, Art and Clarence just laughed and shrugged. They'd seen it all before.

\*       \*       \*

'This, Mr Tompkins, is how you get the mistletoe down if Xander goes all sissy and won't climb up for it.'

And Lydia raised the rifle and began shooting high up in the branches. 'Off you go, Will,' she said, sending him to pick up, as if he was a retriever on a shoot. 'You see, we sell Longbridge Mistletoe— it's quite a nice little earner. Though Xander here insists on taking forty per cent.'

'Fifty,' said Xander.

'We'll talk about it later,' said Lydia.

'Where do you sell it?'

'At the Long Dansbury Christmas market,' said Lydia. And everyone knew that however she and Xander divvied the proceeds, they always donated the lot to the community fund.

With the rifle now safely in Art's hands and the baskets brimming with mistletoe, Mr Tompkins turned to Lydia.

'That date you want—next spring for completion—it's a bank holiday.'

'Well, how ridiculous!' Lydia barked. 'How very inconvenient!'

'Doesn't the Queen have something to do with approving public holidays?' asked Mrs Tompkins, looking hopefully at Lydia.

And they all wondered whether Lydia would be straight on the phone, on some secret hotline to Buckingham Palace, suggesting to the Queen that she change it.

'So we'll have to move it to June,' Mr Tompkins said.

'Do you actually know her?' Mrs Tompkins asked Lydia artlessly.

And Lydia let an ambiguous tilt of the head and a knowing expression widen the woman's eyes.

'Those garden parties at Buckingham Palace can be terribly dull and one never has enough to eat,' Lydia said. 'I think, next year, before I leave Long Dansbury, I shall throw an enormous party right here in the Longbridge gardens.'

Everybody congratulated her on an excellent idea. Christmas was coming. The world looked so pretty. The New Year wasn't far off and it would herald change for them all, bringing with it the growth of hope for good times ahead, the seeds for which had already been planted.

Lydia could sense emotion welling between them all like those silly Mexican waves Will had described happening at football matches. They'd even done them at Wimbledon. Most inelegant and quite unnecessary. She cleared her throat. Now was no time for emotion—they had a busy morning ahead. 'Now, we like to have a little sherry as we divide the mistletoe and tie it with red ribbon. Who's joining me?'

Everyone.

*       *       *

In the house, Mrs Biggins had everything ready. She was standing at the front door as though she owned the place.

Stella lingered behind. Just a little way off. No one noticed.

As she passed the statue of Lord Freddie she stopped. She stood on tiptoes, placing her arms gently around him, and kissed his cold old cheek.

He tried to look unimpressed but actually, today, he regarded her most benevolently.

'Happy?' he asked, as if he had been at the helm of all that had happened to her since they first met back in the spring.

'Very,' said Stella.

She walked on, then turned and retraced her steps to him. 'By the way,' she said. 'You're definitely staying here, Sir. You'll never be parted from Longbridge.'

And as Stella skipped through the snow to join

the others inside, Lord Frederick Makepeace William Fortescue glanced at the house that he'd built and looked out over the gardens he'd planned and thought how beautiful all of it looked today.

# Acknowledgements

I had a ball researching and writing *Rumours*—snooped around some divine houses and met truly extraordinary people. I respect the fact that most wish to remain anonymous—but I thank them sincerely for their time, their hospitality and their memories. It was a privilege. It was riveting. I am honoured. Katey Hugi—a wink and a big high five to you!

Team North, as ever, have been superstars. You wouldn't believe the behind-the-scenes effort that this talented and supportive posse invest to ensure my books reach you. My agent Jonathan Lloyd and my editor, Lynne Drew—wow, a not so dirty dozen. At HarperCollins, I'm indebted to Oli Malcolm, Roger Cazalet, Adam Humphrey, Thalia Suzuma, Ben North, Damon Greeney, Kate Elton, Alice Moore, Belinda Budge and Victoria Barnsley. Mary Chamberlain—thank you. Maura Brickell—thank you.

Writing this novel also coincided with me feeling wonderfully settled into my new life in the Hertfordshire countryside and my own community has been instrumental in this. So here are my heartfelt thank yous. The Cucumber Girls—especially Souki and Lyla. The Little B people—particularly Sandie Ash. The St Jo's ladies—Lisa W, Michelle S, Mel B and Helen B-C. The Tuesday Potters—you never know, you might be next!

To my besties: Sarah Henderson, Jo Smith, Kirsty Jones, Clare Griffin, Jessica Adams, Mel Bartram, Lucy Smouha and Emma O'Reilly—

459

finally we had a year when there was way more laughter than tears.

To my family: as always, you've been a tremendous support. Thanks—Ma and Pa, Dan and Osi, Jane and Jonny.

To my beautiful and extraordinary children Felix and Georgia—what a ride we're having! Hold on tight, kids, it's going to be spectacular.

In memory of Liz Berney 1968-2005